# EAGLES RISING

For Joe

Best wishes,

*[signature]*

## THE COLUMBIAD—BOOK 1
One of seven stand-alone novels about the lives of an Irish-American family in the 20<sup>th</sup> Century

Booklocker.com, Inc.
2007

# EAGLES RISING

## A Novel by

Gerald F. Sweeney

*Columbia...*

*The old earth hears a song, sees rainbows gleam*

*And lifts her head from a deep couch of dreams.*

Harriet Monroe, *Columbian Ode*

(Dedication for the Great Chicago Fair,

1893)

To the Cleveland women who brought me to the dance-

Gram, Gracie and Marge

# PROLOGUE

The day Frank's line of the family somersaulted into the modern age occurred the afternoon that his son Martin was transformed by the sight of the White City.

At seventeen, Martin, the eldest son, was entrusted by his father to accompany livestock to the Chicago market where the family was able to bargain for better prices. It had been his father, standing beside him, who taught Martin everything he knew about farming and living with animals. With Frank supervising the round-up, his farmhands drove the doomed cattle across the Iowa fields to the Mississippi river landing at Long View. There, instead of taking his freight over the rails, Martin boarded the cattle boat to Dubuque where he could link up with the through-train that eventually spilled the dizzy animals alongside the Windy City's yawling stockyards and packinghouses.

In 1893, on one of those journeys, Martin was dazzled by a sidetrip to the World's Fair. After delivering his herd, he found his way to the lake. From there he rode the new elevated train to the fairgrounds and entered the shimmering mecca that was the Columbian Exposition, built to celebrate, a year late, the 400th anniversary of the discoverer's voyage.

Rising from the shores of Lake Michigan, the eye-aching whiteness of the Great Chicago Fair provoked expectations of civic grandeur so tangible that its impact remained with Martin for life. This shining city that bobbed on the sands of the inland sea became a magnet for the young of the midwest, and bound them together by the power of its imagery and the possibilities of its dream. Before them soared the city beautiful, sparking their imagination and hopes. Framed by classical buildings erected alongside lagoons that circulated through the fair, the canals were patrolled by Venetian craft festooned with flowers. In the evenings, Sousa's band serenaded the crowds from a string of gondolas, the melodies drifting under the crowded bridges and across the water. Tuned by American music floating across an enclosed lake, the gleaming white metropolis became the signature vision of Martin's generation.

When he walked into the beaux-arts complex, the contrast to his ritual farm life was startling. Carrying the aroma of the stockyard pens with him, he stepped off the el and stretched out his arms to shower in the fresh lake breezes and after finding a wash-up room was soon windblown and refreshed. Making his way through a turnstile near Sullivan's Transportation Building with its golden arch, a concoction of old Spain and the Alhambra, he was seized by emotions as spiritual as they were aesthetic. Within Martin's Catholic soul, the deep clonging of a cathedral-sized ringing produced a reverberate response that stirred his insides.

Distinguished by his country cap amid a sea of derbies, Martin viewed the Court of Honor with its Pantheon-size edifices. The scene gleamed like a wondrous white confection, a rebellion against the grimy city outside the gates and the mud of his Iowa barnyard. Here, for a few hours, the unreal became palpable and Martin, overwhelmed by its impact, was filled with awe. Approaching the waters of the statue-encircled basin, where the idealized women of his time were represented in heroic stances, he first viewed the monumental fountain in stone of symbolic *Columbia* skippering the ship of her American state through a pond of geysers. Above and beyond, he viewed Saint Gaudens' rendition of the archer *Diana* on top of the Agriculture Building and French's colossal *Republic* at the other end of the reflecting pool. Emotions struggled through his body, physically testing his bucolic beliefs. He felt a visceral alliance with the artists' aims to meld feminine virtues with symbols of power—the torch of liberty, the longbow, the orbed eagle. Within him, there was an emotional transformation. He began to equate the beauty of what he felt and saw with the goddess spirit captured in the statuary—the revelation that women were not only the seed of life but also the antibody against industrial decay. He and smoke-stale America were acknowledging the gender of their ideals.

He entered the Electricity Building where he inspected the massive dynamos, much preferring the full-bosomed marble virgins outdoors. Viewing Edison's kinetoscope, he watched hootchy-kootchy images dance before his eyes. Then on to the Agriculture Building, where he asked his best questions, mostly concerning corn and its generation. Later, he wandered into the Krupp Gun Works exhibit to be iron-struck by the potential destructive power of the enormous cannons that waited ominously to decimate an entire generation of English and French youths still in their infancy. Martin hoped no relative of his would ever face these railway siege guns.

Later in the afternoon, steps away from entering the Midway amusement area, Martin was again distracted by the decorative female forms surrounding another of the imposing halls. On the facade a flag fluttered, announcing a free concert inside. Curious, he entered the Women's Building, and was soon informed by its gentle atmosphere, which contrasted sharply with the castings and mechanical contrivances of the other exhibits. Its spacious central atrium was filled with music. Above on opposite archways, he admired the large-scale wall paintings, one labeled *By Mary Cassatt*, which depicted modern women harvesting the tree of knowledge. The other, illustrating primitive women, was fleshed out by Mary Fairbanks, wife of the sculptor of the central statue sailing above the waters outside depicting Columbia as the country's helmswoman.

Observing the Cassatt, Martin thought to himself, "She makes faces good. Has an eye for caring women."

As he listened to the music and absorbed the soft feminine milieu around him, he began to doubt his own beliefs concerning the female's solely domestic role.

"Too bad Ma didn't have many chances in school," he said to himself. "She's smarter than all of us."

His father would also have been amazed by the splendor of the fair. But who was to teach Martin what these images and impressions meant?

The music's echo resounded as it lifted through the open hall, the harmony of the chorus and instruments a wonder to Martin. Familiar with pump organs and church singing, he had never heard the sumptuous sound of a symphony before; his only previous experience with tuned instruments rested on the quartets played back home by his cousins, the nuns. Beneath the Cassatt mural, the women's orchestra was playing the *Festival Jubilate* that Amy Beach had composed for the Fair's opening day. Enthralled, Martin sat until the end of the concert. As a finale, the women played *America the Beautiful* inspired by the White City itself. The female chorus sang of amber waves of grain and alabaster realms.

After the final notes faded away, he strolled through the hall and fell in behind two attractive women, each with an unblemished complexion. They balanced small tilted hats on their heads that offset their ankle-length skirts and puffed-up sleeves. Martin had never seen such clear-skinned women before.

"What a relief to hear music other than the usual Chadwick," said the taller of the two, mentioning the country's favorite composer.

"I'd have preferred something more modern."

"Something Wagnerian that would make us tremble? Our poor frail bodies couldn't stand it."

"Sweet sister, the two of us left fragility mooning by herself on some back road long ago."

"Cynic! You'll be telling me next that you agree with what Mister Sullivan said at dinner the other night about the fair's architecture."

Martin, walking behind, didn't understand their references, but was fascinated by their refinement, their air of gentle force, unfamiliar traits in the farmwomen he knew.

"You mean about all those fake Greek temples and oversize bank buildings around the Court?" the taller one asked. "What did he call them? Decorated sheds?"

Martin followed the women like a silent shadow.

"Young man, are you trailing behind us?" the taller woman turned and asked.

"Why no. . . . Actually yes. I mean no harm," he said, cap in hand.

Though in farm clothes, Martin displayed a hardiness sufficient to attract most females his age. Tall and thin with muscled limbs, there was a yeoman's honesty sculpted in his face. Fortunately, Chicago women were sympathetic to rural ways, aware that they were surrounded by a thousand miles of farms in every direction—plow fields that needed civilizing. Many of these modern millies took their country cousins into protective custody once inside city limits, especially suffragettes like these two, born proselytizers, who reacted favorably to incipient male sensitivity captured by the aroma of their seductive perfumes. That's how Martin Mahoney for five full minutes entered the emancipated sisterhood of these North Shore beauties.

"What made you stop by?" one of the women asked.

"Mostly the music and the statues," Martin answered plainly.

"See, it works," the smaller woman said. "We need something to entice people. We should give concerts every day. Maybe twice a day. Serve refreshments. Even charge."

"It's fine to snare this young man but women shouldn't require an invitation. They should be motivated to come on their own," her sister said. "Aren't they obligated to visit their own exhibition?"

"That's unrealistic. Not with a Wild West show and a Pygmy village just around the corner—to say nothing about that big iron wheel flapping around out there. Or those Arabian persons! Or that wild-looking locksmith. And Professor Tesla—all lit up like a firebug—creating home-made thunderstorms right through his body over in the Electricity Building."

"I liked that one," Martin mumbled. "Scorched his collar running all that electricity through him."

They weren't listening to him. The taller sister was saying, "Why are we always competing? Confrontation is such a nuisance. We need to take charge of ourselves instead of arguing and begging for everything. It's so distasteful. . . .What do you think?" turning full face to Martin, who had never been so close to such beauty before.

"I hate to fight," he said. "Unless I have to."

"But what do you do when you're forced to?"

"Punch first. Then run like a scared hare," Martin said.

"That doesn't sound very gallant."

"Saves a lot of doctor bills."

"Do you have any sisters you could bring to the fair?"

"Only brothers—five of them. That's how come I know about fighting. I had a sister but she died. She had problems." He didn't want to say they were mental.

"I'm sorry. . . . Perhaps you could invite a cousin or someone. Bring them along to see all the possibilities opening up for women. . . . Don't forget," she said, bidding him goodbye.

The language of the feminine future wasn't the only new voice he heard that day; he was soon introduced to the latest in popular music as well.

A variety of sounds stirred the evening air as Martin drifted through the Midway carnival, the summer home of Buffalo Bill, as well as belly dancers from the Mideast, and a certain Mr. Weiss from Brooklyn who called himself Houdini. Soon enough, amid the pennywhistle sounds of Irish bands and the drumbeats of the African Village, there came a flight of music that startled him with its quirky surprises. An altogether new sound—a piano with a sparkling kind of rhythm, one of the first ragtime numbers—*Elite Syncopations*. The music lit up Martin's spirit as no music had ever done—rollicking rhythms so disguised that the listener could barely discern the soul of released slavery in it, didn't know that the beat partially derived from the slave dance tunes that his immigrant father, Frank, had heard as a boy in New Orleans, the same sounds that would lead to jazz and all its progeny.

The rambunctious rhythms sprinkled on the summer air, the music reminding Martin of high-stepping trotters, or arched-back minstrels shuffling along with a shoulder-shaking strut, parading toward a jamboree, cake walking. Martin felt an eruption in his body that set his spirits tapping. Even the new electric lights seemed to jitter. Though Martin was unaware, the kinetic energy that was to burn up the twentieth century was here and in the nervous images of the moviola—flickering mechanical marionettes inside black boxes that illustrated the stuttered, frenetic life that was on its way. Hurry up, *wah-wah*; it's a, *wah-wah*, new century coming. With a herky-jerk to it.

The music came from a beergarden beneath Mister Ferris's giant wheel. Entering the grove, he saw a Negro gentleman banging away on a tin-pan piano. Martin took a seat nearby and began swaying to the rhythms, listening to the cascading ragtime tumble out of the upright like starshine on a clear black sky, twinkling with the boisterous urban patterns of postfarm America. The black man noticed Martin's reaction and played to him, acknowledging Martin's interest with a tip of his derby—the shy of the world improvising their special signals. Martin sat with his schooner of beer for twenty minutes until the ragtime man arrived at a natural break.

Martin rose and walked over to him, "Your music woulda made my grandpa dance."

"I try to give it a lot of sass," the pianist replied.

"Can I buy you a beer?" Martin asked. "Only right after such fine entertainment."

The Negro smiled, "Not in here you can't."

"How 'bout next door then?"

"There neither. Maybe sometime in August when they have Colored Day."

"Why don't I just buy a couple mugs, and we'll sit someplace?"

"OK. I'll meet you out back. You can walk around by the fence."

They pulled up camp chairs when Martin returned and sat in the evening shade of a kitchen oak that backed up onto other attractions. Jugglers lounged there along with cooks and chorus girls. Martin failed to observe that his companion never touched his brew.

"Your music sure does sting the senses," Martin said when they sat down; unaware of the looks the pair were receiving from the other performers and potato peelers. "Did you make up some of those tunes yourself?"

"Most of them. . . .But a few of them," the black man said with a smile, "I repossessed."

"What do you call that kind of music?"

"Part minstrel. Some African. All spliced together in Saint Louis—mixed up in the ginmills on the back side of town."

"I don't know much about music," Martin said. "But yours has a nice finish to it—like a well made cabinet."

"I hope the tunes take with the crowds. People don't always actually see us coloreds. But maybe we can at least get them to listen. Later on, we'll help them grow eyes."

The pianoman had to return to work and they soon parted. With the sound of ragtime skipping in his ears, Martin stepped out onto the raucous Midway and gazed up at the giant Ferris wheel turning on high. The cars above came tumbling over the top of the sky and seemed to overflow like a song. They came dancing down, cartwheeling into the new times.

It had been a wonder-filled day. But he came to the realization that he would have to teach himself more about the world, learn about things beyond his father's comprehension.

Some of America's dilemmas were beginning to unravel at the Chicago Fair. Choices between gold or silver currency, between an indentured southern class or not, art versus commerce, voting women or domestic slaves, isolation or world power, native music or Europe's. Decisions would soon arrive that would burden and excite the lives of its youngest generation.

The nineteenth century had been one of the most prosperous times that any country had ever known—America sitting high and dry on the western ocean. Its tenets already laid down by Jefferson and Emerson, its basic literature established by Melville, the younger James, and Twain. Its new music was about to explode with Ives, who would acknowledge the black-inspired folk music already fingered by Joplin in his Chicago beergarden. Sullivan's Auditorium downtown glowed with the possibility of native architecture, Wright not far behind. Poetry redefined by Whitman. Its Civil War already fought. Legal slavery, the ugly crack in the Liberty Bell, behind. All the country had to do now was build on its foundation, match the deeds of the doers that would not be denied—the Irish who dug the canals, the Chinese who built the railroads, the Germans and Scandinavians who tilled the midwest, the Slavs who worked the ore furnaces—the active ethnics. Foreign-born and first-generation immigrants—forming three-quarters of the population—were reworking the continent. America was stretching awake, opening its front door and gazing out on a bright morning of achievement. It was a country set up and ready to do the business of the twentieth century.

But in the back of the American house, there was a cramped door low to the ground—crabbed out of the muck of the yard, the dark side already visible in the despair of unreconstructed blacks who were being thrown back into servitude by southern legislatures. Women everywhere in cotton chains. The government interfering with brown breeds below the border. Union-busting monopolies. Chinese exclusion. And maybe worst of all, the final fencing in of the Indian nations.

And in between the light and the dark, the front door and back, between the hopes and doubts, dreams and nightmares, intelligence and stupidity, nobility and corruption, most people like Martin, his father Frank, and his future son, John-Arthur, would be divided by courage and fear, with few answers except those offered by religion or a fifth-grade education. People suffering in confusion. But in that middle room, humor, civility, frilly curtains, a player piano and pictures of Abe Lincoln offered stability and a moment's joy between a dirt hard life on the one hand and the search for economic and social freedom on the other.

One of the first things Martin saw on this day of his whitened vision was the sight of MacMonnies's *Columbia Triumphant* riding her ship of state above the fountains alongside the gleaming splendor of the Court of Honor, and before the day was out, he came to feel that America's future could only be achieved by the full participation of its women and the creative force of its blacks. Dynamos be damned.

When Martin left the White City that night to catch his westbound train, he could see the lights of the fair blazing in the sky for miles. Tesla's new electrical reflections, radiating from the immense glass roofs and from the light bouncing off the white surfaces, shimmered in the summer haze. He knew that he had to redirect himself, even though his only points of reference were his affinity to his family and the sacristy of his Catholic beliefs. As he rode the night coach back to Iowa, he was ready to admit to himself that he wasn't cut out to be a farmer. When he arrived home, Martin told old Frank he wasn't going to work the crops much longer.

That fall, he entered the seminary, the sacrificial eldest son.

## THE (O') MAHONEYS

Great James the pioneer - John-Arthur's great-grandfather.

(Wife - Bessie)

Frank, the Iowa farmer - John-Arthur's grandfather

(Wife - Ellen)

Martin, the Chicagoan - John-Arthur's father

(Wife/Mother - Kitty)

John-Arthur, their son

# Chapter 1

The deep black soil pushed up a golden crop far across the rolling fields; the burnished roof of maize melted into a blue sky. Above the far shore of the great river, the plains spread all the way to the mountains a month's ride west. Here, above the river bluffs, the fertile Iowa sections were fractionalized into a patchwork of family farms, among them the thousand acres tilled by members of a single Irish family—the O'Mahoneys from Fermanagh. A plat map issued before the Civil War delineated their seven farms spreading from the Mississippi toward the church the family helped construct a few miles inland along the road to Strawberry Point. On a day in late August with the advantage of a bird's eye view, the whirling motion of the O'Mahoney clan could be seen plying the dusty roads as they rode their farmcarts and horses toward the homeplace, the original farm of Great James, to celebrate the annual family reunion.

Heralding this dusty commotion rose the sounds of the songbirds whose melodies were the essence of Iowa's lyricism. The year was 1856.

By 1896, during the following forty years, owing to a combination of agrarian competence on the part of the more industrious German farmers and too much whiskey resulting in too many mortgage foreclosures on the part of the Irish, the O'Mahoney lands had been halved. But whether in debt or in clover, the family steadily reaped a wealth of relatives. The children of Great James, who had sailed with him from Ireland, now called the pioneers, had produced forty-five native-born citizens of the New World, and they in turn had tripled the number of Mahoneys in the next generation, who by now had left their patronymic "O" behind. But the farms could not physically maintain that many limbs, so the migration off the land to other parts of Iowa and Wisconsin and to Dubuque and more distant cities had been going on for years. It was to the original homestead that Martin, the fair-going seminarian, now unfrocked, arrived from Chicago with his new wife and baby boy for this year's get-together. The child, John-Arthur, born on the eve of the 20th Century had come to meet his clan.

Martin and his family spent the night of their arrival at his father Frank's farmhouse, nested in a stand of trees downstream from the homeplace. At sunrise, as the curtains in his old room billowed in a prairie wind, he rose, and then bent down to kiss his sleeping wife and baby still curled in the comfort of his old bed. Martin, the eldest son, looked out across the fields and renewed his choice, unashamed of his decision to abandon his birthright, confirming to himself that much of life's ultimate direction was a matter of hard selection. He had known better than to commit himself to all the things he loved, including this farm.

Later, combing his neat beard, Martin prepared his wife, "You'll have to pretend you're a good listener. . . . "

"You know how much I'll like that," Kitty said, winking at him.

"It's just that the old folks squawk on. Trot out all the old stories."

"Just comfort me to know they'll be nothing said against the Germans."

Irish Catholics had arrived in America with their hatred of the English intact, but ethnic squabbling with the Germans was a newer phenomenon. Conflict between the two peoples had crossed the Mississippi on the first ferry, their quarrels transported to the unclaimed territory, embedded in their wagons and in the saddlebags of those that swam their horses across.

It was as if the Germans were sustained by old traditions in their new land—challenging themselves to reproduce the same high standards followed at home. They created communities of industrious people in America—reconfirming their beliefs by founding an orderly society based on strict custom. Meanwhile, the Irish were driven inward by their church, Anglo oppressors, their poetry, and their dislocation. Stabbed in the heart at birth, they were compelled to find laughter and mead to treat the wounds of self-denial, reckless behavior, and hopeless dreaming. Forced to function from a wholly emotional base, they found their joy in others. By extending their love, they redistributed themselves into a tribe of seekers, not settlers.

"Try to find the humor in it all," Martin said, propping the baby up on the lumpy white bed. "Forget the old feuds between the Germans and the Irish. They've all been settled in this boy's blood."

If it were only so, Kitty thought to herself. Within her own well-ordered, urban family, she had been the bright star, able to express herself in bursts of explosive affection. She had been shown daily, almost hourly—usually within the confines of the family kitchen— that she was well loved by her parents and siblings. Buoyed by such warmth, she had grown strong and independent and learned how to overcome adversity. Through humor, she developed the knack for broadening and enlivening relationships. Worldlier than her husband, she might have eventually prompted her children to excel in a more competitive way if she had chosen another. But she had married a gentle man, often blind to the hostility around him. Feeling duty-bound to replicate his softness in their offspring, Kitty had made a commitment to herself that in order to be true to Martin as a matter of faith, she would strive to regenerate his ways and pass along his quiet, loving code to their son, John-Arthur.

Theirs had been a complicated courtship; one fought out in the silent precincts of prayer, amid candles offered, some burning with hope and some with sadness. Martin had been called to the priesthood shortly after the closing of the Chicago Fair and intended to give his life to Christ, but on one of his homecomings before ordination, however, on his way through that hell-bent-for-growth city, he met, fell in love with, and eventually married Kitty Rapp of Chicago, whose talents were ever afterwards exalted as the protectoress of Martin's line.

Martin had been stunned by the passion he came to feel for Kitty, whose olive-colored face and small wiry body interrupted him along the cloisters of his spiritual ambition. Nurturing feelings so strong that he could not deny her, he was overwhelmed by the warmth of her understanding. Still she had no intention of interfering with his agreements with God. She had come to love him suddenly and completely, but it had to be his choice as to with whom he would share his soul, almost afraid to hope that it would be herself. Where the strength came from to make such a decision, neither knew. But he came to believe that only death or madness could separate him from her.

Now sharing both bed and the right to love as one desired, after rising and dressing in her one good outfit, Kitty retreated to help with breakfast in the kitchen, leaving Martin to finish details upstairs.

"Let me give you a hand," Kitty said greeting her mother-in-law, bent over the woodstove—the younger woman confidant of her culinary skills, stepping in with authority.

"You've enough to do with the baby," said Martin's mother. "But if you're free and don't mind, why don't you manage the flapjacks while I handle the eggs." Hesitating before speaking again, drawing a dozen eggs from a brown-glazed crock, Ellen asked, "And how's married life been this past year?" She was not known for her timidity.

"So many changes," Kitty said, not intimidated by Ellen's questioning, knowing that his mother was specifically interested in the well-being of her eldest son. "I guess the big thing for me was wondering if the baby would bring me and Martin closer or start us snapping at one another. I'd say it's worked out because Martin's never been happier. Having a son was important. Like it verified something in him."

Satisfied, Ellen asked, "And yourself?"

"Truly fulfilled," Kitty replied, without raising her head, smiling to herself.

"And how is the grocery business going?"

"As good as can be expected," Kitty said, with less enthusiasm. Then greeting her new kin, "Here they come."

After breakfast, Frank and son Martin had a chance to share a cup of coffee on the porch. The old farmer, not as direct as his wife, circled around the question, "And how's Joe doing?" referring to another of Frank's sons living in Chicago.

"Dead tired from work, but he's game and accepts the drudge in his usual stoic way," Martin said of his brother. "He's still knee-deep in gristle on the slaughterhouse floor. Hoping to get into the packinghouses where it's a little cleaner."

"I don't blame him. I remember the trouble you had. . . . How's it going at Kitty's deli?"

"The store's still a struggle, but we do our best."

Frank said, "With all the learning you've had, it would please God if you could use some of it."

"Pa, I'll have to learn about making money by sweating it out like everybody else."

When they were washed and packed up, they drove to the reunion at Great James' homeplace, a white clapboard house surrounded by farmyard and barns—a busy enclosure within

100 acres of cropland. The home represented the spiritual center hall of the family's encampment in America. Here Martin was embraced by his wider clan. As a baby, he had been cared for by his grandmother, Great James' ancient widow, and though he couldn't remember her, that tie constituted his main claim to family fame, that and his youthful self-removal from the pigsties and aching work of the corncribs. He and his young family were warmly greeted and baby John-Arthur was dandled from lap to lap, grandparents to great aunts to cousins twice removed, until by noon, young father Martin had difficulty detecting which apron his child occupied. None more proud than the new grandparents, old Frank and Ellen, who insisted on the boy's uniqueness.

"That baby's an O'Mahoney," Frank said, using the old form, "or my name's not Francis after the saint."

Frank, the youngest son of patriarch James, instantly connected with his grandson and they, the old farmer and the city baby, seemed naturally to bond. In his extended family, Frank still counted one living brother and sister, who had all arrived as young children together on Great James' pilgrimage. The trio had been witness to dark prairie truths and the bountiful harvest of a thousand Irish dreams, including this newest baby.

To the accompaniment of shrieking children's games, the farmyard bristled with talk of earlier days as food began to pour out the kitchen door in ever increasing streams. Clumps of uncles inspected the barn with much commentary on bovine and other wonders, while the town kids chased the chickens to distraction. The uncle who owned the saloon in nearby Long View had tapped into his reserves in order to relieve the thirsty element in the congregation, and his actions had not gone unnoticed by his cousins, the nuns of the Blessed Virgin Mary, the BVM's. As to male clerics, owing to Martin's defection, there wasn't a priest in the family, even though there had been a seminary in Dubuque before an ox cart carried old James to the acres of his dreams.

For the reunion, ancestral stories were unwrapped and confidant new ones invented. Some were tales of present prosperity and defeat; others foresaw the future with its promise of machine-made progress. Yarns about Indians were relayed to the wide-eyed young ones along with stories about the early lead miners and the hardships of pioneer farm life. There was talk of husbandry and bee-keeping and quilting and the quality of their church choirs—tales growing out of their home soil like a garden of family flowers.

"Have you seen that young Martin from Chicago, the one with a baby, who was to be a priest?" one of the gossipy relatives asked her sister.

"With the pretty wife? From a German family I think she said. He's trying to straighten her out about the family, addling her with the names of dozens of cousins. Over by that new girl, come over from Donegal. That Maeve O'Donnell. The one with the sharp tongue. . . .Chased out of Ireland, they say."

"I think that one has revolutions in her bonnet."

"They say she goes to the Grange and sits with the men. And even talks up."

"Bad enough that she looks like her hair's on fire and wears suspenders. ... Some people are born to trouble."

"And some to drink, and I can see my Festus trying to suck the jug inside out."

For the midday meal, the senior members of each line gathered their offspring, arranging them around the outdoor tables. Seating was tight on the narrow boards; the planktops were likewise crowded—with plates of heaped-high steaks and chops and serving dishes of corn on the cob and mounds of buttery mashed potatoes. Within easy reach were beer kegs as well as cider in tall glass pitchers. Above them spread a prairie blue sky.

"Come sit by me, Maeve. You don't want to be scrambled in with those hens from Matthew's line," Frank said.

"You mean I get to eat with the handsomest of the lot," Maeve sang in her lilting brogue, nudging him over.

"Very observant, I might add. . . .Like one of them evolutionists you hear about in science."

"Frank, you'd be my proudest experiment."

"I'd be like putty in the good doctor's hands."

Her words came flying out like sparks, offering Frank a taste of the bantering black humor of his boyhood home when the O'Mahoneys still thought of themselves as Europeans, giving Maeve an opportunity to practice Iowa prattle with someone who shared her roots.

The BVM nuns insisted on grace, and as Frank prayed, he looked across the fields bequeathed by Great James that had been the backdrop of his life's work

Maeve, halfway through dinner, in an attempt to suspend the toothy gnashing of corncobs, asked the old farmer, "Tell me again, Frank, about how it was you dealt with the jury system when you were young."

"Better than all them lawyers with books piled to the ceiling—just like you have. Asides everybody's heard the story before."

"Not me," said Kitty, holding the baby in one arm. "Nor John-Arthur here either."

"Go ahead, Pa," Martin encouraged him.

"Stop me if it's boring," Frank said. "I don't want to be bragging on myself. . . .It happened before Abe Lincoln's war when everybody in Iowa was on a rampage ready to burn out slaveowners—current or past—and anybody siding with them. Boasting the way big-hearted Americans do, standing up for the Union, ready to show off the flag.

"Back then, I had been going around saying how my Da had been this big rebel in Ireland before he came over. Pretty soon, word got around that I was yapping about rebellion. Not about over there, but right here. That's when the grand jury in Dubuque said how they were going to indict me for treason because I was a reb. Had nothing to do with the land I owned on the other side of the Ridge Road. . . .my foot.

"So, I hired lawyer Friedman and we go in court with a suitcase full of precedents. They asked me if I was a Copperhead, and I told 'em no. But didn't the prosecutor get a couple old Krauts—sorry Kitty—to testify and say I was a threat, and how they had no eyes on my lot over east. That's when I started to get mad. When they actually voted to indict me, I roared up and stormed over to the jury box and started throwing punches, yelling I was as loyal as any man in Dubuque County. They were all trying to fly out of the box but I kept strangling them and throwing them back in. The judge and bailiff are hollering and lawyer Friedman is on my back but I kept whacking them until I had eight of them collared and told them I was going to beat them some more if they didn't pull the indictment right then. Finally, they allowed as that was a good idea. And I walked out of there with barely a blemish."

"What do they call that, Frank? Frontier justice?"

"I don't recommend that kind of behavior for all, but sometimes you have to stand up."

"Who else did you punch out, Frank?"

"Don't get me wound up."

"Go ahead and fire away."

"I only tell these stories to remind you how hard it was for the family these 50 years. That's no time, of course, compared to the eons that the Indians managed it. . . . Best of land, here and across the river—truly sacred to the Sioux and the Sauk and the Fox until the 1830's—before we came and tore up their holy ground. Back then, Indians prayed straight away to their Great Spirit. . . .Deer roamed the forests—hickory mostly and black walnut. Further west past the woods were the grasslands and the buffalo. . . .I'm telling you all this for your own edification you know. . . . Though I don't see anyone taking notes."

Maeve answered with mock innocence, "Frank, how could we ever forget a word you said?"

"You're pulling my britches."

Frank knew his history. Iowa farmers spend long winters raiding their local libraries, and he understood the context in which his family had grown. The first whites to arrive were French explorers from Montreal waving the cross and their trinkets, bargaining for God and fur. They came paddling into the old Indian empire by way of the rivers and streams that flowed over the continent past great falls and immense lakes that led them west. Following the rivers' flow up and down the rapids, they carried canoes across the Fox-Wisconsin portage eventually spilling them out onto the broad Mississippi at Prairie du Chien, just up the river.

Frank continued, "What would become the Iowa territory— they called it the Savage Lands back then—was part of a sharp deal we made with Napoleon, and when the Black Hawk War ended in 1832, there was a run of settlers across the river, staking their property. Farmers from the eastern states and Ireland and Germany came rushing in while fifty miles to the north across the Neutral Ground were hostile Sioux. . . . Closer by Sauk and Fox camped to the west and Iowas to the south."

The O'Mahoneys came, surveyed, and planted themselves there in the great emptiness that was the Mississippi valley. Even though they would claim their acres and later buy their farms directly from the land office of the great republic, what the settlers came to believe was that their holdings had been protected by the thousand-year trust maintained by the tribes of the plains.

Old folks have no monopoly on stories. After the picnic lunch, the teenage cousins readied themselves for their annual performance, something less than a pageant and more than a tableau. A dozen of them hurried through dinner and in a scramble of excitement, escaped to the house to dress up as pioneers, borrowing children along the way as props, including baby John-Arthur whom they overwhelmed in a girl's bonnet. Unnoticed, two farmboys, painted as Indians, entered the barn where they untied a pair of horses.

The clan was invited to sit and rearrange themselves on blankets near the springs to view the homemade play. A line of linen hung fronting the audience; the makeshift curtain screened the performers noisily assembling their roles. The BVM nuns, familiar with the foibles of teenage productions, helped manage things behind the scenes and soon, out came a reader—a tall Irish-pretty girl in pioneer garb. In clear tones, she began, "The first time that Indians appeared along the creek running through the O'Mahoney land was after the first harvest in 1842."

The curtain opened to a re-creation of a one-room log cabin, fashioned with more quilts than furniture. Simultaneously, two made-up Indians rode up to the creek flowing away from the spring.

The girl continued, "When old James looked out and saw the Indians, he quickly hid the youngest children under blankets, beds and even the washtub". . . .There was a scurry of activity on the set. . . ."And as many guns and weapons as he could find, he thrust into the hands of the older children and Great Grandmother Bess. Then out James walks alone and unarmed to confront his visitors."

A wide-shouldered young man representing Patriarch James complete with a cotton beard approached the Indians whose horses took the opportunity to drink from the stream. Across the backs of the horses, the riders had strung dressed chickens and ducks, along with other obscure species of fowl plus a stuffed squirrel. They began a pantomime. The Indians offered their game in exchange for wheat that the family had stored following their harvest. After repeated gestures and eyeing the audience for signs of recognition, the actors appeared pleased that everyone grasped the storyline.

"I was the one under the tub," Frank said.

"See, he's trading with 'em like old James did," volunteered one of the onlookers.

"Hush up and let them play it out," came a response.

In the end, the Indian braves rode away with baskets of grain, and James returned with arms overloaded with game. The girl who was reading added, "And so began a trading of wheat for game that would continue for six or seven more summers between the native Sauks and the farmers from Fermanagh. . . ."

Maeve couldn't resist, "Both feeling a little tight in their leather pants about such an unequal land transfer."

The reader concluded, "In time, James would lend his guns to the Sauks who repaid the family with extra provisions." Dramatically, spreading out her arms to indicate the family's good fortune, "And this meeting place was evermore called Indian Wells."

The use of the word "evermore" is always a clue for the audience to applaud, and they did so with vigor. When they began to clap, the noise frightened baby John-Arthur, but instead of crying, he looked out from beneath his blanket in wide-eyed amazement at his kinsman, waiting for the sound to subside. Then he cried.

The girl-reader, anxiously looking back at the bawling baby, announced, "Stay nearby, Uncle Matthew is going to read from his new family history book, so round up here in a half-hour after we get all the quilts back in the house. . . . And later this afternoon, we'll have another play for you."

In due time, with help from Kitty, the baby stopped crying, while the set was struck and the clan dispersed for a refill of coffee, only to regather soon after for the reading.

Uncle Matthew began, "This piece I'm going to read is about the ones who answered the final summons and are buried in the churchyard on the hill. Any of you want to see a copy, I've deposited the pages over to the college library at Loras if you care to read it slow. So, here goes. . . . " he said. *"Our Family History."*

He told how the Irish came in great numbers, walking their rows, plowing Celtic civilization into the deep black soil, longing for the Old Country and their friends, never tiring of their own legends, trying not to forget their own history—the lamenting melodies sung anew, replayed each night. But the dreamers too tired to linger long in the past. Before them, prosperity beckoned and sometimes it came and sometimes not.

The first O'Mahoney to cross the ocean was John, son of patriarch Great James who sent his favorite son to scout the New World on behalf of his numerous clan. James had grown up under Ireland's Penal Code, which prevented Catholics like himself from owning land, or voting or even attending school. Furious at his oppressors, he rebelled.

To James, the Anglo-Irish were like a giant oak on a summer day, its rooted knees half visible under an immense lawn on a treeless meadow, the single tree waving its mammoth branches in a vast pasture where sheep grazed. The oak cast a comforting shadow, a protecting oasis under its spreading arms, as if harboring the wealthy families in the shade's circumference. But this safe haven was surrounded by acres of turf— everywhere in the direct eye of the sun, its green-shine brilliant against the manicured shade of the oak's shadow, a dark spot of privilege in a sea of emerald despair.

Mesmerized by the promise of free land in America and refired by thoughts of Jacksonian democracy, James scrimped stone by stone for forty years until he accumulated enough money for passage. In 1839, when a wild wind blew the thatch off the roof of their church at Aghadrumsee, James viewed it as a sign to abandon his shorn land. John, the appointed son, as family messenger to America, sailed west in 1840 with ten other young men of the parish, while James, whose life's dream was to provide farms for his sons, patiently waited at home on his seven acres of leased land, regularly praying at the high cross of the ruined sixth-century abbey for his son's safe return. John and his party, meanwhile, circulated for a year through the old Northwest Territory, finally determining that the rich soil west of the big river held the best promise. Back to Ireland they went to gather their families, carrying stories of Indians and geography unmatched in their known world.

Uncle Matthew related how scout John awed the family with his tales, "John told them, 'The grandest sight I ever saw was along the Mississippi. I was standing on a high hill north of the Indian mines, and saw great flocks of eagles over the water. And I've seen them all rise together, you know how birds do, late in the day, thousands of them, the sunset staining their white feathers red, squawking and circling with their wide wings. A powerful sight and you'll be seeing them soon yourselves.' "

As the time for their removal from Ireland approached, and as a mark of respect for sixty-year-old Great James, John the messenger raised a memorial stone in his father's name at the Round Tower graveyard in Clones, so that his daring would stand upright on his home soil. Struck by a favored son.

In the summer of 1841, James, his wife Bessie, seven sons, and two daughters—five of the children including Frank under the age of ten—along with six neighbor families, left Ireland forever and set sail for New Orleans. When they reached the Crescent City in late October, they embarked from steerage and set out along the docks. They hovered together, protecting their assets, viewing the riotous ethnicity of the new world—French traders, black slaves chanting African work songs, brown men from the Islands, red men in buffalo skins and yellow men with pigtails, all toiling on the barrel-crowded quay—a scene that widened their Irish eyes in wonder. With wobbly legs and carrying their sick children, this bundled wash-up of new Americans huddled along the waterfront and with slow pace shuffled toward shelter, the arrivals dense with hope and apprehension. They moved as a body along the cobbled streets and taking the advice of their ship captain found a boarding house a few blocks from the wharf where they settled down and made plans for their winter encampment—*the same year Stephen Foster wrote the first of his songs, many borne on a gentle and too darky air.*

They soon learned from the rivermen that owing to ice on the northern stretches, there was little they could do until winter eased. So the family set about visiting supply stores, checking on prices for seed and saws and stock, and attending local stock auctions in order to acquaint themselves with the intricacies of local bidding, while the women shopped for cloth and household goods. Though shy, they would approach passengers traveling down the river to ask about conditions in the higher latitudes: Was there ice where the river Ohio flowed in? How much did a milk cow cost in St. Louis? Slowly a mental map of the Mississippi valley emerged, whose capital was here in French New Orleans. They spent hours questioning the keelboatmen on the levee, listening to their stories of adventure along the river's broad path. Only ten years before, Schoolcraft had discovered the source of the Mississippi, thanks to his Indian guide, Ozawindib.

The O'Mahoneys waited in the delta town until late winter, trying to restrain one of the older sons from falling in love with a worldly-wise mulatto woman. At night, they heard the Creole/Negro music, wondering at the bright syncopated rhythms, exchanging their Irish-Scot songs with free blacks and bayou men, and listening to the melodies of a local boy named Gottschalk away studying composition in Paris. On special nights, they heard an orchestra playing on an offshore riverboat, and once at Christmastime attended an open-air "monster" concert with hundreds of instruments and voices—a noisy din. As if America could be raised up by its ears.

For the most part, they stayed away from the fashionable part of town, as no resident there spoke English. But on a mild day around New Year's, the parents and older children, including Frank, set off on a stroll through the elegant rues of New Orleans. They passed by mansions and open gardens, as the sun set west towards Mexico, and came upon a great house in the last evening light. They could hear the candle enflamed music weaving through the louvered windows, an orchestra playing a sketch left behind by the boy in Paris, a reverie piece recalling tropical nights. In its yearning melody were echoes of guitars riding on soft, swinging rhythms, a musically gentle place, latin, with mild winters, passionate flowers, bright birds and exotic green hills—coloring images of the sun flaming behind hundreds of Spanish-named mountains into the Pacific sea along a 10,000-mile coast. Embedded in the music was an echo of the American national anthem, *Hail, Columbia!*

One Sunday after mass, the Irish brigade, organized into a moving herd, followed the sounds of African drums until they came upon a large congregation of blacks in an open area known as Congo Square. There the slaves, who had been allowed a day off from their labors, blasphemed the French Sabbath with sensual native dances called bamboulas—whose rhythms young Gottschalk would recall in his later scores. The jig-prone Irish children, energized, came forward to step to the sweltering music.

James, taller than his surrounding convoy, was the only member to scowl at the sight before them. The other parents were awed by the dense and exotic scene, as their children, released by the spirit of the music, began to imitate the moves of the blacks. But James reckoned the emotional arc that spanned the slave's suffering, imagined the degraded life they endured, recognized the pain that was lightened momentarily by this reconnection to African customs. He had already begun to despise the blight that slavery had imposed on an innocent continent. All the venom and mortification he suffered and attributed to the English blasted angrily to the surface.

Matthew said, "James yelled out, 'Stop it! You'll not dance to any slave songs. We don't belong here. And if we stay, we'll be obliged to fill their heads with our own bile.'"

The sounds of those lilting bamboulas would remain in the family's collective memory until, in another generation, they would begin to hear those same tunes emerge as minstrel songs. For fifty years in their snow-covered cabins and frozen camps, the O'Mahoneys would remember the blood warmth of those black melodies played through the tapestry of its attendant French culture.

When the ice broke in the north, the new immigrants rode steam flatboats upriver, arriving in Dubuque before Easter. There, James bought a team of oxen and a rig and with John and another of the older men rode overland on the brightest, happiest day of his life. His dream was about to be fulfilled— the promise he had sworn to himself on the last night of the old century that he would provide and protect his own.

With James that day rode one of the Connollys who was especially knowledgeable about soil, and as they progressed slowly up the road, his friend would jump off the wagon and run out into the field to test the quality of the soil.

Uncle Matthew said, " 'Very good but not good enough,' was always the answer."

Late in the afternoon, they came to a settlers' camp pitched beneath a stand of pin oaks, and around the campfire that night inquired where the good land lay, and were advised to travel the next day a little farther west and north, up towards the north fork of the Little Maquoketa, back from the ridge road that ran along the cliffs of an older Mississippi.

In the late morning of that glorious day, they came to an unclaimed place of exceptional fertility in the eyes of the old farmers, the air heavy with spring earth smells, the birds caroling in the high branches of the hickory. James himself tested the earth, and noticing the course of a creek, came to a place of low rolling unbroken land that seemed perfect. Observing no stakes, James marched off about 60 acres, the edge of the northern enclosure located near a spring that fed a stream that wandered between the boundaries of the property.

They established the homeplace alongside the outflow, planted wheat and built their log cabin over the summer. They endured their first harsh winter when a blanket of snow covered the great silent basin from the Alleghenies to the Rockies and turned the great rivers a frozen white.

The next Easter, in commemoration of their survival, and as a reminder of the high cross they had left behind at the old abbey, the O'Mahoneys and their neighbors raised a large wooden cross on top of the highest rise so settlers could look up and see their sign of Christian faith from the surrounding fields. James had redeemed his promise that his children need never lease land again.

"That same year," Uncle Matthew inserted, "the first of the wagon trains reached the Columbia River in the Oregon Territory and a couple of actors rehashed that song about the *Gem of the Ocean*, lifting it from an old English tune."

The next year they built a church of white oak on the spot where the farmers had planted the cross, a church like the one the Germans had constructed the year before in neighboring New Vienna. Remembering the sacred symbol of their old and new home, they called the church Holy Cross. Within a few years, James officially confirmed title on the seven farms he had acquired at $1.25 an acre, settling up with the government land office, and parceling a thousand acres among his sons and daughters. During that same period, they built the first of the stone churches and the first of many schools.

Soon, their township appeared imprinted on a map with the name Concord, in honor of Emerson and the New England literary flowering. On the east, the boundary touched Jefferson township and on the other Liberty—the land a swath of Americana.

Matthew finished by saying, "And that was only the beginning. . . ."

During the history reading, the teenagers had kept a respectful distance but once Matthew finished, they smartly re-hung the curtains on the line, set up scenery and maneuvered themselves into position to resume their theatrics. Rising over the top of the curtain, nailed to a tree in the background, rose a rude painted paper reproduction of Holy Cross's old stone church. Meanwhile, the nuns reappeared to smooth down the hormones of the young, who were running in noisy circles. The cowbell soon clanged out an invitation.

Noticing the spires, "No doubt a religious play," Maeve said as she and Frank answered the call to assemble.

"Might help some heathens I know see the light," he said, eyeing her sideways.

"What light is that, Frank? Fairy dust?"

After the clan had resettled on the grass, the reader-girl emerged to present a new drama.

"In some branches of the family," she said, "being poor had special meaning."

The curtain opened and three girls and a pillow-stuffed mother lovingly examined a washed-out dress.

"These three sisters learned to share things including the one dress they owned between them."

One of the girls wearing a shift strategically placed over a full set of clothes raised her arms so the dress could slide down her limbs and thin torso.

"On Sundays, with clouds of petticoats whirling on and off, their mother holding the pins, the girls would help each other in and out of that one dress."

Mother and sisters primped over the girl wearing the communal gown.

"Then, one at a time, they scampered over the fields, bows streaming, trying to keep up with the itinerant priest who said early mass at the old stone church."

The chosen sister bolted from the cabin and rushed towards the painted church where the clergy awaited her. Joined by fellow worshipers on the way, she proudly modeled her dress for her friends. Then some prayers and mumbo-jumbo stayed the action, and after some mime, the girl ran back and the dress was transferred to the next-in-line.

"The undressing and hair combing continued, then the second sister was sent scurrying to Uncle Maurice's cabin where the priest said mass for the older folks in that section."

Away went the middle girl to repeat the scene.

"Then back again in holy procession to the church for a high mass came the clergy."

The nuns, already in costumes of a kind, joined the throng. Meanwhile back flew the dress so the remaining sister could oblige her Sunday duty. One of the girls brushing, another tying and the scheduled daughter whose time it was to wear the dress set to dash across the fields. Off she went.

"They were always late, of course. In the last relay, the mother ran behind, holding her hat. The treat for the sister on the final run was that she not only got to hear the choir but was allowed to stay after and mingle among the buggies."

There was a minimum of praying during this interlude as the choir sang out *Tantum Ergo*. Then a big climax when several traps were wheeled onto the set.

"They and the rest of the O'Mahoneys rotated—the girls, the dress, the crops, the seasons and the generations, adults and children alike confidant that they were creating a nation that had forever been the dream of man."

General socializing ensued among the actors, bringing the playlet to its conclusion. Everyone applauded on hearing "forever," the virtual ending.

Soon thereafter a general lethargy fell upon the family. The annual gathering of the Mahoney clan was deflating in the long afternoon sun following the entertainment and the pressure that the storm of food had generated among the hungry host at midday. The women retired upstairs to sleep three to a bed in their underthings. The men lay quietly snoozing in the grass.

After their naps, the men talked politics, Populists almost to a man. They believed in free silver and nationalization of the railroads and popular elections and the adoption of the referendum and the recall—building blocks for a farmer's movement that would plow the way towards the battles ahead.

Their antagonism against the robber barons of the east was intense, this after years of panics, speculation, corruption, and mortgage defaults, based on currency fluctuations and rampant capitalism.

Seeing that his bride was cared for by an old aunt, Martin decided to carry the baby along the stream that rambled past the fields and rows of corn behind the house. Memories flooded back to Martin as he carried young John-Arthur along the brook that flowed through this and the adjacent farms, including the one on which he was raised. He remembered how when they were children, he and his brothers and cousins played on the stream bank during its brief tree-lined journey across the fields. There they acted out Indian stories and pioneer tales—the creek stimulating their imaginings of steamboats on the river, Confederate raiders, and wagons fording west.

"See, along the bend," Martin said to his infant, "is where we fought the battle of Vicksburg, and that big tree down there was our Indian camp."

The whole of young America was played out here—the crossing of the ocean, the Battle of New Orleans, the building of the canals and the buffalo hunts—until the dinner bell rang across the fields and the stream each night was remanded to the frogs.

Martin said to baby John-Arthur, "I can't promise you much. Being a cartman selling vegetables in the alley doesn't pay much but we'll make do. You'll grow up in the city and have opportunities. And you'll spend your summers down here on the farm, so you'll see both sides."

The stream, though reduced and downsized from the eyes of his childish imagination, would remain the most important body of water that Martin would ever know, and he affectionately followed its course as it carried through the fields.

"You'll grow up to see it all. Big events like the Chicago Fair where they showed us the future. Your own children and grandchildren will have riches I can't even dream of. And be educated. And make a difference in the world."

As Martin walked back along the creek toward the homeplace, he swore the promise—the ever-recycling American allegiance that fathers make to their children—that his offspring would prosper to a greater degree than himself. Made in 1896, after years of depression, when America was switching from its dream of Arcadian enchantment to the harsh reality of its world power.

In the late afternoon as the heat of the reunion day began to perish, the Sisters of the BVM brought their instruments outdoors and near a shed with an overhang began to tune up their strings. The gathering clan took their chairs or spread out on blankets across the lawn. Some of the kids hopped up on the roof of the chicken coop or hoisted themselves into an elm and sat in its branches, while the quartet of nuns arranged themselves in a half circle that allowed them to signal their musical entrances through eye contact and breathy beginnings.

In her small soft voice, Sister Bern said, "We would like to play something Anton Dvorak wrote after visiting the Great Chicago Fair. It's one of two pieces he wrote a few years ago just fifty miles north of here, up on the Turkey River near Spillville. We'll do the first movement of his *String Quartet Number Twelve in F Major*. It's Iowa's song—about the land, and the old times, and even the Indians. We've been practicing all summer so I hope you like it."

The main theme came floating out, reminding Martin of stories about the billowing prairie schooners that sailed across the land a half century before. That theme meshed directly into an Indian refrain and then a sweet melody, an expression of remembered unity, like a family embracing its past. There was appreciative applause from the adults, which gave some of the boys an opportunity to whistle loudly and start an apple fight, followed by some parental interchange. Then an encore performance—the sweet theme an Iowa hymn.

The next morning after mass, surrounded by dozens of kinsmen, John-Arthur was christened in the red brick church.

## Chapter 2

From across the fields, John-Arthur could make out the top of the hill where his great-grandfather had raised the high cross. Wherever he wandered throughout the township, he could easily sight the white steeple that pointed upward from the red brick church that had long ago replaced the rugged cross, the log enclosure and, the rough stone church that preceded it. From any farmyard or patch of woods, wherever his adventurers led him, he could quickly orient himself by a turn of the head. On some warm afternoons, when he missed his parents back in Chicago, he would sit inside the immaculate sparseness of the church under the stained glass window presented by the Irish Young Ladies Society and pray. In these soft hours of the day, he quietly acceded to the impulse to surrender himself to a higher power, more meaningful because he made his supplications within walls built by the hands of his own kin. Familiar and comfortable here where he was baptized, each Sunday during his summer visit, he would don oversize red robes and a white lacy top and assist at mass. It was 1906 and John-Arthur was ten.

The boys arrived on their grandfather Frank's farm following the spring planting and departed before the fall harvest, but there was plenty of weeding in between. Though they had chores at the beginning and end of the day, there was time to play with their cousins in the middle hours—games in the barn on rainy days or the production of inventive dramas along the creek. There was a free-swinging hinge on his imagination because Martin had convinced his son that ten was a perfect age. Then true intelligence was unblemished by cynicism, there was a sense of values and fairness uncorrupted by experience and feelings of wonder and expectation that would never come again. Unburdened by sexual desire, tolerant of all, fair to a fault, courteous to old and young and stock alike, ten-year-olds like John-Arthur faced the world with unbridled curiosity. Later there would be a concern about larger people.

Each summer John-Arthur and his brother Francis named after Old Frank would visit the farm, offering their parents relief during the hot Chicago weather, allowing Kitty and Martin to renew their closeness. The boys would board the westbound train and travel across the Illinois prairie, span the Mississippi, and be met at the Dubuque Station, set on the flood plain below the Victorian mansions that looked down over the city from the bluff above. They then transferred to the local Long View train and, upon arrival, drove the remaining few miles to *Sunny Slope*, Grandpa Frank at the reins. The old farmer had not been well but kept his good disposition and the daily work habits that had described his life.

The boys were unable to comprehend any concept of the abundance they saw around them—the wide fields of corn, and black earth arcing in quarter circles etched in geometric color on a blue-sky canvas, the land undulating away into infinity. But they were aware of a bucolic richness that filled their eyes; their senses awakened to the sounds of field birds and the dank odors of the animal birthing bins.

There was much excitement when they crossed the threshold of their ancestral home. The boys would be swept up in the musty smells of Grandmother Ellen's apron that would mix with the downwind fragrances from her stove—warm and pungent. Then they would race up the dirt road to the family homeplace to see their country cousins—the four boys and three girls of James III, who ran the local general store and saloon and, with help, found time to manage his own farm. The city boys would burst into the house with great enthusiasm and then once in the presence of their small relatives, shyly move from one to another, with smiles and much thumping of backs.

The endless days that followed unfolded from first light until Uncle Leo came in from the barn long after dark, carrying his lantern. The boys' jobs, feeding the chickens, gathering the eggs, pumping and carrying water and slopping the hogs, were tiresome tasks but relieved by more adventurous chores like shepherding the herd out into the yard or brushing the horses. As luck would have it, they were excused from the milking parlor, happy to let others handle that sticky job. If needed for weeding, they turned into the fields to mind the corn and barley and oats. But the best part of the day was the lazy stretch from eleven until four when they were on their own, free to ride Blaze or Gin or wander wherever their imagination took them. Within days of their arrival, they smelled like the barn itself.

Their mornings began at dawn with a call up the narrow stairs to the third floor where John-Arthur and Francis slept under the roof. Grandma Ellen had the woodstove crackling by the time they descended and Grandpa Frank, his big farmer's frame  dominating the room, sat behind the small breakfast that preceded the larger one a couple of hours later. The kitchen table held a medley of items in the center, a shifting cluster of salt, pepper, toothpicks, cinnamon, creamer, napkin rings, a butter dish and preserves—a kingdom of condiments. And a jar filled with wildflowers.

Joining them was the old couple's unmarried son, Leo, who helped run the farm, and a hired hand, a Glasgow carpenter named Scotty who, though he wobbled in the morning, held a steadfast hammer by midday, a man whose love of his daily liquor determined the course of his wandering years.

"And how are my city angels this morning?" asked Grandma Ellen.

The boys nodded sleepily.

"They'll earn their keep," said old Frank.

"If they don't, we could always hoist them on top of the silo and let them fry awhile," Leo joked. He was a big, shambling man with a forced sense of humor that masked a darker laughter.

"You don't have to scare them on their first morning," the grandfather said. "What they more likely need is a treat. Maybe they should look along the creek for one."

That woke them up. "What treat?" asked John-Arthur.

"You'll have to see for yourself."

After breakfast, they ran down the path along the stream about a hundred yards from the house and saw that their grandfather had dammed up part of the creek to provide a small swimming hole for them. Elated they ran back to the farm but the men were already on their way to the fields.

"He must have kept it a secret from the cousins," John-Arthur said to his brother. "Come on. Grandma's waving."

After lunch, they gathered the cousins and headed for the dam and were waterlogged by midafternoon. By then, armed with willow branches, their bony limbs sticking out of their bathing suits, they reenacted a schoolbook battle of the Civil War, the girls protesting their Confederacy.

"Talk southern like they do in Saint Louis," commanded Emmett, the eldest of the seven, and the leader.

"Why do we always have to die?" asked Gen, the only one of the girls brave enough to sass her older brother.

"Because it's the rules," answered Emmett with finality.

A "who says—I say" confrontation ended in compromise. Francis, under protest, was sent over to the girls.

Emmett and John-Arthur were fighting halfway up the bank to "Vicksburg" and the girls and Francis were showing their courage in the siege when they were noisily distracted from the din of war by the sound of a bawling calf wandering up the middle of the stream. Close behind the stray appeared a large redheaded farmwoman, chasing down her prey. She caught up with the brown calf and after tying off a line on Martin's Indian elm, approached the battlefield.

"And what's this?" asked the farmwoman. "The Vikings and the Saxons?"

"The boys always make us lose," one of the girls said.

"We'll change that right away," the woman answered.

"Can you give us another game, Maeve?" asked Emmett's sister.

"With a good girl ending. . . .And maybe a Spaniard or two in it as well. . . .Some turned-around story my granny told me," the woman said. "And here's a new face…What's your name?"

"John-Arthur."

"A good name for this story." Removing a silver necklace, she said, "You'll be in charge of protecting this. It's a charm that keeps you safe from those in power that cook up a life for themselves without caring for others. Now here's how it goes."

Arthur looked down at the pendant hanging from the silver strand and saw some curlicue markings on front, and inscribed on the backing, the word "TARA."

She re-arranged an Irish myth in such a way that the girls ended up defeating the boys, much to the one's delight and the other's chagrin. She had entered their imaginary world and swirled it around. Then she left, waving; she and her brown calf started back down the path beside the creek.

The next afternoon, drawn by his attraction to the Irish farmwoman, John-Arthur walked downstream towards Maeve's farm and found her in the yard among her cattle. He hailed her across the field and she welcomed him with a big open waving of her arms as he approached the fenceline.

"My gallant John-Arthur," Maeve said. "Come inside."

She lived in one of the foursquare O'Mahoney houses built around the time of the Civil War. She had decorated the rooms in a plain, spare style, lining the halls and rooms with bookcases and stacks of volumes. In the parlor, a musical machine sat in idle expectation, one the boy would come to associate with her—a rat-a-tat banging, tinklebright player piano that was her favorite possession. The pianola was constructed of light oak, and portrayed a stained-glass image of an outspread eagle on the sliding doors that opened onto the tracker mechanism—the bird a symbol of her newfound land.

"Come, we'll load up the magic box and I'll play you a tune," she said, sitting him next to her on the edge of the up-pitched bench, reaching down to adjust the levers.

As she pumped organ-style, the roll began to turn and the keys to bounce like popcorn and out sprang the sounds of *To a Wild Rose*. John-Arthur sat fascinated, watching the automatic fingering. Nickelodeons were coming into favor in the Chicago arcades and he had seen a variety of instruments plucking their way through the musical vocabulary—autoharps and unmanned banjos— but he had never before sat abreast a pianola or was so intimately surrounded by its nervous energy. Breathing a quiet lyricism, MacDowell's melody sang a gentle air not only reflecting the composer's soft soul but reflective of front-porch and back-garden America.

Maeve said, almost to herself, "That song. . . . It reminds me of how I feel on a day in spring when apple trees wear their brides' dresses." She hesitated and said dreamily, "I sometimes wish I could catch their blossoms and pinch them back on. And how all summer long when the green leaves shine through the veil, I can still see in my mind's eye, robes of white."

John-Arthur, not understanding, remained silent.

Continuing, Maeve added, "Wild Rose, that's me."

"Can you play this thing yourself with your own fingers?" John-Arthur asked.

"Sure," she said," shuttling the lever and lowering the bench. "What would you like to hear?" thumbing through her stack of sheet music. "How about *After the Ball?*"

She played in a forthright parlor style, getting the melody right with a minimum of poking around. John-Arthur, entertained by an attractive adult, responded and smiled as he watched her red hair bounce to the rhythms of the song. She began singing and prompted him to join in, and they soon filled the house with music.

"That was grand," she said, hugging him.

He felt her softness envelope him. Then and there was born in John-Arthur a sense of romantic exaggeration whose soulful yearning for the beauty of women entered the Mahoney strain with such strength that it would carry him and his sons well into the next generation.

She then selected the *Maple Leaf Rag* from among her music rolls, a tricky tune written by Scott Joplin, the same pianoman that his father, Martin, had heard at the Chicago Fair. Joplin had taken Gottschalk's cakewalks and spun them into ragtime, which in turn would create the fabric of jazz—all fashioned from Mississippi river towns.

*Unknown to the pair, Joplin, after his summer tour, would arrive in New York with the expressed intention of writing a second grand opera, which he managed to complete, even in the face of racist skepticism. The newspapers, thwarting Joplin, said that a Negro wasn't capable of composing a real opera. But Joplin's music would be redeemed and blacks would eventually sing out its rhythms on royal stages. And ambitious parents would be energized by women like Joplin's freeborn mother, a maid, who took her boy along to the big houses where she cleaned, and there negotiated benchtime with the landed ladies, allowing Scott to practice on their big squarebox pianos while his mother mopped. Borrowed palaces where they could dust and dance.*

"Would you like to learn to play yourself?" Maeve asked, and John-Arthur nodded with enthusiasm.

For the rest of the summer, each mid-day, John-Arthur tramped over to Maeve's farm and the two of them sat at the upright and he learned his exercises. She was patient with him and kept up his interest not only at the piano but also by sharing her books—many of them illustrated by the new color process that brought the myths she fancied alive. She loved the old tales, any legend, Greek, Roman, or Asian, and she passed along her enthusiasm to John-Arthur by regaling him with stories filled with the sometimes arbitrary doings of gods and heroes and the like, classical representations of the virtues and vices galvanized into action through the device of some old plot. He would sometimes sit there after she returned to the fields and practice his scales and then peer in the books again and revel in the heroics of Irish and English children's literature.

"It's all right to read those English stories about Avalon and all," she would say, "so long as those bloodsuckers are fighting among themselves and leave us alone on our own green island," she laughed, "where we had plenty of opportunity to murder each other."

She taught him the Celtic myths including tales of the little people of the underworld and tales of the enchanted woods. He drank it in like a thirsty runner.

She would say, "We're reading so many of these tales, I'm beginning to feel like the Queen of the Fairies myself."

At home in Chicago, he told her, his parents read to him and his brother Francis each night, no matter what the traffic in their store. But Maeve's exploration into the mysteries of these Anglo-Irish legends encouraged John-Arthur to learn more and soon the connections began to spread, their patterns and the themes became more transparent, illuminated as they were by their common virtues and evils. Soon, his reading greatly elevated the quality of the games played along the creek.

Maeve would add, "You young ones should start reading these tales earlier than you do. I don't know what parents are waiting for, holding back their children. For what? It's not like you're gonna be flying off with Peter Pan to slay pirates."

When John-Arthur would return to his grandparents, he would delight them by repeating stories they had not heard since childhood.

"I remember that one," Ellen would say. "My old Aunt Margaret told it to me but with a different ending."

"Has Maeve told you this one. . . . ?" his grandfather would ask him.

"Tell me that one again. . . ." Francis would ask his older brother when they had settled under the eaves.

Story cycles opened and were repeated.

His brother enjoyed John-Arthur's storytelling and came to accept his advice and opinions on most matters. This reliance had been solidified one day that spring on the St. Anne schoolyard back in Chicago when some older kids were ragging Francis, whose meekness was viewed as a sign of weakness, the bullies thinking him easy prey. When John-Arthur saw them punching his brother, he waded into the melee with fists flying. Reliance on the protective arm of an older brother—Irish law.

* * *

On the first Sunday that John-Arthur visited Maeve for his daily piano lesson, an older man was seated comfortably in the big couch in the parlor. He was both a piano partner and literary-society friend of Maeve's.

"Everybody calls me Ed," he said to John-Arthur. "Might be easier if you did too."

He lived in a nearby town, a widower, and enjoyed Maeve's company. They liked to play two-handed piano and afterwards he would turn piano rolls with her. What bound them together aside from music was their interest in the legends and though they would mainly concentrate on knightly English tales and the ones from Grimm that Ed could read in German, they discovered other lush accounts in translation, including ones from Russia. Into this Sunday circle, John-Arthur entered at full tilt, flags flying, guided if only in imagination by the glory of St. George and all the other monster killers.

The power that legends held for mature adults back then was part of the attraction of the Romantic movement, so opposite the reality of daily life. Fables from the chivalric system still possessed the power to lance insensitivity. Wagner's music and Yeats' poetry confirmed this madness for fairies, woodland sprites, and other-worldlies. When Ed with fire-breathing passion read these spirit-cleansing tales aloud, John-Arthur thought he could almost see the knights' horses and fair maidens bouncing through Ed's brain.

The following Sunday in June, Ed brought along three piano rolls that he treasured, one spun out the dotted calibrations of the middle section of MacDowell's *Keltic Sonata*. They listened to the music, drowsing in its Irish lore, for hints of Cuchullin and Deirdre, even Mab herself.

After playing this American version of Celtic airs, Ed said, "Here's another from MacDowell. . . .The shame the poor man lies dying in New York. . . . It's a piano version from the middle movement of the *First Concerto*. Music that could calm a banshee."

"Is he the one who loved Indian music?" Maeve asked.

"Composed a whole suite of it."

After listening to the *First*, Ed said, "I get so filled with some kind of yearning after I hear that middle section, I can hardly speak."

John-Arthur had never heard anyone talk like this before—confiding emotions about something artistic.

"Here's my last one from MacDowell—his *Indian Idyll*. . . .Listen to the love song. One from the Iowa tribe."

They were his first adult friends, and in the next month, they helped escort John-Arthur outside of himself. He felt freer because of them—less restrained, as if they assisted him in unwinding the bandages of self-interest that bound his stiff soul and offered him the looseness to stretch his mind and imagination. When you have older friends, he thought to himself, you feel like you belong in the world.

The following Saturday night, Ed invited Maeve and John-Arthur to his nearby German village of New Vienna to view a locally advertised *Opera and Extravaganza*, presented by a traveling company from St. Louis. It was the first theater performance John-Arthur attended, one he was destined never to forget. How could he, sitting among the sizable farm families who were uncertain about any music other than Wagner and the three Teutonic B's? Titled *Columbian Fair*, the opera was produced by a black troupe and, amazingly, played in ragtime. The syncopation pursued by the composer, who worked the keyboard, delighted the trio. Enjoying the music, Maeve asked for and bought a copy of the score, and on the way home she and John-Arthur sang one of the principal themes over and over until the melody came to reside, as all good melodic guests should, in their musical mindstrings. That score was presumed lost by the time death overtook the youngest member of the audience, but musicologists searched for it the entire century. Unfortunately, the opera had a short run, owing to the times and disposition of its audiences. The opera troupe broke apart and sashayed back into minstrelsy, where man's higher and lower aspirations were able to seek comfort with one another without skipping key changes in the ragtime signature.

* * *

His Grandpa's confidence in him was another reason John-Arthur felt that he was growing up. He appreciated the fact that Frank never talked down to him, always spoke to him as if he were conversing with another adult. Before dinner it was Frank and Leo's habit to take a few minutes to read the paper and catch up on the news and then after dinner, prior to their last chores, the family would sit around the empty plates and discuss the day's doings. In the beginning of summer, the boys avoided rummaging through the spreadout newspapers so they could scamper home at the last possible minute, but John-Arthur enjoyed lingering after dinner and listening to his family. Before long, he began to arrive home earlier and would help Frank read because the old man didn't like to wear glasses and was always misplacing them. On Mondays, a river-borne copy of the St. Louis *Globe Democrat* would appear, a paper that floated up and down the tributaries and creeks of the Mississippi, a journal guided by a famous managing editor that held the riverwest in his sway. From those pages, the larger world began to emerge for John-Arthur.

This was also the time of day that the boys were treated to Frank's weaving of family yarns. They listened intently to their grandfather's stories, especially the ones about Indians.

"Back in '48, when I was twelve," Frank said, "the government got the Winnebagos to give up their privileges in the Neutral Ground. . . . That's because there were so many new immigrants crowding them off the land. . . .And the army wanted to resettle them far north in Sioux country, even though that was enemy territory for them. I was working over in Long View the day the Winnebagos came downriver towards Dubuque—where the steamers were waiting to carry them away to Minnesota. It was the most remarkable sight I ever saw in my life—two thousand Indians in full dress in hundreds of canoes drifting by our side of the river. Proud, sad, afraid—a whole nation displaced. I felt miserable for them because I knew how it was. We were practically thrown out of our own country by the English. Now it was our new government's turn to chuck out the Indians, sending them away from their own river. My Da, standing next to me on the shore, shouting, 'Don't go. Don't let them do it to yese.'"

The boys absorbed the local stories, how once a steamboat caught fire off their patch of the Mississippi. Or how all the O'Mahoneys had traveled across to the Illinois side to observe thousands of bald eagles rapting through the sky above the river. And another one about how the men sometimes crossed the wide waterway on ice in winter. And one more about how the leftover Indians would set up toll booths along their old trails, offering passage for a few bites to eat or drink.

"Grandpa, tell us again about going to the Gold Rush."

Ellen said, "Did he tell you he was three times unlucky there?"

Old Frank said, "Persistent at least. Call it what is was—pure greed. One chance in a lifetime. I'd go out—three or four months to get there—and I'd spend all my money and come back and raise more cash and go out again. Nothing like a fool to take three times to learn."

He continued. "It was a Rush all right—men laying down their plows and racing by boat and wagon around and across the continent. . . .The itch to make a lot of money fast. Ditch the poverty of dozens of generations, shake the muck of the yard off your boots and be able to build a big garden with a brick wall around it. And have all your children schooled."

"Like we did with our Martin," Ellen said, alternately expressing pride in this accomplishment and confusion about its impractical consequences.

"Some men," Frank continued, "would leave their family grubless, take their only horse and trail two thousand miles to California. Or slip down the river and over to the Pacific at the isthmus or around the Horn and sail a schooner up into San Francisco Bay. When they got there, the bay was filled with empty boats abandoned by their sailors as well as the passengers—all of them following their pipe dreams up into the hills.

"Tens of thousands of us from all over the world, with a shovel and a pan and a dream. First time I went, I ran out of money in a month. The prices were sky high; it cost two dollars just to eat dinner, one you would have thrown out the back door at home. But I was young and unmarried and didn't want to kick myself later for not going. . . .Places with names like Sonora and Mariposa and Jackass Hill and Angel's Camp. . . .Even El Dorado itself. . . .You had to take care of yourself though— fights all the time and looting. It was a brawling place.

"You had to wait for the gold to come to you and it was back-breaking work—the cold water in the streams cramping your limbs but you stayed with it because you knew if you turned your head at the wrong moment, a fortune could flow between your legs. You'd even go out at night if there was moon enough and a lantern because you couldn't sleep for the riches floating down creek.

"But what good was it anyway except it made you crazy? Even the real gold was fool's gold because it didn't make a country of us. It couldn't heal the wounds between the rich and poor, or between black and whites, south and north, whites and Indians, gringos and Mexicans. All it did was make you go around busting your buttons in storebought clothes. And even they'd make you look silly.

"Course people thought they could see the gold shining in the hills all the way back here to Iowa. . . .You have to remember that California is the end of the earth. Think about it. Figure the day begins when the sun comes up over China where most people live and it rolls over all of Asia and Europe and Africa and the Atlantic and comes back around again and the last of the day's reflections leaves its colors on the high Sierras—all red and gleaming—with a million specks of gold shining out. We were like slaves of some evening sun god who had lit up the end of the day in a great storm of color.

"The farmers back home thought that if they climbed high enough on their barns they could see the gold glowing from their own roofbeam, but it was all a myth except for a handful. A rush to nowhere. All near the American River south of another one called Columbia. Flag-waving rivers."

In that parlor John-Arthur learned what it meant to have a country. Passed down by an old Irishman.

\* \* \*

Next day, John-Arthur was working with Scotty in the back of the barn. The old Scotsman was adept at fixing things and handy at carpentering, though he didn't like working with machinery as much as with his wooden maul and adze. Frank would say to the boys that Scotty was more wedded to trees than to mowers.

"Pass me the level," John-Arthur said absentmindedly.

"No Scotsman likes to take orders from an Irish lad, but I guess I'll have to oblige seeing that your people got here first," the carpenter said, teasing the boy.

"What part of Scotland are you from?" John-Arthur asked trying to place the map of the country in his mind's eye.

"Glasgow, the part facing Ireland. Little wonder I'm bothered by the spirits. Must have caught something from across the sea."

"Is it far between the two countries?"

"A good day's sail on a quiet day. Some say the best Irishmen were from Scotland, the ones that sailed over as gallowglass."

"What's that?

"Paid soldiers. To keep the Hibernians from killing each other in their everlasting battles."

The Scotsman, a stubby pencil behind his ear and sawdust in his hair, hesitated, then said, "I'd be interested to know if you can keep a secret, lad."

"Probably can," John-Arthur said.

"If so, I may have an idea for you."

"I said I could, unless it would hurt somebody."

Scotty said, "No, it can only hurt myself."

John-Arthur scanned his basic moral precepts and landed, as usual, on church grounds, "Do you have the same church as we do in Scotland?"

"God in heaven no. We've got prune-faced Calvinists instead of your smoke and oil."

"What's a Calvinist?"

"A Calvinist? One of John Knox's men. Calvinism is what the earth looked like before man got here. Lumps of boulders is what they are. . . .People parading around as stones."

"I don't get it." John-Arthur said.

"Does a rock in the heather ever take a little drink? Does a highland boulder know his country's beverage is whiskey? No! He practices Presbyterian prohibition. . . .Don't get me started. I don't know why they've come here looking for freedom anyway when they can stoke hell's fires at home. They surely prefer purgatory on earth with no hope of heaven. Do you know what purgatory on earth is, son?"

"No, what?"

"Abstinence!"

"What's the secret you want me to keep?" John-Arthur asked, unable to contain his curiosity.

"Maybe you'll come with me one day on a run over to Long View and we'll go to the back door of your Uncle Jim's saloon and then we'll see if you can keep a secret or not."

Francis and Scotty were actually better tuned to one other. The old carpenter offered to teach Francis, age seven, tricks of his trade in much the same way that Maeve taught John-Arthur the piano. Francis would follow the Scotsman around the farm and join in whatever task Scotty confronted, often as much nuisance as help. But the Glaswegian was patient and soon Scotty was teaching the quiet boy how things worked and how to fix them. Quickly enough, they found a Sunday avocation. Situated on the same hilltop property as the new brick church and the pioneer's cemetery was the old abandoned rock church that had served the original settlers. A low, primitive building, long deconsecrated, served as a shed of sorts for the forty acres of church property. In its dark cavern, the old Scotsman and Francis conspired to mend the roof and walls of the former stone chapel.

"It's as good as him going to mass," Frank would say approvingly. "Of course he comes home that night and gets drunk and wanders into the ice house where just before he freezes to death, he bolts out and falls head first into the stream. Sobered him up quick enough."

\* \* \*

One night, his grandfather told John-Arthur that he was welcome to attend a meeting at the Grange if he'd care to come along with Uncle Leo and himself. The boy quickly agreed. They hitched up Gin and rode into Holy Cross. Squashed between the two men in the buggy and later on the benches of the dancehall, John-Arthur felt secure between the two family men with their heavy clothes and layered smells, packed in among dozens of other farmers, including a variety of his kin, some full-blood, some by marriage, plus his Uncles Vince and Matt. His Uncle James was there with his chum Emmett, and his Great Uncle Maurice, Frank's last brother.

The Grange movement was linked to the writings of Edward Bellamy, a Massachusetts newspaperman who published *Looking Backward* about an ideal socialistic community. The group sprang as well from the active mind of Henry George, a Philadelphian, who edited newspapers in the west, a single tax advocate who wrote *Progress and Poverty*. The Grange coexisted with the Socialists at a time when the latter's discussion clubs stemmed from the same writings, organizations that eventually formed the nucleus of the People's Party, which evolved into the Populist Party. They in turn promoted an eight hour day, the secret ballot, income taxes, women's suffrage,

free silver and nationalization of the railroads. The Grange, half
hard politics and half idealistic, offered a podium for Irish and
German dreamers.

A few rows forward, John-Arthur noticed his piano-playing
friend.

"Tell me about Maeve?" the boy asked his grandfather.

"Maeve O'Donnell? Been running one of our old farms for a
few years. Related to us through the McCloskeys. Pretty good
farmer. . . .Though they say she trained as a nurse in Dublin.
Would argue God out of heaven. It's said she was turned out of
Ireland."

She herself would say that it was good she had come over
when she did because soon after her arrival Congress passed an
immigration law that denied entrance to anarchists and women
of ill-repute. "Got in just under the wire," she said laughing.

John-Arthur's Uncle Jim, the one with the general store and
saloon, stood up in front of the audience and the chattering
diminished as he went through some notes and announcements.
"Welcome once more to Fidelity Grange. Glad to see the
participation. These Grange meetings are the only way we have
to get together and express ourselves and take up the issues, so
I'm glad to see such a good turnout. I see Walt Beiderhaus is
feeling better and. . . .Oh, and Charlie McGuire. . . .Arm's

looking good. . . . .And I think I see a little shaver here and there. All welcome."

His Uncle Jim set the tone of the meeting, "When my granddad, old James, came over, you could live without money and not be tied up by bank loans and mortgages and the craziness of currency. He came before the robbers from Chicago laid down a single piece of railroad iron on Iowa soil. In those days we shipped produce downriver to St. Louis, and they may even have eaten our corn as far south as Memphis. But when the railroads came, we were in Chicago's noose, and of course it's been a battle ever since. It's us short haulers that's paying more than those shipping from Kansas and beyond. Now they say they're going to raise prices again. Maybe it's inevitable."

Maeve hollered out, "Some things aren't inevitable. I've heard that even Niagara Falls itself went dry a few years ago."

Her face, with its high forehead and solid jaw, sloped into a neck that throbbed like a pillar of emotion, a conduit connecting her heart and head. Striving through her rough clothes, her wide hips were carved out of a smaller waist, beneath a muscled back. There was something lusty about her, full-blooded. Her eyes were penetrating when she spoke, constantly evaluating the other person's courage or intelligence. Her eyes now blazed at this latest injustice announced by the railroads.

She continued, "Only one marker for a public service, whether it's railroads or police or the army. Is it fair and even-handed for all alike? That's the test in a country like this. The rest is ear corn. We live way out here in nowhere to enjoy our freedom. We pay for it with a hard life but we wouldn't live anywhere else because we want to be left alone—and that's how you lived until the railroads came pressing in. Bad enough to remind us of the times back there," she said, tossing her head to indicate the four thousand miles that separated them from their native lands. "It took a surge of courage for us to come over and live like exiles—some of us booted out of our settled lives. But it's the only place we can live in peace, so don't ask me to sit by and be abused by some railroad lawyer from Chicago."

"What would you propose?" asked James Mahoney.

"The only thing they understand is a fight—even though we know what they'll do to us if we organize. Same as they did to the Haymarket and Pullman strikers," Maeve said.

They listened to her as an equal because she had proved herself in the fields. But they had to be encouraged to action. "In Ireland, we'd tear up their tracks," she said.

James said, "Jail's not that appealing to most of us, Maeve. The national organization's gonna take it up and we'll have something to tell you fairly soon, I'm sure."

Sitting down, she said, "I only want to say that when people walk away from the farmer, they walk away from their own best interests."

The meeting drifted to other topics like crop prices and milk distribution in Dubuque and after an hour or so, Jim gaveled the meeting to a close.

Frank said, "Them damn railroads."

"Yeah," John-Arthur said, not really understanding why they should be damned, but agreeing.

Afterwards, as was their custom, the Mahoney men came together in an awkward circle—the five men and two boys—part of Great James' progeny. The two eldest, Frank and Maurice, had been raised in Ireland. In the higher registers of their voices, there was still a touch of the brogue.

"That Maeve, she's something—tearing up the tracks!"

"Think it's true what they say on the other side—she was the leader's other girl?"

"Told to leave Ireland, that's all I know."

"Hard to figure such a feisty woman."

"Harder still to live with one."

"And I guess no man's learned how to do that yet. Surely not that Ed guy."

"We ought to send back for some scrappy lad that's looking for a row to hoe."

"She'd be too much for any man."

John-Arthur took in everything, all the while watching Maeve, who with no circle of her own, touched the edges of all. Then she came over and put her arm around his shoulders while she talked to his kin.

* * *

The big event that summer, so it would seem this early in the season, was a show of power by the United States Navy. On July 1, long before dawn, the local citizens on both banks of the river were up and dressed. Coffee was brewed early and biscuits came popping out of the stove, and by five nearly everybody in the countryside, except for the animals and a few herders, bore down on the river.

As soon as they arrived along the shore, they could see the ships coming out of the mist. They came in single-file fleet parade, smaller ships that had been able to work themselves through the locks downstream. With their distinctive knife-edge prows, came a flotilla from the Great White Fleet that was on its way to an around-the-world display of U.S. force. White on white in the early haze, the ships floated south past the awe-struck farmers. John-Arthur looked on in amazement. He had never seen such power before.

The tour of the White Fleet had been one of Theodore Roosevelt's greatest ambitions—not as important or as permanent as his Panama Canal—but a gesture for the entire world to see that America had matured into a world power. He was sending out his Navy to display the country's prowess—sailing to the Far East toward Japan and across the Atlantic to alert Europe—a warning for both to stay on their own sides of the ocean.

Here was a string of the fleet's smaller ships, a squadron that had steamed to the Minnesota line and was now tracking back to St. Louis to celebrate the Fourth of July.

The sight of the ships formed an important image in John-Arthur's mind. He would never know if he should rejoice in his country's strength and boast of it or simply fear and question its hostile strength. He would ask lifelong questions as to whether or not we should have gone to war to imprint our manifest destiny on such places as the Caribbean and the Philippines—or if instead we should remain a beacon, not to torch the world but encourage it. Or some balance of both. For a person who would face one of the brutal events of the twentieth century, this was his first glimpse at his nation's power. And he never forgot it. The fleet came to symbolize his time and place just as the White City did for his father and the exodus of the Winnebagos for his grandfather and the rise of the eagle flock for his Great Uncle John. Woven into the fabric of America, these images were knitted together in cross-stitched confusion.

# Chapter 3

On the morning of the glorious Fourth, Frank's household, minus Scotty who was assigned to stay home to watch the stock, climbed into the wagon and headed for the Long View station. They were on their way to a holiday picnic and it was the job of Leo and the two boys in the back to protect the food. They listened attentitively while Ellen, who had been up half the night cooking and baking, offered instructions in her soft voice. There were jars in this one and pies in that, and no tilting please. Tucked in one of the baskets were the strawberries that the boys had picked as their contribution.

"Everybody in? Maeve's waiting. HEY ! UP!" instructed Frank, shaking the reins.

Surrounded by baskets that smelled like Christmas morning, their grandfather began to fill the boy's heads with jams and candies. "For years I've wanted to picnic at Eagle Point and I figured this was a good a year as any. We'll take the 7:05 downriver and get off close to the park and climb the hill before the day's along."

"Will we have treats, Grandpa?" Francis asked.

"What do you think's sitting on your lap? Maybe you can have some root beer if you want. Or popcorn. And maybe even one of them new ice cream cones. But mind that you listen to your stomach."

"It's like going off to the fair in the old country," Ellen said. "I can remember being the young one. All the excitement of sailing over to Galway City for the auctions. Do you remember the fairs, Frank?"

"Vaguely. Best I remember were the boxing matches on the Clones Square."

Leo said, "Nothing wrong with the Fourth right here. Flags flying along Main Street. Remember last year's opening of the water works and the big dance? Even a new fire cart."

Back and forth went their memories.

Ellen added, "Parade lasted all of three minutes if I recall. Best part was Maeve all dressed up like Miss Columbia, riding her horse, wearing the sash that read 'Suffragette.'"

Frank nodded, "It's lucky we have those social clubs in town or you'd wink and the whole thing would be past. . . .Course the dancing's the important thing. Tells you something about Holy Cross when the biggest building in town after the church is the dancehall."

And Leo from the back, "And don't forget the ball teams, all ten of 'em—that's one-third of the population right there."

"More people marching in the parade than watching," Ellen recalled. "Town's growing too fast. If we don't watch out, they'll be adding sidewalks."

Ellen, like Frank, was as Irish as the green earth, but she had been transformed since arriving with her family as a girl. Transformed into an Iowa farmwoman down to her catalog-bought shoes, she had become practical and slow to judge, stubborn and tuned to the seasons. The pig's litter was so, and the return of the tanager thus, and when to pick the first corn on the cob. Alert to judge when the quality of chopped wood in the stove was seasoned just right, what speed to churn the butter and how deep to plant the bulbs.

Her year was as productive as the seasons except in the years when the rain didn't come. Those were offset by the fertile years when the children arrived—her Martin, the third James, Joe, Vincent, Leo, Mary Ellen the sick one, and Matt. She had been as fruitful as the land; her life with Frank a trial and a blessing. She was without rancor and loved Christ and His mother. About her was a sweetness that everyone remarked on, with an inner toughness wrought from adversity. Frugal and shrewd with money; she was indebted to her father, who had taught her how to negotiate at the cattle market back in Galway. Even though she had spent most of her life here and was as loyal as any native born, Ireland was and would ever be her home.

When she first came over she worked as a serving girl in Chicago, and she brought to her husband Frank a lace dowry and the famous fact that she had once served dinner to Abraham Lincoln. Now the midwest was under her nails and packed in her lungs. If she lacked a sensitive streak, her plainness was without malice. It was her love for her firstborn Martin that helped identify her, so intense she allowed him to tune his own strings. He had opted to negotiate the complexities of his emotional and spiritual life by entering the priesthood. Then, after he removed the robes of the church, she was forced to throw her own mantle over him, to try and protect him; his weakness in her eyes was that he was deficient regarding money and property, something that bothered both his practical parents.

At the crest of the hill, they looked down the incline where they saw Maeve O'Donnell standing by the side of the road, her red hair shining in the early sun, her ample frame attired in a long flowered dress over a body with few traces of fat. By her feet lay a large basket. Ellen couldn't recall seeing her wear a dress before.

"Once," Frank said, "when she first came over. 'Course if she came to mass…"

"Maeve, you look so nice," Ellen said when they reached her gate.

The dress was a size tight on a body that would have pleased Artemis. Straight back, buxom, the blood that flowed through her hourglass figure brightened her cheeks.

"Healthy at least," she said, climbing into the wagonbox next to the boys.

John-Arthur felt her warmth and the smell of roses. Her basket was overflowing and decorated with grain.

"You did a nice job sprucing up your basket," said Ellen.

"I must look like the Harvest Queen, wouldn't you say, Frank?….And I suppose you're going to have these young ones listen to the speeches that explain how this country was so brave in Cuba and how we never cared a lick for their sugar crop."

Their arguments were local legend but they had managed to remain strong friends.

Old Frank answered, "Maeve, we have all day to fight."

John-Arthur asked, "Where's your necklace, Maeve?"

She said, "Do you know the sin of it, I can't find it. I haven't seen it since the day we played our game by the stream."

"Maybe you dropped it there."

"You look for it around that swimming hole of yours, OK?"

Arriving in Long View, they unshackled their horses. As prearranged, Frank left the animals in the barn behind his son's saloon and they walked to the railroad station. Once seated on the train, they watched the wide Mississippi glide by, a panorama of attached postcards, the river so powerful there seemed no horizon, only the bulging image of the moving fore-plane. They scooted down the tracks and were left off near the entrance to the park. They walked away from the river towards the stone gates and were pleased to find buggies waiting to transport them to the top of the hill. Maeve and John-Arthur, holding hands, walked up alongside. The sky was a dark blue, the way it was before automobiles.

Eagle Point Park soared above them, with large trees and sunny meadows spread over a hill and a half along the Mississippi. The concessionaires were opening their stalls as they mounted to the crest where they could view the river rolling beneath them on its way to the Gulf of Mexico. A hundred rickety chairs waited expectantly by the outdoor stage—the grandstand decorated in the day's tricolors.

As a point of privilege, the wealthiest families had sent servants ahead to reserve the choicest locations. The town fathers, acting early, land-grabbed the grassy space nearest the speaker's platform. Spreading out their wooly blankets, they plunked down their claim against the unfriendly aliens. Thus entrenched, the established citizens were able to cushion their politicians against any Socialist claptrap from the bellicose orators who planned to stir up the immigrants on the other side of the park. It wasn't the city's society folk, of course, who had rushed out in the morning air; rather they sent their maids and handymen, up before dawn, who came bleary-eyed to occupy stage center. Prior to the arrival of royalty come their carpets.

"The Irish will be to the south," Frank said, pointing downriver, "nearest to the chute that drops the drunks right into the confessional box."

"Frank, no need for stage Paddys today. No sense confirming people's prejudice," Ellen said.

"No need for the Bishop's temperance men either," Frank replied.

They settled themselves apart from the gentry, allowing the farmwomen time to organize their baskets as the crowds began to gather. Over on the baseball field, they could see the teams in their striped black and white stockings, cracking their bats. The boys, John-Arthur and young Francis, off on discovery, went foraging among the tents and came back to share their news. The Senator would speak at two.

"That'll be a good time for a nap," said Maeve.

The boys said they came across a photographer's tent with a real goatcart in which the children could pose. And a notice pinned to a tree that there would be a spelling bee for youngsters ten and under.

"If I'm to enter the spelling bee," John-Arthur said. "I have to go now for the test."

"What test?" asked old Frank.

"First, they make you take a spelling test and then if you do good, they ask you up on the platform to spell more words for the prize."

Maeve said, "I think this bears looking into, Frank; I'll go along."

The two walked over to a table set up near the speaker's rostrum behind which sat a prim Victorian teacher lady.

"Name?"

"John-Arthur Mahoney, ma'am."

"Address?"

"Holy Cross," Maeve jumped in.

"Take a seat over there and in seven minutes, they'll be a written test," said the severe-looking registrar. "That'll be twenty-five cents entrance fee."

Between John-Arthur and Francis, they only had a dollar. After a moment of hesitation, he gave up his coins.

More than forty children—ten and under—sat clustered together on the wobbly chairs, whose legs alternately sank into the grass or tilted precariously. Early-arriving parents and aunts, as well as Maeve, sat aside.

"Did your mother make you sign up?" the girl beside John-Arthur asked. She had red hair like Maeve with flaming curls and firelicks, a background to blue eyes and freckles.

"No, I did it for the five-dollar prize," John-Arthur said.

She noticed his scuffed shoes and wondered what her father would think about those.

"What would you do with all that money anyway?"

"Give it to my Ma," he said.

"That her?" pointing to Maeve, redheads careful to notice others of their kind.

"No, that's my neighbor, Maeve. My Ma's in Chicago with my Pa."

"You from Chicago?"

He said, "South Side—5600 South."

"No wonder you don't have red hair," she said, knowing nothing about sides or southness. "Do you live in a big city building?"

"No, but my Ma takes my little brother and me downtown every Christmas."

"Must be something."

"Yes, it's something," John-Arthur said.

"Let's be friends," she said. "What's your name?"

"John-Arthur Mahoney. What's yours?"

"Caroline."

It was that natural. Two unafraid ten-year-olds, jabbering on as if they were already close. Both excited without knowing why, perhaps by their difference in gender, or their sheer enthusiasm. They instinctively perceived the clarity of truth in someone or were able, contrarily, to deduct duplicity. Intuitive enough to tell who was a potential friend, they were fully able to gather in a relationship of their own. There was an easy, open attraction for one another—their questions and answers about the world pierced by pairs of bright eyes.

The spelling judge was a huge man who wore a rough shirt under his coat. The two new friends both passed the written preliminary test, and John-Arthur was pleasantly surprised because his spelling was essentially mediocre. There were two dozen bright-looking rejects that appeared more capable than he. They were complaining to the spinster that they had been unfairly tested. At ten o'clock promptly, John-Arthur and his red-haired friend sat with twenty-three other candidates for the five dollar prize. John-Arthur's first word was "sickly" and he spelled it correctly. She spelled "bridgework", and after the first round there were eighteen children left on stage. He next succeeded with "thyroid"' and she survived with "incendiary". But then he fell on "longevity" and was fifteenth out. She managed to spell "larboard" but just barely, only to stumble on "cascading", which it turned out, didn't have a "k" in it.

John-Arthur had listened to the red-headed girl's voice chattering through the alphabet in a clear, confidant tone. When she muffed her word, she shrugged good naturedly and walked straight up to him and said, "That little kid really knows how to spell," indicating a dwarfish child of seven or so who eventually won the five dollars.

"Come meet my folks. They're sitting right back there," she said, leading Maeve and her new friend.

The girl had never been out of their sight. Behind the chairs, amid a crazy quilt of blankets, they came upon the encampment of the Knoxes, whose daughter she was. Arranged on a blanket behind the parents was a governess type or perhaps an unmarried aunt The red-headed father and the seemingly gracious mother eyed Maeve and John-Arthur with curious and critical eyes, all the while maintaining settled smiles on their faces, as if they were practiced at meeting others and making quick social judgments behind their masks.

"This is my friend, John-Arthur Mahoney," Caroline said. "She's not his mother."

"I'm Maeve O'Donnell, John-Arthur's neighbor on the farm."

The mother heard the brogue.

"Hello," said the mother, eyeing Maeve's dress critically.

"John-Arthur's from Chicago. . . .South something," said the girl.

"I'm John Knox, Caroline's father," the man said. "Visitors, are you?"

"Yes," John-Arthur said, "staying with my Grandpa on his farm."

"In Holy Cross," Maeve contributed. "A pioneer family."

"And you? Over from the Old Sod?" When Mrs. Knox asked the question, there was an army of marching English in her voice and Maeve heard their hoofbeats.

Maeve nodded, waiting for the inevitable.

Mrs. Knox, continuing her social selection process, asked the boy, "And what do your people do?"

John-Arthur answered, "They run a delicatessen."

Mrs. Knox said, "I hope they don't eat up the profits—must be a temptation to bulk up on the bologna."

Maeve looked at Caroline's mother sharply; she was crossing the line and wouldn't quit, "From Ireland, my dear? Will you be going back?"

Maeve answered, "Not likely. And yourself? Did you come from that other island—downwind from us?"

"I can't imagine why I'd go back after four generations. I might even be careful in choosing which one to visit," Mrs. Knox snipped.

"One of those islands had to be blest, didn't it?" Maeve asked. "Not likely England."

"Can we play?" Caroline asked, sensing this interaction wasn't going well.

"I don't know," her mother said vaguely. "The Bennett children will be here soon. And your friend Elaine."

"Anyway, he shouldn't be going around with two redheads," Maeve said. "People might think he had all the fun."

Caroline's mother said. "It's not envy I worry about. Overstepping maybe."

Maeve saw no reason to remain civil and asked, "The Knoxes? Are you the family that owns the streetcar company downtown?"

"Why, yes," said the father. "Why do you ask?"

"I'd think you'd want to maintain the tracks," Maeve said, "Else people might complain and petition the city to take over the cars on their own."

The gauntlet thudded to the ground. Municipal ownership was socialism.

"Yes, well, enjoy the day," the mother said, dismissing them.

Maeve said, "We will. Always a pleasure to celebrate the Fourth of July. . . .Reminds people of their right to rebel."

The father who had stayed above the fray now joined in. His surface smoothness evaporated in the fat and muscles of his face. "Miss, best not play with words you might not understand. We don't tolerate talk of revolution here. We quash it."

"Be sure you wear spikes when you go around stomping on people's toes. Some of us don't take to heel," Maeve said. "Where I come from, we've learned to deal with those who tried dancing on our boots."

Knox couldn't know that she had already piked a soldier; but she may have underestimated him as well.

Maeve and John-Arthur walked back among their own people, who were spread across the far side of the park—the laughing, full-barrel-in-the-morning Irish of the midwest. Strolling past a meadow that included diggers from the lead mines donning their baseball uniforms, a few flirted with Maeve as she walked by. From out of the pack of shortstops and outfielders, with baseballs hopping in their right hands or swinging hickory bats at imagined fastballs, a big blade stepped forward to answer her counter-jibes.

"So, Miss, you'll have a chance to come see us paste one over the fence at the game this morning, giving you the courage to shout your lovely lungs out."

"Or laugh at all the blatherers who puff themselves up and fan the catcher."

"Beg pardon, Miss, but this is the Leadville nine and we are the toughest band of batters to beat in all Dubuque County."

"Or brawlers, more likely," Maeve replied.

"A sharp tongue for such a well-rounded woman. Reminds me of a lass I once heard of from Connaught. But you'll surely come see us play at eleven, will you not?"

The trio had stopped. John-Arthur, feeling protective of Maeve, stood in the shadow of the gigantic lead miner who could, if he wanted, hold the boy in the crease of his arm. Even

Maeve, as staunch a womanly figure as could be found in the whole park, appeared smallish next to this giant miner.

Maeve said, "I suppose you take it as a matter of pride to so easily distinguish between the physical and mental attributes of a woman, or is it that saying things without thinking about them is less challenging for a simple person?"

"Sometimes, a man is so blinded by outward beauty that he doesn't immediately see the soul," he said in a half-mocking tone.

"You'll have to practice more."

"O'Malley, batting fourth," he said with a sweep of his ill-fitting cap.

"Mr. O'Malley," she said, with a twinkle, "I just might come by. Then again I might not. But I wager you'll show the girls some muscle before the sun crosses the noon sky."

Behind him, listening to the exchange with their small-peaked caps and striped stockings, the baseball boys whistled appreciatively. For John-Arthur, who was feeling less intimidated, it was better than watching a show.

O'Malley bowed turning his leg out, and she with a mock-reproving smile, walked on.

"I love them sassy girls," she heard him say to his mates. "How they love to polka."

The holiday had given the miners courage; they hoped to fashion a few memories to lighten the daily harvesting of their ores. Rising to the occasion of a holiday, they sought relief from their ordinary drudgery. On their national day, untried personalities came flying out of repressed spirits.

Maeve and John-Arthur found Ellen and Frank and Leo and young Francis waiting.

"Any five-dollar pieces?" Leo asked John-Arthur.

"No silver but he's come back with a lesson in social puffery," and Maeve told them about the Knoxes.

"You were right to speak up, Maeve," old Frank said. "Take none of their guff. They'll not turn us back again."

Frank and Maeve—it was as if they had a compact. On Frank's part something gained from his father, Great James. She, in turn, had inherited her defiance directly from the Troubles themselves. What they shared was the union of the poorborn after a thousand years of feudalism. They had disestablished themselves from the prerogatives of the royal rich and had weathered the storms of rebellion to seek the leavening of America.

After a moment they looked around for John-Arthur and figured he had gone to sulk over his rejection. Instead he returned to the Knoxes, and in his innocent way, he asked for a review of the family's decision. He was not aware of scuffed shoes or unfashionable knickers or that his words sometimes tumbled out back to front. He was not conscious of class discrimination except that certain families that patronized their delicatessen caused his parents to jump faster than others. John-Arthur had no need to be afraid of people. As he walked up to them, Caroline saw him first and her eyes flicked between the faces of her parents to study their reactions. The mother was surprised; the father's jaw tightened.

He walked straight up to Caroline and offered her a small basket of berries. She didn't know whether to take them or not.

"What have you there?" the mother asked.

"Strawberries, ma'am. I picked them myself."

"She won't need them," the mother said. "Why did you come back here?"

"So she could have the berries."

"Young man, don't you understand. We don't know you. . . God knows where you come from. And you don't know Caroline," the mother said. She looked about to be sure none of her friends were within hearing as she spoke.

"I'm from Chicago," the boy said, "and her and me want to be friends."

"John-Arthur," the father said. "You seem a nice boy but Caroline is special—like I'm sure your family feels about you. We don't know your people, but if they talk like your redhead friend, we know how to protect our own—chief among them this girl."

John-Arthur did not grasp it all but he understood the gist.

"Boy, you simply cannot appreciate the kind of life she leads," said Mrs. Knox.

John-Arthur, who had no problem understanding his own beliefs when he sat in church, found it more difficult to distinguish subtle differences out on the street. He was respectful toward adults and was not so much stung as embarrassed by what Mrs. Knox said. More by the tone of her voice than the words. He had offered himself for their disregard and now felt he earned it, so he placed the berries by Caroline's side, and walked off.

"Young man. Take them with you. Don't leave them here."

He did not turn back.

John-Arthur's ears still burned when he returned to his own turf. He took his brother Francis by the arm and followed the Leadville nine across the park to the baseball diamond whose outfield sloped towards the river. On the way there, he could see Caroline sitting by her parents wearing a scowl above her crunched shoulders and folded arms. When she saw him, she dipped her hand into the berry basket and smiled.

Meanwhile, Maeve walked with Ellen to the bluff and sat on a bench watching the lazy water, three hundred feet below, slip by. Washing the sides of old Indian land—Minnesota, Wisconsin, Illinois— these states fastened together by the rolling river, sliding its way towards sinful Louisiana. Past the caves of Huckleberry Finn and the blown bugles of Vicksburg. Past Chickasaw Bluffs where DeSoto became the first white man to view the Father of the Waters on a May day in 1541, three hundred years before Great James led his family out of Clones. 'Ole Miss continued past Big Bear Country, dissipating in a hundred chutes of deltawater south of the clanging streetcars of the French Quarter.

Southward, the women could see the steeples of Dubuque and the two bridge crossings to Illinois, one a railroad bridge. They looked out on flag-draped Mississippi riverboats and could hear the singing and music of the banjo bands resounding across the river, echoing along the cliffside. Late that night, through the dim gaslight, passengers would create silhouettes, shadow dancers whose quicksteps would flicker across the moon-sprinkled river.

John-Arthur had fallen in behind the baseball team as they sauntered across the park in an impromptu parade. Near the field, O'Malley came over and walked with the boys—Francis no bigger than a bat—awestruck by this friendly giant.

"And that red-headed sister or aunt of yours, she's not coming?" O'Malley asked.

John-Arthur, his eyes wide, staring up past the huge arms and shoulders, said, "She went off to sit by the river."

"I suppose there's no competing with a force of nature. What's her name, lad?"

"Maeve, sir"

"No wonder," said O'Malley.

"She said she might follow," John-Arthur volunteered.

"Then sit along the third base side," O'Malley said, "and I'll keep an eye on 'ya. Give me a nod if she comes by. Maybe there's an old glove in it for you."

And the giant watched for five long innings until Maeve climbed into the stands between the two boys, which action caused a series of hand signs to whip around the infield, signals flashing across the diamond that had nothing to do with sacrifice bunts.

O'Malley came off the field and soon abat made the air explode with his striking out. Maeve paid no attention, accepting his humiliation without comment, but O'Malley slunk down on the bench. But he had another chance in the final innings and on a three and one pitch, hit the ball so hard that it sailed whistling through the blue green air over the fence at the river's edge. The ball kept flying, finally arcing down over the Mississippi to splash far below and sink and cork-bob back again and water-rumble south—past all the rivers, the entering Illinois, the Missouri coursing from the western mountains, the Ohio from the eastern hills and the Arkansas—to come ashore the next year in Mexico, its dark brown spot still showing where O'Malley had bruised the once-white cover.

The Irish cheered and the German team was downhearted but the beer that each team brought to assuage their sweaty innings quickly revived both the losing and the victorious teams—the cool kegs set in great pans filled with ice. O'Malley motioned them down from the stands and soon Maeve and the boys were standing among the teams. O'Malley poured Maeve a beer and root beer for the boys, and while Maeve only brushed the glass by her lips before she set it down, the boys bolted down their fizzy concoction.

"Mister O'Malley still batting fourth, I presume."

"Your servant, ma'am. Over from Mayo."

"No greater place, I'm sure, Mister O'Malley, unless it's Donegal."

"And now we're living the American dream, I believe."

"And grateful to be doing so," she said.

The conversation was general. He was a foreman at the mines; she ran a farm. He lived on the south end of Dubuque. Her place contained seventy acres. He was a joiner—Irish Society, sports teams, rowing club. She liked to read—about the legends people left behind and the myths they handed down. She believed in women's rights and he stood with the unions.

No sooner had the beer begun to flow when three big-wheel circus wagons plowed across the outfield and a dozen men began erecting a big tent out past center field by some woods.

"See them, Maeve."

"Probably a circus."

"Where are the animals?" Francis asked.

O'Malley said, "Not that kind of a circus. Actually not a circus at all. They've dressed some 6-year-old kid up to look like a saint and I hear, he spouts off for the unions."

"As if he knew anything about them," Maeve ventured.

O'Malley added, "The labor movement's behind him. Trying to drum up some publicity. The kid must have a good memory. They crank him up and let him rip."

"A boy? Can we see him?" John-Arthur asked. "Is he special?"

Maeve said, "I'm sure he is. What does the sign say?"

A worker was nailing up a broadsheet:

*"...out of the mouths of babes...*
*Thou hast founded a bulwark against Thy foes"*
*GIANT FARM- LABOR REVIVAL CAMP MEETING*
*Hear the Boy Wizard of Nebraska Give His Vision of the*
*Working Man's Destiny*
*1PM & 7PM—Fourth of July—Eagle Point Park Ball Diamond*

As they walked back towards the picnic area, John-Arthur watched Maeve and O'Malley, and he sensed he was losing her to another power, that their morning closeness would be interrupted. The boy absorbed the hurt of it but hardly felt the pain. He must have possessed some counter-rejection function enabling him to turn his attention elsewhere, so he just grabbed Francis's hand and ran ahead. They passed the booths and crowds and hawkers and flags as the size of the crowd increased and listened as the band warmed up for the first concert of the day, the brass of their instruments shining in the noon sun. First there would be the fireman's band and later a military one and lastly, in the evening, the pride of Dubuque, the River City Band, with members from the Philharmonia Orchestra.

Passing the podium, the high school chorus was singing Dwight's old anthem.

*Perfumes as of Eden flowed sweetly along,*
*And a voice as of angels enchantingly sung*
*'Columbia. Columbia to glory arise*
*The queen of the world and the child of the skies.'*

The lunch rituals of the first families and those of the German and Irish immigrants differed, the latter separated on the south end by a spacious beergarden, the difference being that the food for the wealthy was transported by servants who commuted back and forth between the mansions on the bluff. Carried by servants in highly polished wood hampers, the boxes contained puritan plain food, distributed discretely and served on fine linen. The immigrant families, on the other hand, tended to bring their ethnic foods and smelly delicacies in wash baskets and tubs, a lunch served on cotton and washed with beer. In various corners of the park, there were smaller congregations, each with its own foods—the Bohemians, Balts, Jews, and the rest of the tribes from the Austro-Hungarian and Russian empires who became the best Americans of all because they had so much to gain.

"Go ahead, Maeve, take your basket and sit with the Irish boys," Frank said, indicating the team, sitting nearby with their dusty uniforms and dirt-smeared faces, where girlfriends, wives, and mothers were unboxing provisions for the hungry nine.

"No, I'm settled where I belong," she said. "Maybe I'll bring them chocolates later."

Unexpectedly, a potential victory appeared. It was John-Arthur who saw her first, wearing a smile and with a small hand in her father's paw. Mr. Knox approached and confidently presented his only begotten daughter to the democratic race of Mahoneys. Behind him, observing among the elms, stood Miss Giles, Caroline's governess.

"Is it Mr. Mahoney?" Mr. Knox asked old Frank.

"It is, sir," Frank replied.

"My name's John Knox," he said, "and this is my unhappy daughter who's in mortal danger of ruining her day for lack of friendship with young John-Arthur here."

Knox said it with style and a nice tone, but Frank did not immediately put aside his natural restraint. Still he retained his civility. Maeve, on the other hand, eyed him as the enemy, scowled and moved to the background, but never out of hearing.

If Frank needed support, she'd be ready to stride in with flared nostrils.

"I'm sure they're a harmless pair," Frank said introducing Ellen, Leo and young Francis.

"Wouldn't hurt a fly, that boy. Almost a priest's son. Doesn't need a certificate of acceptance from any house," Maeve intervened, unaware of the clerical irony.

"Exactly," Mr. Knox said, ignoring her. "It seems that in the past couple hours the spirit has retreated from this very animated child, which in turn has brought on a case of mortification of the flesh under the guise of a hunger strike."

"A common occurrence on national and other holidays," Frank ventured. "Like a touch of Christmas constipation. But the right ingredients might cure the cause."

"Exactly, so if I may suggest, would it be possible for Caroline and John-Arthur to play together under the watchful eye—the cliff being so high and all—of Miss Giles who's hiding there behind the trees."

Frank, who had not risen, said, "That's up to John-Arthur, I'm sure," watching the boy's eyes light up. "And may I propose a spoonful of some of the best potato salad in all of Iowa to help the child recover and a dish for yourself, sir."

And the lion lay down with the lambs. Quietly, John-Arthur and Caroline sat aside while Frank and Mr. Knox positioned themselves for class warfare. The women dealt with the clean-up a few yards away. And young Francis played with a deck of cards. While Leo, interestingly, eyed Miss Giles.

Because, like serfs before him, Frank counted wealth in terms of land and tillable soil and because he and his family had more of that than almost anyone else, he never envied those with fortunes, because they could no more chew their wealth than Frank could eat all his crops. Yet there was fear and hostility between the rich and the rest of the country in those years and only the beginnings of a middle class. The immigrants often arrived from overseas with radical beliefs packed in their crumpled valises, and were normally spurned for a generation upon arrival. By necessity, they joined in common causes and rose in power knowing their unions were able to threaten owners on their behalf. The eastern banks still held most of the country in thrall and the railroads controlled the hinterlands, but their corporations were greedy and were eating up farm profits and the older settlers were beginning to join with the unionists. It was a new kind of politics urged on by necessity—the Farmer-Labor movement. Few negotiators were able to close the hostility gap between adversaries without anger. But Frank and Mr. Knox were both sure of themselves, and personal confidence, whatever the societal differences, remains a powerful instrument in the hands of mediators who chose to bridge the classes. For those that succeeded, attainment was mostly a matter of character and lack of fear.

"A day like this," said Mr. Knox, trying to rely on patriotism as a first defense, "brings to mind an older America."

"Indeed," said Frank, "when I was a boy we heard the settlers from the east tell about those once happy days, as they called them. Figured the country to be as fair as Eden. That must have been the first of our old Americas—the good feeling one—the bygone days. Before all of us Irish and Germans came splashing across the sea in numbers"

"My people originally came from the east," Mr. Knox said.

"We sailed directly to New Orleans, skipped over that whole Yankee Doodle part," Frank said. "Just leap-frogged over it. But I remember after the Civil War, people were always yearning for those old days—boys walking beside the Erie Canal and climbing high steepled churches in the old towns of New England."

The Mahoneys had never been afflicted by the religious views that emerged from Harvard Yard or influenced by its Pilgrim or Congregationalist values. Nor did they pay much attention to federal Washington, or red-brick Philadelphia, or tree-lined New York. Indeed, they had never seen the Appalachian chain. Neither Martin's father nor grandfather had been obliged to travel down the Ohio from Pittsburgh or across the lakes from Buffalo. They had never transferred west. They started here beside the river.

"Nowadays," Mr. Knox said, "People look back towards some horse and buggy America around 1890, before the automobile when there weren't so many factories. Another old-fashioned time. I guess we didn't lose old America just once; we're in the process of losing it a second time. No matter how much some of us are trying to hold onto it."

Maeve piped in, "They'll be no real America until the workers are in charge."

"And own the railroads as well, you'd say," answered Mr. Knox.

"That and a lot more," she replied.

The gauntlet was still bouncing along the ground.

Frank said, "Sad part is we lost something important. Lost part of our heritage, even its symbols and maybe the reason for who we are. I'm talking about the pride we once had in Columbia. Bountiful as a corn goddess."

Knox replied, "Afraid she's had her day. I prefer Uncle Sam myself. More up-to-date and hard-boiled. A good symbol for an unsentimental age."

Frank said, "That rascal's too much the bully. . . .It's Columbia for me. She's more about the heart. A holdover from a time when enlightment turned to rebellion. Uncle Sam is more about factories and navies—doing business. Myself, I prefer the old girl. An easier America to like. Softer and with less arrogance."

"But the good Uncle has the energy and drive to boost us abroad and find new markets. Not so interested staying home on the farm. Better able to help us come up in the world. Raising dust around the globe."

Frank reacted, "That Uncle Sam does have a bit of the empire-builder in him. Just like the man in the White House. . . . But I say that if we don't keep Columbia alive, I don't know who'll remember our beginnings and who we were designed to be. Business isn't so much in Columbia's line. She's more apt to spend her time healing."

"Give her a hatchet and she'll be arguing for prohibition and suffrage. More reason for a strongman."

"Don't worry," Frank said. "Our girl has sinews in her backside as well as her mind. Like Maeve here."

"Who will, I trust, use her strength—you should convince her—in a constructive way," Knox said.

"What's that?" Maeve said from the outskirts.

Frank said, "About that Sam—I never trusted a man who wore striped pants. To me, he's a puppet for your railroad gang, you'll pardon the expression. The way I see it, Mister Knox, is that Uncle Sam is more the Republicans, and Columbia favors the Democrats."

Frank went on, "I'd prefer America be a woman. Chances are the country might last longer. You get that Uncle Sam up and running and he's going to shoot every Chinese or Philippine that moves. And they would only be the beginning."

"Think I'll take my chances with a real man. Keep the factories going. Might better hold the economy in line."

"Watch out you don't dry up the fields instead. Once you start meddling with nature's birth canal, you're going to wish you stuck with the 'ole girl. . . .She may be the last best hope and even though it's not turning out that way, America may still have the potential to be the place that the rest of the world can rely on and trust for justice. I'm afraid we're beginning to savage that hope, but Columbia with her woman's touch is still here to remind us that we just might be able to stumble our way back to paradise. Not just for us here but for everybody everywhere. . . My prayer," Frank said, "is that women remain our beacons and teach us to balance ourselves."

"Wasn't old Columbus a disease bearer and gold smuggler?"

"Columbia's his opposite. She was the one who was here before he came, here with the Indians, and she'll stick around to care for us. He only named her."

While the others were politicking, Miss Giles and Leo traded admiring glances, eyeing each other to determine if anything remained in life's barrel for people like them, two lost souls afloat on life's picnic plains. Finally Leo, driven by piled high irritations, approached her and said outside of the others' hearing, "Pa's always showing off and I wish he wouldn't. Always jabbering about things he doesn't know about."

Being underclass herself, she heard something in those few words, mumblings of discontent, so she answered, "And that Mister Knox isn't as nice as he pretends."

Their aggravation sealed a contract.

Mr. Knox was saying, "It seems, Mr. Mahoney, that we've come to agree on getting along, no matter our differences, thanks to the behavior of a willful child."

"I think the girl simply had an advanced case of disappointment, soon enough cured."

They watched John-Arthur and Caroline skip off, Miss Giles not far behind.

The rest of the day Caroline and John-Arthur were inseparable. Within an hour, they were fast friends because there was no guile between them. By afternoon they were as free with one another as siblings, running, pushing off and telling secrets. When she ran, ribbons flowed behind. More sure of herself than he, she called most turns—which tree to climb and when to hear the band play, which of the races to participate in, which potato sack to choose. They were underfoot, then they'd be gone twenty minutes with Miss Giles in perspiring pursuit, appearing at one or the other of the family blankets. They raced through the park. As if they owned it.

Mr. Knox was still testing Frank, so he prompted the old farmer to talk on. "And which political party do you favor, Mr. Mahoney?"

"I vote progressive wherever they are, maybe Republican next time, maybe not depending on young Roosevelt. I used to be Republican mostly because of the Union, and maybe I'll be again if Teddy keeps fighting the trusts and quits scaring other people with his navy. Being wealthy himself, he knows how to control the rich, beg pardon, probably because he's had to wrestle with those devils all his life. He picks good fights, I must say, and battles the right people. Knows the tricks the rich use. Some of us will never forgive the wolves that made their money on Union soldier's graves."

They talked on. Once when John-Arthur and Caroline returned to hang about the blanket, the boy heard his grandfather talking about his Dad. "That young one's father, my boy Martin, always talking about how impressed he was by the White City. I tell him it was a plaster front, a stage show, a trick of the eye. A backdrop for violence, ending with the mayor's assassination, just like McKinley murdered at that other fair in Buffalo. And when the Chicago Fair closed down, the only thing those leaky halls were good for was for squatters who had no jobs. And then that next summer, during the Pullman strike, the whole thing went up in flames, scorching the sky like a scene from a war picture while the workers battled with the company thugs. I keep telling him his White City was an illusion viewed through a screen of fire."

"The ones that did the shooting were deputies appointed to protect the trains," Knox said. "Lawful deputies." Few things could separate Knox from the working class as much as his support of Pullman.

It was politics that interested the two of them, the younger traction magnate curious about the views of the older farmer, satisfied to listen and learn what he had to say. Meanwhile Frank, whose entire social life comprised the airing of his views and maybe a little drinking besides, responded to the interest shown him by the younger man. They had little in common but they both had the character of their diverse personalities as sure guides to their beliefs. Both had exercised their civic duty on this patriotic day. They had stretched out their poitical ideas for investigation. When he felt certain that his only daughter would not be butchered by barbarians, Mr. Knox returned to the sanctity of the upper class.

Frank, as he was leaving, rallied one last remark, "I know I'll probably fry in hell but I've always believed more in Mister Jefferson that I have in Saint Patrick."

In the flurry of people moving around their blankets, none of the Mahoneys had noticed that a small boy kept edging in on their space eavesdropping on the conversation between Frank and Knox. Tumbling about in the nearby grass, the children in their own excitement failed to recognize the winner of the spelling bee hanging about—a child on whose mind Columbia was painted that morning in her full star-studded, blue-robed glory.

Having returned to his own circle, Mr. Knox told his friends, "I was talking to this old farmer and he still believes the poor should have all manner of rights. Kind of quaint."

Ellen meanwhile had gone back to the cliffside to view the river, leaving Maeve and Frank alone with young Francis. Leo, in pursuit, had disappeared among the trees after Miss Giles.

Leo, mostly underfoot, had always been inconspicuous. Speaking last and often interrupted, perhaps harboring darker thoughts but who would ever know, Leo was one of the easily dismissed. But he showed he had a heart after all and wasn't anybody's fool, because he had struck up a relationship with the shy Miss Giles and was making a little holiday headway himself.

Maeve stepped back into Frank's circle, saying, "I get mixed up between all those Libertys and that Columbia you're always talking about."

Frank said, "It's the cartoonists to blame. . . .All our symbols, at least the female ones, are based on Marianne of France—and she's all about revolution and equality, wearing a funny cap and all. Here, we've dressed her up with shields of stars and torches and eagles for bonnets. We've got liberty flags, and statutes of liberty and liberty coins, but they're all Columbia in disguise. Columbia's the real name for America.

That Vespucci guy gypped us out of being called right. Columbia's who we are."

The spelling bee winner rose from the grass and ran towards the big tent.

## Chapter 4

After lunch, John-Arthur and Caroline moved towards the ballfield to hear the child prodigy, their contemporary, preach the word of the union man. They fell in with a crowd moving in that direction but were stopped at the tent opening until faithful Miss Giles appeared along with Leo and escorted them into the warm interior whose side flaps had been raised allowing a small breeze to circulate the heat. Inside, a band played sprightly circus entrance music as if clowns might momentarily tumble down the aisles. Such were the expectations humming through the crowd that John-Arthur would not have been surprised to see Buffalo Bill's herd of Rough Riders and Indians storm the tent.

"That music," Miss Giles said, "comes right up to you and pulls you off your seat."

*A boy in faraway New England had already attended a circus where he savored the band sounds of the Grand Entrance—marching elephants and tigers and rouged-up ladies on white horses along with trapeze artists— and carefully saved those images in his memory. Later they were destined to pour out and be compacted into a one-minute circus march with all the om-pah, drum rolling, coronet blowing fanfare allowed in a single second hand sweep of his grandfather's pocket watch. . .*

. *The older Ives had already written* Circus Band *but it was twice as long.*

The audience was multi-tongued and carved from a dozen ethnic blocs and into this babble of voices emerged a small boy in an immaculate white suit with an off-the-shoulder white cape. Everyone craned to see him until he was lifted up and put on view by a giant of a man, who hoisted the boy on top of the drum normally used in the dancing elephant act. To the normal person, his delicate voice would be a tad high, but for John-Arthur and Caroline and the excitable immigrants, they hardly noticed that he had a slight squeak.

If the tent had the look and smell of a circus, it was left to the boy to perform the equivalent of a highwire act, standing as tall as he could in his tiny shoes. Lion trainers were not as fearless as when he raised his short arms and asked for quiet from the growling audience. He had the translucent, unearthly, ageless look of some wonder of nature that had escaped from a Barnum show. Managing the crowd and his own composure was this six-year old chirper—the Boy Wizard from Nebraska.

"He's not even ten," John-Arthur said.

"Maybe he's a midget," Caroline ventured.

"I've heard of boys going out front to preach and they open their mouths like they're talking but it's really someone behind the altar saying the sermon," said Miss Giles.

"He looks familiar."

"Hey! He's the kid that won the spelling contest and that big guy was the judge."

"Quiet, children," said Miss Giles, shuffling her skirt, to provide Leo a seat beside her.

The boy in the white suit waited until there was silence and then said in as loud a voice as he could muster ". . . .When Socialist Jesus went into the Temple, he threw out the moneychangers. And that's what you union men should do—toss out any moneymonger that doesn't respect the working man."

The place exploded. They had been waiting for him to say something provocative. It took a full minute for the place to settle back down.

"Give it to 'em, little man," said a farmer in the row behind.

"You tell 'em, kid," shouted Leo.

John-Arthur and Caroline jumped up with surprise on hearing the racket. One of their own had lit a fire under the adults. There was a spate of yelling and carrying on. Something had unzipped.

The boy continued, ". . . .When Jesus was a boy like me, he went to preach to the Elders, and what do you think He would say today if He went into some big fancy church downtown filled with all the windbags that operated the monopolies and the trusts—He'd say, 'Give your working men an eight hour day'...."

Another eruption. The cheering had started early.

". . . .And the right to bargain."

And grew louder.

". . . .And health care and workman's compensation. That's what Jesus would say."

With each new prevarication, the crowds yelled louder until the whole tent was ringing and it wouldn't be a wonder if folks had heard the racket all the way to Peoria.

". . . .Did you ever hear that rich J.P. Morgan's boast— 'America is good enough for me' he says—And do you remember what Bryan, the poor man's champion, cracked back at the banker, 'Whenever you don't like it, you can always give it back.'"

The people roared.

". . . .And do you know what that bag-a-bones Rockefeller had the audacity to say, 'God gave me my money'—as if a hundred thousand working men hadn't made it for him."

Grand booing.

"You know what's wrong with the rich? They think they've got God in their pocket. You heard what that railroad president said, 'The rights and interests of the laboring man will be cared for—not by labor agitators, but by Christian men to whom God in his infinite wisdom has given control of the property interests of this country'. . . .God with all his brains did it, you see."

"That's not my God," someone shouted out, followed by a sudden attack of applause.

The Wizard continued, ". . . .Nor mine. But here's what another said. This is what the rich really believe: 'We own America. We got it, God knows how, but we intend to keep it'. And I say to the rich: We intend to take it away from you."

The place erupted. From all over the park, people looked up at each other. The noise from the ballfield caught them by surprise. Must have been a homer.

The Boy continued, ". . . .You know what to expect when you're a union man and you organize to strike for a decent wage. Same as the Reaper Guild harvested from the bosses on May the First in '86 when labor called for a General Strike and one of our men was killed. And what happened three days later when three thousand protested at Haymarket Square and a Police Inspector sent a hundred and seventy-five of his force to scatter protesters. That's when a bomb was thrown that left seven policemen dead and four of ours shot? There was a reaper there all right. Not the Virginia Reaper nor the McCormick made one either, but grim fate nevertheless, sent against the laboring man. And Judge Joe Gary, making a mockery of justice, executed four of our leaders, some of them weren't ever even there, for no other reason than they had the courage to stand tall and proudly proclaim they were Socialists."

The crowd hooted against anti-unionists.

". . . .And in '94 just south of Chicago City, Debs and his American Railway Union protested a cut in wages at the Pullman Car Works. Honest workingmen trying to be heard. But do you think the owners lowered the rent on their homes in the company town when they cut their pay? Of course not. Old Mister Pullman wanted to exploit them on the job and in their kitchens both. So, the company sent in Federal troops and deputized gangs to bust up the strike and sent Debs to jail and crushed their union, while the bosses toured Saratoga and Bar Harbor in their gold-plated sleeping cars."

The audience jeered again

The Boy Wizard went on for thirty minutes until his lungs began to give out. In that short time he managed to out-bluster Teddy Roosevelt and out-quote William Jennings Bryan in his prime.

After the band stopped playing and the crowd standing around the little creature dispersed, John-Arthur and Caroline approached the boy wonder. Standing behind the miniature wizard was the huge man who protected him. John-Arthur saw that he was dressed like a lumberman. People called him Big Jack.

Jack said, "I'm glad to see you children. You'll make the little fellow feel at home."

Looking at the Boy, Caroline asked, "Do you have hair between your legs?" much to Miss Giles' horror and the boy's discomfort.

"Little girl, what makes you ask such a thing? This Boy is but six."

"If he's a wizard, can he do magic?"

"Change you to salt if you ask any more about his privates."

"He seems older. Does he play with other kids?" she persisted.

"You just come with me and find out," Big Jack said.

They waited in the back of the tent while the Boy changed out of his white suit, surprised to see the schoolmarm who had registered the spellers earlier in the day now folding the boy's clothes. The woodsman led the four of them and the Wizard toward some shade along the left field foul line and sat them under a grove of elms. Big Jack quickly realized that he would have to take charge of the social amenities.

"How did you get the little tike to talk up like that?" Leo asked.

Jack said, "Boy's a genius is the truth of it, and a wizard like him can do just about anything another man can do, and most times, a lot more. Everybody's surprised at the Boy's learning. I tell people not to doubt him. You just can't understand it and that's all there is to it. It's like he was born in a special state."

"Is he your boy?" Leo asked.

"No, he came to me." Jack was used to answering questions about the boy. "I was managing a one-ring circus back a few years ago and I was in charge of advance publicity. We'd go ahead of the other wagons, trying to drum up business. Blow into a town and boost up support from the newspapers and local businesses and hang posters and banners all over town and give out some free tickets. And we came into this one place, Zenith, Nebraska. I'll never forget it. Just as it was getting dark, I spotted this tower. Weren't a water one but a tower with a big clock on top. I always liked to hang my banners high so I asked the Mayor if I could pin one up there and he says go ahead, and I asked how to get up and he gives me the key and up the stairwell I go. Halfway up I hear a baby crying and I get up there under the bells and when I look around, here's this kid— the Boy here—with the biggest head I'd ever seen on a baby. . .

.So, I hung up my banner—that was my job, right?—and I pick up the kid, rolled him up in nothing but old newspapers. He's snuggled up in a big write up on how some big canal in Chicago was going to open the next day.

"So I take him down and show him to the Mayor, who has a fright when he sees the size of the boy's head. We show him all around and nobody knows who he is and nobody wants him neither with the swelling and all. Most people thought he'd have a short, hard life and that would be the end of it. But he fooled all of us, like he always does. So I waited around for a couple days for the troupe to come through. Meanwhile we put a story in the paper about a lost baby but nobody comes to claim him. So, I stayed for the set-up until it was time to move on—and I left him with a friend of mine in one of the caravans…"

"That was Ginny, the Wonder Girl. Right, Big Jack?" the Boy asked.

Explaining, Jack said, "She was the Human Clock; her trick was to swallow watches—dozens of them that the rubes gave her. Well, some went in her mouth and some went in her pocket. She ticked so loud most times she sounded like somebody plunking on a bass fiddle.

"We raised him, Wonder Girl and me. She had a heart of gold—people used to say it was probably from all the watches. Truth is, she was a little noisy to live with. In a couple years, she had to quit minding him. He was so smart, he drove her crazy asking questions. She might have stayed if she could have kept up with him, but he stumped her every time and she couldn't take it. She wasn't no dumbbell, either."

Miss Giles asked, "But you were able to keep up with him?"

Big Jack said, "Oh, sure. I used to head up the Chautauqua circuit east of here. I've spent time with them all—Theosophists and phrenologists. Hell, I even belonged to a Transcendental Club, so I had a history of philosophizing."

Leo said, "I was never up on all that stuff."

Big Jack said, "Some people don't take to it, but the Boy, he sopped it up Mozart standing in front of a keyboard. He was up to Emerson by the time he was four."

"What was it that Mister Emerson said again?" Miss Giles asked.

That was a signal for the Boy to take his playmates aside because he knew once Big Jack started on the Concord School, he was good for a half hour. It was like throwing Mister O'Malley a slow pitch over the heart of the plate.

"You never heard tell of the Oversoul?" asked Jack.

The children moved aside while Miss Giles and Leo paid for asking too many questions. No sooner had they sat down than the Boy, Al was his name, reached into his tiny pocket and pulled out a big cigar and lit it. John-Arthur and Caroline were as surprised as their chaperones nearby, but Big Jack waved off any apprehension saying that it kept the boy's size down.

The Wizard said, "I've got a couple hours. Why don't we have ourselves an adventure?"

After checking with the adults, the three children bounded across the park. As it was getting onto two o'clock, they noticed that most activity now centered on the gaily spangled speaker's stand where the senator was due to speak at this very hour, but it had been announced that his magistrate was delayed enroute and would be late. The crowd had already gathered and most of the chairs in the grassy arena were filled. Off to the side, a military band practiced.

"I've got it," the Nebraska Boy said. "Follow me. Nothing better than a ready-made crowd. Like coming off a bad road trip and finding the table set for Christmas dinner."

They raced back to the tent and found the old schoolmarm.

"A quick job, Aunt Em. I need a red wig, a blonde wig and some of your best greasepaint."

There was a flurry of activity. Al pulled on a yellow mop and with a few deft lines on his face with a make-up crayon he took on a few years and soon looked older than his accomplices. Caroline not only received a black wig but a major ethnic overhaul; she was turned into a black girl, including an apron costume that made her look like Cinderella after a coal delivery. Aunt Emily transformed them in a professional circus way, to such an extent that no one, not even their relatives, would recognize any of them.

"We'll have to hide her, so we'll wrap her in this big cloak to cover her head. Now, this is what we're going to do. . . ."

And away they marched. When they approached the rostrum, they could see that the senator had not as yet arrived. Al told Caroline to stay out of sight around back, and as brassy as the ship's propeller on the new Lusitania, up on the stage walks the Wizard, pulling John-Arthur behind him. There were a few members of the reception committee milling around the platform, consulting their watches, but they hardly noticed the pair of kids mounting the stand.

Al told John-Arthur, "Now, remember, you just go 'Tick-Tock, Tick-Tock.' Got it?"

Al, with all the confidence of a traveling preacher, walks up to the front edge of the stage, stands on his toes, and lifts his little arms and says in a normal voice, "OK. Quiet. Thanks. Quiet now."

John-Arthur looked out on the hundreds of people sitting in the audience and all he could see was his grandfather walking across the lawn in their direction.

As the volume of noise began to decrease, and the committee people turned to question the lower level of sound, it was then that Al projected his high-pitched voice so he could be heard by all. It was going to be an irritable throat day for the little trouper.

"My name is Billy Smithers and my daddy is the senator from here in Iowa."

A welcome applause rose to greet them. Weren't they cute?

"And this is my brother Petey."

Of course, no one on the reception committee had ever seen the senator's children. And wasn't it so that the senator had a slight russet color to his hair, which might account for red-wigged John-Arthur, now Petey?

"My daddy asked me to come up here—he'll be along in a minute—to keep you entertained for a bit," says Al.

Again they received a hand.

"Aren't they the limit, those two?" John-Arthur heard from out front. "Will you just look at 'em?"

Al began, "You know my daddy's against the eight-hour work day."

There were rumbling sounds underneath the applause.

"And you know he voted against every pro-labor bill that ever came onto the floor of the Senate."

Mixed hurrahing and hissing.

"He's against the unions too."

Now, a few shouts for and against began to reach the boys.

A big farmer in the back of the crowd yelled, "Get those cretins off the stage."

Al continued, "You know, my daddy also voted for those immigration bills to keep all the Asians and other undesirables out of America."

Now there was big applause up front and a roar of disapproval from the immigrants standing in the back. Old Frank was shaking his fist at them.

"And you know he tries to keep the colored in their place too."

Again a mixed response.

"Now we'd like to do a recitation for you. My daddy will be here real soon, so we're going to repeat some of the nursery rhymes he's taught us—but first I'll bring my little sister up."

Al goes over to the side of the stage and calls out for Caroline to come up and join them. She's gone through a black transformation, made up as pickaninny poll with cotton rags in her hair and wearing an ashen embroidered apron.

"Here's our little sister now," Al said. "She doesn't get a chance to get out much. Daddy keeps her in his closet."

Caroline's blackface was so convincing people were gasping.

"And now we're going to do the rhymes daddy learned us."

Al raises his hands as if he was conducting, and in response to Al's metronomic beat, John-Arthur and Caroline begin chanting "Tick-Tock. Tick-Tock. Tick-Tock."

Before the audience could guess what was coming next, Al begins to recite:

". . . .Hickory, Dickory, Dock

Rats ran up the Clock

The clock struck Oh-One

Our President's shot in the lung

Hickory, Dickory, Dock

And a Cowboy rides into the White House dung."

The audience looked on in shocked silence.

". . . .Hickory, Dickory, Dock

A Rat ran up the clock

The clock struck nineteen-ought-two.

A mine blast in P.A. kills a hundred two

Hickory, Dickory, Dock."

People couldn't believe their ears.

"....The clock struck nineteen-o-three

The Wright Brothers fly—a-Whee!

Hickory, Dickory, Dock

Two hundred Wyoming miners perish. Oh! me."

"Tick Tock. Tick Tock," recited Caroline and John-Arthur.

"....The clock struck nineteen-o-four

Two hundred miners in P.A. are entombed. Oh Lor'.

Hickory, Dickory, Dock...

"....The clock struck nineteen-o-five

A hundred miners in Alabam choke alive..."

"....The clock struck nineteen-ought-six

'Frisco quakes in a fiery fix.

Hickory, Dickory, Dock

And a hundred thousand children sweat in the shops."

Along about 1906, a portly, slightly florid gentleman climbed hurriedly up onto the stage. The crowd, recognizing their senator, began to applaud, though a healthy dose of jeering accompanied the greeting. Al, realizing the jig was up, backed his troops towards the other stairs, smiled weakly at the elected officials, tramped down off the stage, and away the trio fled into the woods.

The senator, forced to redirect the unruly crowd, began laughing, "These kids today. Young ones. Knicker-wearing kids."

Appealing to the crowd, he says, "I appreciate a practical joke as much as the next man but whoever put those children up to this foolery should be looked at by the police. We don't tolerate socialists around here, or anarchists either, to spoil our glorious Fourth."

Not much response.

"Because it's a star-spangled kind of day."

Slowly, he gained control.

\* \* \*

An hour earlier, Maeve was at the cliffside where she noticed a file of baseball players moving down the path towards the shoreline. Squinting, she watched them cross the railroad track that ran beside the water. Recognizing the striped stockings of the Leadville nine, she laughed to herself as she saw them uncover their flashing fannies, dropping their dusty baseball uniforms in heaps behind the bushes while they worked their swimsuits over their similarly-striped bodies. Like two-toned animals, she could see their brown arms, necks and faces and lily-white trunks. Some including O'Malley chose to wear nothing and she could see dots of crotch hair on the few sports who dared the conventions of this Iowa time and place.

Maeve paid particular attention to O'Malley as he dove in the river and then began splashing the others, the edges of his voice discernible up and across the face of the cliff. A passing boat whistled as it chugged along and they swam out to ride in its wake. When a freight train passed, they mooned the engineer who tooted back at them, his greeting rolling in waves of thunder across the wide Mississippi.

Not modest, Maeve walked to the north end of the park and into the woods and found a promontory where she could look directly down on the swimmers, making out O'Malley as he sported like a water dragon, his penis waving up and down like a catfish jumping upstream. Behind her were flaming red flowers and she picked an armful and back at the cliff's edge, she began sailing the wild roses down the outblowing west wind. Spotting her red hair, they began hiding their parts except O'Malley who opened his wide arms welcoming her, the others darting out behind the bushes to catch the flowers cascading down the cliff, O'Malley in his full glory catching bouquets.

Maeve, excited now, ran back into the woods, stumbling with laughter, and returning to her perch, flung another half-bushel down on them, the flowers floating gently in the breeze, a daytime fireworks. O'Malley motioned her to come down the path but Mister O'Malley, batting fourth, wasn't going to get away that easy. And the pair began an aria to which neither could distinguish the words of the other, allowing them to shout to their heart's desire.

She: If there were only a man with a big enough heart.

He: Where's the woman whose blood boils?

She: Can any man raise a fire in me again?

He: Is there a woman in this country not afraid to live?

Maeve returned to the picnic area from her flowerperch to find her companions resting. Music from the bandstand drifted across the park as the warm day pressed down through the defending trees—a lazy afternoon stretched ahead. Frank and Francis were still sleeping, while Ellen guarded them between her own drifts in and out of consciousness from her seat on a camp chair.

Ellen indicated to Maeve that she should nap as well.

There is something so sensual about a woman preparing to fall asleep in public that all the impressionists in the world would never get the picture right. Whether soft or strident, she will look quietly around and settle herself within the modesty of her own precincts, touching her hair, perhaps her thighs, ensuring their careful passage through loss of time and control—safe in the protective world she has taught men to adopt for her, surrendering to the civility around her that her daily compassion helped create, knowing that all depend on her decorum. Confident that the love she feels and engenders will still be there when she wakes.

The image of O'Malley's white body appeared behind Maeve's eyelids, his broad shoulders and tall muscled frame—a picture with hardy details. Would there ever be a man in her life again, she wondered, after her years as the mistress of the old Irish chief? Or anything to match the excitement of their cause and battles back home? And instead of someone old whom she revered for the purity of his purpose, could there be some young stripling, free and easy, careless of himself but never of her? How she yearned to be with a man who knew how to laugh. Someone who never disappointed his friends or those around him for he would surely be a leader, surrounded by others who deferred to him. A man with ideas and one who lit up any company with his spreading good cheer, shining his miner's lamp on morbidity with coal-black humor. What would it be like to have hours filled with mirth, elated by someone whose only duty was to please? A man filled with compassion and alert to injustice? The kind of man that people would talk about;

a person ready to amend history, feeling that he was destined to do interesting things. That he would find riches and explore some faraway sea and never have the time to sit down to remember his last adventure because he was already preparing a new one. And whether a man like him even needed a single loyal woman was a real question. It wouldn't be easy to create such a man in America. For a longer time than their compatriots in the east, before social compression began to dampen their horizon, the men of the west held out; their virility lasted well into the century, but many were beginning to lose their sense of generosity, the special quality that marked them as naturals.

She slept while across the park, the river bathers returned.

O'Malley entered a shed behind the ballfield, carrying his street clothes, after he and his mates had climbed back the hill. He wondered as he undressed if there was a woman out there to match his vitality, someone who could absorb his rocketing enthusiasms. A responsive heart where he could hear the sound of his own good cheer vibrating in another soul. A woman with animal instincts and of purpose who could center his scattered life. She would have the power of laughter and the confidence to act on her faith. And be knowledgeable as if all the ambivalence of nature were somehow balanced in her instincts.

She would understand feelings before they were manifest. And contain his lust with a lust of her own.

Maeve awoke to find O'Malley sitting beside her.

"You've been watching me sleep," she said, smiling, not really annoyed; pleased that he was there.

"Sometimes you have to invade a woman's privacy to let her know you've arrived," he said. "And me amazed that gardens grow in the sky, because this very day, I saw an entire botanical garden floating in the air, a shower of flowers raining down the cliff."

He had changed from his uniform into an outfit featuring a striped summer jacket; a straw boater cocked sideways covered his curly black hair.

Maeve, resting on her elbows, enjoyed his closeness and felt no restrictions or trepidation within herself. Her impulse was to touch his face but she rested her eyes on him instead and then sat upright, their shoulders touching. When he had first approached, Ellen motioned him to sit down. He had watched her pelvis and breasts moving against her light dress and he could sense the strength of her body.

He was twisting blades of grass in his fingers when she said, "To take a nap. Such a luxury. I think I'm ready to face the afternoon now."

"I thought we might take a walk," he replied.

"That's a fine idea," she said and she reached out her arm and he arose and their strong hands clasped as she glided upward with ease.

"You'll notice by the pull that farm girls don't come in small sizes," she said.

"Save us from those thin, nervous nellies," he answered.

"Don't be too sure. Soulful women often live in thin bodies," she said.

"I prefer rounder lasses."

They waved goodbye to all those sleeping as well as awake and began to walk away.

"You've left the farm for good, Mister O'Malley?"

"Yes. I like having a regular job. Free to spend my own time—to fish and hunt and take river trips—not those life-long chores on the farm."

"It's industrial working, is it? Turning your back on the land?"

He said, "It's machines for me. Leave the mind-soaking drudgery of the barnyard to those who prefer it."

"I farm," she said, "and take comfort in it."

"I find excitement in the factories and mills too. Railroads loaded with goods, bringing in products that somebody else, someplace else, makes better than we do and our own ore going all the way to Indiana. They're connecting us up."

"Railroads devil the farmer," she said. ". . . .But do you not mind about the health of your lungs down in the mines?"

"No, the sun's at the top of the shaft and a good wash-off makes you new as corn in June. . . .But who minds your farm on a day like this?"

"Neighbors," she said. "I farm it myself."

"Some healthy farm lad will be along to help you someday."

"I'd begun to doubt I'd ever see the man."

They sat beside Mr. Clemens' river exploring the boundaries of their excitement, but Maeve kept coming back to his life in the mines.

O'Malley said, "Knox and his gang—they think they own us all—because they've stock in everything—the mines, the utilities and even a big piece of the railroads. They sit on each other's company boards so you're always dealing with the same ten skinflints wherever you turn. Now they're crying we have to take a big cut in pay and we've warned them we'll strike. That has them up a wall."

"But you have a union," she said.

"We do and we'll strike the minute they put their fingers in our pay envelope."

"Will they send in the Pinkertons?

"Probably."

"Then you'll want to be careful," she said, feeling for the first time in years that she meant what that expression implied.

They talked as well about their Irishness.

"Speaking of ancestors. Let me tell you about mine," he said. "Granny O'Malley. That woman could bend a spar in two with her bare hands—a pirate no less, hounding the English up and down the western shore."

"Oh, that O'Malley. One of mine was some old queen the poets praised," she said. "Remembered like Mary Magdalene."

"A woman with a past, is it?"

Had he heard about her already, she wondered? Notoriety follows every sinner.

Attractions in those days were compressed into shorter incubation times—the work so hard, there wasn't a lot of time for experimentation. Lucky if there was a day or two off a month in summer and then because it rained. Maeve always looked forward to January and February and its white landscapes with less to do except tend the animals—winter days that cast shadows from the tree's unblown dead leaves onto the sparkling snow, a shadowy apparition of the past summer. She wondered what it would be like to be with him on a quiet winter's day.

But now it was high summer and flowers were flying. They walked to the prospect above the river where she had rained down the blossoms and he walked up to the edge. Taking a silver dollar from his pocket—Miss Liberty—Columbia on one side of the coin and an eagle on the other—lofted it high over the river and it sparkled like a diamond as it plummeted down into the water.

"Mississippi tribute," O'Malley said, "for allowing one of the river she-gods loose for the day." They sat on his jacket and he twirled flowers in her hair. They quickly allowed their extravagant imaginations to wander.

* * *

The crowds, gathered around the speaker's platform, eventually settled down after their dose of nursery rhymes. Many of the picnickers on the park's south side had come across the grass to hear the senator speak. Senator Smithers acknowledged the crowd as the polite clapping reached him from the nearby chairs and blankets. Frank and Ellen heard part of his remarks.

"Sorry for the delay. . . .A good Glorious Fourth afternoon to you, friends and constituents. Especially to those of you who have ventured across the river from the old part of the country to trespass upon God's gift to nature which you once called the outlands of the west but which we know now and love as bountiful Iowa."

Having identified his precinct, and following a smattering of applause, the senator sounded his theme: "The question for us is what do we mean when we say America? We know the country is exploding and will bring us great wealth and we all want to partake in its plenty. But what makes us who we are? And where do we go from here?"

His basic theme was that the strong should govern and the rest should follow the dictates of the enlightened class.

"And these leaders will define who we are, bringing us employment and security. And we will be guided by a divine hand in conjunction with men of affairs—for we are living in God's crucible, taking in all the people of the earth, and from this great mashing together—a new American man will emerge. No fifty-fifty American, half good and half something else stored up from the old countries but a new kind of patriot with ambition and Christian faith to succeed."

There was an undercurrent of movement as the senator looked out on the crowd. Children could be quieted for only so long and in the near distance the older kids were boisterous. It was not wholly evident that part of his audience began to slip away towards the beergarden as the three o'clock mark appeared on their big fob watches for it was then that a firebrand from the western mines was conducting a counter-rally for the working men.

As they walked back towards their area, Frank said to Ellen, "Funny the senator should have such peculiar children."

The old couple headed for their part of the patch. They followed the crowd and linked up with friends and took seats around the picnic tables of the beergarden while others sat in the chairs placed on the enclosed dancefloor from which the orator would speak. Pouring into the enclosure streamed the multivariate people of a dozen cultures to listen to Socialist Joe Faye.

He was thin and not tall and he burned with a sense of injustice. Though often afire, there was a controlled calm about him as he began, until the moment came in his speech when the preacher in him would take hold, and then he would emit a scalding blaze of invective against his current aggrievement. He was a revolutionary, his fury spawned by poverty, bad conditions and flagrant violations to women, children and the dignity of his friends. Joe Faye had continued to fight even though the radical Wobblies and other unions were losing ground. Encouraged by new blood coming in from Europe to help him rail against the factory owners and the trusts, he and his ilk would continue the battle until the First War when patriotic fervor swept away all but the most intransigent opposition to traditional conservative views.

He began: "There's probably nothing as coincidental in our history as the fact that Jefferson and John Adams, the two greatest revolutionaries in American history, both died on the very same day—this day of liberty—the Fourth of July in 1826, the fiftieth anniversary of the signing. . . .Showing us that some lives have a symmetry to them.

"What we might ask ourselves today is: Have we been faithful to them—the Virginia planter and the Boston lawyer? Whose country is this anyway where one percent of the population owns more than the other ninety-nine percent combined?

"You know the numbers. Morgan and Rockefeller between them control corporations whose wealth exceeds the assessed valuation of all the states west of the Mississippi. From here, two thousand miles to the Pacific—from the Canadian Rockies to the Rio Grande—the worth of that land is matched by the bank accounts and power of a couple gents sitting on their yachts in Newport harbor.

"But when will we ever learn how to curb their railroads with their nasty rate structure that hurts the farmer and eventually hurts us all?

"We've allowed a ruling class to govern our lives. Sure, they were content to allow cheap labor into the country to turn the wheels of their factories but now that the world is flooding in, the rich are in a panic that their authority will be politically threatened. They've slammed the door shut on the Chinese, and don't think your people aren't next. . . .Like proprietors everywhere, they think they own this country and the rest of us are nothing but trespassers.

"They truly believe they deserve to rule. That the country's theirs. They boast they were the reckless ones, the entrepreneurs, the investors, starting up a business, tearing a living out of the wilderness, and now that its been tamed, they're content to make money out of money. The wizards of Wall Street—earning capital from the steam of your labor. They've developed into a privileged class, with all the trappings of royalty. Arrogant rulers who think they're the only ones competent to govern. They're like actors on a stage we've helped them construct, performers who, I'm sorry to say, dance courtesy of the admission coin we provide. It's us, the admiring audience, fascinated by their daring, that's allowed them to succeed. . . .But you're smart enough to know they don't deem your life worthy or your work honorable because they don't care about you if there's no profit in your exploitation.

"They don't acknowledge that one-third of the world's landmass was saved—this whole hemisphere was saved—from the ravages of the old world, that there was a ready-made paradise waiting here in a pristine state for enlightened man to come and share the harvest its bounty. But the explorers turned ruthless, carrying the sores and plagues of old nations and ideas. They came to exploit—the golden image of El Dorado that was burning in the Spanish imagination."

He was warming to his subject. "Those of you who profess to be Christians might know that on the masthead of his newspaper, Garrison the Abolitionist, printed right under the picture of a slave auction the words of the fourth commandment, 'Love Thy Neighbor'. It was Garrison—the Great Liberator—who understood what those words meant, who said it all when he proclaimed that we were not only free men but endowed with a holy commission to perform a sacred charge. A mandate from God and nature that has been sabotaged by greed. A greed that has denied us fulfillment of our own destiny to share our bounty with the whole world. When will we have the wisdom to recognize God's unacknowledged gift? And respond to His unanswered transaction from us that we bind ourselves to His covenant with America and acknowledge that—'*Our country is the World. Our countrymen all mankind.*'"

A great cheer went up. The democratic standard had been reconfirmed.

"He put it well, I thought," Frank, the senior member, was permitted to express himself first. And those around him agreed, including the big guy, O'Malley.

The speeches ended around four as the heat of the day began to diminish and the women wove their way back to their blankets and began thinking about supper. Following the main meal, a major concert was scheduled, then fireworks at nine. The younger couples like Maeve and O'Malley remained in the beergarden where the German band began to play. Once the political crowd left, the musicians began to supply polkas and czardas and waltzes and the lights came up in the young people's faces, especially the unmarried, eager to hold one another if only in dance. Caroline, John-Arthur and Al, cleansed of their disguises, would alternate between blankets—Ellen's and Mrs. Knox's'—scattering their laughter, then back to watch the young people shuffle around the dancefloor. From the side of the structure, the children, peering through the trellis, could see the square of polished wood and the couples, some firemen stripped down to their flaming red shirts. The pavilion supported a wooden roof with latticed sides where roses grew in parts of the fretwork.

Back at the blanket, young Francis stayed mainly with Ellen as she began to prepare the evening meal—the real picnic. Leo, when he wasn't chasing after Miss Giles stayed with the other farmers, who were now joined by Frank around an open bottle.

The day had spread out its carpeted light through the trees and now the late afternoon began to lay down its yellow threads.

The Irish team sat together in the beergarden at massed tables studded with steins from the local beermaker, Dubuque halfway between the other great German breweries of Milwaukee and St. Louis. Maeve was the center of attention, mostly because she was new to the crowd and had turned the head of their captain.

She didn't know how to polka but O'Malley was patient— neither of them lithe enough to win blue ribbons. As they danced, it was O'Malley who looked ahead.

"Do you come to the city often? It's only fifteen, maybe twenty miles at the most," he said as they hopped around the floor.

"I stock up here two or three times a year, but I hope you'll see me in Holy Cross."

"I would like that," he said. "I could rent a rig and drive out of a Sunday."

"You might even make it for the Saturday night dance at the Grange. Or if you don't want to drive out, you could take the train and I could meet you at Long View," she suggested, "and we'll have Frank and Ellen put you up."

"I'm not much help around a farm," he said.

"That's OK. I'm not much good down a mine shaft."

They confirmed that they would meet again and the agreement was sealed as they bounced and jigged across the floor, as O'Malley waltzed the girl with the strawberry hair.

It was dinner now and plump cold chickens and fat hams escaped from picnic buckets. Holiday breads came forth with olive dishes, applesauce and fruit compote. Foods that had been warm in and above the ground a year ago and faithfully preserved during the harvest emerged for a last time as garnishes and asides—corn relish, sweet chow-chow, tomato sauces, and pickles—for final consumption.

This time Ellen and Frank insisted that Maeve join the other young people and she did so, knowing it pleased them as well as herself, but not before she left the best of her fare with them.

The late day shadows now began to slant through the park, nearing time for the major musical event of the day scheduled for seven at the bandstand. A young composer from far Connecticut had journeyed to Dubuque ten days ago and had been holding secret rehearsals in church basements and fraternal lodges around town and word had begun to circulate that some strange music had been emanating from these sacred places. The composer would present whatever surprises he had in the second half of the program. Earlier in the day, less renowned bands had performed but prime time had been reserved for the River City Band, some of the bangers and tooters from as far away as Galena.

The Boy Wizard headed back to his tent to prepare for his evening performance, but not before returning 25-cent pieces to his two new friends. After parting with the young wizard, John-Arthur and Caroline managed to escape from Miss Giles, who appeared to be more comfortable with the Mahoneys than the Knoxes now that Leo was paying attention to her. The unchaperoned children listened beneath the picketed undercarriage of the bandstand as the musicians tuned up. They knew the day was closing down around them. There were already red shadows in the eastern sky across the river.

Caroline cupped her hand and held it close to his ear.

"Mustn't tell; it's a secret," she said, her hair brushing against his face, the fire curls licking his cheek. "I've never had a boy for a friend before. You're my first."

He brought his lips to the whitened sculpture of her ear, below the pile of red that he brushed aside, "I'll always be your friend."

They ran one last time through the park, he showing off when he could, she clapping her hands in delight and executing perfect double cartwheels, her petticoat fluttering in wide circles. When they returned, they sat aside from her parents but within view of them.

Now the crowd hushed as the stranger, an image of Victorian rectitude and as stern as a New England winter, lifted his baton to play the old marches and operatic tunes that the crowd was waiting to hear along with the latest songs, *Tell Me Pretty Lady* and *In the Good Old Summertime*. The crowd responded favorably even though the conductor seemed bored with these and the other hymns to conventional taste. The crowd hummed along their favorites, the same melodies that stood on their piano stands at home.

After intermission, it came time for the stranger to conduct his own musical appreciation of the holiday. The nervous looks and trepidation that made valve fingers tremble and drum sticks click in anticipation warned of ensuing problems. Then it began. First a quiet rumbling sound. Then slowly a cacophony of harmonies flew out of the bandstand—wild, primitive, crazed musical sounds, the likes of which had never been heard before this side of the river. Dissonance and broken melodies and harmonics that wounded the ear. The audience was dumbstruck as the Connecticut Yankee thumped out the beat and yelled out the rhythms. There was a howl from the audience. What madman had wandered into their celebration? Out of the blast of sounds came the army bugle call for reveille. To wake up whom? All were alert to this musical insult; some began pitching half-eaten fruit; others yelling to stop, stuffing their fingers in their ears to muffle the sound. The kids became unhinged, jumping around as if anarchy gave them permission to go wild. The music had set off a maelstrom.

Then out of the unsonorous soup came a snippet of *Columbia! Gem of the Ocean* played on the ignominious tuba whose sound arose and fell back into a puddle of disharmony.

"Our Columbia!" a woman screamed. "You're slandering our Columbia."

"Praising her," yelled back the conductor, the only words he uttered all night.

Then blasting out of the chaos of sound came a single line from the *Battle Hymn* and now he was on sacred ground. . . . "*And His Truth goes marching on*". . . .Then the line was slammed back into a dense blast of thundering brass played off-key. That's when the leftovers really started to fly.

The Park Manager, sensing a disturbance quickly signaled the fireworks experts from Hook and Ladder #1 to send up a couple of flares into the deepening evening to alert the police and divert attention, but in their haste and lack of experience the pyrotechnical engineers sent up a shortfall, the firestream landing in the middle of the crowd. Mayhem broke out, but the musical stranger, unperturbed by the stampede around him, urged the band to play on. Sparks nestled in the long dresses and big straw hats that were the preferred fashion that year as mothers grabbed their smoky children. Then the next set of incendiary shortfalls sent up by the firemen landed on the roof of the bandstand, and flames flared up between the wooden shingles. The musicians continued to pour out their unpatriotic blasphemy while the crowd, some with flame-tinged clothes, began cursing the culprit. But the leader kept waving his baton, while the fire on the roof spread, and smoke began to filter down among the carefully placed members of the River City Band, who kept one eye on the bandmaster, and the other on the widening conflagration. Soon firesticks began to fall through the cracks of the roof and burn the sheet music and that's when some of the members of the band fled. The bright polished brass began to tarnish on some of the instruments but no amount of yelling from the composer could stave off a thinness of sound that spread through the music as his associates dodged the heat. Trumpeters and wind players were deserting, coughing, until finally, even he began to see the futility of the situation as the flames whipped up and the fire brigade came clanging to the rescue, a sound he dearly loved. Taking up a discarded cornet, he blew a clear melodic rendition of *Gem of the Ocean*, and only then did the crowd in derision begin to cheer him—this mad composer—yelling at him from the safety of the trees well beyond the fireline. He stood and played to the finish, licks of fire sprouting on his cuffs.

After the flames were out, the time was approaching when the Mahoney party had to say goodbye, as smoke settled down into the trees. They picked up their encampment before the others in the park for they had a longer distance to travel, though many others with singed clothes also made an early exit. The sky in the west was red from Minnesota to Texas.

John-Arthur and Caroline walked hand in hand until they found her worried parents.

"Can't you stay for the real fireworks?" the girl asked.

"No," said John-Arthur. "We have to catch the train."

Mr. Knox said, "Say goodbye now. Shake hands like big children."

Instead, Caroline stepped up and kissed John-Arthur's mouth and not to be outdone he kissed her back, because they were confirmed friends, and didn't need permission.

With Maeve and O'Malley, there was more heat in their departure, and though they both wanted to embrace, they resisted, knowing that all eyes were on them as she left the beergarden.

"And no dancing with any of those cheeky Dubuque queens," she said, with a lilt in her voice, just loud enough for his friends to hear.

"I'll be seeing you next Saturday," he said, "even if I have to miss a game or two," also uttered for the benefit of his friends.

O'Malley walked along with the family, supporting Maeve on one arm, feeling her breast against him, and holding her basket in the other. The family boarded a buggy to take them downhill. O'Malley helped the women and children aboard before waving them off on their trip. Down they went to the water's edge to wait at the sub-station as darkness began to roll over the river.

As the Mahoney party waited at the sub-station, they saw and heard the fireworks explode over the riverbank. Smoke continued to seep down the face of the cliff as a result of the gazebo fire. Now rockets went up, and soon they viewed a sparkling crown over the whole scene as an illuminated eagle thirty feet across burst into flame, shining bright. Eagle Point perched high on the dimming cliff, where the west began and where Indians from the same vantage seventy years before watched the encroaching danger from the east—the fearsome settlers. As the fiery locomotive came into view in a spray of flaming red, colored shards of light poured down the cliffside and mixed with the sparks from the engine rattling along the embankment. And as they headed north for the short ride to Long View, the fireworks fell down on the smoking monster, and the modern behemoth and the old holiday's dream were merged.

\* \* \*

A bedraggled band of Mahoneys transferred to the farmwagon behind Uncle James' saloon. Once embedded, the boys fell asleep in Maeve's lap as they rode through the dark countryside. They were soon in their beds while across the fields a refreshed Maeve stood naked at her window and watched the stars grind over the cornfields.

\* \* \*

It was probably just as well that the Mahoneys missed the brawl between the Irish and the Germans after they left the beergarden, though O'Malley would still be showing a few scars a week hence. The fight did not surprise, indeed it was hardly noticed, by the privileged near the bandstand because they knew all those low types would sooner or later make fools of themselves. Besides, the efforts to damp down the fire overwhelmed the hallooing from the south end of the park. Actually, there was little animosity in the uproar; it was just another bloodsport to go with the beer.

\* \* \*

That night, John-Arthur had a dream. He saw Maeve and Caroline flying upward, their red hair streaming behind them— red rockets in air.

# Chapter 5

Next morning, breakfast was served at the usual hour to the sleepy inhabitants of *Sunny Slope*, except for the allowance that Ellen made for the boys to sleep in. The day was warm and there were already voices from the barn when John-Arthur awoke and reviewed the events of the previous day. He had a new friend in Caroline, and Al as well, but he had a different, more ambiguous understanding of his neighbor, Maeve, whom he had come to idolize. His feelings about Caroline were lighthearted while his feelings for Maeve ran deeper and were more confusing. It was the difference between yellow and purple—a just-burst buttery freshness against a majestic shade that signaled Maeve's imperiousness. Princess Caroline and Queen Maeve.

When he looked out the window, he observed that the morning was already marching to the routine of normal farm hours. He didn't rush to join the commotion but allowed the day to filter calmly into him. Over the fields, he could make out Maeve on the crest of a rise far across his grandfather's farm, watched her driving posts with a sledge hammer, the instrument sailing out in a wide arc before delivering its downward stroke onto a trembling fencepole.

In addition to his daily piano lessons with Maeve, John-Arthur saw her again at the Grange meeting that week. She had a pleasant way of acknowledging him whenever he came within her circle, either by touching his hair or putting an arm around his shoulder, interrupting if someone noticed her gesture with "My best beau" or "My gallant John-Arthur." Her green eyes would flash with affection and he was stilled by their luster.

At the Grange meeting a rumor was confirmed that the freight rates were indeed scheduled to increase in time for the fall hauling. Maeve implored the local chapter to pass a resolution urging the national organization to lobby Congress. But what the other farmers noticed and commented upon was not her demands but that she wore her dress to the meeting—a voiced observance that made her wonder if she would ever be taken seriously in this country.

"Will we never learn that they will pick our pockets until we take our knuckles out and show them some fight?" she asked the lethargic gathering.

"Maeve," Uncle Jim said, "you've seen too many pictures with farmers waving their rakes against some estate owner."

"Jim," she said. "Back there, I was one of them in the picture."

She was relentless.

\* \* \*

On the following Saturday, with saucy bravura, Maeve not only waltzed about in her Derry dress at the Grange dance but showed off Mister O'Malley as well. He arrived at Maeve's in his rented democrat and the pair rode to the Mahoneys, where the visitor dropped off his valise, allowing him time to socialize with the family. There were varying degrees of excitement attending his arrival, the kind that any new relationship inspires. Everyone contributed something to the nervousness of the couple and though there were some stumbles as they sat in the Mahoney parlor, there were no outright pratfalls as the pair initiated their courtship dance.

"I suppose you'll be wanting to go to the dance tonight, Mister O'Malley?" Ellen asked.

"Indeed, ma'am., I'd promenade all night if I could skip around the floor with you" O'Malley answered.

"I think you'd rather dance with a sack of potatoes," Ellen said.

"Lovelier spuds a man never held in his arms," he replied.

Maeve chimed in, "You and I better keep him spinning or those hussies from the Young Irish Ladies Society will."

As promised, O'Malley brought John-Arthur an old baseball glove and they were soon out on the side yard playing catch.

"That was generous of him," Frank said.

"Stealing a girl's attention by coaxing the children. An old trick," Maeve responded.

Ellen said, "I'll bet you meant 'heart'."

"This heart may be too wise to be stolen," Maeve said. "Then again maybe too smart to be alone."

When she arrived at the dance, she startled the town, statuesque in her flowered Irish dress. Her skin shone and excitement pulsated through the networks of her throat and blazed through her eyes, signaling her interest in big O'Malley.

The whole town came out for the Saturday night dance, including the children and John-Arthur and Emmett and Francis and Gen and all their other cousins, both distant and near, appeared. The children would mimic their elders and galoop around the floor, hopping in exaggerated steps to the fiddler's tunes. John-Arthur followed Maeve and O'Malley around the hall, feeling special about them and somewhat mixed.

O'Malley, with his hitched pants, fresh shirt and jacket, exuberated a generous spirit—a throaty laugh, gregarious gestures, a cheery face—a boisterousness that put off some and attracted others. He made a show of loyalty to Maeve by dancing solely with the women over sixty, including Ellen.

"The big oaf coulda stomped me into the floorboards," Ellen said to Frank later.

Maeve, understanding something of John-Arthur's feelings, invited him to dance. Hesitating, she reassured him that she would not cause him any discomfort. They danced slowly within circumscribed footprints. She masked his jerkiness with her own big gestures. He unfolded his spirit within hers, lent himself to her generosity as the fiddler played a Derry song.

After the dance O'Malley drove Maeve home through the dark countryside. They sat in the rig in her yard beneath the wide black dome of sky. Removing his jacket, he placed it around her shoulders, and even though she was as healthy and hearty as he was, she left it there, liking the smell of him about her. They sat quietly, enjoying the calm of right unions.

"They were surprised to see you, Maeve," he said, testing out her first name.

"I told you, Kevin O'Malley, that you've joined a select company when we decided to step out. I scare off most of the bachelors because I'm stronger than they are. The ones your size are afraid of my tongue."

"The greater the challenge, the greater the prize, my father said."

"But did your father know that some women don't want to be prizes."

"And what do they want?"

"They want a wholeness."

"And what's that?"

"That, Kevin O'Malley, is everything."

O'Malley said, "And I have a riddle for you as well. What's the one thing that's more important than a man's love for a woman?"

"That's easy. Love *between* a man and a woman," she answered.

"I didn't mean it that way though that's right, isn't it. . . .I mean what's the most important thing for a man to become?" he asked.

"Himself," she said. "You're doomed to roam alone until you discover your own worth."

"I was going to say a man's work. It's important—that part of him is. And not even work so much as a sense of being together with your pals and doing something productive."

She said, "I agree. After you've made a cozy life with your friends and they're busy helping you grow, it's then you're free to go larking about after love."

He said carefully, "I wonder if anyone else would think you and I are full grown."

"What difference does it make what others say as long as we think so ourselves?" she said.

The puffiness fizzled out of him. He had gentled in her presence. There was no need to bluster her.

Maeve said sadly, "I'm whole to myself. But to someone else, I might seem flawed."

"Another riddle?" he asked.

"The life I left behind may make me incomplete to someone else, but within myself, and only to myself, I'm about as complete as I'll ever be. But when I came to America, I expected, for better or worse, to live whole again, if you get my meaning."

"I believe I do."

"Then, Mr. Kevin O'Malley," she said, kissing him lightly on the cheek, "I hope you'll take me for a ride again tomorrow."

"I will that," he said. "Though I suppose we'll have to begin with mass."

"The congregation would expect nothing less. But I'll be a novelty there," she said. . . .Then she hesitated, "Kevin, have you ever been with a strong woman before?"

He saw that she was serious, but he couldn't resist.

"Only my mother. Does she count?"

Smiling, she said, "Well, that's a start."

As he rode to Frank's place, he knew the boundaries between them had softened.

The following week, O'Malley returned and this time after the dance, the pair sat on the swing on Maeve's porch. It was warm and she fixed some cider.

Bringing out the glasses, she said "Tell me about the strike plans."

O'Malley answered, "We're going out in a couple of days, depending on what response we get on the settlement. The men are ready to gamble the whole works."

Maeve said, "Sometimes that's the only way to win."

"My own guess is that they'll close the mines. Exorbitant profit's played out of them anyway. We're trying to think of some way to get even. But the men are OK. They'll be able to find work out west in Colorado or Utah. Get 'em up in the hills; we'll make good Wobblies out of them yet," he said, mentioning the radical union.

"We all know what it is to uproot."

"That's America," he said. "Wages move about."

This night as they sat gently swaying, neither hesitated to touch the other, sometimes holding hands, or running their fingers along each other's arm. She touched his forehead and pushed back his black hair. They knew they were destined to lie together, and they were comfortable knowing that they would fall naturally when the moment was ripe.

\* \* \*

Before his scheduled return the next week and even preceding the receipt of his letter, she read about the strike in the newspaper. The miners sat down in the tunnels on Tuesday, were removed forcibly on Wednesday by guards and the police. So next day unionmen gathered by the gates and this time they brought reinforcements of their own. A fight broke out which turned into a near-riot and there were injuries on both sides. By Friday, an even larger crowd, including their women, appeared, and by then Maeve was at O'Malley's side at the gates. On Saturday afternoon the entire working class of Dubuque turned out. It wasn't a general strike but there would be a full-scale riot.

Maeve, excited to be involved in political action again, showed O'Malley that he had harvested a cyclone. No voice was louder than hers, no ballyhooing so firm. Standing together in the front ranks, he knew he had found his equal. And she saw by his actions as he directed his forces that he was a leader, which allowed her to acknowledge that she had rediscovered a man with a dream of his own.

But it was dangerous business to be part of a mob. Congregating for religious, patriotic, or musical activities was perfectly justified under the Constitution, but labor demonstrations frightened people. There was always an implied potential threat, an edginess that could break into violence. Adherents might parade their sympathies, start out as a happy pack and seek no conflict, but countervailing antagonists often appeared—to throw rocks, or curse maddened epitaphs through exploding red faces, summon the police.

Maeve could afford to attend the demonstration for one day only and so she missed the riot on Saturday. Late that night, O'Malley appeared at her front door. He had walked from Long View.

"You wouldn't want me to miss a Saturday night?" he said.

In her nightgown, her hair already down, she swept him in, raising the kerosene lamp to check the extent of damage on his face and arms.

"They're looking for me," he said. "There was donnybrook started about noon. A couple men were shot. The coppers got my name and everybody told me to light out."

"You can stay here as long as you want. They won't be looking out here in the country."

"I was hoping you'd say that," he said.

She cleared up some of his bruises and left him to sleep on the big sofa in the parlor.

There was now between them a conspiracy of action that hastened the inevitable enclosure in each other's arms. When lovers finally unleash their secrets, the way opens for closer embrace. Believers are amazed when they find their dreams are shared by another, then inhibitions melt away, walls tumble.

O'Malley's name appeared in the Sunday morning paper. The townspeople were curious about his newly acquired celebrity, but she denied knowledge of his whereabouts. Maeve maintained her routine, appearing in town to shop. No one was to know he was at her farm. Arriving early for piano, it was Arthur who found him hiding there, when he spotted O'Malley working inside the barn. Once he discovered the captain of the baseball nine, Maeve swore him to silence, which invested John-Arthur in their deceit. They could trust him; the boy was a friend. They cloaked him in their secret.

The one hitch that required attention was Ed's weekly visit, so Maeve asked John-Arthur to ride over to New Vienna that

Sunday morning and tell Ed that she would have to cancel their visits for a time.

"Tell him anything," Maeve blurted out. "Tell him I've found an errant knight."

John-Arthur rode off, but returned with bad news. Ed had visited Dubuque earlier in the week and while walking downtown was knocked over by a streetcar. His injuries were substantial, and John-Arthur was given the hospital address. When Maeve heard the news, she quickly made plans to return to the city. While there comforting her legend-loving friend, she distributed some letters to O'Malley's union comrades, informing the leadership where he was and how he might be contacted and suggesting certain tactical moves.

Maeve was crushed that her musical partner became mangled by a streetcar. The irony made her sick. This gentle soul, his mind protected by a brain packed with chivalry, run over by a mechanical horse. It was too bizarre—heavy metal had broken his bones and driven the whimsy out of him.

On her return, she was dejected. "Smashed his leg and cut him up bad. Worst is, it broke his spirit."

O'Malley said, "It's that damned Knox's' doing. Works his motormen nearly a hundred hours a week. It's a wonder those cars don't knock over half the population."

\* \* \*

After a day when the young couple had grown close, they opened their vulnerability to one another. She touched his face when he came in from the barn, he came from behind and put his arms around her as she washed the evening dishes, She lay her head on his shoulder when they read the newspaper—"No sign of ringleader. May have escaped to the west."

"They make me out to be a circus bozo."

"They got the leader part right. Lead on, MacMalley."

"Leading you is all I'm thinking about."

She came downstairs that night, unable to sleep. Hearing her, he rose to meet her and they embraced on the stairway. He was naked and she in her gown and they could feel the blood thickening as their flesh merged and she led him upstairs and that night, they both came to arrive at pleasures neither had known before. They rode through the night on trembling bodies of full desire, carrying them in again and out across the boundary of some new exploding upper space.

They became insatiable. The stock would low in the pastures, and weeds grew in the cornrows but nothing interfered with their lovemaking.

"Oh, 'lor, I hear nature calling."

"Calling you right back under the covers."

The intensity continued day and night for a week until word came from Dubuque that his co-unionists were wondering if he had skipped out.

The couple had slipped into a dreamworld. They offered themselves completely to each other, even as the world was campaigning against their isolation. People had to be seen. Plans to be made. They delayed the coming reality, savored the remaining moments, and finally allowed the pressure to steam out of them. It had been a free and open love; they had only been able to think of the other. They glowed in one another's company, at work, at rest, in the aftermath of marathon lovemaking.

Cradled in their farm bed, two immigrants, merged in an emotional storm, fused blood and fluids. The settlement of America, the greatest chemical mix of all time. Hungarian shopgirls with Portuguese sailors. Bohemian hop growers with buxom Italian girls. A Polish teacher with an adventurous Greek vinyarder. Sloe-eyed Egyptian girls with Welsh captains. Fat Russian girls with skinny Danish bakers. A great democratic pie dreamt up in heaven and baked in the oven of hell's own sweat and labor, the festival held together by the bountiful plenty offered to the cowtenders and greasy machinists and milkmaids of the new land.

It was not easy for John-Arthur to keep O'Malley's hideout a secret; he had never had to harbor such immense news before. In order to discipline himself, he found it necessary to visit the couple regularly, often finding them in unusual pieces of clothing. Once Maeve came to the door in a blanket; another time in O'Malley's shirt.

Late one evening John-Arthur ran down the creek to her place after dinner, but seeing a number of buggies in the yard, he cautiously approached the front door where he heard voices arguing in the parlor. As the light faded from the sky, the heated conversation made him hesitate so he detoured to the back steps, listening to what seemed to be a dispute. Three voices could be distinguished from those of Maeve and her swain.

O'Malley was saying, "Where's your spine, man? They're going to ruin the miners and the farmers both. I say hit them on Labor Day; that will send a working man's message."

A familiar new voice said, "You're risking your own freedom. They'll know it was you. Even if you're not caught right away, you're in for a hard time."

Maeve said, "John Knox and that gang of his will wake up once we hit their source of revenue. We'll close down east/west traffic for a year."

What did Caroline's father have to do with the discussion, John-Arthur wondered, now listening closer?

A man who seemed to be concerned about farm issues, said, "I'm with you, but how are we going to get our stock and crops to market if we blow it up. Knox will try to block us. And do you have enough dynamite?"

John-Arthur now listened in fear. Blow up what? Caroline's house?

Maeve said, "I've started to buy some charges and I've been setting off some blasts on the property. I'm telling the supplier and the neighbors both that I'm widening the creek."

Another said, "We can take our crops downriver to St. Louis. Cheaper anyway."

The farmer said, "Can they handle the excess?"

Another said, "They're short right now with the drought elsewhere."

O'Malley said, "Any more questions? Can we get on with it? Fact is nothing will convince you if you don't feel the heel of their boot on your chest."

A new voice said, "What good's blowing it up if we can't get through to the mills in Indiana?"

Maeve said, "The ore'll stack up so high they'll either cave in or close out. Either way, you'll know where you stand. Pay off your mortgage and scat out."

O'Malley said, "Are we agreed?"

John-Arthur was in dread. They were going to use dynamite against Caroline's family, maybe her house on the cliffs. Aware that the wrangling had ceased, he presumed that the meeting was over, and now didn't want to be seen. He wanted to get closer so, covered by the increasing dark, he rounded the corner of the house and looked in the parlor window. He saw four men and Maeve examining something, but he couldn't see that it was a model of the Mississippi River railroad bridge that crossed from Dubuque to Illinois. When one of the men turned, John-Arthur clearly saw that it was Big Jack, the Boy Wizard's guardian.

John-Arthur stumbled home in the dark, conflicted and afraid and so excited that he couldn't sleep. If they were going to harm Caroline or her family, he had to warn her but how could he betray Maeve? He hated the railroads because his people hated them. But what Knox property were they going to blow up? He finally fell asleep but he bolted up stark awake at five and went over the problem again. Surely Maeve would not hurt Caroline. The only thing he knew was that he had to warn the girl. He didn't know how to accomplish that and protect Maeve at the same time, but he had to try.

Without waking Francis, he rummaged through dresser drawers for money and his knife. Then he quietly descended and left a note saying he would be out early for a long hike and would be back by dinner. Don't even think about chores, he thought. He folded some bread and cheese in a paper bag and went out on the main road and began walking the sixteen miles to Dubuque. He arrived after four hours of hiking and hitching rides with farmers on their way to market.

As he made his way through the center of town, all that he could remember was that she lived in one of the big houses on the bluff. He looked up towards the top of the cliff and could see a line of mansions overlooking the city, hanging like steamboats in the sky. The river port spread behind him as he trudged uphill. When he looked back, he could see the last of the Diamond Jo two-deck paddlewheelers at the wharf.

He would tell her he had a dream—a warning that she would be hurt. No, dreams don't count, he said to himself. He would just lie and say that he overheard it in the market that morning. It had been a few weeks since they watched the bandstand go up in flames and he hoped she felt as much a friend as then. If not, he'd have to warn her anyway. She didn't abuse farmers like her father did, so it wasn't her fault, so why should she suffer? It was the fairness doctrine of ten-year-olds that brought him to her elm-laden street.

John-Arthur went around the back of one of the big houses to the stables and asked about the Knoxes, and within five minutes he was standing by her gate, hoping that her mother wasn't about.

"Caroline, honey, who is that boy out there?" the maid asked. "I've been looking out the window and I sees him. He be trying to sell us something?"

Caroline looked out and when she saw it was John-Arthur, her face lit up and she tore down the stairs, out the door, excited, crossing the porch, running all the way to the gate.

"John-Arthur."

"Caroline, hello."

"Can you come in?"

"Sure. I was looking for your house and some boys said this was the one."

"They were right. Musty old place."

They went up to the porch and sat on the steps.

"Can you stay for awhile?" she asked.

"A couple hours. Then I'll have to get back."

"How did you get here?"

"Walked mostly."

"You must be thirsty. I'll get you something to drink."

"No, wait," he blurted out. "You and your folks. Are you going on vacation at all?"

"No, we're just back."

"No more holidays before school starts? Will you be around on Labor Day?"

"Labor Day? I don't . . . .Oh, Labor Day. Yes."

The "yes" made his heart skip.

She continued, "We're going on a boat ride downriver and we're doing something, a party, on an island with a bunch of other families. Gone for a week."

A great weight lifted from him.

"For sure?" he asked.

"For sure! Why?"

"Just wondering where you'd be on the holiday," he lied. "And nobody will be in the house at all?"

"No, it'll be empty. We'll all be on the river and the help will be away to visit their people."

Cripes, he thought, nobody will be home. She said it's a musty old place anyway. Besides Maeve is never going to do anything harmful.

"And when do you go back to Chicago?" Caroline asked.

"We'll be leaving the middle of August after the family picnic."

"And you walked all that way just to see me?" she asked again.

"Sure. We're friends, aren't we?"

"Best friends. Come on, I'll show you around. First I'll comb your hair and you can wipe off your shoes. Then we'll surprise my Ma."

Caroline showed John-Arthur around the house; he had never been invited into a mansion before. There was even a small room to make ice cream. From the upstairs porch there was a river view. She insisted that he see her room, even though the maid was busy there.

Embarrassed by his audacity but clever enough to see their attachment, Mrs. Knox was disturbed by the sight of John-Arthur. But neither of the children noticed her displeasure. They sat outside and had sandwiches and John-Arthur, not wishing to alarm Ellen and Frank, did not stay long. But before he left, they climbed the giant apple tree near the bluff and he cut his initials with his knife high up on one of the branches, high enough to hide them in a tent of green where they kissed each other, away from prying eyes.

Her father had come home for lunch and as an accommodating gesture to his daughter, drove John-Arthur to the northwestern edge of town on a circuitous way back to his office. People bowed to the magnate as they made their way through the city. Residents were deferential and slightly wary.

When he got back to the farm, Frank said, "We got your note. Where did you go?"

"Went walking. All the way to Durango," Arthur lied.

"What for?"

"Oh, just for the fun of it."

It was an early lesson. John-Arthur understood that split loyalties are complicated and make you lie a lot. What he was to discover was that not everyone accepts the lies one tells and the result is that trust can be damaged.

\* \* \*

It was August now and the corn grew full in its sheath—a bright yellow hidden in a light green gown, topped by a tousled fright wig. The sun was still hot during the day but one evening in the second week of the month sweaters came out of boxes stored beneath the beds. Meanwhile there was an acceleration in plans for the annual homecoming of the Mahoney clan at Great James's place where the III of the line lived with his family, including cousins Emmett and Gen.

The children had gathered at different rendezvous points during the course of the summer. The dam Frank built was one, the meadow behind the church was another, also the small village with its ten commercial buildings, one of which was the General Store commanded by Uncle Jim. Emmett was old enough to tend the register for a few hours each day, and John-Arthur, trained in his parents' delicatessen, helped out while the younger kids played on the dusty road where they waited for their ringleaders to come off duty.

Inside the store, surrounded by pickle and cracker barrels and crocks of butter and cheese, and canned goods piled high in great pyramids, the older boys practiced their retail skills under the genial, but tough, supervision of Uncle Jim. The mixed aroma smelled something like caraway, cheese, beef and dill on the side. Behind a glass showcase for bread, and crates of eggs and rows of bottles, the boys began their long climb to manhood. In the same way that the migratory farm population was headed for the towns, country boys were learning ways to prepare themselves for the transition to possible retail service when they grew up, and in the transaction something was lost and something was gained. Individualization was changing over to socialization, where different skills were needed.

\* \* \*

Unbeknown to any of the Mahoneys except John-Arthur, the clandestine meetings about the dynamiting continued at Maeve's. Meanwhile, the passions of O'Malley and his red-headed mistress only enflamed their recklessness as if nothing could change their good fortune, not even railroad police.

Between chores, John-Arthur continued to visit Maeve for his piano lessons, noticing that a greater number of love songs were appearing in her repertoire and that there was a good deal more singing. Because the boy knew that O'Malley, wanted for inciting a riot, was a truant from the law and because John-Arthur could be trusted to retain their secret, Maeve no longer hid the big outfielder from the youngster's view. And in that way, the two males bonded, though Maeve was quick to defuse a total attachment between them, not wishing to draw the boy too deeply into their conspiracy.

But the inevitable happened, and Maeve was forced to go to Frank and ask if John-Arthur could ride into Dubuque on an errand for her. The old man agreed remembering a like adventure of his own at the same age when Great James himself entrusted him to cover the same distance to accomplish a piece of business that the old homesteader needed to settle. Saddling Maeve's horse, John-Arthur made his second solo round trip into the city. After delivering the letters O'Malley prepared at the first two assigned houses, he was amazed to find a familiar face at the third stop. Answering the door was Big Jack and behind him, the Wizard Boy.

"Hey! John-Arthur. You in on the plan?" Al asked.

"No, I'm just delivering stuff."

"Come in. How's Maeve?" Jack asked, taking the envelope from the young messenger.

"She and. . . ." John-Arthur hesitated. "She's fine."

Scanning the letter, Big Jack said, "I see that you know O'Malley's visiting with her."

"Yes, sir, I do. But I'm the only one who knows."

"You've seen him then?"

"Most every other day," John-Arthur answered.

"And are you going right back?" Jack asked.

"Yes," said John-Arthur responding slowly. "Though maybe I'll visit a friend first."

Big Jack said, "You've got to be careful. Can't tell anybody where you've been."

"I know. Maeve told me."

"This friend of yours. You'll tell him you've come all the way into town just to visit him?"

"I've come alone before to visit," John-Arthur said.

"So who are you going to see?"

"You remember her. Caroline Knox from the Fourth of July picnic."

"Knox?" Big Jack asked with surprise.

"Yes, up on the hill."

"John Knox's daughter?"

"Yes."

"Who lives next door to Mayor Gage?"

"Don't know about that," John-Arthur said.

Big Jack looked at Al knowingly and said, "That's where they keep their anti-riot plans. We've already snuck into his office downtown trying to find them. We think he must keep them up at the house. He's always having Knox and his cronies in there for meetings."

Jack thought for a minute, then said, "You two boys sit down here and visit while I go out for a half hour. Show him your piano, Boy, and I'll be back soon."

"So, what have you been up to?" John-Arthur asked when Jack went out into the kitchen to negotiate a number with the telephone operator.

"Still doing our Wizard thing for the unions. That's usually good through Labor Day, but then the crowds fall off."

"What do you do then?"

"We're thinking about going into vaudeville to tide us over until the tent season begins again next spring. . . .When the roads dry out, we can always go back to the circus."

"What will you do if you go in the ring?"

"Jack's the strong man. I'm usually the midget and sometimes I get to be a clown."

"That's something."

"Come in here. I'll show you the piano."

They walked into the parlor and a few seconds later Jack stuck his head in to say he would return shortly.

"Do you play?" John-Arthur asked.

Al said, "Yeah, old Jack makes me practice. Sometimes when we have a big crowd in the tent and the pail's not full, we get the crowd singing. Loosens up their pants pockets."

"Hymns or tunes?"

"Everything," Al said. "A little opera. Marching songs. Anything to get 'em hopping. When we're in a tightfisted place like Kansas, that's when they screw the chair way up and I start banging away. I'll give 'em gypsy music if I have to. . . .You play too?"

"Just learning," John-Arthur said. "From Maeve we're talking about. She's got a lot of good rolls."

"Come on, we'll knock out a few songs. . . .Want some coffee? I'll make some. Helps stunt my growth."

"Will you have a cigar with it?"

"That's for after dinner," the Wizard Boy replied.

The pair entered the kitchen and Al prepared coffee in a blue speckled pot. There was a wood stove going and the usual assortment of cabinets and cutting tables were in evidence. Plus curtains on three sunny windows. A small blackboard sat on a peg next to the telephone poised to accept incoming messages.

Al asked, "So, Artie, what do you see for yourself?"

That was the first time anyone had ever called him Artie.

"You mean after I get out of school?" Al nodded and John-Arthur continued. "I'll probably go in business with my Dad. He peddles from a fruit wagon and I already help him some."

"You can't make any money at that. You got to come up with a scheme. An angle. Get on the road like us."

"I don't think I'd like that," John-Arthur said. "I'd rather be home with my folks."

The coffee pot was on low rumble.

"Let's see. . . . What kind of a thing could we get you to do? . . . . How about this? Looking into the future is always a good gimmick—crystal ball kind of thing, tarot cards, anything. Jack's good at all that swami stuff—we get him all dressed up like a camel driver. . . . But what do you see for you and your family? What's the family plan? Like Jack and me—in another ten years, we're going to the South Seas and pick pineapples."

John-Arthur said, "My folks talk about insurance and something about a burial plan."

"Art, you've got to improve your chances. Tell me. . . .No, wait, I got a better idea. We'll get Jack to give you a legit reading. We con the rubes but there's something actually rings true in all our prophecy hokum—and Jack'll get you connected with the other side. Stars or whatever. He's got the knack. Me too. Never can tell what things we can conjure up."

"Like ghosts?"

"More like impressions from outside. But you have to know what you want and ask the right questions in order to get the spirits moving. General stuff—like where you want your family to go for vacation— isn't enough."

"My Pa keeps talking about some White City."

"We'll ask Jack how you get to go there. Not like a right turn, left turn, and then another right. But how you get eased into things and make 'em simpler to find. He's good at that. . . .This coffee thing boiled long enough?"

"Let it go another minute," answered the son of the delicatessen owners.

"See, we got to ask the question just right. . . .Something like. . . .'What will we do after the family gets to the White City?'. . . . It's not 'Is there a White City?'—because your Pa already says there is. . . .And not "How do I get there?'—not 'Follow some cobblestone road' or anything. . . .But it's 'Where will my family live once we're in the White City?'"

The coffee was popping and bumping.

John-Arthur repeated, "Where and when will my family live in the White City?"

At that the blackboard clattered to the floor.

"Oh, god, the blackboard trick," Al said.

They walked over and picked up the slate from the floor and saw amid the notations for grocery items, phone numbers and future appointments, recipes and other reminders the words *Only in your dreams*.

The blackboard was trying to tell John-Arthur something.

"What does it say?" Al asked in a state of agitation.

"It says, *Only in your dreams*, and down below it says, *Never buy. Always rent*. That your handwriting?"

"Nope."

"Jack's?"

"Nope. You got fresh tracks."

John-Arthur set the blackboard back on the hook. "I'll ask my Dad what it means. He went to seminary."

"The coffee!"

Al heard the thumping. He set the pot, exhausted and grumbling, off to the side and reached for a cup and some milk and sugar. He lifted the pot and tilted the spout over the cup, but nothing came out but vapor.

"How did that happen?" John-Arthur asked.

"I hope that weren't just hot air."

They walked into the parlor to entertain themselves with some music. Starting off, they played a duet of the *Wild Rose* song. Then they cranked up some rolls. In a while, the music began to lose tempo. The keys, which had been popping up and down, suddenly hesitated and then quit altogether.

"There it goes again," Al said.

"What's the matter?"

"I've been tinkering with it—trying to jigger it for a bigger response—but it backs up on me. Just wait a second."

At that, Al searched for some tools, then lifted the topcover and began tweaking the knobs inside. That didn't work, so he pulled the upright away from the wall and started playing with the tracker gears, soon the keys began hopping again. John-Arthur kept his nose right in the action until it was repaired and the rolls began to turn once more and they could enjoy the tunes.

"You sure are handy with fixin' things," John-Arthur said.

Jack walked back in. He had a plan. "This is what we're going to do. . . ." He proposed that the two boys, without Caroline's help, break into the Mayor's house and pilfer the strike breaking plans from his library.

Up the hill the boys rode, two astride Maeve's horse, seeking out the Knox home on the bluff. They rode up to the house and tied the horse to the post, and this time, Caroline spotted them first and came out.

"Hi John-Arthur. Al, hi. What are you two doing around here?"

She asked a boy from the back of the house to look after the horse and began escorting her guests around.

"This big old place is yours?" Al asked.

"Sure."

"Who owns that one next door?"

"That's the Gage's place. He's the Mayor."

"Oh. . . ." Al said.

They sat in the swing in the sideyard and Al surveyed the house across the lawn. He noticed that in the back of the house a chimney popped out of the roof covering the one-story kitchen extension. He could see a trail of smoke steaming from it, a signal that a meal was in preparation.

Al said, "Why don't you two play off by yourself. I'm a bit tired from the ride. I'll just sit in the gazebo for a few minutes over there—near where that ladder's parked."

"OK," John-Arthur said, happy to be alone with Caroline, and added, "We're going to climb the apple tree out back."

"Good. I couldn't get up there anyway," said the Wizard. "My legs are too short."

John-Arthur and Caroline climbed back into the upper quietude of the apple tree branches and found the initials he had cut on his last visit. He noticed that she had chipped out her own initials under his. While they were occupied in their airy lair, Al, with a pail and ladder, did some climbing himself. Short legs or not, he trudged up the rungs onto the short roof off the back of the Gage house and covered the smoking chimney with the pail, in effect stopping the flow of exhaust. He then gingerly retreated, leaving the ladder in place and sat on the swing and waited for the inevitable.

In a few minutes, a wisp of smoke came seeping out the back screen door, and then a minute later, a white curl came drifting out the kitchen window.

Soon there was commotion from inside the Gage house. As smoke began to billow out the open spaces in the back portion of the house owing to the backed-up chimney, an alarm went up among the inhabitants. First a few shouts, then more cries. Al waited until he could see smoke coming out the front door, then started bellowing, "Fire! Fire!"

He ran around to the street and shouted some more, alerting neighbors, hollering across the lawns and fences, "Fire! Fire! House on fire."

Pandemonium broke out as the covered chimney blew back smoke into the interior of the house. Neighbors rushed to help as smudge began pouring out of every orifice in the dwelling. Arthur and Caroline hearing the noise scampered down to join the spectators.

"The boy went into the house," someone yelled.

The fire department came clanging around the corner, the horses at full speed, rattling their gear. Just as they arrived at the front door, eyes straining through the smoke, out came little Al, covered with soot, carrying the family cat in his arms.

"Oh, you saved our Snooty," one of the Gage girls said.

"Nothing to it," Al said. "Had a pet once myself ."

Navigating the growing crowd, Al told John-Arthur, "Go up the ladder in the back of the house and take the pail off the chimney cap. Do it. Now."

John-Arthur did as instructed, up and down the ladder he went, looking for all the world like a volunteer junior fireman, descending again into the yard, hot pail in hand, as the firemen inside doused the Gage dinner in a flood of fresh water.

The smoke soon dissipated and aside for an acrid smell that remained in the house for a few days, there was little damage. Caroline helped scrub the boys down on her back porch, served them some refreshment and saw them off down the hill. In Al's pocket rested the anti-strike plans against the miners, drawn up by the local and state authorities.

Big Jack, greeting them, said, "I knew you two could do it."

Next day there was a picture of Al in the newspaper, grinning, holding the cat with the headline, "Boy Wizard Saves Mayor's Favorite Pet." The smile on his face was priceless.

"You never could resist a little publicity," Jack scolded him.

Back in Holy Cross, John-Arthur gave Maeve and O'Malley all the details, feeling like a full participant in their plan.

\* \* \*

As John-Arthur's vacation neared its end, Maeve and he traveled to New Vienna to see their friend, Ed.

Maeve lamented, "I hope we find him in his garden fighting nothing more dangerous than snapdragons."

When they reached Ed's house, an elderly woman, an aunt who minded his cottage, greeted them. "You'll find him changed, I'm afraid. He just sits by the window and turns pages in his books, not so much reading. . . .just reciting by heart the parts he remembers."

They entered the library and there in the window seat with the sun pouring in on him sat their friend. Flowers growing outside, mostly roses, framed the sash; light filtered through the flowers and cast a dusty rose color on him and his book. Oversize, the book lay on his lap opened to a colorful print from the English legends—a scene filled with knights and ladies of the tournament class crashing headlong into a story of deceit and conquest. Maeve went and sat beside him and even though he failed to recognize her, he knew she shared his interest, and she began reading to him. Though he hardly responded, he seemed happy to watch her mouth and touch her hair.

They left him there in the rose light.

Maeve was sad. "He was my link with the old stories and now I'm missing one of the strings that holds me together. He just sits there imagining he's away in another country . . . .The two of us grew up reading the same verse. I'm so vulnerable with love now myself, I need all those people and their dreamy stories. I need to hear the rhymers and minstrels. Ed and you are my only contact with them. Such a dear man! He played out his dream through music—and I hope he hears MacDowell still. Forced to stare into the abyss courtesy of John Knox's traction company." She hesitated, and then took his arm, "John-Arthur! Help me find my Tara necklace."

They were riding home to Holy Cross in silence until she remembered the songs they harmonized on their journey home from the ragtime opera performance, the one they attended with Ed. They reprised the lively arias once again in a show of bravado—ragtime prancing through the tall corn country.

* * *

The annual family homecoming coincided with the early harvest, the abundance of Iowa August. Pies and tubs of corn came flying out the kitchen door as in previous years. There were smells around Jim and Anna Mahoney's stove that could be savored in the memory passages of the mind for a lifetime. Roast chickens in tarragon, sausage, roast beef and peppery gravy, roast pork with heaps of apple sauce and mashed potatoes, butter and corn, all supported by fresh hot bread and biscuits, surrounded by sliced red tomatoes. For dessert the fragrance of apple pies, cherry tarts, meringue and fresh cream, laced with tastes of molasses and cinnamon—all covered in the warm steam of the original homestead kitchen with its big oak table, carpentered by Great James himself, and piled high with the offerings from his progeny's fields.

Martin and Kitty had arrived two days before and were reunited with their sun-drenched boys. They listened intently to all their stories, except the secret one that John-Arthur kept to himself. Old Frank and his son Martin had time to take a walk, neither knowing these were the last few days they would spend together. Kitty, a magician in the kitchen, stood at the stove with Anna and Ellen for hours on both the afternoon before and the big day itself, the women in long dresses with upturned sleeves. Other wives and cousins were happy to oblige the unspoken rule that this was not a time for women of medium cooking skills to be in that hot room. The buggies and rigs began arriving early. Later Maeve O'Donnell made a token appearance around the noon hour. In response to a formal letter that Frank had sent to Mr. Knox, requesting Caroline's company, the girl and Miss Giles appeared, courtesy of a door-to-door ride with the family's nuns who had been given permission to make the trip, seeing as how it had been a diocesan privilege for the Mahoney-related BVMs to attend the event for forty or more years.

Out in the yard, planks were resurrected from their winter slumber from back of the barn and set across barrels from the General Store, while folding chairs from the church basement were placed beside.

Kitty welcomed Miss Giles and made her feel comfortable by introducing her to likely bookmates—though there had been no need, since solicitous Leo quickly intervened. John-Arthur, anxious to reconfirm that there had been no changes in Caroline's Labor Day schedule, was relieved and relaxed when she assured him the boat trip was still planned. Kitty took great interest in Caroline once her cooking chores materialized, anxious to meet the girl about whom her son had written. The girl needed little coaxing and before the day was out, Kitty had made a friend of the child. When Maeve first appeared she was cautious but her natural ebullience quickly emerged; she had been looking forward to spending time with Martin, owing to her strong attachment to both his father and his son. Martin, not accustomed to attention from women other than his mother and wife, tried his clerical best to keep up the conversation, but barely succeeded.

The gossip among the men revolved around the railroad rate hike and the violence surrounding the strike at the lead mine. The Knox faction had practically closed the mining operation down, and as a result entrepreneurs in Dubuque were complaining about the loss of business. All actions having a reaction, complaints arose including those heard from Mahoneys who had moved away from the farms and now covered insurance and ran retail and wholesale operations in the city.

The BVM nuns performed again for their secular cousins, having expanded their repertoire thanks to some of the novitiates who had taken up brass instruments. With trepidation and courage, they had decided to play a larger work this year.

Sister Bern, still conducting, rapping for attention, said, "We've decided on an American piece this year, a work by Chadwick. . . .On the title page, he's written:

*No cool gray tones for me!*
*Give me the warmest, red and green,*
*A coronet and a tambourine,*
*To paint* my *jubilee!*

Here it is: *Jubilee*."

As they played the mellifluous middle section, Martin, remembering the poignant Iowa song from the Dvorak piece ten years before, thought again, "Must be America likes sweet honey music."

When the time came to say goodbye, the Chicago Mahoneys thanked Caroline for her effort in joining their festivities and tried to show how much they appreciated her trouble for making the long journey by preparing a harvest basket for her family. She would be in the care of Miss Giles and the nuns on their return trip to their convent. Surrounded by both the holy women and his family, Caroline, to everyone's surprise, stepped up and kissed John-Arthur.

"I'll be thinking on 'ya," she said.

"Won't soon forget you and this summer," he answered.

Then she was gone, down the dusty farm lane towards the main road.

Late that evening, John-Arthur walked along the stream to Maeve's.

"The rest of the summer won't be the same," Maeve said, leading him into the house.

"Will you write me a letter?" asked John-Arthur.

"I'm not good at writing," Maeve said, "but you know in your heart I'm thinking about you, don't you?"

"Suppose so," John-Arthur said, suddenly shy.

"And remember now—like in the games along the stream—you're to be chief of all of Iowa, and you have a special job to find that lost locket with the Tara name on it."

"We'll find it for you, Maeve. If not this summer, next"

"And what is that necklace supposed to mean?" she quizzed him.

"Tell me again."

"It gives you the right to be yourself. . . .and where did the power of it come from?"

"I forget."

"From all the people who came here to live free like me and Frank's Da."

O'Malley joined them.

Maeve said, "So let me take a good look at you so I remember you over the winter, because when I see you next, you'll be up to my ears. Give us a hug and tell your parents to buy you a piano. I'll save this one for you until you come again."

They hugged and O'Malley stretched out his big paw, as large as a first baseman's mitt.

"Thanks for keeping our secret. You've given us time to be together without bother."

John-Arthur, fretting, asked, "Maeve, you'd never hurt Caroline Knox, would you?"

"What makes you to ask such a question? I'd give my life for that girl."

"OK," John-Arthur said.

The next morning, after mass, Martin, Kitty, John-Arthur and Francis said goodbye to Frank and Ellen and Leo and Scotty and headed home to Chicago

# Chapter 6

Kitty had enjoyed her five days of vacation in Iowa, and now she was ready to go back to work for another year. But first she would rest as the train rumbled across the Illinois plains.

When John-Arthur and Francis and their parents rode home to Chicago, the city had grown to be twice the size of the metropolis that Martin viewed when he visited the White City thirteen years before. Back then, as Martin wandered through the glistening artificial city by the lake, migration off the farm was well under way and waves of immigrants from Eastern Europe were rolling over the midwest. In a city where many of the poor worked in the slaughterhouses, the meatsaturated population had jumped from one million to two in the interim between 1893 and 1906. Downtown, horse-drawn streetcars had been replaced by electric conveyance.

The Mahoneys arrived that day at one of Chicago's great railroad stations, all of them both a dead-end terminus and initial embarkation point. Passengers were required to change trains here, and the only glimpse of Chicago most travelers beheld was the blur registered through a cab window during their race across the city. Arriving on an eastern train, en route passengers scurried to one headed west or south or north at a totally different location. They had no time to sightsee. Frantic people, riding in carriages heaped with overflowing luggage, could be viewed at all hours of the day crawling through the traffic eager to meet the timetables of the continental through trains, their departure times sometimes slipping away as they moved in slow motion through the crowded streets, wishing their drivers would speed up the horses.

The Mahoneys, carrying their bags, walked outside into the din of whistle-pierced Chicago. There was a smoke and electric smell in the air, and a pleasant whiff from the lake.

"Appears to be a new headliner in town."

"I hear vaudeville prices have gone up a nickel."

The city's buildings were the first in the world to reach up and scrape the sky, and Sullivan's architectural magic had already been bestowed on what would become the Carson, Pirie Scott building. Other creators were developing their craft. Frank Lloyd Wright now from Spring Green and Georgia O'Keefe from Sun Prairie, born two counties apart in Wisconsin, were perfecting their styles. Wright had finished his work on the Rookery Court and O'Keefe was a student at the Art Institute.

"Look," said John-Arthur. "I count twelve stories on that one."

Chicago was already the steelrail bulwark between the east and the west; its crossroads would retain its position as the nation's switchyard for another fifty years. The city would both guard the through-track of religious and political conservatism that ran between the Appalachians and the Rockies and at the same time give right-of-way to the literary locomotion of the 20th Century. The writers of the midwestern flowering were still in knickers playing among the tall elms—Fitzgerald up in St. Paul, Hemingway in nearby Oak Park. Eliot, wearing longer pants in St. Louis, was preparing to enter Harvard, the boy in him still in love with the river, calling the Mississippi a god. The new American language would transfer here onto the modern stage. Except O'Neill who would transfer from the New Haven line. And downriver, Faulkner from the Gulf and Chicago.

Passing a bookstore, Martin said, "There's the new book about the stockyards that everybody's talking about."

The great families of Chicago were already established, many of whom were choking on the Sinclair book—the Armours, Pullmans, McCormicks, Fields, Swifts, and Potter Palmers. The lives of these people held little interest for the Martin Mahoneys but they did influence commercial markets like meatpacking, and so in turn dictated food prices, which affected Kitty's store. In a larger sense these prominent families, along with their counterparts in the east, gambled in the same risky monetary practices that led to the regular financial panics and downturns that plagued the rest of the country. But the ways and means of the rich were part of the mysterious forces that the Mahoneys neither comprehended nor devoted time to follow.

Martin and Kitty, though they accepted the status quo, found it difficult to maintain their business and provide for their family. They had a good marriage because they were both givers and they were gentle without being timorous, but it was hard going economically. Martin believed what Christ preached about humility and charity and practiced these beliefs within the circumference of his family, and as best as he could on Chicago's streets. He wasn't interested in impressing other people and tended to stand back from quick exchanges. Having spent part of his youth in the seminary at a time when his peers were running amuck, he skipped the wild-oat-sowing stage that included drinking and whoring around, and because he had never participated, he never missed it, and wouldn't have wanted that kind of life anyway. There was a shyness about him except when he was with Kitty, whom he urgently enfolded in fierce embrace. Or when he would swing Francis through the air in wide merry-go-rounds. He was tall, spare but toughened by years of hoisting and lifting crates onto the wagon. Though his life's work was hauling cabbages, he didn't begrudge it. His children would remember that he wasn't very good at making money, coming from the priesthood and all, because he tended to overtrust his customers and often indulged the overdue.

Kitty, like most women, was more proficient in the social graces and she employed her talents successfully, running the delicatessen while Martin plied the back alleys of near and distant neighborhoods. She was small and brunette, with long hair below her hips and with a dark oval-faced prettiness, sturdy but still stylish considering she had borne two sons.

Everyone knew the pair was devoted to one another; between themselves they kept their love whole because their separate instincts told them that even if life was short, it minimally offered the plenitude of this one abiding relationship. For both, this was the singularly rare one. When they married they had challenged their God and were forced to live a life of unknown consequences. Martin was within months of his final vows when he felt the power of Kitty Rapp's emotional pull and decided to exchange an ascetic life for a conjugal one. He had been chosen for holy orders, but there was no power on earth or in heaven that could separate them from their passion—a brave love in the face of God. They silently prayed for compassion.

Her family, the Rapps, stemmed from a religious core. A distant cousin of Kitty's father led an army of five hundred souls from southern Germany to the New World to establish a religious community where all would share equally in the commonweal. Renowned as a prophet, George Rapp led his Protestant band out of Bavaria, and these plain people of the Lord set up their tabernacle in western Pennsylvania in a place they named Harmony. By hard labor and devotion, they developed it into a version of the city of God. Then two things happened. Like the Mormons, George led his followers further west and created New Harmony, Indiana, but somewhere between these modulations, he declared that the laws of celibacy would henceforth govern the sect. Outsiders scratched their heads when both the Shakers and the Harmonists introduced that law, because it surely meant the destruction of their congregations. But what others did not accept or understand was a reckoning that had always been clear to the brethren. Nonbelievers simply did not understand that the world was scheduled to end by 1900.

Though the Chicago Rapps never accepted their famous cousin's prophecies or his plan to communally develop God's real estate, the family sprang from the same Wurttemberg strain and sang the same German hymns. In the blood of Kitty and Martin's sons, John-Arthur and Francis, prophets and mad folks circulated.

Kitty had been a model daughter. Though old Rapp and his wife were a dour industrious couple, their Catherine grew up with a sweet, mildly saucy disposition and a sterling character. When Martin broke his pact with God and came to tell her parents of their plan to marry, the seminarian was still wearing black. The Rapps were stunned and hostile toward the marriage, not only because of Martin's ecclesiastical background but the age difference, and the certainty of his current and future impoverishment. When Kitty informed her parents that she was converting to Catholicism, it was as if she told them baptism water could run uphill. It was only after Kitty threatened a total break with her family did they accede to her willfulness. Though she was only eighteen and the groom still had one foot trailing along the altar rail, both parents feared her iron resoluteness and could see she was destined to be the fallen priest's wife with or without their consent.

There had been other suitors, bull-chested German businessmen. She had waltzed them around but always kept a few spaces open on her dance card. When she and Martin bedded down, their emotions burst in wild explosions, and rested in afterstorms of inner peace. Burdened now by children and work, Kitty was still able to retain her centered self and applied her good disposition to her family and the customers of her store. Not that any of it had been easy. Her parents, who ran a delicatessen themselves, had reluctantly lent them the money to open their daughter's offshoot store on the first floor of the apartment house they owned and occupied, but the venture had not been a success. Always more tired than she could bear, Kitty's routine was continually interrupted in her pursuits. There were never-ending things to do, until finally she collapsed in Martin's arms for two or three minutes' quiet rest before falling to sleep. Sometimes in the morning, she would wake and for a few seconds half-dream she was still a schoolgirl with a day off until she bolted up remembering all the things she had to do in the next hour.

Their acceptance of things-as-they-are lay embedded in their obedience to the church and by the long history of their agrarian ancestors and, in truth, by the country's sluggish economy. The spunky spirit of westerners and the life of hard-drinking roustabouts that characterized the lifestyle of whooped-up Rocky Mountain speculators illustrated an unfamiliar formula to them. They didn't understand the spirit that sent men clambering over the peaks for silver and gold, to places where a man might start up six kinds of businesses before one caught on or before he conceded defeat or bankruptcy, and even then would start a new enterprise again. They were unlike Frank of *Sunny Slope*, who sped after the Gold Rush three times, inspired by his youthful quest in favor of riches. The family's sentiment for a stable middle class was encouraged by only a few institutions—unions and granges—filled with Jefferson's idea that happiness meant a square deal for the family. But work and struggle without the assurance of long-term economic prosperity became the Mahoney's reality and they chose not to rebel against the system.

Passivity was ingrained in the world's poor, whose numbers practically amounted to human kind's entire population. Where strands of moral fiber existed, as in the case of Martin and Kitty, its force was usually expressed defensively. To them aggression connoted ruthlessness and was to be avoided at all cost. What John-Arthur made of all this was easy to comprehend; basically, he went along with the sheepishness of his father. If the boy rebelled, he might have been a different person. He might have chosen to engage in an active life, but for the present he and Francis opted to sink into a dreary form of modesty. The Mahoneys seemed to be more comfortable being acted upon than acting on others.

Characteristically, to be a whole person in the early 20th century meant to establish personal integrity and derive strength from within. So what if a new American in these years didn't knock down forests or change the course of rivers? A person could always maintain one's dignity and sense of self and personal honesty. Those qualities were important to this family. So passivity was part of a wall people built to protect the treasures within themselves as well as a bulwark against the mad intrusion of aggressive behavior from without.

The day of their return from Iowa, the family navigated the trolleys and el, transferring through the structured cable and transportation grid—a series of electrical transactions—toward the South Side and emerged late in the afternoon in their own neighborhood, somewhat closer to Back of the Yards than Hyde Park, south enough of the Stockyards to breathe clear but too far from the lake to enjoy the breezes. The neighborhood was German and Irish, mostly foreign-born or first generation. The ethnic differences between these two northern European territories were fading. Germans doublenumbered the Irish throughout Chicago but that was not true here in the Garfield/Ashland neighborhood, where the balance was approximately equal. The family alighted from the streetcar at that intersection. Further north was the Irish stronghold of Bridgeport and further north again the old German neighborhoods near the river with names like Schiller and Goethe on the streetsigns.

On Laflin Avenue, the stone and wooden streetside facades might have been the subject of an architectural photograph, static with little movement, while in the rear of the houses, facing the alley, the scene was operatic. Wooden porches running on both sides of the alley presented a bustling soundpicture of flapping laundry, wailing kids, and neighbors calling over their banisters to one another. In the stables, there was much hammering, part of the process of transforming these structures into automobile garages. Chants rose from the horse-drawn carts or pushcarts rumbling through the alley, offering goods and services from passing icemen and knife grinders and the ever-present carters that called for "rags and old iron." The chilly fronts and the boisterous backs of these houses matched the cold front parlors and warm rear kitchens of the apartments themselves. It was in the back of the house where life flourished.

The Mahoneys climbed the back stairs to the second floor and entered the elongated flat, and the boys headed for the front bedroom next to the sitting room overlooking the street. In the rear, the largest room was reserved for cooking and most of the eating; a tiny bedroom off to the side was reserved for the parents. Connecting in the middle was the dining room where holidays and Sundays were observed. The big table, with the leaves left permanently in place, became the battleground for games of hearts and rummy, or the place to spread out newspapers or homework, puzzle pieces, sewing or ironing or the fragile pieces of the model racing cars that the two older males were always building. Their delicatessen was located downstairs, and in the rear yard, their stable and horse.

Kitty, laying her large hat on the bed, called out, "Boys, did you see your Dad painted your room?"

The boys dutifully carried their bags to the front of the house.

"Can you believe how they've grown?" Kitty said. "They'll be Art and Frank soon and six feet tall." She sighed, watching after the boys, breath of her flesh, and said, "I think I'll go down and see how things are in the store."

"Go ahead," Martin said. "I'll follow shortly."

Delicatessens are a little like America. Some German sausage. Milk from a downstate Irish farm, ham from the Milwaukee Polish, neighborhood Jewish rye, olives from the

Italians in California, butter from the Scandinavians in Wisconsin—tubs of food from all the cultures of the world, mostly sacked in blackman's cotton. Sometimes even a bit of French bakery. Early Chicago, abundant with the dream of inclusion and a concomitant reactive fear of it, believed that some kind of eventual bounty would come from this mixed bag of peoples. Most looked ahead to some flowing ethnic cornucopia, but for the present they kept their eyes glued on the glass case of today's offerings and current edible delights.

When Kitty entered the store, her sister and brother-in-law, who had substituted for them while the Mahoneys enjoyed their long weekend at the farm, greeted her. They chatted between customer visits, catching up on gossip. Donning her long apron, Kitty automatically began arranging dishes and sopping up crumbs and easing back into her regular place behind the counter. She asked after their parents. . . .They were fine. . . .And Milly showed Kitty where she had hidden the weekend receipts. Milly, as willful as her older sister, expressed part of her stubbornness by maintaining a distinctly unfriendly attitude towards Martin, blaming him for her sister's conversion to Catholicism, going as far as to refuse the role of bridesmaid at their wedding.

"One strange thing happened," Milly said. "Some tough guy came in asking who owned the place, and I asked him whose business was it, and I thought he was going to climb over the counter for me, but just then Fritz came out of the kitchen with a meat cleaver in his hand and the guy skeddaddled."

Kitty replied, "Some of the other storeowners have been complaining about a bunch of bums with a new dodge. Maybe he's part of it. They must think we're fair game."

Within fifteen minutes, Kitty thanked them, paid them, and saw her relatives off.

Kitty was a good cook, a prime reason they had decided on the venture in the first place, that and her experience in her parent's own deli. The delicious smells emanating from the small back kitchen provided customers an appetizing welcome when they entered the store. In the summer, she would save her cooking until closing time when she prayed for a little air through the rear door. Now, between trips to serve customers, she began rattling pans in preparation for the food that would be presented to her customers the next day, a working Monday. Looking forward, she began to mark down her needs from the wholesaler. Kitty was still trim, and she danced behind the ice cases with quick steps, her smiling face and tidy apron top visible to customers above the displays, where her bountifully arranged delicacies tempted all comers.

Winter and summer, Kitty was up at 4:30 and in the store downstairs by 6. The bread and milk deliveries were awaiting her when she arrived and sometimes there would be an empty space in the milk container and a nickel or two conspicuously placed by some early bird. In the winter, the cream would freeze out the top of the bottle, lifting the cap to form a milky mushroom.

Martin and the children soon joined Kitty. Francis occupied a stool near the front window and would help by shelling peas or scraping carrots, while John-Arthur went out back with his father to check the horse and cart. The small stable in the yard, which gave off to the alleyway, housed their gray, Gin's dame, who survived in a grimy stall, still dreaming of Frank's pastures out in Iowa. Whiskey, the old horse, was caught up in the same migration to the city as her owner, and like him, hardly ever touched a blade of grass or turf. John-Arthur kept suggesting that they ship Whiskey back to the farm and buy a gasoline combustion truck—a few had begun to appear in the neighborhood—but his father would have none of it.

John-Arthur's job entailed finding clean boxes from the rafters to stack in the wagon for Martin's Monday morning run to the supplier up by the stockyards. Most Saturdays and all summer, he would join his father on his rounds and they would ride through the alleys singing out their wares, "Fresh tomatoes, fruits and greens," waiting for customers with their small change to emerge on the back porches. "Melons. Nice melons."

Martin never complained about his discomfort over the job. He kept his feelings to himself like most men of his generation. If this was defeat, pushing an old horse through the alleys, he accepted it. The reason he could do so was because he treasured Kitty and the boys. Without them, he would have been alone, and he might as well have taken his orders.

Still and all, Martin was the least likely peddler ever to roam the alleys of Chicago. College trained, he faced life without expectations of success. He didn't have the vaguest idea how to make money. When Kitty and he became engaged, Martin wandered aimlessly through the offices of the charitable and humane societies downtown but could find no work. He volunteered at Hull House but no paying job ensued. He had no skills and never did find employment. He was too shy to teach and few businesses needed an expert on New Testament commentaries. So, he had agreed with the Rapp family recommendation to open a store, but finances were soon so shaky that the young couple was compelled to amend their plans and settled on the idea of adding a fruit and vegetable route. That way the produce with its limited freshness could be sold on the street, or if rejected, cooked that night in the store.

Everyone liked Martin; he was an easy touch, but few admired him save his wife and children, for he was a poor tradesman and that was a trait no midwesterner could abide, for the sin of Chicago had always been its scorn of an impractical fool. His life was altered irrevocably by his decision to wed Kitty, and he never regretted that choice, so he accepted his lot quietly. Meanwhile, he enjoyed the boys and their innocence and was fierce only in his family's defense.

The payoff or disappointment for the week came on Friday night when the couple sat down at the dining room table, with their separate sacks of money—one from the store and one from the vegetable route—along with their receipts and bills.

"We'll pay the store rent," Kitty said, "but we'll hold off on the apartment."

"Just as well your father's the landlord."

"Can you hold off the the food terminal's bill for a week while I pay the butcher?"

"Sure," said Martin. "They'll just be a touch of brown on the lettuce for a while."

"Martin, don't joke. Help me with these columns."

* * *

On summer evenings, Martin liked to read to the boys. Once the store was closed and they had all gone upstairs, out came an oversize book. Their father had faithfully read at least two books a year to them. This summer, he choose the *Wizard of Oz*. Francis was the steadier listener; John-Arthur tended to be distracted. Martin enjoyed the boys' response to the story, and for a shy person, he could be positively animated and original in the confines of his sons' bedroom where he now followed the adventures of Dorothy and her pack with creative flair. And when he got to the part about the Emerald City, he summoned up all his powers and compared it to the White City that he had seen as a teenager. And in the minds of the children, the two became synonymous—the father's vision of the White City revived in the Wizard's castle, and what had been Martin's dream was reshaped on the minds of his children. But whereas the first city had no leader, the Emerald City was run by a fraud, and John-Arthur came to comprehend the notion that there was humbug at the civic center.

* * *

The last two weeks of the summer passed quickly. The end of August was always a busy time. A few untried summer activities were scheduled before the weather turned cooler, including a last trip to swim in the lake. There were school clothes to mend and a round of visits to relatives. In all these endeavors, the boys went with one parent while the other minded the store, because delicatessens have a habit of never taking a day off. Another daily reminder for John-Arthur of the end of summer was his dread of the planned Labor Day bombing in Dubuque.

* * *

On the day after Labor Day, John-Arthur was at dawn, dressed and out of the house while his folks were still closeted behind their door. As he walked towards the candy store, he could see the morning editions tied in bundles by the front door. He pulled out a copy of the *Journal* and the headline confirmed all his fears. It read: "Anarchists Blow Up Mississippi River Bridge." In plain sight of the jellybeans that gleamed from a glass jar in the window alongside root beer barrels, he read the sub-head: "3 Die in Blast" and below that: "Explosion Claims Girl's Life."

The article went on: "Before dawn on Labor Day, explosives tore apart a section of the Mississippi railroad bridge connecting Illinois with the city of Dubuque, a blast causing three deaths, one a child. The two adult victims were said to be responsible for prematurely setting off dynamite that blew a twenty-foot hole in the structure. They have been tentatively identified as radicals associated with the local mining union. The other victim, a ten-year-old girl, suffered a fatal freak accident when portions of the bridge exploded in a hail of steel and timber that poured down onto her father's yacht moored below the span. Witnesses said that the man and a woman who were blown up in the fiery inferno were observed at the scene shortly before the blast. A woman with red hair was identified…"

John-Arthur went and retched in the gutter.

With a stained mouth, he read on: "A freak accident directly connected to the blast took the life of a ten-year-old schoolgirl. She was sleeping on a yacht owned by her father, a Dubuque traction magnate, when the explosion lit up the night sky, hurling debris down in a fiery storm. The boat had been berthed overnight at a pier beneath the bridge when the explosion ripped through the darkness sending flaming timbers and pieces of grillwork down into the water. A piece of iron tore through the deck of the yacht killing the sleeping child, identified as Caroline Knox, age 10…."

John-Arthur collapsed on one knee, screaming, tears pouring from his dazed eyes. He could no longer read; he was stretched over the pile of papers when his mother found him. Shaken, she took him in her arms.

"Dead," he said. "Caroline and Maeve both dead."

"What are you saying?" she asked unbelieving, until he pushed the paper towards her. "Oh, my god! Explosion! No! It can't be."

She read a few lines and then threw the paper away and they sat there in the doorway holding each other, sobbing. Martin, discovering the store locked, looked up the sidewalk to see his distraught wife and child sprawled on the concrete.

A competing paper confirmed that the other victim was a Socialist union official by the name of O'Malley, traced as the writer of a note left in the middle of the night at a Dubuque newspaper office: "Bridge explosion related to mine dispute over unions."

As the day and weeks followed, other details emerged. Maeve and O'Malley had tripped off the explosion prematurely and were blown up in the ensuing blast. John-Arthur later came to believe that it was better that they died together, without ever knowing they had also caused the death of Caroline. If he couldn't bear it, neither could have they.

All that first day John-Arthur sat distraught in his room, hysterical with grief. The only thing his father could think to do was to take him straight away to St. Anne's, where the priests tried to console the youngster.

He kept repeating, "They didn't know she was there. They didn't know."

No trace was ever found of the two revolutionaries at the site or downstream, but no one ever returned to tend the stock at the O'Donnell farm. The city was outraged by the death of the child and its citizens came to despise the Irish, both the miners in Dubuque and the farmers in Holy Cross, and it took another generation before that wound healed.

Goods and crops were re-routed across the river while the bridge was being repaired. South of town, the mine was closed for good, and the union snuffed out. Now John-Arthur's dreams were all nightmares: red rockets and exploding body parts. It was a long time before he was well.

He felt helpless and overwhelmed. He didn't understand life's dimensions, but death had stepped in to become his depriver. Life had now taken away his first unrelated adult supporter and his first friend from the other sex. Unable to fathom the complications of fate and other people's action, he began to blame himself for keeping their activities secret and that perception began pounding its message into his guilty brain. He entered a lost place, dark and lonely. The edge of reality widened and blurred. What was inside him struggled out but reality lay at a greater and more remote distance each day. He learned to internally contain his own bitterness.

Francis was wounded as well. The sorrow that inflicted itself on his older brother stunned him with its pain. What had been shyness became lifelong meekness; what had been caution when it came to relationships became fear. He revered John-Arthur and now sank with him as the life-force deserted the older boy.

Francis said, "Can you make the pain go away?"

"No," John-Arthur said. "It's stuck to me."

* * *

The next summer, John-Arthur and Francis returned to their grandfather's farm but it was a painful time because Frank died in July, and that led John-Arthur to relive the past deaths. Hearty Ellen went on and lived to be nearly ninety but that's not to say that she enjoyed it. After the funeral, his parents took John-Arthur and his brother home to Chicago, and they never returned to the black slopes until they were adults, breaking loose one strand of Great James's tribe. In time, Ellen decided to sell the farm to a young German couple, as everyone agreed that Leo was a good helper but couldn't handle the responsibility of managing the entire operation. Maeve's farm was sold first. When they sold off Frank's place, it meant that there were only three of the family farms left in the Mahoney name.

In Frank's obituary, the Dubuque *Times-Journal* said, "Mr. Mahoney was engaged at farming sixty-seven years. He lived during a most interesting period in which the development of that vicinity occurred. He was of the sturdy type of his countrymen, a man of genial manliness, in whom the traits of humor, integrity and righteousness were identified in all his dealings. During his long life in the community he merited the esteem and respect of all who knew him. He loved his family and his home and his retiring and modest life will remain as an inspiration in the memory of his friends."

Many years later, Ellen's obituary read, "Mrs. Mahoney, called home to God, was a devoted mother and her life was one of devotion to her family. Hers was a life rich in good deeds."

While still in Holy Cross that summer, a time of constant tears, John-Arthur went stumbling down the creek seeking Maeve's lost necklace. One day, near the point where Maeve had first engaged the children just a summer ago, he found the silver chain in some weeds on the bank and placed it around his neck, and continued to wear it the rest of his life as a reminder of his lost friends.

When it was time to leave, Scotty, the old carpenter, who would soon be moving on, had something for Francis. Stone sober and now homeless, the old Scotsman handed the boy his favorite hammer and chisel that he had brought with him from Glasgow.

"You never know when you'll be trussin' up another kirk, lad."

But John-Arthur's would never worship the same way. Death and guilt were destroying his will.

## Chapter 7

Martin and Kitty worried continuously about John-Arthur. They tried to keep him within the tracks of normal development and at the same time help him explore the anxiety that seemed to be inhibiting his natural growth. Kitty hovered over him constantly and even allowed him to see how concerned she was by displaying her own wounds—the conflict she had with her family over her wedding decision, the struggles for profits in their business, how she had to sublimate her Germanity among the Celtic horde— as if an honest revelation of these blemishes would help heal him. Meanwhile Martin sat patiently for hours whittling and gluing while John-Arthur lethargically watched his father work on their model car kits, the father trying as best he could to rally the boy's spirits.

But John-Arthur had been jolted out of a regular boyhood by the devastating force of his experience. He was obsessed with the deaths and was unable to expunge the fiery trauma from his mind or unscramble his part in it. The suspicion that he shared responsibility haunted him and caused a guilt he couldn't digest. Endlessly recycling the facts, he wondered if he should have told his grandfather or even Mr. Knox himself. His unswerving loyalty to Maeve affected his emotional growth, though some days he loved her less than others, especially when he contemplated Caroline's loss. It was all an accident but what if this or that. . . .All the what-ifs were preventing him from capping off his childhood and getting on to adolescence. He took to staying in his room after school and not running after his friends.

His parents despaired as they watched their son retreat within the veldt of his animal instincts. It was as if he had sealed over his natural exuberance, leaving himself vacant— inside and out. Nothing stimulated or excited his interests, not automobile rides, trips downtown, or cruises on the lake. The deaths ripped and sawed into his soul.

That same fall, the family faced another problem. Kitty was in the store one day when two burly men walked in off the street. One was a huge man with reddish-blonde hair and a big Irish face. She didn't recognize either of them and asked if she could help. The smaller one went to the front door, locked it and pulled down the shade that said "Closed".

"What are you doing?" Kitty asked.

"Are you alone?" the big man asked in a quiet voice.

Realizing that she was in trouble, she lied, "No, all my helpers are out back. What are you boys up to?"

"Thank you. I don't get called boy very often. Must happen when you start parting your hair different," said the big guy.

The other man, Danny Moriority, checked the empty kitchen and bolted the back door.

"Miss, we don't mean to alarm you, but I think you need some protection. There's all kinds of bad elements around nowadays and we want you to have the security of the Clancy organization."

"Gang of thieves, you mean. I don't need your protection."

The little guy took a wrench out of is pocket. He reached in and took a pickle out of the big glass jar on the case, and began munching it. Then he whacked the jar with his tool, scattering glass and contents all over the case and floor.

The big redhead said, "You clumsy chump. You'll get pickle juice on my shoes." After he removed a handkerchief to tidy up, he continued, "Miss, can't you see that you need our help? Must I spend all day here demonstrating it?"

Kitty was so frightened she didn't know what to say. "What do you want?" she asked.

The big guy saw that he had her attention, so he made his pitch. "So many bad people out there. They can come walking into your store any day and cause trouble. But if you'll support our cause for the Irish Society, we'll see to it that no harm comes to you. I'll even give you a telephone number to call, and quicker than a flash, certainly quicker than the police, you'll have an army of us over here to help."

Kitty tried not to panic.

"Who are you?" she asked. "I'll go to the police myself."

Moriority raised the wrench.

"Will you put that thing down," the big guy said. "My name is Owen Clancy. I help out the Society by operating a protection company."

"It's like having insurance," the one with the wrench said.

The big guy said, "How many times do I have to tell you never to interrupt while I'm making my pitch? Don't you know it confuses the customer?"

There was a knocking at the door.

"Closed," Kitty shouted. "Inventory morning. Sorry. Come back this afternoon."

"See already you're losing business," the smaller guy said.

Clancy said, "Your weekly premium is only ten dollars."

Summoning all her courage, Kitty said, "Get out of here. My husband's very well connected. He's a personal friend of Alderman Tooley. And my father. . . ."

The wrench came down on the metal case, carving a big dent that would mark her fear of them. She wanted them to go, anything to get rid of them. She walked over to the cupboard where she kept her cash and pulled out ten dollars to give to them.

"Before I take your contribution," Clancy said, leaving the money in her hand, "I want you to know what it will be used for. Aside from dues to the local club, for team uniforms and social events and picnics which you're invited to attend, some of the money goes back to Ireland for helping the Cause, and some to help the political situation right here—especially for the Mister Tooley you mentioned."

Only then did he take her bribe money. He didn't grab it or snatch it. He took it with just a sliding motion of his fingers, a gesture of gratitude. As if he was accepting an offering. Then he tipped his hat. "Every Wednesday about noon."

Kitty was shaking with fear and anger.

After they left, she cleaned up the mess, and spent the rest of the afternoon trying to decide what to do. Forty, fifty dollars a month. That would not only take away their profit, it would eat into operating and home expenses. Finally she called her father and old man Rapp came over and advised her to pay the money but not tell Martin.

"He vouldn't understands," her father said.

For a month, she paid the Clancys. Then, one Wednesday, John-Arthur came home early from school and was in the store when the hoods walked in, the guy with the wrench and some other punk.

"Where's the lady?" one of them said.

"My Ma's out back," John-Arthur said.

"Get her in here, kid."

John-Arthur didn't like the tone of his voice, but working in retail is like life at a hospital—all the specimens of man, whatever their ailments, were entitled to walk in the door.

Kitty looked out into the store after John-Arthur relayed the message and she asked him to stay back and watch her pots while she went out front and paid them off.

When she came back, he asked her who they were and she looked at him sorrowfully and burst out crying. The boy had never seen his mother show that kind of emotion before and was alarmed and scared.

"Ma! Ma! What is it?"

She settled down, and in between trips to the front of the store, she told him the story. "But you mustn't tell your Dad," she admonished through her swollen eyes.

"I'm telling him tonight no matter. I don't want any more secrets," John-Arthur said.

"Your Grandpa Rapp doesn't want you to," she said.

"I don't care," said John-Arthur. "I'm telling him anyway."

That night, he let his mother tell her tale, and Martin was appalled. He offered no recriminations. He simply said that they weren't going to do that anymore. They would have to prepare their defenses.

When Martin decided to protect his family, he knew that all the new forces that were rising in the burly city might cause his undoing. Because they lived in a mixed ethnic neighborhood, he didn't have the tribe support that a shopkeeper would have in Bridgeport where all the residents were Irish, though in fact he knew the same pressure for political payoffs existed there but the bribery took more subtle forms. The problem in this neighborhood was that rogue gangs like the Clancys were willing to compete with German gangs, or Jews, or any other nationality with enough incentive to operate in this open territory. Gangs emerged here because no one group was strong enough to resist the scavengers. With some logic, Martin concluded that if he once paid a given gang, he might be vulnerable to all the others. With the arrival of petty extortion in Garfield/Ashland, Martin was woefully unprepared when these rougher types came in demanding protection money and cut rates, so he decided not to pay. He went to the police but quickly grasped that they would not help him. One of the sergeants there was a Clancy, father of six boys. He went around to the political committee and finally to Alderman Tooley himself, but he was rebuffed, probably owing to the fact that the same hoods that were harassing the Mahoneys were recruited to muster votes around election time.

The Saturday evening after they first refused to pay off the Clancys, Martin was alone putting Whiskey down for the night and emptying his crates, when four heavies came in and beat him up in his own stable.

In his half-conscious state, Martin heard a voice say, "Mister Mahoney, one of our very own. It doesn't make sense for you to go tattling around to the police and the committee. Because we are the committee, don't you see that? So, pay up and no more trouble."

Martin stayed in bed all day Sunday, nursed by Kitty, who with good grace made no criticism, just helped him through the day, easing his pain and giving him comfort. The boys looked in on their Dad a couple times but kept very quiet. Francis was confused and John-Arthur was unstrung by this additional violence, the older boy again confronted by actions that stemmed from his insistence that his father be told about the extortion. The Rapps were not as kind.

The next day, Martin went to the parish pastor and told him his story, and though he might not know the language of the street, he was positively loquacious in the sacristy. It was the church that tied the Clancy gang's arms. Negotiations were soon concluded. There would be no further violence against Martin, the former seminarian.

Yet, the family was still menaced. The hoods didn't come by for money, but they hung around to verbally harass Kitty, so Martin took all the night shifts and they kept John-Arthur from school some days so he could stay with his mother to offer her some minimum protection. They even had the boy make the alley run by himself for the next few Wednesdays so that Martin could stand behind the counter in case there was trouble. They also drew on the support of some of Martin's relatives, part of Frank and Ellen's clan, Martin's brother Joe, who had moved to Chicago after his own escape from the cornrows.

By now, John-Arthur was doubly crushed—an eleven-year-old struggling to overcome the violence he had seen in the last couple years but unable to forget any of it.

One Sunday, Kitty came home and smelled a burning odor. She went sniffing through the house thinking Mrs. Exstrom must be burning her roast downstairs. From room to room she went until she came to the closed door of the boy's bedroom. She tried the handle but it was locked,

"John-Arthur, are you there?"

"Yes."

"I smell something burning. You're not smoking are you?"

"No."

"Please open the door."

She heard the scrape of a chair and the door lock open.

She pulled open the door, and John-Arthur was standing there in blackface. A piece of burned cork was on his dresser.

"John-Arthur. . . .What?"

"It's just cork."

She saw the pitiful look on his face.

"Why?. . . .Why did you do this?"

"Just remembering how Caroline turned black."

After that incident, the parents doubled the time they spent with their oldest child, fearing every day they might lose him, that he might crush any balance left in himself and imperil the family, that they might be defeated by the beast beyond the door, that the beast might actually find a way in.

The business with the Clancys was not over. Retribution followed but quick action on the part of both parents prevented Whiskey from a fiery death, though the hoodlums did succeed in smashing up the family fruit cart. An uneasy peace was declared only after the pastor threatened to mention names from the pulpit and publish them in the church circular. As a result of his defiance, Martin became something of a celebrity among the local retailers for standing up to the gang. His fellow alleymen raised money at the fall fair so he could buy a used cart by raffling off a complete Thanksgiving dinner for four, a feast prepared by Kitty, including homemade sausage dressing.

Like ants in the summer and mice in winter, the Clancys kept coming back with some new form of disruption. Now they decided to tax all the carts in the alleys, this at the same time that the city inspectors were shaking down the cartmen for failure to process a license. It wasn't an accident that the supervising city inspector was another Clancy.

To offset the pressure from both the gangs and the city, Martin recommended a meeting with the other alley cartmen. They thought about organizing but didn't know how, so Martin invited a few of his cohorts over late one Saturday afternoon and told them to bring along their wives so that their coming together appeared to be a social event. John-Arthur cleaned out the stable and tied Whiskey to a stake in the sideyard, and along with Francis, hauled some wooden chairs from the church basement. Meanwhile Kitty prepared ham and pork sandwiches and set out some beer to greet the tinmen and fruitiers. Ten or more of the cartmen appeared and it reminded John-Arthur of the Grange gatherings in Holy Cross, except the villains weren't the railroads this time but officials abusing municipal regulations and members of a gang with a preference for wrenches.

"Martin, you can talk good to people, so you take charge," the iceman said.

"No, I don't have the stomach for it," Martin said, evaluating himself better than he knew. "Let's just talk among friends and see if there's any common agreement."

They soon broke into two camps. The negotiators wanted to go over the heads of the inspectors and the alderman, directly to the mayor and the newspapers, while the agitators wanted to battle openly with the Clancy gang. They washed down their sandwiches with some zesty Crown beer and decided to meet again. Meanwhile, they'd mull over their options.

By the next spring and after a rash of beatings and overturned and destroyed carts, the alley brigade had suffered enough. Luckily, Martin was not one of the victims in the latest truce breakdown, but he totally supported the labor action now under consideration.

On Easter morning with Martin, wearing his old seminarian outfit in the lead wagon, the trek began. The cartmen had been unable to convince any priest to ride with them, so they made Martin the holy man, only two years after another priest led thousands onto the streets of Saint Petersburg on Bloody Sunday. Almost a hundred wagons pulled out of their stables across the South Side and headed for Garfield/Ashland. There were few if any guns, but hundreds of clubs in the carts as they began to gather at six in the morning along Laflin Avenue. They had kept the protest a surprise. No newspapermen. No early clashes with the police or the gang. But as they headed east, the police soon picked up their movements and tried to find out what was going on. But the cartmen had anticipated the probability of various countermoves, so while the police stopped the head of the column, the tail began sliding off, ever eastward, along parallel streets and alleys, As many police as were sent out, as many flanking movements were made by the peddlers, until the entire convoy finally converged on the block that Alderman Tooley called home. They did not stop in front of his house. They raised no banners and shouted no slogans. They simply circled the block over and over. The police, busy trying to stop the demonstration, were unable to control the flow and spent most of their time trying to avoid the manure on the slippery streets. There was no sign of the alderman, his house was quiet except from time to time a little girl wearing a new bonnet would appear at a window until a rude arm yanked her back. Round and round they creaked. Martin was driving Whiskey with John-Arthur at his side. In the wagonbed were four healthy Joe Mahoney cousins.

Police reinforcements came but witnessed no violence. Chicago cops were still stinging from the judgment made against their actions at Haymarket Square twenty years before when, after killing a protester on a previous day, they harassed the crowd again a few days after. Before it was over, seven from the same precinct were blown away by a bomb thrown by a demonstrator. This Easter morn, the police kept their guns in their holsters.

Soon enough, the Clancy troops arrived, about forty of them, hauled out of church and their various other post-Saturday night service centers to menace the cartmen. Randomly, they began to haul men down from their seats and beat them. That's when the reserves sitting in the wagons sprang into action and soon there was a donnybrook. There was a good deal of blood on the street and alleys but within fifteen minutes, the Clancys had been dispersed and a couple of iron and ragmen brought their leader, Owen, around to the front of the alderman's house so the city official, now peeping from his window, could see his field general in the equivalent of chains.

The iceman said to Owen, whose face was swollen and who was resisting any move to contain him, that the cartmen had no other choice, and that he hoped a lesson had been learned. The prisoner was defiant, suggesting that retribution was inevitable and that they would all be picked off one by one in any alley any time.

"You ragmen will never be done with us," Clancy shouted.

The iceman said, "Don't make us come back, because next time, we'll come into your own streets and yards."

John-Arthur carefully watched the big Irishman with the blonde-red hair and for some reason thought of O'Malley.

It was soon over, and the horses began to turn for home, Whiskey among them. The injured were deposited at hospitals along the way. By nightfall, throughout the entire city, by word of mouth, the events in front of Alderman Tooley's home had been repeated a million times. It had all happened on Emerald Avenue, and when His Honor finally came out on his porch to survey the field of battle, all that he could see was horseshit.

To John-Arthur, for some reason he could not understand, the event had been like an act of forgiveness. He came to understand that if you fought your devils, things could come unfrozen in the fray. Slowly, he began to come around.

That wasn't the end of the street battles, of course. Random acts of violence followed and there was talk of the cartmen bringing down the Irish gang from Bridgeport to protect them, but they knew that would only encourage a new set of bribe collectors. They tried to organize a union, but there was so much disagreement that the establishment of a loose federation was as far as they got. The Clancys, trying to regain control, finally did burn down the Mahoney stable with Whiskey in it, but the wind direction luckily blew away from their apartment and store.

The result was that the Mahoneys leased a gasoline engine truck with an open bed behind. It came with a top that covered the fruit and vegetable arrangement and had the advantage of providing father and son shade while appleselling.

# Chapter 8

As the boys grew into their teenage years, Martin would sometimes take a Sunday off and they would visit the new Comiskey Park to watch the White Sox play or their mother would pack them on the bus and head for the lake. Kitty and Martin, seldom together during the day and often separated in the evening, lived for the boys. Once Martin took them to the Field Museum—formerly the Columbian Museum opened at the time of the Great Fair—but the boy's father had no idea what to look for, often elbowed out of the way. He discovered that the natural behavior of museum herds abhorred a directionless member. Nevertheless, John-Arthur adored his parents. It never dawned on him that it mattered if he became, like Martin, indifferent to industry, ambition, and finances, because as the boy progressed, he never came to know or feel anything as significant as that which had already happened to him. No man, priest, or friend however close, or even his brother would ever affect him as deeply as he had been touched by those early deaths.

"Do you think much about your cousins down on the farm? I think Gen has a birthday coming up and would appreciate a line," his mother suggested.

"Maybe Francis and me could write one together."

He didn't tell her that he secretly wrote letters to Caroline, then burned them.

His father continued to be patient with him and sensitive to his continuing grief. Martin felt that the best way to teach was by example, and the virtue he thought most important to project was a sense of steadiness. In his role as father, he tried to offer a calm and assuring even-handedness, no matter what the ups and downs of the day. In that way, he believed the boys would learn self-discipline, and, if he did his job well, they would learn self-worth. These were the years when manliness was much admired and stressed in a number of beefy ways, but Martin's way of illustrating the strength of adulthood was to react to disappointment by accepting pain stoically or success quietly. He and the other shy members of his generation survived among their more exuberant and flamboyant brothers by patiently outwaiting them. In that way, American men, often devoid of a native culture or confused by their ethnic roots, lacking a good education or verbal and intellectual ability, developed as easily into strong, silent types as often as hale fellows well met.

There was a patina of Christian gentleness on men in those times that would not survive the bluster of boosterism.

Gentleness was a virtue that could be passed to the next generation if a family's center was strong enough to hold. Though none could prevent rough patches along the way or the loss of a positive family outlook, members sensed that heavy hearts lurked outside the door ready to snatch away their easy grace if a family ever stumbled. But change was the constant that affected families' lives.

With the arrival of the new truck, a powerful force came rumbling into their lives bringing the father and his oldest son closer together. The automobile craze came chugging into the modern world, sparking new attitudes and enlarging horizons. Reacting to it, Martin rented a garage along the alley and John-Arthur and his friends, grease to their elbows, learned how to pull a car apart and put it back together. Henry Ford's assembly line was already producing Tin Lizzies by the tens of thousands, and a new industry blossomed in a storm of after-farting smoke and dust.

The boys attended St. Anne's grade school, maintained by the nuns, and went through the Chicago ritual of preparing for the right Catholic boy's high school, but John-Arthur's grades were indifferent and a scholarship was not in the offering. Besides the store was losing money, so Arthur in 1911 at fifteen exited the classroom to work full-time with his parents.

That was the same spring that Kitty delivered her third child, a girl, whom they named Marie. For a time the baby's entrance into the family brought them all together. The boys adored her, a younger and rosier version of their Ma.

John-Arthur was feeling better now. He had a job to help support the house, a hobby with time to pursue his interest in automobiles, a warm kitchen to go home to and the freedom to poke around his neighborhood as he wished, associating openly with his neighbors, celebrating publicly any occasion. He took all these things for granted unaware of the cost borne by a hundred generations that allowed for this standard of life.

Aside from cars, he continued his interest in two additional pastimes, one was playing the piano and the other was speed skating. One of his aunts on his mother's side, not caustic Milly, owned and taught piano and offered to continue John-Arthur's lessons and train Francis and Kitty as well. Over the years she helped them all become moderately successful at banging out the latest songs. When John-Arthur began to pay attention to girls in the neighborhood and attend parties and dances, he was able to entertain friends by pounding out the newest hits. When he began to appreciate the boost provided by this rise in popularity, he doubled his practice time, and the family eventually convinced Martin to purchase a used upright from whose not-so-white keys they all learned to play the ragtime numbers of the day. Sometimes, when he ran across a song that he had played with Maeve, the piano became a painful instrument of memory for John-Arthur. Other times, if he let his imagination wander, he could still feel her arm around him.

John-Arthur had always been fast on the ice because his father, who enjoyed skating, had early-on trundled the boys off in winter to the local parks with their frozen ponds and rinks. Bundled in wool, they would walk to Sherman Park and speed across the ponds on whose banks they would picnic in the summer. Martin entered both boys in the children's' skating races, conforming to a Chicago prescription that encourages sports competition among the young. John-Arthur, who developed quick starts, won a number of ribbons. In order to encourage him, Martin bought him a pair of long-bladed racing skates at Christmas and John-Arthur became one of the neighborhood boys, encouraged by a city-wide newspaper-sponsored tourney, to race in the Silver Skates competition. On a good day John-Arthur sometimes managed to do well enough to qualify in the quarterfinals in downtown Grant Park or at Lincoln Park or Garfield Park west of the Loop—Chicagoans remembering and respecting the heroes of the Civil War.

"Who was Garfield, anyway, Dad?" John-Arthur asked.

"A good and thoughtful man and a Civil War hero. Like Lincoln, assassinated while President."

As time passed, there were some days John-Arthur might not think of Caroline or Maeve at all, but there were a lot of bad days when death's rattle continued to be the sinister rhythm underscoring the horrid secret in his life. He kept his guilty and deadly information from everyone including the dark presence in the confessional box, and like the Chinese ate his bitterness. There were other quiet times at home, when his mother and father listened intently to him, that he would have liked to share the agony he carried regarding the bridge explosion and his foreknowledge of trouble, but the grief in him and the fear of exposure would not allow him to unbend.

That winter of 1911-12, a letter arrived reopening the wound from that turbulent summer in Iowa. It was from Al saying that he and Big Jack would soon be playing the vaudeville circuit in Chicago, and sent along four passes inviting the Mahoneys to a Saturday matinee in February. As the weekend approached, John-Arthur relived the memory of their days together in Dubuque with Caroline, and it was a somber juvenile that entered the gaudily bedecked American Music Hall downtown where the family, leaving the baby and store in the hands of Rapp cousins, took their seats in an upper box.

It was the heyday of Vaudeville. Even Sarah Bernhardt and Pavlova and Ethel Barrymore took a turn. Every day except Sunday, the singers, dancers, comedians, magicians and animal acts entertained twice a day, often more. Drop-in customers could watch a couple of acts after work and come back to see the rest of the bill on Saturday night. Acts usually lasted up to fifteen minutes, and there were six or seven of them, plus the two-a-day headliner routines that filled out the allotted time slots. The backstage was a maze of big-hatted mamas, chorus girls in their risqué tights, clowns in oversize shoes, bird acts and jugglers. Dressing rooms were more like quick-change rooms. A pair of clowns could enter, doff their street clothes, go out and hoof about and work up a few jokes, exit, and be back in their saloon having missed only one or two rounds. The orchestra members weren't so lucky, so they amused themselves by playing too loud or too slow for performers they didn't like.

Vaudevillians were always the first ones in any crowd to play a prank, often contorting themselves to make people laugh, all the while waiting and expecting rejection. Many youngsters from New York's Lower East Side, cobbled with dirty boots, who thought a shoeshine was the first mark of success, began their careers by running errands for one of the stars. Or studied the top-billed acts and learned routines on the run. Untutored, one silent screen star remembered with fondness the one day in his life when he attended a real school. Agonizing road trips led them from one dusty burg to another. These were kids who, en route, learned their geography from a train window. Performers lived in boarding houses for five dollars a week, including meals—at a time when 75 cents had a jingle of affluence in the pocket. They were applauded on stage. However, once on the street they were viewed as slightly dangerous because they were feared in the bedrooms of the middle class. Rootless. Trying to please. Polishing their delivery, hoping their skills would lead them, if not to stardom, at least to a permanent one-bedroom apartment somewhere in Brooklyn. They sought success in the talkies or on Broadway but few escaped the road. Vaudeville would flourish long past the introduction of the talking machine, but it was the movies that finally dissolved the traveling troupes and confiscated their theaters.

The Mahoneys sat excited in their theater box. The opening number on the bill featured a dancing sextet and the second act presented a woman in a broad-brimmed hat with fluffy pinned-up veils, along with her tenor swain, singing flippant songs about their several beaus and belle-annas. That was followed in succession by a comic, and then out came Big Jack in his swami outfit introducing his partner—the Boy Wonder of Nebraska. Here comes Al in another white suit, waving his wand over a variety of boxes and objects and pulling out multi-colored cloths and rabbits in tune with the orchestra—Ta Da. Then following a drum roll, the Wizard made Big Jack the victim of a disappearing act. After spiriting away another unsuspecting lady who had come up from the audience, Al said, "Now we're going to read minds, searching out your innermost secrets."

"What did you do with my wife? Don't tell me she's gone for good," came a voice from the audience.

"Sorry, sir, I thought you wanted to get rid of her...No? Here she is now."

Out walks the lady who disappeared, and takes a little bow to the applause and shakes her finger at her husband.

The band helped Al segue into the next part of their act. The orchestra leader took up his baton and launched into a raucous, blowzy set of numbers that carried with them the wide-open sounds of 14th Street and the Bowery theaters, music that burst out in a combination of ragtime, jazz and tin-pan alley tunes all mixed together—the new sound that would rise to the Broadway stage.

Jack soon returned from the missing and appeared in the back of the hall. Then he and the Wizard began their telepathy routine. Jack would wheedle some hidden information out of one of the audience members, who confidentially whispered a secret to him, and then Jack through a series of call and responses, mentally signaled the hidden message to the blindfolded Wizard on stage, who by word and intonation could discover the person's secret and broadcast it to the world.

"I have a member of the audience," Big Jack said.

Already, Al knew it was a man.

If Jack began—"Say hello to a member," etc.—that would mean that the innocent standing in the aisle needed advice on one of the verities: love, death or money.

Altogether there were sixteen openings.

"Here's a well-dressed-looking customer," Jack continued, signifying that the unwitting man wanted to know about his chances for prosperity.

Al would say, to show his power, "I sense a man with a desire to increase his wealth."

If Jack hesitated, Al would put his hand on his eye covering, signifying he was on the wrong track and say, "No, that's not right. It's something specific he wants."

"Yes, specific" responded a hesitant Jack suggesting Al dig a little deeper.

Al knew then that their mark wanted a major acquisition: a family, a bigger apartment, a new job. So the pair of swamis by selection of word or idea would narrow the options until finally Al would say, "This young man wants to add a baby to his family." and the man would shout, "That's right. He got it," and the man would hug the lady sitting next to him and they would beam and it was as good as a billboard on their front door advertising for an addition to the nursery. The audience would applaud and ask each other how the Wizard had divined the truth. If it were near payday, sometimes the members of the audience would take up a little collection in that part of the house and pass it along to the young couple in a handkerchief and then the couple would think about naming the baby after the theater but would later reject that idea when they remembered the name of the place was: The American.

Jack next choose a woman with an eager face and quickly noticed that she didn't wear a wedding ring, that her shoes had heavy mileage and that the ribbons on her old hat were new. She was young and attractive and whispered her secret to Jack.

"Say hello to this person in the audience, "Jack said, "who would like to consult with you on a matter of immediate interest."

Al said,"I sense that you're talking to a woman who needs help on a financial matter."

"Why, yes," Jack would say. "But don't we all?" That meant it was employment related. When he added "She could use the money"—that obviously meant there was external pressure like debts.

"About the job. . . ." Al said, fishing.

"Yes?" Jack asked. "Not out of the question." She had no job.

"I believe she's down on her luck and looking for employment right now."

"My, you're right. . . .But what kind of a job?"

Al then put his hand to his ear, signifying a heady job like a librarian or teacher.

Jack said, "He's trying to get the message." It wasn't a brainy job.

Al began twiddling his fingers, which meant a secretarial or bookkeeper position.

"I know you're concentrating," which meant that office work wasn't the answer.

Al touched his stomach.

"Yes, I think he's beginning to get the answer."

That narrowed it down to cook, waitress or grocery store clerk or somesuch.

Jack continued, "It will serve him right if he misses this one."

Al: "Yes (serve), she will soon be the hostess in a fancy downtown dining room."

And the girl would jump up and kiss Jack, believing he had given her a new lease on life. Their predictions would often come true because they armed people with the belief that they were being directed by fate and it gave them the confidence to do what they only dreamed of doing in the first place.

"We simply encourage people to pursue the things they yearn for. It's like a service," Jack would tell Martin and Kitty later.

Once for laughs some fresh shopgirl said she wanted to be a streetwalker and poor Al was touching every part of his body before he got it right. Sometimes they failed to communicate through their personal brand of wordheavy telepathy like the time an undertaker wanted to be buried alive for an afternoon like Houdini. But on an especially clairvoyant day, Al could actually "see" what the people wanted and Jack would again wonder about the boy's origins and genius.

While Jack was working with his last customer, he looked up to see hanging over the side of the box, his young friend from Dubuque—a sad, smiling face that lit up when Jack nodded to him. Both Jack and Al had forgotten that this was the day the Mahoneys were in the audience, so the old lumberjack was caught by surprise at the Mahoney's presence. Jack liked to test Al once in a while and he decided not to parse John-Arthur's wishes in their regular way, though he later regretted this impulse.

When he finished with the last person, Jack said, "You'll have to wait a minute while I run up the steps." The giant dashed up and a moment later appeared in the Mahoney box, asking for the spotlight.

"OK. Here I am. . . .Let's have your secret."

"Give him a hard one," said his brother Francis.

John-Arthur dutifully whispered his secret desire. Jack looked at him peculiarly because the boy wanted someone, maybe Al, to intercede for him. Jack knew there were times when the Boy Wizard could travel past reality into another state and he hoped this was going to be one of them.

Jack began, "I have bright-eyed member of the audience."

The garish light made John-Arthur appear more vulnerable than usual, but he wore a trusting look as Big Jack put his arm around him. The boy shivered with excitement.

"Might even be a tenderfoot," Jack said, giving Al false clues, not wanting him to guess the right answer. "Sensitive area. . . ."

The Wizard responded, "I feel the sorrow of a young man with a personal wish. . . ." putting his head in his hands. "Tender, you say?"

"Something about a revival, a spiritual revival," Jack answered, totally out of their pre-arranged word patterns, ignoring their code.

Al, confused now, and knowing that Jack was challenging him, soared out of context and rose to another plane. He was struggling for clarity, his mind scenting the unknown.

"I feel something terrible has happened," Al said, keeping up the act, suffering for an answer. "I see destruction. Ahead and behind. Ammunition. No, no. Explosions."

John-Arthur's heat was rising.

Al's mind rose to a place somewhere before or beyond the detritus of this yet unbroken decade with its coming horror of war. He cast a light into the darkness where the sun never shone. Voices babbled in that darkness, millions of voices—

shells, gas explosions, collapsed time, twisted trees, shattered earth and fire.

"Bodies flying," the Wizard said almost in a trance. He pressed his fingers to his skull.

"You'll never be able to bring them back," Al finally shouted.

With that, John-Arthur fainted.

"It's all right, folks," said Jack, trying to steer the spotlight away with an arm motion. "It's the excitement. He's just a boy."

His mother, as big as he was, took John-Arthur in her arms and held him.

Jack, hastily exiting the box, mumbled to his parents, "I'm sorry, folks. My fault. I should have never cast him loose like that."

It was as if John-Arthur had opened the door, allowing fear and confusion to claw its way in, a beast no Wizard could allay.

After the mind reading, the pair demonstrated their ability to induce somnambulism through mesmerism by putting folks from the audience to sleep and then suggested that they do foolish things; for instance, they hypnotized an unacquainted couple and suggested that they kiss one another when they awoke from their woozy sleep. Exhausted mentally, Al's heart wasn't in it. John-Arthur, coming around, watched from his mother's arms.

After the performance, the family walked around to the stage door, and soon the vaudevillians emerged amid a flurry of floradora girls.

"Hey! Art. What were you trying to do—get in the act?" Al asked.

John-Arthur was sheepish but felt better when his weakness was out in the open where he didn't have to wonder if other people were clandestinely thinking about it. Francis kept looking at his brother; he had never seen him collapse like that before.

"I heard your message walking up the aisle, right up on the stage. The manager asked me if we planned it in advance."

"C'mon, let's go have a bite," Jack said.

Kitty intervened, "Instead of today. . . .Will the two of you be able to come over for dinner tomorrow? We'd love to have you."

"Home cooked?" Al asked. "Can I come for breakfast too?"

"Al, you're a card," Kitty said.

"Ace of spades," he answered.

"Sure, we will," Jack said. "What time?"

"How's noon?" she said.

"Perfect."

"In that case, maybe we'll skip a bite now," Kitty said. "We have to get back to mind the store anyway, but tomorrow we'll have all day to talk."

That Sunday morning, the Mahoneys were up earlier than usual because the pots were boiling at both locations. They all managed to attend one mass or another, open the store, and by ten Kitty was back in her home kitchen, the flat soon filling with her flavorsome doings. Jack and the Wizard arrived by mid-day and by two in the afternoon, five males succumbed to Kitty's specialty—roast beef and noodles. The vaudevillians praised her home cooking and began relating their adventures. Their travels had carried them through opera houses in dozens of towns watered by the Mississippi and its many tributaries.

Jack said, "We opened in Memphis, and then onto Saint Louis. . . ."

"We slayed them in Saint Louis. . . ."

"Then Keokuk and Davenport and then Peoria and after that...we wound up where?"

"In Dubuque."

The name itself made John-Arthur's blood run cold.

"What kind of a life is that?" Kitty asked.

Jack answered, "It's all lights and hoopla and on to the next place before you're settled in the last one, but it's a free life. I don't recommend it to everyone, but I wouldn't have it any other way myself. Show folks—we're all just grown-up children, spending the whole day entertaining. Practicing over and over, hoping to please a bunch of tired people. Performers all dressed up looking like they're off to see the queen, and most of them simple, sweet people you wished was your sister or your brother."

"Is it all right for the little guy there?" Martin asked.

"Him? He was born to it. You remember he was a baby when I first took him into the circus. That boy had sawdust in his diapers. You'd be surprised how a child adjusts. I think we pamper kids too much, always saving them for something. . . .For what? Hold them back from finding out their own selves? Or what they're capable of? Actually, I recommend running away to the circus. We'll be taking John-Arthur from you one of these summers if you don't watch out."

"Oh, no you won't," said Kitty good-naturedly. "He's got a good job and we need him right here with us. And he doesn't have time now. He and his Dad are building an automobile out back. Besides he can't sing or dance. Plays a nice piano though."

"You must have seen a lot of the headliners along the way," Martin said, star struck like most people.

"You bet," Jack said. "We mostly work the midwest but we made it to New York once and even met a bunch from the legit—Trixie Freganza who does the shimmy act and Lillian Russell, an Iowa girl. Billie Burke, and, oh, actresses like Oza Waldrop. She'd have us falling down laughing one minute, crying the next."

"That's a funny name—Oza," Martin said.

"Yeah," Jack answered. "Must be a girl from the Emerald City."

"Certainly exciting," Kitty said.

"Yeah, a bunch of risk-takers. Crowding the footlights. But we never think we're good enough. It's like a gamble every performance. What we really want is appreciation, not that the money hurts."

"People must have lots of sass, risking getting dumped in the middle of the country with a poor show," Martin added.

Jack said, "Fearless. Talk about ambition. All those girls running away from the farm where their foster fathers beat them, sneaking over the transoms of their locked rooms— walking through deserted streets, waiting at the station for the midnight milk train. Sitting up all night in day coach, barreling past frozen towns—arriving some cold morning in a Chicago snowstorm. You got to hand it to them spunky girls."

"C'mon, Art, "Al said. "Why don't you and I take a walk and let the folks talk. Maybe you could show me that car you're working on."

It was the moment that John-Arthur dreaded, but he had to know what happened that night in 1906 when his world blew up.

Downstairs, he said, "Sorry I fainted. I hope I didn't ruin it for you."

"Naw. Like I said, it's all part of the act."

"How did you know what I was thinking about?"

"Sixth sense. Don't worry about it."

As soon as they were out of hearing, John-Arthur asked, "What can you tell me about the bridge explosion that night?"

"That was long ago."

"Not for me it wasn't," John-Arthur answered.

"We saw them both the night before," Al began. "There was an upstairs loft at the old union hall and Jack and I went for the final meeting. They had the dynamite and caps and wire stored down by the river and the idea was to go up on the Dubuque side of the bridge and string the sticks along. They started up— the two of them. . . ."

For a moment John-Arthur was able to think of them as still alive, walking and talking, and the thought almost drove him over the edge.

Al continued ". . . .Big O'Malley carrying the box of explosives and Maeve paying out the wire. It was dark, of course, and they had to light a lantern and the last anybody saw—we had miners guarding the bridge on the Illinois side—was the light bobbing up and down and then the explosion. Standing there with probably a half-full box, it ripped away part of the bridge and them with it. The miners standing on the Iowa end ran down the tracks but couldn't see any trace of them. They waited as long as they could and tried to blow the rest of it. We had been staying awake to hear it go off, but I fell asleep and all I can remember was Jack saying, 'Too soon.'"

"What about the boat—the one with Caroline on it?"

"Some of the miners went to help but she was gone before they arrived."

"Who were the people who saw Maeve? One of the papers said someone saw her."

"Some old biddy living by the tracks. She never squealed on the miners, but she told about Maeve."

"Why weren't they more careful? Why didn't they see the boat with Caroline? Could you have stopped them?" John-Arthur asked.

"What could we say? They were hell bent to go through with it. Cussing old John Knox. Nothing could have stopped them. They were crazy to die for it."

"It was all so useless," his tormented friend responded.

"Listen, Artie, you got to get over it. I know it was hard for you, but you're not doing yourself any good hanging onto it. You have to accept it. And get on."

"I'll never accept it. I'd rather have it bend me over double, so as not to lose it."

Back in the flat, the adults were talking about the Iroquois disaster, a theater fire in Chicago some years back that killed six hundred people. Jack was telling Kitty and Martin about some of the strange stories he had heard backstage over the years about the Iroquois inferno—about the mayhem and tragedy, about firemen carrying people out black with death and stacking their bodies into carts alongside the raging maelstrom.

"Let's not talk about it," Kitty said. "I've had enough excitement for one weekend."

"How do you do that mind-reading trick?" Martin asked, trying to change the subject.

"Sometime the Boy is able to read somebody's mind. Like yesterday. I thought I'd let John-Arthur trick him, so I didn't lead him like I usually do. Al just knew it was him. He could feel him. Mostly it's just hokum, but sometimes the Boy's in touch with something out there."

That night in bed, Kitty said to Martin, "It all sounds unsavory to me."

# Chapter 9

In the fall of 1913 when John-Arthur was 17, the telephone rang one day reopening connections with his friend Al.

"Are you in town for a show?" asked Art. That's what his friends called him now.

In a deeper voice than Art remembered, Al said, "No, we've given up the road. Jack's got the gout and we're pinned down here in Chicago. I'm working at the *Journal*."

"No kidding? Newspaper work? You're here permanent?"

"Yeah. I thought maybe we could get together and chew on old times. I just started work here and I hardly know a soul and Jack's sort of down all the time, so I'm looking up old pals."

Art said, "I'm working on my car today but how about Saturday afternoon? That OK?"

"Deal! I work until one. I'll meet you in the *Journal* lobby and show you around."

In the early years of the century, newspapers were the principal source of information and entertainment for people prior to the rise of broadcast; this at the same time that moving pictures were just catching on. The Hearst, Pulitzer and Scripps chains of papers dominated the country and aside from parading America into a war in Cuba and Manila, they were the chief outlets for news of the Powers that were edging toward conflagration in Europe. The competition between these giant news chains was fierce. They were in the habit of creating daily hysteria, haranguing their readers with stories of ax murders, exposed lovenests, anything to excite the public. Truth suffered when feature writers cavalierly invented maniacal tales of terror in creative bursts of lurid fiction. The penny papers dealt in bent facts with their ink-smudged rivals, themes barely differing from dime novels. While the even hand of honest journalism circulated among a privileged few in Chicago, there were a dozen newspapers scratching for gullible readers in this final spring of the old world, this twilight of civilization that Europeans had fought to build for a hundred years that would come crashing down in the next four years.

In the Loop's cityrooms, the local editor most admired by the ward-wise reporters was Joe Medill, who by the end of the old century was in control of the *Tribune*. Joe, as important a figure as Pulitizer from St. Louis, spawned a spread of inklings—the Pattersons and McCormicks, including Bobby, the future scourge of the midwest. This last menace, promoted eventually to Colonel, was the nemesis of a fellow Grotonian by the name of Frank Roosevelt, and in due course, his underclassman's mortal enemy. Waiting ahead was both despair and triumph for this latest Roosevelt, who by 1914 was Assistant Secretary of the Navy like his cousin Teddy before him and not unlike Churchill of the Admiralty. Though he would be crippled by polio, FDR would manage eventually to win New York's governorship at a time when his schoolboy challenger was beginning to subvert the *Tribune*.

Al toured Art around the pressroom. Then he said, "Let's go meet the gang."

When they entered King's Restaurant, a cloud of smoke met them and the pale, enlightened ghosts of Chicago's glory days gestured in slow motion through the white haze. At one large table, the ruffians of the press, at another a mixed company of literati and at a third the zealous spirits of the China-bound.

The boys joined the ink wipes, a riotous crowd of friendly drunks and burned-out reporters, most of them spiritually devoid, harboring a lost sense of poetry and feelings of guilt, stemming from the fact that each day, they were required to impale innocents with their flesh-creeping narratives of strangulation, rape and mayhem. These scribes of the dark side who often incurred the wrath of publishers, politicians and would-be holy men, believed in little except the surety of the day's deadline and the week's paycheck. Indeed, running through them was a fatal dead line—a cynicism mixed with a few wispy strands of lost hope and sentimental values. They enjoyed their reputations as Chicago's prime customers at liquor outlets and brothels and as walking reliquaries of buried bones and forgotten tales of the streets.

Yet, there was still a touch of the truth in all of them, some reverence still for the facts of a thing as well as respect for their own language and the cutting edge of Mencken's wit. But having witnessed so much calumny, they distrusted everyone and set their defenses against the bores of life. Theirs was a peculiar line of work—their type-trays spilling out with overused verbs that could be soldered into printed shibboleths to bombard dullness, which was the despised vice, though many of them could be sappy, cherishing sticks of bad poetry, a doggerel a day, soon lost on yellowing paper. If these journalists of the day's events could communicate the riotousness of daily life and spice up their media sufficiently that a streetcar motorman or elevator operator could entertain their passengers, what was the harm? The conductor/operators could then tuck away copies of the bulldog edition in the corners of their ironclad cubicles and bring the crumpled news home at night to share their tall tales with the missus. If so, the spinners of fiction could stoutly defend their papier mache fortresses as instruments of diversion. Words were their weapons of choice. If they could stir the swill around them, perhaps they could survive and live to fill another edition, though their work was mostly an extortion of truth, not its preservation.

Another table was filled with the shadowy lights of the Illinois Renaissance. They weren't all there, of course, that night—Sherwood Anderson, Harriet Monroe of *Poetry* and sexy Margaret Anderson of *the little review*, the poets Maxwell Bodenheim, Vachel Lindsay and Edgar Lee Masters and the Socialist Swede, Carl Sandburg. Here, at this table, ideas were more lasting and didn't lose their potency overnight.

At still a third table sat the American romantics—those who would save China, zealots who put their words into action, who could barely get through their veal without performing good works. If they were busy eating, they would ask the waiter to tell them his life's story, relate the progress of his family, and ask how much he earned. At the end of the meal, they left him a big tip for taking them on his sociological tour. Ideas at this table were meant to be translated into action: political ideas (rouse mankind through revelatory action) or religious (come all you heathens and sing under our Christian tent) or exotic (I am in tune with mysteries whose song I hear) or adventurous (join us on our trip to the abode of imperial mystics and mad monks worshipping in temples built thousands of years ago where the truth of existence resides).

Visiting King's restaurant that night were the diverse elements of the American soul: included were the unrepentant; the artistically imbued; and the socially activated. Emerson would have been appalled by their common bonds, but never Whitman.

The boys were casually invited to join the soulless newspapermen, taking seats behind the chairs of the first rank at one of the many tables that had been pushed together in a vaguely circular configuration.

"Has anybody seen that blackguard Delaney around lately?"

"I saw his sister at the Fireman's Pension, but not him."

"Someone said he went out west."

"Anything to get away from the snow."

"I hear he was pretty good once."

At any reference to the past, or what had been true, fashionable or only fiction, they all turned to Joe Johnson, the managing editor of the *Journal*, who took a sip of his beer and said, "He was never right after the fire."

"Which one?"

"The big fire at the Iroquois."

The name, Iroquois, struck as much terror in the hearts of contemporary Chicagoans as the Indian name had done two centuries before to frightened French missionaries camping on the Saint Lawrence. During Christmas week a few years back, the city was immobilized by the tragic matinee fire.

Johnson continued, "He was one of the best, always went the extra step, not like some of you palookas. He had a fine hand and a good command of the language. The day of the fire he was on call when the alarm came in—around New Years it was. He hustled right over there and comes upon a scene of hell awake. Hundreds of dead strewn across the road—half-burned, lying frozen in the snow. So he makes an attempt to get in a side door, but it's blocked with bodies. But somehow he manages, crawling over the victims. He's choking and he can see the fire licking through the smoke in roaring waves. They say you could actually hear the fire. He picks up this child and carries him outside—where he sees a nurse he knows—who gets the kid some help. Back in he goes; it's like an inferno. It's black as a closet; he gets disoriented, and he can't find his way back to the exit. He's stumbling around but losing consciousness, nevertheless struggles to the door and collapses in a heap of half-burnt dead bodies just as the firemen start loading the corpses on a truck, piled ten deep—Delaney, still alive, among them. He was near the bottom of that hell's pit and you can imagine what it was like. It was hours later as the hospital tried to sort out the corpses, they find Delaney alive, sort of wild and mad, caught at the bottom of death's own cart. . . . He was never the same after that, and he lost his fine hand."

Art was listening bug-eyed.

Al said, "Didn't I tell you there'd be good stories."

On this the night Art had his first beer.

The penny-a-lines were soon talking about the Medills who owned the *Tribune*.

"Old Joe from the *Trib* was the best of the lot. He backed Lincoln when he was still a local bumpkin downstate. Even helped put the Republican Party together. . . .But he met his match when they made him mayor after the cow kicked over old lady O'Leary's lantern. He rebuilt the city but quit the minute the dolly parlors and saloons reopened."

"Do you remember the girls?  Not the hookers. I mean old Joe's daughters?"

"A pair of midwest mollies. Talk about aggressive women—those two could have started a revolution."

"'Here come them suffragettes,' people would say. 'Better watch your mouth.'"

"Matching tempers and no keeping them down."

"None of that eastern girls school fol-de-rol. Those two would arm wrestle the cook for the kitchen money."

"I saw them once at the big Fair, riding—for a lark—with Buffalo Bill."

Women of the west, bred to make their way without masculine help if necessary. Hands-on-hips vixens. Short hair before 1900.

Kitty had once read something about them to her Martin, but she dismissed them as rich eccentrics, spoiled and bossy and certainly unable to juggle two customers and a mess of cole slaw at the same time or ever cook a tasty ham.

The reporters, poets and would-be missionaries who came to King's didn't come merely to eat and imbibe; they came to argue and listen, to hear and share the gossip and stories, the jokes and foibles and pathos that made up their Chicago days. When they spent time together, they knew they were in for the afternoon and probably most of the night. Consequently, there wasn't any sequence to the food and drink service. People came and went. Dinner turned into supper. Rounds of food came floating on headhigh trays carrying a clatter of dinner platters and side dishes. Some were having soup, others fish, some fowl, choices ranged from beef to chocolate cake. The same at the other tables, though the missionaries were somewhat better aligned in food sequence, owing to their regular hours. King's was principally a place to bloviate; consumption was secondary and haphazard. When Al and Art finished their first beer, they decided on the soup and the waiter pulled a side table over and pressed it against the wall as a place to rest the tureen. After they finished, the table's convenient placement made it an ideal dropping-off place for half-consumed biscuits, roasted bones, stale beer and melted ice cream, until the whole would be swept clean, ready for fresh clutter. As a result of this mixed bill of fare, paying the check oftentimes took a week to sort out, and sometimes the luckier young members occupied space at the table rentfree. An office pool often settled disputes over charges.

There was a sudden explosion of applause at the next table, loud enough to divert the attention of both journalists and missionaries alike, as well as the regular members of the Saturday afternoon dining community, as if someone were celebrating a birthday.

"He's going to recite."

Tough as a tree, with the broadest shoulders Art had ever seen, the poet in the shiny vest stood, looking rather doleful but alert, scanning the audience, seeking the responsive connection of other eyes, figuring out whom to read to. He was so impressive that even the jaded journalists put down their glasses and listened.

"I'd like to read a poem I composed after living six months among the Winnebagos."

He began to speak in the language of the Indians and his entire demeanor changed. His personality expanded and he became theatrical, as if he lusted after acting roles, throwing his voice, moving his hands through the air, the thumb and pointer fingers touching, like priests do when they gave benediction. The sounds chopped the smoky air. Then stringing together songlines with shifting rhythms, he spoke-sang in a Native American voice, wise sounding as if from a spirit chief, speaking directly, like Chief Seattle himself, his words seemingly riddled with truth.

When he finished, there was silence and then applause.

"This next one is in Creole."

He recited his playful ballad with great flourishes. Roaming the vocal scale from guttural jumps to pleading soprano, he related a love story. He began moving around the room, flirting with the women, kissing their hands, acting, first a virgin, now a suitor. Dancing between tables, he let his exuberance fly out unimpeded.

The room roared its approval.

"Better than a show," Al said.

Then he performed a song in old English, one that he had composed after a visit to the eastern mountains, hiking back into the hollows where the language hadn't changed since the time of Queen Anne.

Then another hymn in the Negro dialect. And an Irish ditty. And then he sat down, depleted of the energy spent pouring into his multi-ethnic reading.

The old editor, Joe Johnson said, "You see why we have no national papers in this country—too many languages, too many voices. Just listen. A babble of tongues."

There's a bit of the chronicler in every newspaperman, as if each knew his daily diary might be part of the national record if only the editors weren't so stupid and provided better assignments. It was owing to this instinct to create historical precedents, whether it matched the truth or not, that led to the day's principal amusement.

It started out by someone from the Obituary Department saying, "Somebody should write down all the ruckus about old times. Make a good book."

"Hell, we could write something better sitting here tonight."

"What'll we do with it? Send it to the Library of Congress?"

"No, stuff it in a box and bury it near some Indian mound."

"Sell it for a half-dollar a copy and pool the money for a month of suppers."

"We could call it—*The Print Enterprise.*"

That's how the idea to publish a commemorative issue sprang up, celebrating and deriding the last century—the Era of Good Feelings, the Civil War Era, the Gilded Age, the Gay Nineties, the Mauve Decade and all the other color and times in America whose significance since the Louisiana Purchase had sprouted above the timeline. During the afternoon and into night, the journalists began and later invited the adjoining writers and missionaries to help out, at different hours in keeping with the staggered distribution of food and drinks. Bearing pencil to paper, they scratched out an outline of their memories of days past—before the automobile and telephone, before tall buildings and airplanes, back when the country was a ripe green.

Joe Johnson, the senior editor, laid down the rules. It would be a six-page paper. Page one and the overleaf would herald the triumph of democracy in the woods of America.

"Somebody should do Lincoln and Jackson and somebody should do the brain stuff at Concord, and somebody. . . .Stern, aren't you social editor? You should do the business about Saratoga and Newport. Then the back should carry the bad

parts. . . . Antietam, things like Donner Pass and the way we treated the Indians. In the middle, they'll be a single sheet insert. Pages three and four. . . .That'll be for you issue guys. . .
.

The fights over the unions, how hard farm life was, the way immigrants had to live in the tenements. . . .How life was for most folks."

"Why do you want to remember all that old stuff for?" one of the men asked.

"Tell me again why we're doing it, aside making beer money? What are we aiming at?"

Joe said calmly, "If I get it right, we want to show the old times we knew of or heard of. And if it's too hard and you don't want to do it, just order another round and tell us a story about your crib girls."

"Let's call it *Old World.*"

"Piss on the old world. Why don't we do a section on what's ahead, not what's behind. Screw the past. We'll do an insert on all the things that's up and coming—wireless and biplanes. I'll bet we could even sell ads in it. Make us some real money."

"Yeah. The hell with the past. Let's go with the times."

Al piped up, "How about calling it *The American Centennial?*"

"Not bad, kid," Johnson said.

In the end, they decided to publish a version of the past. A few of them got busy right away while their brains were still clicking, assuming that their creative faculties would diminish in the hazy alcoholism of a Saturday evening. Some of the more intuitive writers let it lie, contemplating which editorial team to join. Joe kept running layouts, drawing out the columns on the immense once-white tablecloth that covered the slapped together forty-foot irregular oval. Many simply returned to drinking and eating. Sometime in the late afternoon when the effort began to bog down, the journalists brought the writers at the next table into the project, thereby elevating the rhetoric, as well as the wordcount, owing to the fact that the book writers had not been trained to be pithy quick with their paragraphs. It was only a matter of time before the Asian specialists joined in, though some of them had to leave early in order to perform good works.

There was a lot of milling around as the scene changed from sitdown conversations to a highly flavored mixing of intellectual salads. China-bound doctors stood toe-to-toe with police reporters, *little review* editors were buying drinks for missionary wives, biographers shared pretzels with Hull House workers, cartoonists polka'd with playwrights. Several nonparticipants swerved over to one side, shuffling the deck further, young female poets whispering verbs into the ears of healthy young sports editors. Al quickly joined in with a lively group putting together the entertainment section, show business types soon arguing over themes and plot. That left Art free to wander by himself where he soon found himself next to an attractive actress.

She had probably seen him walking toward her, perhaps even noticed his tongue moving across his lips when he caught sight of her.

"In all the commotion, I can't see where my friend has gone," she said to him as he walked by. Art, with foreshortened trousers and high-topped shoes screeched to a halt.

"Beg pardon, miss."

"I'm looking for my friends," she repeated.

"I'm sure you'll find them."

"I suppose. Meanwhile, tell me which of these three cults you belong to?"

Women, especially pretty ones, don't like to stand alone in crowded rooms. Why she picked out Art lay hidden in the mysteries of adult feminine behavior, though she had sensed his quick reaction to her. On his part, he merely accepted his good fortune.

"Are you a newspaperman or poet? Or on your way to Shanghai?" she asked.

"I've hardly been above North Avenue," he answered.

She laughed in an open way, leaving him with the impression that she was glad to be with him. He couldn't remember when he last experienced that kind of reaction, an intimation that they would surely be companions and soon. More was said in her facial expression than in the indolent tone of her voice or the actual words she spoke. It was in what lay behind, in her bright eyes, shining outward, capturing and holding Art in their focus. There was a warm invitation in her open, upturned lips showing the whitest of teeth hiding within the intimacy of her moist mouth. John-Arthur was so transfixed by her face that he could have counted the number of her eyelashes.

"Have you ever seen a more unlikely den of scribes?" she asked looking over the crowd—a few spirited, some colorful, others plain.

"I don't know what they're talking about most of the time," Art confessed.

"That's OK," she said. "Neither do they. . . .We should give them all numbers like a team. . . .Let's see. The newspapermen can be zeroes. And the artists can be tens. And, what's the

Asians favorite number? Eight?. . . .My name's Alice by the way"

"Art," he said, testing out his new moniker.

She quickly saw that he wasn't up to word games, so she got personal. "Are you here with your girlfriend?"

"Don't have one," he said.

"Good. Then I can flirt with you and be as outrageous as I want. . . .And I want."

She seemed free in a sensual way, as if not tethered to current popular norms; she appeared to be outside the usual standards, having let them go, having abandoned mores though never fashions. She concentrated instead on the immediate prospect of romance with the tall teenager, teasing him, catering to him, making him feel wanted. They were standing near a ledge designed for eating stand-up free lunches and she leaned back, spreading out one elbow in a casual way, opening the front of her body toward him.

"Is it too smoky in here, or what?" she asked after a few moments of conversation.

"About normal," he replied.

"It's a little bit too much for me," she said, affecting a small cough.

"Would you like a little air?"

"I have a better idea," she said. "Why don't we go over to my place? It's just around the corner."

She had offered him all the signals, but he wasn't reading her, couldn't twist the latch on the opening. Instead, he stated that he had to remain with his friend, who was busily involved with chronicling the years from minstrelsy to the Little Theater.

So, she left him to his own devices. Shrugging, she thought, "He didn't even have the sense to ask me anything about myself."

Soon afterwards he saw her engaged in a corner with a sculptor, who was probably better at modeling short-term relationships.

He couldn't activate himself. He told himself that he might become engaged later, but afterwards was going to be too late. An opportunity passed—as if he held a willing girl in his arms and told her that they would get together tomorrow. Missing the "now" of it. A way had opened but he didn't pursue it. Al, meanwhile, entered into the tempo of his times, engaging the others in the show business, riding the rhythms of today.

It might have been a defining day and night that could have turned John-Arthur around, given him something to aspire to and emulate, a starting point for development, a rationale for leaving the cold cuts of Laflin Avenue behind. But the image of a different life, as stunning as it was, bounced against his rocklike lassitude like a rubber ball off a concrete stoop. He took home the excitement of potential adulthood, but he couldn't help himself from resisting its attractions. He was getting better, but he wasn't ready for the big world. From time to time, he still had to endure the nightmare of fiery bodies colliding through the air.

Later in the week and thereafter, he avoided Al's calls, and they would not meet again until the whole world was on fire.

A month later, a copy of the one and only edition of *American Centennial* arrived in the mail.

# Chapter 10

Far away, as a contemporary remarked, the lamps of Europe were going out.

Only a few years before, it seemed possible that an era had arrived in Europe when the task of western history seemed near completion, monk-preserved, a rich textured tapestry glowing with the tradition of troubadours and tyrants. Romance and chivalry had flourished amid the simultaneous corruption of disease and poverty; two millennia of Christian civilization had encouraged adventurers to seek silver chalices, encouraging knights to believe that they could actually drink from the grail of human fulfillment. Their aim to reproduce heaven on earth in an English or French or Italian or German garden, a picnic-site of grace and aesthetics, hoping the achievements of the species by the end of the 19th century might culminate in a gorgeous bouquet of beautiful souls in the after-bloom of Victorianism. By 1914, the rise of romanticism and science and urban poverty had been sheltered in some places by a hundred years of near-peace. Cities had grown mellow along wide boulevards, filled with unheard-of elegance and out-of-the-way squalor.

America, however, had not followed the same trajectory. Here there was a new kind of culture that leapt directly from the green forest and brown prairie that blanketed the early continent. Settlers moved into their nation's first full century armed with a backwoods logic and daring practicality that made overseas civilizations appear slightly irrelevant, too distant to comprehend, and counterintuitive. Sprung directly from nature, America nevertheless soon joined the industrial revolution ready to throw filthy black smoke and ash into its rivers and air, rationalizing the cost of pollution in its cashbooks, reaching the conclusion that if materialism warranted its destruction, who needed to guard natural resources?

The country had other, greater assets. It was fortified by a cultural blood-mixing from the world's most adventurous stock set free from arbitrary restraint—no church, no army, no royalty checked its progress. More importantly the U.S. was not burdened with the weight of a million old ideas, or by generations in habitual servitude and soul-killing spiritual fear. In Europe, the aristocratic life was about to die; in America, the door was opening to empire.

At 17, Art was tall and thin. He was unaware and totally unconcerned that he would be a pawn in moving events. Rather, in the late winter of 1914, he was prescient enough to discern the difference between various complimentary smiles as he sat at the piano in the church hall and banged out his quirky ragtime rhythms at the Friday night dances. Gawky, he had outgrown his hand-me-down trousers so that their bottoms rode above the laces of his boots. In the lapel of his mismatched jacket, he wore a Boy Scout pin; higher up he was ringed by a detachable collar, which lassoed his neck, appearing to stretch it, making him look even taller and thinner than he was. He had outgrown some of his childhood inhibitions, but he was still wounded and suffered his old pain silently. He had clear, good looks and a quiet smile, the look of a serious, morally brought up boy that other Catholics recognized in a growing kid. This is the youth that Gracie Cleveland found at a church social before the Great War.

Gracie joined her friends around Art's piano and vocalized in her fellowship soprano, laughing an open toothy smile through the more amusing lyrics, then posing in properly sentimental fashion at the sadder songs. She and her girlfriends would hold each other around the waist in youthful support, knowing that the group bravery that had sustained their sisterhood would eventually unravel and they must soon impose their individual will upon some excitable youth.

Not a beauty, Gracie made up for a lack of stunning good looks with vivacity, a zesty personality, and a good figure. A number of Fridays would pass before he asked her to waltz, but meanwhile they circled each other in an elemental courtship dance. Whatever part of the hall Art happened to occupy, Gracie was not far off—and the opposite. Their eyes began to meet in an excited way as if chances were to be taken, and they both began holding late night imaginary conversations with the other, usually in front of a mirror where they would be considerably more daring than they would be in person. Because she had a loud voice that she learned to pitch through the heavy weather of her father's shipping operation, she tended to be boisterous and because she was naturally ebullient anyway, her presence was always noted and sometimes resented by some of the quieter members of the sodality. She made sure Art could hear her even if she were across the room, and though she sounded loud to others, for him her voice carried a penetrating warmth. She was 14.

No church social could live up to its reputation without some form of entertainment or games. One night, the teaching brothers and nuns, referring to their own childhood, decided their wards should bob for apples. A barrel was filled with water and floating upon the surface were dozens of red, shiny McIntoshes, bubbling about the tub, nudging each other for floating rights. The boys held back, judging their options as how best to snag one of the spheres, before committing themselves to ridicule, the poison of teen-age boys. But the girls, unafraid of failure, knowing it was all a lark and chances had to be taken, stepped forward to try their luck, none more eagerly than Gracie Cleveland.

But some other girls beat her to the rim. Hands behind their backs, the players weighed their options, strategically eyeing their plump victims, devising various approaches. Some took a sidewise swipe, mouth open like a steam shovel, their ivory prongs skimming along the surface of the water in cold pursuit of the slippery orbs, the apples skidding across the water, sliding harmlessly from their attacker's grasp. Others would utilize the overhead approach, plunging directly down on the bobbing apple, claw-teeth poised, but that contestant usually came up with nothing more than a mouthful of water. With various young people gulping and gasping, the girls with dripping wet hair, Gracie pushed forward. Her tactic was to trap one of the apples against the side of the barrel.

"No hands, Gracie. No hands."

She had involuntarily brought an arm from behind her back to grasp the side of the barrel to steady herself. Then, she plunged her head into the water, bending far over and she emerged with an apple in her teeth. Her face was streaming and the crown of her head was wet and her long hair became untangled and avalanched down the back of her neck, her red highlights admired by Art. The front of her blouse was wet and rosy nipples erupted through her chemise, and before she embarrassingly covered herself, her eyes captured Art surveying the soft structure of her underpinnings. She laughed, flustered, and retreated with a girlfriend to dry off.

As she walked away, she appeared overripe and blown apart, and though she carried the title of Grace, others may have been more suited to the name. She lacked the understatement of private school girls, or the sophistication of the debutantes from the North Shore who went Christmas shopping in New York, but she possessed an energy and fearlessness that made her special. Although she had a know-it-all reputation, she was, as midwesterners say, up front in her dealings. Her cardinal vices, or some would say virtues, were her stubbornness and pride.

At one of the Friday socials, as Art was playing a sprightly ragtime number, he held her in his gaze. She blushed and whispered to her girlfriend afterwards, "The way he looked at me while he was playing, like all he wanted to do was grab me."

That night the couple found themselves standing alone on the same patch, with no one else near enough to divert their attention. Beneath them, whitened sprinkles of wax remained undisturbed on the dancefloor, spread there to help awkward shoes slide with greater ease.

"I sure like your piano playing," Gracie said

"Thanks," he said stiffly.

"I see your brother Francis over there. They say he's the quiet one."

"Yes," Art said, "He doesn't say six words on a Sunday. He should join up with one of those silent orders."

"I've seen you in the window of your store. Maybe one time when I'm going by, I'll stop in."

"Yes, and if I'm not there, say hello to my mom."

"She'd think I was fresh. I'd want to make a good impression," Gracie said.

"She'd like you, I can tell."

It was as if he himself had said he liked her, and that gave her the confidence to go on.

"I've heard you like to skate in winter. My friend Alice told me she's seen you at the pond. Sometimes, I go with her."

"Maybe we could meet up there sometime," Art said, imagining holding her, pressing next to her, arms linked, gliding through the dark.

"You probably don't remember, but I've seen you for years, working from your wagon. Sometimes when I was a kid, I even bought things from you—melons, I think."

"Must have been September. When they come in sweet."

All it takes for a twosome to congeal is the announcement in their eyes of an unspoken agreement to accommodate each other and to offer the other person a chance to respond favorably. That and two or three turns of the tide to allow the excitement to wash over them. The pair provided time and space to dissolve their natural shyness. Soon Gracie was talking to Art in the same voice she used with her sisters and friends and he began to speak in multiple sentences. There was no fear involved in opening themselves to each other, because there was no censor or criticism standing between them, other than normal American Catholic repression. Rather there was relief in finding someone from the other sex who resembled a friend.

They danced through the end of one song, and stayed together on the polished floor, holding hands as couples do while waiting for the music to return. A lovely interlude, hands clasped tightly, excitedly aware of the touching. When the music rose again, they opened their arms for one another as if to express their new feelings.

"How about yourself," he asked. "What do you. . . .?"

"I'm going to secretarial school and at the end of the school year, I'll be out working steady. Probably downtown. My Dad's dead now, so the rest of us have to work. That's my Mom, two sisters and two brothers. It's kind of tight but we all manage to live together though it's not always roses."

She was forthcoming and he was not, but the more she jabbered on, the more comfortable he felt, the air vibrating with something more than her personal chatter. Soon Art began to open up as well. She led the conversation and later that night, his recurring image of her was that when she spoke, she held herself proudly. She was sure of herself and that was appealing. For her part, she felt warm in his dancearms, and loved the looks of his tall frame and became comfortable with his quiet ways. She was about to exchange her transpiring girlhood for the role of young workingwoman and along the way, she would need someone like him. Earlier, when the record player had fired up *They'll be a Hot Time in the Old Town Tonight*, they clomped around the hall, laughing and he could feel her shifting breasts moving with the uptempo, just as she could feel his scrumbly parts.

The following Friday night, Art walked Gracie home and they held hands along the darkened streets between the pools of light, uncomfortable to show their emotions in the glow of the globe.

"Do you like to go to the beach?" she asked.

"Yeah. My family goes sometimes in the summer," Art replied. "How about you?"

"Love it," she said. "How about fishing?"

"No. We haven't done that much. I did some on the Miss-a-sip when I as a kid."

"They rent boats down on the lake."

"So, you like to?" he asked. "Fish, I mean."

"Queen of the Fish. That's what my Pa said. He was captain on a grainboat and when I was a kid each summer, he'd take me out with him, up and down the lakes, Detroit, Milwaukee. Once all the way to Buffalo. And I'd fish the day long and some weeks my Ma was with us as cook, and she'd fry up whatever I caught, so I kinda got the hang of snagging them in."

"That's something. Better than working in a deli."

She said, smiling. "My Pa said it made me a tomboy, hanging around with sailors."

"Do you still go out on the lake summers?"

"No. Not since my Dad's gone. He took me off the boat anyway when I got older. Said I was distracting."

"Must have been fun out there," he said

"We had adventures, I swear," Gracie said. "One of my uncles, one of my good uncles, was our first mate—my Ma's brother—and he was my hero. Big Uncle John. He was always getting me in trouble or out of trouble. . . .My dad's from an English family way back, but Uncle John still had his brogue and was no friend of the British."

"Sounds like the two of you had some good times."

She said, "I believe we did. Uncle John of mine loved mischief. Once near Windsor, opposite Detroit, we pulled alongside a British ship and all day while we're loading up, Uncle John is watching the English swabs moving around the decks. At dinner, he lays out his plan. We're going to board it and steal their Union Jack. He was crazy like that."

"You musta thought he was nuts."

"I did. And do you know what? He talked me into it. . . .He wakes me up before midnight, and we go down the docks and climb on board and slip around the night watch. Uncle John, he makes me run the colors down the halyard and we grab the flag and start to hightail it out of there. But not before he goes and raises a black flag up the pole just to let the Brits know they had been attacked by a pack of pirates. And ever since, he's calling me Grainy instead of Gracie after some old Irish lady pirate."

"I had some adventures too when I was a kid, Out in Iowa. One Fourth of July, my pals and I. . . ." and he told the story of Eagle Point Park but left out all the bad parts.

* * *

They began seeing one another regularly, certainly each weekend. Soon after, they started to appear at each other's Sunday family dinners. At the Cleveland's, they would play cards with her brothers and younger sisters and Gracie, sharp at games, always won.

When summer arrived, and after Gracie settled in her new job, they would spend part of each Saturday or Sunday afternoon at the beach, and it became the highlight of their week, to see each other unclothed, frisking in the water, touching. One evening, when the beach was quiet, they rolled over to one another and kissed a full-body kiss, and the aching emptiness that followed confused and excited them

Time and new feelings were healing the loss of 1906. Meanwhile across the ocean, the Somme and Flanders were shrieking for blood.

# Chapter 11

In the late summer of 1914, the young men of Europe erupted in spasms of patriotism, swarming recruitment offices. The poor, not knowing they were signing up for self-immolation, waited impatiently, pushing in line for glory. Emulating the nobility, they sought esteem in battle with the same fervor as the portraited gentry, the aristocratic young hoping that their valor might bring with it life-long respect by a chance show of bravado.

The German/ French/ Anglo/ Italian/ Russian/- hyphenated Americans of Chicago felt a burst of pride in their old mother/fatherlands when the guns began to roar. A few rushed to Canada or into the ambulance services or risked a return to their native country, but transatlantic war fever diminished when the columns of murderous statistics began to line up, tranquilizing the urge to enlist. Most were content to contemplate the advantages of the American side of their hyphenation when compared to the brutality of trench warfare. Although there were varying degrees of ambiguity regarding loyalty to their adopted country among these national groups, and even though President Wilson advised neutrality of thought and spirit, public opinion coalesced against the Germans, who were the aggressors in Belgium and France. A deep prejudice developed towards the Central Powers, presidential caution notwithstanding, that was soon carried to excessive lengths— parents rechristening their William-named babies so as to distance themselves from Kaiser Bill.

Though forewarned against foreign entanglements by law and by our original and most illustrious general, an idea emerged in Washington's city that the New World, given the chance, might somehow redeem the corruption of the Old— even though the euphoria of that idea propelled an epidemic of false idealism that would eventually collapse and help create the skeptical modern age. Agreement would soon prevail that the bloodbath of World War I was the most savage act of gross stupidity in the history of the planet.

Even knowledgeable people in England were fooled by the tricky notion that the war might reap enormous benefits for laborers—miners and factory workers that had spent their hard lives battling poverty. Liberals imagined that these workers would finally be recognized as true back-home heroes, guilded smiths and yeomen, delivering the food and materiel that would help win the war. Consequently many reformers pushed for war in order to ensure labor gains, but what was the sense of it if England, as well as France, Germany, and Russia, paid with a lost generation of their young men? All dead in Flanders and Picardy or buried along the Marne and Meuse never to partake in the new social contract.

Locally, older Irish-Americans, anti-English anyway, were against the war and fervently hoped the British Empire would collapse in the tumult. But their Americanized children were belligerently opposed to the Prussian militarists, whom the newspapers overly castigated as cruel and inhuman barbarians. Martin, technically first generation, because old Frank was born in Fermanagh, clung to the Irish half of his lineage, whereas Art was attracted to the idealism of the day. Sons like Frank's Martin felt the pull of their heritage but John-Arthur wasn't as clannish about the old ways. For the first time, there was a political rift between Kitty's men, and Art's attitude, spurred by an eighteen year old's emotions and normal sense of rebellion, widened the breach and led him to oppose his father's views. This parental battle allowed Art an opportunity to increase the sense of his own individuality and independence. Combining that attitude with his feelings about Gracie, there was a tentative arrival of early manhood.

\* \* \*

When John-Arthur turned eighteen earlier that spring, his parents pondered over a birthday present. Celebratory gifts like a gold watch or an automobile were out of the question, so they decided to approach him directly. When they sat down with him, seeking a less expensive solution, they were surprised by his answer.

A new concert garden was about to open on the South Side and there had been a flurry of speculation during construction concerning its exotic appearance. Imaginatively conceived, it was designed to be a walled arboretum offering patrons the opportunity to hear classical music under the stars in an atmosphere somewhere between Egypt and a time that had not yet arrived. Over by the lake, Frank Lloyd Wright was building one of his most dazzling creations—the Midway Gardens.

"I think I'd like to take Gracie to that new place over by Washington Park when it opens," John-Arthur said.

Washington, and its neighbor, Jackson Park, were famed outposts for city enjoyment. The Great Chicago Fair, which had turned the corner on the twentieth century, rose originally from the bog that became Jackson Park. A corridor connecting the two parks was the site of the Fair's original Midway—an amusement area in 1893 designed to lighten the gravitas of the Great Fair that portrayed America's coming-of-age strength and its bold entrance into world affairs. The less serious Midway—a place name that spawned a thousand carnivals.

These parklands bordering Lake Michigan had been urban playgrounds for years. Even before the White City, there had been a famous racetrack at Washington Park. Immense beergardens seating thousands of revelers had been part of the area's gemutlicht history—Old Vienna, the Edelweiss Gardens—and now the Midway Gardens, a place where American music might bloom.

Gracie was excited by the invitation and both she and John-Arthur went out and purchased new clothes: she her first dancing dress, he his first suit. On a balmy June night they rode the cars east and on arrival, breathed in the cool fishy smell of Lake Michigan, so familiar to them that only the freshness of the breeze slid over their senses. As they walked along Cottage Grove to the new pavilion, they viewed recessed terraces rising one upon another from a low-slung Prarie-style enclave. The façade lifted numerous horizontal balconies toward high perched belvederes, all sheathed in statues and cascading flowers.

"I never saw anything like it," Gracie exclaimed.

"Yeah. Like something out of a story book."

They walked beneath a statue of the Queen of the Gardens, a saucy deity rising amid symbolic skyscrapers, a modern nymph. Inside, they walked beside the Winter Garden under low arches and through darkened passageways, tunnels of expectation, and then burst into the wide expanse of the Summer Garden—an outdoor amphitheater with a series of terraces sloping down to a dancefloor beneath the largest bandshell either of them had ever seen. Arcades ran along each side, flowers streaming from every railing and arch. Stone waterfalls of light guided them. Along the wallways, cylindrical brass columns held great sprays of gladioli. And everywhere statuary of Asian sprites, some serene, some laughing. The young couple was greeted and shown to their seats, the pair walking stiffly and somewhat self-consciously through the crowds. There were no eagles here. No Americana. Only fey spirits wearing sly smiles in a hanging garden.

"Like walking up the aisle on Easter Sunday," Gracie whispered as they headed for their table.

The impact of the garden's vision was so overwhelming that they felt they were walking through a dream. Their eyes didn't know where to look first. The oasis held multi-layered balconies where guests were gathering for dinner and a concert. They looked up and in one of the dining boxes saw animated groups of young people their own age.

"Must be the college crowd. On their way to Lake Geneva."

They sat under trees, sculptured and potted and surrounded by plants flowing from great urns. The young couple marveled at their good fortune to be one of the first customers to share this manifestation of Wright's imagination.

Lying on the table alongside the bouquet was tonight's program; a glance informed them that American works would be featured. They looked around and smiled at neighboring guests, who beamed at the girl and her beau, so obviously innocent and out for a special occasion. The pair studied the menu while peering around, then ordered. In time, the food would arrive and the plates disappear between symphonic selections. The orchestra was warming up.

"Look at how many music players they have. Must be fifty or more," Gracie said.

Eventually the lights dimmed and on to the stage came Max Bendix to lead the National Symphony Orchestra. They began by playing Gottshalk's *A Night in the Tropics*, capturing the allure of balmy nights beneath the stars, a fitting response to an evening in Mister Wright's pleasure palace.

After the music and applause faded away, Maestro Bendix and his players relaxed while a piano was wheeled front and center. The announcer suggested that more Gottschalk was in order, seeing that the crowd reacted so favorably to the last piece. The soloist came forward with the conductor, tugging on one of his cuffs, and they proceeded to play Gottschalk's *Union*.

"Old Al would have liked this one—*Yankee Doodle* and those others," Art said. "When we were young, he played an upright that as good as danced around the room."

"You don't say."

"It's true. That old pianola would sometimes bust 'cause he tinkered with it so much but he'd doctor it all up so'd it could play by itself like a brass band."

"Mercy, no."

"Literal," Art said

After intermission and their first course, the orchestra returned to warm up. They next played the opening section of MacDowell's *Suite Number 2*— the *Indian*.

"That soft melody tears at the heart," Gracie said.

"Yeah, old Ed down on the farms liked this one."

"Who's he again?"

"Maeve's friend. The one who lived in a dreamworld. . . .Maeve and me used to play some of MacDowell's songs. His name always brings her to mind."

"She taught you piano. It's only natural."

Gracie understood his sensitivity concerning Maeve. She hesitated before she asked about something that had been on her mind, but she wanted to know.

"Art, you think her death cut you off from something?"

"Yeah. Sort of. And Caroline both." He was silent for a moment. "It's like a pain locked up inside me that can't come out."

"Or doesn't want to."

" I don't know. I try to get by with the hurt."

Gracie pursued, "But can you? Replace them?"

"Probably not," he concluded.

She was not happy with the response but was so excited by their evening in paradise that her disappointment soon evaporated.

After playing Amy Beach's *Gaelic Symphony*, the orchestra finished with a piece by Chadwick. His *Jubilee* began with a bright and lively fanfare that woke both of their imaginations.

"A jubilee," Gracie said with feeling, "just like we're celebrating." Hesitating, she said, "Art, I wish we could live our life with those kinds of feelings."

Art failed to hear Gracie's meaning but the music was affecting him. Something about the Chadwick music began to move in him. Had he heard it before?

"It sure's got the spirit," he said. "Sounds like a victory. You get a march, then you almost hear Indians and then it sounds like someone slipping down the Mississippi in a steamboat on the way to some old plantation and all you can see are cotton fields. . . .Then a warning like something's afoot and the music comes crashing back with the big theme. Then the calling back of the river again like an afternoon you don't want to end— sitting with your girl and friends, and you realize without really knowing that this is going to be one of the really important days of your life and that maybe you've come this far and maybe you're not going much further. That the day itself is some kind of triumph that makes your goosebumps pop. Then the music tries for a feeling ending and another celebration. Like you're back home with yourself in a way you've never been before."

He had taken a deep breath and sung every one of the thirty-two bars in him. Gracie was amazed. It was like he had lit up. But he quickly closed down again after the explosion lunged out of him in a burst of confused emotions, all tied up with the splendid night and setting and his yearning for Gracie.

John-Arthur wondered if the deeper-than-ragtime music he heard that night could reach his center self, but the melodies that initially stirred him did not resonate in his heart very long. It was as if the borders of his soul were sealed from the insides against more complicated ideas. He couldn't even examine himself or hear himself through the din, not able to taste the tears in his own mouth. As a consequence, he would continue to play only popular tunes.

\* \* \*

Congress entered the war in April of 1917, when the conflict still had nineteen grisly months to run before the Armistice was signed. The day after the country joined the fray, the newspapers praised the ideals and aspirations of President Wilson destined, according to the editorial writers, to redefine the balance of power in a democratic world. They called upon young Americans to show their spunk and enlist in the cause. By our support of England and France, we would be repaying old bills—thus crediting the nation state of our mother tongue. And France as well for a different reason—for helping us win our own revolution. These national debts would be paid by the young who would help shift the weight of the world around to the Western Hemisphere. America went wild with patriotic zeal at the announcement of hostilities, but could not know the horror of war, especially this war, unaware that flowers planted with enthusiasm that spring had the stain of death on them.

The night after the war declaration, in a spontaneous demonstration, the streets of the South Side filled with military-age young men, giddy with enlistment fever. The young boosted by national pride proceeded to run about and bang pans and ring every available bell, including the ones on the streetcars. Art, Gracie, and Francis joined the crowds that swept up and down Ashland. Musical bands materialized to play English war songs and bonfires were lit at the major intersections. Old-timers donned the uniforms they wore in Cuba and a few old men doddered around in their Union campaign hats. Word circulated that Alderman Tooley would speak at a rally at the local high school, and that's the direction the trio took. By the time they arrived at the school, the auditorium was full, and large crowds milled around the halls and in front of the building. Before the alderman arrived, the students began chanting, "Close the Schools! Let the boys enlist!"

Art felt himself moving from an almost frozen passivity toward an urgent stance regarding war service. Certainly some of his reasoning was owing to the cartmen's action against Tooley—a realization that violence sometimes stemmed violence. Tending towards Wilson's persuasion, he chose not to be carried away by the waving banners—perhaps owing to his innate modesty. But he would be the first to caution others that his meekness should never be seen by others as a sign of weakness.

The next day, he joined the Illinois National Guard.

The night before Art left for camp, he suggested that Gracie pursue her regular routine and not join him downtown when he was sworn in. At City Hall, on the morning of his induction into the U. S. Army, the first person he saw was the neighborhood terror, Owen Clancy, and his sidekick, Danny Moriority, the one who had wielded a wrench when the pair threatened his mother. Art's stomach turned over when he saw the runt, and could feel the blood fear associated with potential combat. The new enlistees were sworn in by a contingent of alderman, including their own Honorable Tooley. A Clancy clique had come along to send off Owen, their leader, and he responded boisterously with big-handed gestures. His crowd was filled with patriotic zeal and carried little American flags, which they waved when the bus left for training camp. Along the route, Clancy's eyes narrowed when he recognized Art.

At camp, drudgery and fatigue soon diminished the spontaneity of their enlistment enthusiasm. Up early and marching all day and then up late for indoor instructions on tactics, the recruits were soon sleep-deprived and exhausted. Because they had no weapons, their training consisted of a few basics: how to march in close order drill and how to tramp about in other people's pastures and how to spread out at night in tents under the elements. There was a minimum of time spent at rifle target practice owing to a lack of ammunition. Their battalion had no mortars, machine guns or artillery and when there were not enough rifles to go around, they used broomhandles. Luckily there were a few grenades available— the preferred close-up instrument of death in France.

Clancy, Moriority, and Art were bivouacked in the same tent complex, part of a training company whose commander knew little of military lore and nothing of war. Clancy, because he was knowledgeable about firearms and naturally shrewd, became a cadet leader and within a week was acting as one of the assistant squad leaders in the same platoon as Art. He soon caught Art in his net, transferring him to his own squad where he could utilize his newfound power over the neighborhood brat whose family had helped thwart his gang's revenue stream.

Clancy leaned on Art, assigning him to the dirty details in the garbage tents and grease pits and latrines. Art, as always, responded slowly and patiently to the forces around him, including these harassments, which were compounded when Moriority was made acting assistant when Clancy moved up. He began riding Art, in an attempt to break him. But Art completed the assigned jobs, got along with his other tentmates, and caused so little trouble that the pair of gang members had no excuse to place him on report. They couldn't humble him; life had already flattened him. They couldn't tweak his ego, because he didn't have much of one in the first place. They didn't have the ability to understand the contents of his heart and they couldn't grasp what motivated a person so meek. His aloofness didn't appear to be related to fear. The truth was that Art had early learned the lesson of passive resistance and had become a natural hider.

Individuals are quick to show their true selves in places like the army. Among the three, it was Clancy who first demonstrated the particulars of his manhood. What happened occurred in a grenade pit. Four men at a time were assigned to climb into a trench where they proceeded to bobble small balls of destruction in their hands. The training quartet included an instructor from the regulars, Clancy now the squad leader, and a rotation of two men from the platoon. The idea was to take a grenade in hand, remove the pin, count to three and throw it the hell and away out of the pit before it exploded. One nuance in this procedure was that half the *pineapples*, with their corrugated surface for easier gripping, didn't work. Many were duds that would burn harmlessly for a moment and extinguish themselves in the target area. The question as to which ones would ignite was a mystery until the moment of explosive truth.

Another one of the recruits and Art jumped into the trench to join Clancy and the instructing sergeant. They reviewed the procedure quickly and a grenade was handed to Art, a veritable hot potato. Art wiggled the pin out of its socket, released the trigger mechanism, waited and flung it out as far as he could, then they all ducked down to wait. A blast followed shortly and the earth kicked up a few clumps that landed back in the pit. Then it was the other recruit's turn and when he was ready to propel the grenade, he didn't throw it sidearm as taught, but instead instinctively tried to chuck it overhand, but the grenade slipped out of his grasp at the top of his delivery and wobbled five feet up in the air and returned to land at their feet.

"Cover," the sergeant yelled as he and the two latest arrivals in this potential deathtrap dove through the air into the corners of the trench, lifting their arms to protect their heads.

Clancy, without hesitating, leapt towards the sizzling grenade. With his life in the care of pure chance, he grabbed the activated handbomb and tried to throw it out of the dirthole, but not before it sputtered and burned his hand, luckily a dud.

Art, wondering if the end were near, heard his nemesis swear as the grenade burned him and then Clancy turned to give the recruit who misfired the rocket, a furious kick in the leg with his heavy boot.

The sergeant raised his head and said, "Nice work, Clancy. Here! Wait! Leave him alone. God, kid. . . .You could have killed us."

The recruit stood, shaking, rubbing his leg, fearfully following the whereabouts of Clancy's fists. Art rose slowly, listening to the tumult rising from the rest of the platoon. Then the sergeant picked another deadly iron-apple from his basket and bounced it up and down in his palm.

"Now, son, pay attention. This is how to do it this time... Ready? Sure you're OK?"

The kid wished he were at a White Sox game.

A few moments later, the greenhorn properly lobbed the grenade over the parapet and it exploded with deadly force, out of harm's way, violently disturbing a number of worms.

As the pair from the platoon climbed out of the pit, Art heard the sergeant say to Clancy, "You're some tough-ass kid, mister. I'm going to recommend you for Corporal. That was a brave thing you did."

That's how the scourge of the Prairie Avenue gang became Art's official by-the-numbers squad leader.

They went off to France, having learned little more than how to march in a parade and line up for chow. Off to the slaughterhouse of Western Civilization.

By the time American troops arrived, a million and a half French were dead, nearly a million British, a million and a half Germans, and untold millions in Russia, not to mention the losses to innumerable allies associated with those no longer great, now depleted, nations. Totally, 15 million soldiers had died. Blown away at Ypres, at the river Somme, around Verdun, at Chemin des Dames and a thousand other ridge roads and towns.

American forces fought in France for six months before the Armistice—that fateful season of 1918 that introduced 175,000 Yanks to perdition and eventually crowded the veteran's hospitals for three generations with wounded, gassed, and shell-shocked victims. Reckless American kids, eager warriors, seeking herodom, dying in piles, adverse to caution, they filled the valleys and fields of Northeast France with early aspirations and quick remorse. They created the chronicled myths that separated them forever from their peers and family by their gambles with death—the Marines at Belleau Wood, the new troops at Chateau Thierry, the final victories along the river and woods of the Meuse-Argonne.

When the Prairie Division arrived in France, they were shipped in 40 and 8 boxcars far to the south of the actual fighting to undergo advanced training. This included mock gas attacks, combat exercises, and instructions on how to use British and French rifles and grenade launchers. They even learned to operate German guns, knowing captured machine guns could always be turned around on a fleeing enemy. They were training to kill now.

In a month, they were shipped north behind the lines in the English sector on the northern Flanders front, past shattered villages and roads clogged with refugees. Under combat conditions, final training began with instruction from British non-coms who had survived four years of purgatory. There in the relatively quiet trenches seven miles behind the front, they began to experience the horrors of war firsthand. Brutalized bodies moving to the rear, the crumpled land and shorn trees, the sound of active artillery in the near distance and their limbless instructors reminded them of the fragility of life in pock-marked France.

They then moved forward into abandoned trenches, still far back of the forward lines, but filled with ominous smells of gas and blood, and were soon lost in an interconnected under-surface maze that had seen live action in past engagements and bore little relation to the artificial training sites they left behind. With full packs, they slid down the muddy embankments and came to the clammy end of their journey, slipping into the dampening reality of their previous dreams of glory. Ahead, toward the fighting, from time to time, a wandering shell would burst at night scratching up a flame like an ignited match. Because the front lines in this sector had been quiet for months, their commanders judged this to be as safe a mudhole as any to boost the courage of green troops.

Training now was designed to save their own lives by killing Germans. Battle-smart British sergeants instructed them on the usage of the Lewis gun and Stokes mortars and gave them tips on how to handle their bodily functions under stress, relating stories that resounded in the pits of their stomachs—tales of body parts rotting out on the barbed wire. One bow-legged Brit, having delivered his gory message, and with a smile from hell, wished them well when their moment of truth came as they went over the top, "All I can say, Yanks, is: Up and over wiff the best of luck." And left them with a snappy Colonial-garrison salute.

They listened to the gallows humor of these veterans of Mons of '14, where the regular British army was decimated and those of the Somme of '16 where the Empire lost its civilian army and of the stupidity in Flanders in '17 where the fearful orders to attack were delivered by maniacs on the British general staff, causing casualties that sometimes amounted to 20,000 a day. Such realities began to erode the new troops' false confidence, replacing it with sturdier stuff. They listened as well to the stale cracks about the scarcity of coffins and rats as big as raccoons.

In another week's time, Art's outfit was inserted into a tertiary defense line a mile behind the forward positions, filing in while weary Australians moved to the rear.

"Look at those big blokes. Must be farmers." they heard the Aussies.

"Look as green as gangrene to me."

"Mind them hot showers up there, mates. It's not always warm water you get."

"Piss down your leg more likely."

"Show us how you curtsy to the queen," Clancy shot back. "Maybe we can give you a few lessons on how to start your own country."

The French troops merely bleated at them like sheep as they rumbled towards the lines.

On their right was a battalion from a different regiment of the 33rd, and now they could feel the earth shudder with incoming artillery; maybe once an hour a shell landed in their sector. The first of the Illinois wounded began their bone-rattling bounce to the rear.

Four days later, they moved into the main trenches and at night were amazed that they could hear the Germans singing from three hundred yards across No Man's Land. It's what the world had come to: remembered melodies across a lost earth, a planet that could no longer tolerate man's stupidity, or care about its survival. When the Germans first heard that fresh Americans were posted opposite, they began lobbing in shells, but after a day or two of scrimmaging, the two sides settled into a comfortable stalemate. After all, this was a quiet section of the front and they might as well enjoy it.

Dug into the side of the trench and down ten stairs, the platoon's quarters lay submerged in the bomb-disturbed, bone-strewn earth where the quickly buried sometimes re-emerged in grisly, smoky resurrection after a shelling. Below, there were empty ammunition boxes for chairs, a rickety table holding the debris of war, candle holders, their bases swollen with old wax, plus cooking equipment and a variety of thin and foul blankets in the corner. Pegs in the dirt wall allowed the squads to hang their gear. Nailed into the mud was a chalkboard with foul messages that some Catholic boy erased. An hour later, a near hit close to their sandbagged roof shook the dugout, pots and pans flying, knocking the chalkboard on the greasy floor. Art read, *"Either God is dead or a sadist."* And below, *"Change your socks daily."*

As the troops toughened to fighting readiness, the 33rd began to hear stories of other American troops, specifically the Marines' 2nd Division charge into Belleau Wood, a tangle with death. There the explosive noise in the woods drove men mad, their ears bleeding. The crazed French general, who ordered a night attack utilizing his newly assigned fodder from America, refused to heed the cries of the untended casualties still suffering on the battlefield from an earlier attack. He ordered another advance, the gunfire and shell blasts too intense to remove the broken bodies, soldiers pleading for death—split in pieces, lying in red heaps. In the dead woods, lives evaporated.

The rain brought cold to Art's dugout. Keeping dry in the laundry-strewn pits was their principal concern, civilization having returned to the mudcaves of their primordial ancestors where this newer species now played cards and wrote dirty-fingered letters. To alleviate a false sense of security, company commanders sent half-squads into the moonscape in front of them to scout the bruised earth, checking that the barbed wire barrier was still intact, always seeking talkative prisoners. The night that Art went out on his first patrol, flares went up illuminating the entire area, followed by ten or twelve bursts of Hun fire. Against the manual's advice, he dove face first into the mud of a crater and stayed there as a necklace of hurtling invisible steel passed overhead. He remained until he heard neighboring whispers, calling for a withdrawal.

While on patrol, his rifle kept banging into his canteen, creating a clonking noise. Back in the trench, the patrol was dressed down by every level of authority up to battalion, demanding to know who had made all the noise. Art had been so fearful that he didn't even realize he had caused the commotion.

The weather warmed up for a day and then the low rolling clouds returned in the typical way the overcast in northern Europe creeps thick and close to the ground. On their fifth night at the front, Labor Day at home, a strange spectacle appeared in the sky about ten at night. Clancy stuck his head into the dugout and called, "If you want to see something weird, you better come up here and take a look."

It was a movie made in hell. Projected against the low, roiling nightsky, a searchlight beamed a picture, a cartoon of fools. Silhouetted against the dark clouds appeared a picture of generals from all the major powers and top-hatted capitalists arranged around a green table. On their lapels they wore dollar signs and deutschmarks, and before them on the eating board lay dead soldiers served up from all their armies. Across the lines, when the Germans saw this sky show, they cheered; the Americans were amazed by the outburst, unaccustomed to displays of treason and unaware of socialization among the troops. Officers up and down the line were heard shouting and fuming. When the brass detected that the images were coming from behind the American line, they went crazy, their careers in jeopardy.

Then a pantheon appeared, a series of portraits flashed up onto the black scurry that served as a screen. The German immortals descended from heaven—Beethoven and Goethe, Kant and Mozart, Bach and Nietzche, Schumann and Schiller and even Freud. The Germans sent up a roar and in their excitement shot off rifles like Bedouins at a camel auction.

American lieutenants and captains kept running around cursing and shouting, "Who are they? Who are those guys?" and some little guy from Peoria thought he recognized Ty Cobb and some other Detroits among the all-star German immortals.

The images seemed to be flashing on the sky from some point behind the battalion on the right and eyes turned back towards a section in the near-rear where the searchlights and telephone equipment of the Signal Corps were parked. But before eyes could determine the cause, new constellations appeared, pictures of Washington and Jefferson, Adams and Jackson and even something for the French in tiny Lafayette. When the picture of the Great Emancipator broke upon the heavens, the 33rd Illini sent up a rousing cheer, echoing the name of their state's hero, Lincoln—the outburst heard all the way back to Division.

"Where's it coming from?"

"I want to find out," said Art.

"Are you crazy? They'll haul you to Courts Martial."

"No, it's like a holiday. I'll get a pass. Who cares?"

One last picture flashed up in the sky. It showed the military and munitions tycoons again from the first image. The generals and capitalists now had full mouths. They were feasting on the dead corpses on the green table.

With unaccustomed initiative, Art wangled a pass from Clancy on the pretext that the Company should have an exact report on these shenanigans in the sky. He trotted to the rear, duckboards squeaking in the mud, until he arrived at a Signal Corps caravan only moments before the Division's chief of staff. To Art's wonder and surprise, he found Al the Wizard Boy of Nebraska drifting through the encampment.

"Al! Al! It's me. Art! Art from. . . .from Holy Cross."

"Art, what are you doing here? Did you see my skyworks?"

"Was that you?"

"Who else? But play dumb. The brass's is calling for blood."

Al, except for a small moustache, looked the same as he did the night they dined with the newspapermen back in Chicago. He was posted with the battalion on Art's right and was essentially a telephone, telegraph, lighting troubleshooter. He had always had a knack for the technical.

"How did you rig it up, the show, I mean?" Art asked.

"Nothing special. Tricks of the trade," Al said. "Easy if you have the knack. . . .Did you like the German hall of fame? Couldn't find Mahler. . . .Figured I'd give Fritz a dose of his own doctors."

"How's Big Jack."

"Oh, bad news there. Old Jack died last year. Caught in a gun fight out West, up in the hills in Colorado, between the miners and the Pinkertons."

"Oh, god. Were you with him?"

"No, I was out on the circuit. So, no South Seas for old Jack after all."

They talked for fifteen minutes as staff officers snooped around the perimeter looking for the skylighter.

"I'd better get back," Art said. He gave Al his exact sector.

"I'll look you up. I string telephone wire all up and down the works."

The next day, the brass faced a different problem. Medical advisors circulated among the troops warning against an increasing influenza problem. All the armies of the world were sick, the pandemic having radiated from this infectious gash of vermin-hosted trenches that saw-toothed across France, a grid of land separating rutted earth from the purposes of humanity, a foulness, perhaps born on the streets and rivers of excrement in China and transported by coolie laborers working for the French, that spread the disease around the world.

The next time Art saw Al, "I" Company was in reserve eight miles behind the lines. Art had walked over to the next battalion area looking for the Signal Corps detachment and came upon Al standing with a group of soldiers near headquarters.

"Come around here, on the other side of this building," Al said to the other soldiers. When he spotted Art, he waved him around shell-blasted walls. A few of the other soldiers and Art followed Al, who halted, overlooking a stream where other doughboys were bathing, a channel that fed the river Oise.

Al was telling them, "You guys'll be rotated back into the trenches in four, five days so you need these green colored glasses I bought in Paris that I'm going to sell you. Makes things look a lot prettier up in the trenches. Wouldn't want you to have to actually see all that crud and damnation without some help. Don't want you to lose hope when the French start bawling at us like lambs to slaughter when we're moving up. Take a little comfort from these green specs. . . .The Frogs have already mutinied once, so maybe they'll need 'em too. They just said, 'Sar-ry. Not going to war today.' Biggest damn sit-down strike in history. Make any union man proud."

"Watch it, Al, there's a non-com."

Al and the rest of the men turned to watch the other soldiers swimming across the narrow river, and when the non-com passed, Al continued, "Because when you have to look the dragon in the eye, you'll be glad to have these goggles. I'll auction them off."

One big guy said, "Listen, I don't want those things. I don't see President Wilson wearing any fairy glasses," Others encouraged him to speak up against Al.

Al said, "President Wilson is a pudding-head. First he wins an election by saying he's going to keep us out of the war because it's none of our business—it's all about European munitions money. And as soon as he's reelected, what does he do but jump in the war. What the hell difference does it make to

Americans if Germans and French society officers puff themselves up like toy soldiers—like some cavalry show? Prancing around behind the lines so they don't have to get their brass dirty—decked out for the King's birthday. They ride around back here like they're looking for a parade to march in. Those fancy thoroughbreds probably eating all the artillery horse's oats because no sane general is going to send the cavalry against machine guns like they did in '14."

One of the soldiers shouted out, "Mister, you better watch your mouth. You heard Congress passed something called the see-dition law and you probably busted it a half-dozen times already today."

Al said, "That pickle of a professor in Washington—Wilson—and his bonehead cabinet, let ém try to kill free speech. They've hired a quarter million paid snoopers to go around the country and sniff out subversives in every Boy Scout troop and Rotary Club in America. I'd like to see them try to shut down Sam Adams or Tom Jefferson. That'ed be a war you'd be glad to fight in—a revolutionary one. All our government wants is the power to bury the unions, so they can kill off the IWW and put people like Debs to jail."

"What about when they sank the Lusitania?"someone asked.

"A British ship filled with munitions. What the hell do you think the Germans were going to do? Fire torpedoes made of knockwurst?" Al asked.

"Wise guy, what are we supposed to do, get shot for mutiny?" someone asked.

"They'll never shoot us if we all stick together," Al cried. "When the day comes, drop your guns in the mud and go home. Just like the Russians did. Just quit."

"Here comes Sam Browne."

The members of the crowd, now numbering about fifty, saw the officer approach, and they all turned towards the river.

"What the hell's going on here?" the lieutenant asked. "Somebody stirring up trouble?"

"No, sir," said Al. "Just betting on which one of those guys is going to win the race to the other shore."

"You better get some sleep," said the officer. "We're back up the line after dark."

He heard the moan of disappointment as he stepped away.

A week later when they were again back on the front line, Al came trudging down the trenchways, trailing a roll of wire after him, and located Art's dugout. He lowered the spool from his back and descended into the designated mud cave and was soon welcomed with some weak coffee brewed from acorns. Art was pleased to see him again; the long periods of boredom interspersed with intense artillery attacks had kept him jumpy.

"Did they ever catch on about the skyworks?" Art asked.

"Artie, by the time they fill out the paperwork trying to explain what happened, the war will be long over."

"How's the revolution coming? Any converts?"

Al said," We're waiting for the right moment. If they ever close down the Western Front, the generals will try to re-assign us to Russia to fight against the Reds. That's when all hell will break loose. Right now, we're just planting the seed."

"Whose 'we'?"

"Union guys like me. Brothers. There's no name for it. Anyway, they'll be no revolution today. . . .The only thing we're getting out of trench life is a permanent stoop."

Art said, "When I'm not shivering to death, I'm mainly wondering why I'm here."

"You're asking the right question at least," Al agreed. "Weirdest war that ever was."

Art said, "I had this dream. I saw these great ships, every one of them pure white, sent to help us, like hospital ships or something, floating across No Man's Land. Come plowing through white water, clean looking, like they were built in fresh sea air. Big American flags flying from the topmast. Heaving through the mud between the wires, and as they went by, the wake splashed all over the front and painted everything white— all the filth, all of us who had been caked in mud, Germans too, all splattered clean, wearing white uniforms, the ships sailing over the trenches in a white landscape. Like we had all died and were waiting around for angel wings. Then, as the ships went down the line, the white all disappeared and all the cleanness just dripped away from us and evaporated and we were all lousy and filthy again, wallowing in this blood soak. . . .Killing each other again because no white fleet could save us after all."

It was one of the longest, continuous set of sentences that Art had ever spoken, sitting in this black then white, then black, again hole.

# Chapter 12

Back on the South Side, the Mahoneys struggled through the war. Kitty was working too hard, taking care of the house, the store and her young daughter; nevertheless she found time to add parish war work to her schedule. Both parents worried not only about their son overseas but also Francis, age 17, eager to join his brother, all of them absorbing whatever war news became available. Martin volunteered his services and his truck to help haul goods to the camps and bases that were growing like weeds in the midwestern cornfields. The country had mobilized and was in a fury to train millions of combatants, so that both soldiers and materiel could be bundled up and shipped as rapidly as possible to France in order to relieve the burden of the exhausted French and English armies.

One weekend, Martin and Francis were assigned the task of delivering an express load of trench mortar guns to an outfit in Iowa whose training had been suspended owing to a lack of equipment. Without begrudging the long trip, they loaded the truck at the army depot near the West Side train yards one Friday afternoon and headed out. Driving most of the night, they parked the truck when they reached the Mississippi and slept for a few hours. As dawn and the birds of the river woke, they freshened up along the shore and crawled through Davenport until they found a breakfast shack. They reached their destination in the afternoon and received directions to the officer training camp at Fort Des Moines. A black soldier, wearing his tin hat, guarded the post gate.

"Colored soldier, Dad," Francis said.

"Looks like he's strong enough to carry a cannon," Martin replied.

"Good afternoon, sir," greeted the gateguard, with a smart, if unnecessary, salute.

"We've come from Chicago. With a load of mortars. Here's the papers."

"These look fine. Pass through. Quartermaster's basically at the back of the camp. Keep bearing right. They'll be signs up ahead. The main avenue curves around so just follow the natural contour of the road and you won't miss your warehouse. You might want to have the Supply Sergeant sign your papers before you leave."

"What kind of a camp is this, soldier?" Martin asked.

"Officer's training, sir."

"Knows his business," Martin said, as they progressed through the barrier.

They drove past rows of tents, stretching as far as the eye could see, in a neatly planted symmetry that would have gladdened the heart of any Iowa farmer, as straight on the diagonal as in rows. They appeared to have been laid out by survey. Even the company flags flapped in unison. In the open spaces, they could see black men marching in formation or drilling or huddled in the grass in circles listening to an officer describe the grim attributes of the Springfield rifle.

There were hundreds of soldiers, all black, the candidates polished and straight-backed. This was the one place in America where John Pershing's army was training its negro officers, Black Jack himself having derived his nickname from the color of the troops he led up San Juan Hill. It was the greatest convocation of educated men of color in the history of the country.

Martin took a detour in order to view the prospective officers as they marched through their paces, different platoons at different chores. They parked by the side of a makeshift parade field, the motor idling, observing the maneuvers. Absorbed by the military drills, Martin turned off the engine and watched the exercises. Some soldiers walked by and Martin asked one of the passing men what was happening in the woods on the far side of the field away from the tents.

"We've dug lines of trenches out there, and they're learning how to scramble through the wire. Sometimes we even get to play the Germans," the soldier said, his black satin face shining in the afternoon sun.

Puffs of smoke could be detected through the far-off trees.

It looks like they're practicing an attack now," he said. "What's in the wooden boxes back there?"

"Says mortars on them," Martin answered.

"Good. We've been waiting for 'em. It's probably a state secret, but the fact is we're missing a lot of equipment."

"I guess it's hard to go from no war to the real thing overnight," said Martin. "My Dad used to say it was the price you paid for separating the politicians from the generals. You were probably a civilian yourself a couple weeks ago."

"True enough. They're going to turn us all into officers and gentlemen." He smiled. "Someday, I suppose, we might even get shuffled together with the rest of the army, but I guess the country's not quite ready for that yet."

Martin asked directions again and was sent on his way. Many of the college-educated black males in the country were here, preparing to lead recruits now training elsewhere, segregated from the white doughboys, but tough rye, eager to prove themselves in France.

After delivering the gunboxes, the Mahoneys were directed towards the mess tents where they were offered an off-hour lunch. It was downtime and the lights were low on camp ovens, so the mess sergeant came and sat with them and he was the one who told them about the black military band stationed at the base.

"They are the best band in the land. They're out practicing on the ball diamond now. Wouldn't mind hearing them myself." He hesitated and said, "Yeah, what the hell, I can afford to go out for a while. Not time yet to put on the stew."

"Johnson," he shouted to one his aides-de-spaghetti, "keep those genta men busy on them victuals." Then to Martin, in a lower voice, "It's the best part of the duty round here, ordering them future officers around."

"Jump in our truck and show us the way," Martin said.

That's how Martin and Francis got to hear jazz for the first time without going to the expense of visiting Reisenweber's Café back in Chicago. Every riverboat trumpeter, whorehouse clarinetist, and perambulating saxophonist deckwalked up the Mississippi to join this, the hottest band in the country, inland from their native river. To see them march or listen to what they were playing offered listeners a preview of the coming age. For those who chanced to see this cadenced band in stepdance, there would have to be a new description of the word strutting. A military cakewalk. Body language would have to be redefined here; it was like a shambling walk in the gardens of old Louisiana.

Francis was amazed at the sounds and sights of the black encampment; he had never seen anything like it and the thought remained with him—the coming concept that his educated betters from the underclass would rise and surpass him in his lifetime. An early indicator here in the boot-crunched cornfields. All this many years after Martin first heard Joplin's piano music at the Chicago Fair. Now it was the white man's turn to acknowledge the treasures of a Black City.

After they dropped off the mess sergeant, whose footwork had been greatly animated by listening to the band, the pair headed their truck north of east towards Martin's boyhood home. Arriving in Holy Cross around midnight at Uncle Maurice's place, whose death marked the passing of the last of the pioneer children—he was old Frank's brother—they found the farmhouse black with the deep sleep of working farmfolks. Instead of disturbing the two-legged occupants, they settled in the hayloft above the musing, milky beasts. And that's where Leo found them in the morning.

They were welcomed into the big kitchen like prodigals from a lost urban tribe and were taunted with questions as to when they would regain their senses and return to farmlife. The visitors promised to stay through dinner scheduled at noon. So they washed up in the big tin basins and all the Mahoneys attended mass in the red brick church. They then went to visit Ellen and afterwards laid flowers at the graves of Frank, Great James, Bessie and John the scout.

Sunday dinner, in those years and for the next twenty, was the high caloric and social point in every family's week, spread with the fruits of the field and enlivened by a review of neighborhood gossip. Young Francis was disappointed to learn that he would be unable to see his cousins, because they had recently sold the store and the farm—lock, stock, and barrel—and moved to Milwaukee to take advantage of the high war wages. His grandmother asked about John-Arthur, and recalled that long ago Labor Day that had shattered so many lives.

It was Leo who told them about Maeve's player piano. He had acquired it in the auction that followed the long probate after her disappearance, and it was sitting in the back of the parlor. But the tracker didn't operate any more, though the keys still played, and if Martin wanted to haul it away in his truck and have it fixed in the city for John-Arthur, he was welcome to take it, rolls and all. Thinking of his son, Martin with the help of many hands laid the player piano sideways in the back of the truck. They soon bade farewell. As a treat to Leo, they brought him along, giving him a few days' break from his chores.

When they arrived back on Laflin Avenue, they lifted the piano off the truck with the help of some bystanders. Then Martin rummaged around the neighborhood trying to rustle up some other broad-shouldered guys to help maneuver the massive machine up the narrow staircase into the Mahoney apartment. And while it was sitting there alone on the sidewalk, with no mortal help, the piano began to play *When Uncle Sammy Sings the Marseillaise*.

## Chapter 13

On the night of September 25th, 1917, nearly a quarter million Doughboys (so named when covered by the white adobe dust of the Mexican wars and later the chalk-hill powder of France) were stretched across a twenty-five-mile front between the Argonne woods and the Meuse River of France, and began moving up into their jumpoff positions. Nine divisions, including the already famous Rainbow, Keystone, Ivy, and Statue of Liberty Divisions, were set to begin a major war-ending campaign along the German border. Two weeks before, the now exhausted Yankee and Big Red One Divisions, plus the racehorse brigades of the Second Division, had helped initiate this eastern campaign at Saint-Mihiel and had then been pulled off the line, waiting in reserve. It was seven weeks and many deaths until the Armistice, but for the first and only time in the war, the Yanks were together under Pershing as a single American army.

The 33rd, the Prairie Division, waited on the army's right flank, close to the river Meuse, near Verdun where in 1916 nearly a million French and Germans had been killed or wounded. As the offense began, Company I's battalion moved quietly into position across the marshy fields, the noise damped down by the rain. Before dawn, bombardment from four thousand Allied artillery pieces, whose objective was to soften the German defenses, shook the ground and tore fiery sheets of explosive blasts from the night air.

Art was frightened half to death, his body shivering so badly that his canteen and belt clips sounded to him like his father's fruit wagon jangling through the alleys. The dry taste in his mouth was bitter, and his nose and eyes ran. He kept up with Clancy and the rest of the squad until they settled on the line awaiting the 5:30 AM attack. This was to be a day of heroics and cowardice. One guy would actually throw himself across a string of barbed wire and have others trample over him in the advance, stamped down on a crown of thorns.

As soon as they stepped off, the German artillery began exploding around them. Art moved from one depression to another, keeping low, his buddies the same. In some places a group of them would fall into a shallow spot at the same time. Once seven of them sprinted towards a likely burrow, and it was there that a German shell burst nearby. Blinded by the explosion and lifted up, Art's body rotated in the air, tumbling, and then landed with a hard thud. When he tried to open his eyes, he saw unclearly through black streaks that he was covered with the gore from the men around him, lying in the churned-up crater of dirt that had buried some of them on impact. He began screaming in terror, unable to distinguish life from death in this instantaneous grave dug for the other members of the squad and himself. Pinned below the other bodies and covered with debris, he was suffocating.

Noise and shouting continued, and then he passed out, the stench and juice of death soaking him. Awake again and screaming, he felt movement, then he heard the sound of a voice and saw brightening light that let him know he was still alive. He wasn't even aware if he suffered pain or not. Someone was dragging the pulverized bodies from on top of him and scooping away the dirt. Some of the screaming now came from someone near him.

"Shut up!" is what he heard when he began to distinguish sounds. Then, "Stretcher bearers! Get them free."

When the remaining wastage of the bloody pile was extricated, Art rose on his knees, lurched sideways, then dove a few feet away.

It was Clancy's voice he heard next. Art, terrified, leapt further away as bullets whizzed by, shocked by the reality of a familiar face. "Get down," Clancy yelled, pushing Art aside. "Get a hold of yourself."

He recognized that Clancy was staring at him, evaluating him. Then Clancy moved over to check the others, survivors and dead. Coming back to Art, he said, "You're OK. Take this," throwing him a rifle. "And when you're ready, keep moving."

Clancy had broken all the rules. As a non-com he had clear orders to keep going forward during an advance and let the dead lie, but so many of his people were trapped in the pile-up that he had broken stride to help them.

Art rolled over, scraped himself off, revolted by the matter stuck to him. He vaulted from the shower of death from which he escaped uninjured and moved aside. He sank into the earth, until an officer from a following company ordered him forward. Catching up with his company an hour later, Art crawled into his platoon sector and resumed his place on the line. Enemy fire had pinned down his buddies.

Clancy came snaking up to him. "You OK now?"

"No." Art almost shouted.

"Then stay back a little until you catch your breath."

"I'll be where I belong," said Art.

Then they spent the next seven hours in hell. The company had to fight their way through German machine gun nests, with overlapping fields of fire set up deep into their defenses, so that no sooner had the Yanks taken out one emplacement, they were already in the sights of Boche gunners ahead. Art crawled through a marsh and across overgrown brambles of barbed wire strung out in previous battles and topped with new flesh stickers. He waded through the swamp, his boots making a sucking sound as he slogged along, ever mindful of the morass of the Somme where the British had literally drowned in the mud. He hurtled into any available hole when the German guns began to send their flying metal beads against their sector, bodies splitting around him.

That night, they slept in whatever holes they could find or dig. The next morning, they were off again. Clancy would motion to Art and two or three others and they would burrow along the flank of an opposing machine gun pit, lobbing grenades and finally running towards the gunners before they could swing their mounts or reach their rifles. Art and Clancy ran together knowing that their lives quivered precariously around them, bayoneting and kicking and punching their way into the sandbagged death mat where they killed two before the third surrendered.

Art was appalled at what he had done, but a crazed need for survival allowed him no time to meditate.

They moved forward from one depression to the next, jumping quickly out of some that stank with flesh and blood, and one that was filled with the trunk of one of God's holy vessels. During the course of that black day, Clancy and Art saved each other's life at least once. It was the day Art saw bloodied bodies flying up through the bomb bursts in reddened somersaults, allowing current reality to match his childhood nightmare.

In the murderous days that followed, Art saw a nearby shell burst dissolve a fellow human being; the soldier simply evaporated. One day as they were bombed by a German plane, Clancy raced forward into a disabled tank and used the still active machine gun to knock the slow moving bomber out of the sky. They were surrounded by acts of bravery and the opposite, and in this cauldron Art established the spine of his own manhood.

At night, stories of their fellow countrymen reached them. They heard about the Indian shoot of Alvin York, and the story to end all war stories, that of Dan Edwards, who amputated his own right arm to free himself from rubble before marching his prisoners away.

The American military advance proceeded slowly, pushing to close the creaking hinge that would slam shut the Kaiser's door, sweeping the stagnated western front forward on its fulcrum, knocking the Germans back across the threshold of the

Rhine. They were mostly untrained men, Wisconsin farm boys and New Hampshire mechanics, offering their lives in such great numbers that the sight of their piled bodies staggered the war-bloodied French and English, as if these New World cowboys, caught in the twirling coils of European history, had to pay their way into the global rodeo with an admission of blood. This the red baptism of power that gave America the right to conduct political services on the world stage, bringing with it the sacrifice of domestic innocence.

Metz was to the east, but the objective was Sedan to the north, so Pershing's newly formed army pushed forward toward martyrs' deaths along the Hindenburg Line, attacking with the Meuse River on the right, the Argonne woods on the left. Standing as a barrier on the other side of the river rose "Corned Willy" mountain, providing the Boche with a clear field of fire down onto the advancing American divisions that were stumbling through the marshes below. The men of the Prairie Division were ordered to turn and take the mountain.

After a major firefight crossing the Meuse, I Company moved toward the base of the hill on whose heights withering German artillery fire pulverized the Doughboys below. By platoons they fought ahead, coming in the late afternoon to an upland rise and, peering over the brink, saw immediately before them fields and woods descending towards a fast- flowing tributary that measured about thirty feet across. Their objective that day was to cross the cold white water and fan out for the next day's assault up the mountain. From across the stream in the trees, they heard machine gun fire a couple hundred yards to the left and right but luckily none directly in front of them, though the German rear guard in its retreat from the Meuse surely had constructed nests on the other bank that their own lieutenant was unable to detect with his field glasses.

"Hey! But look. A little to the left. They've left us a bridge."

It was a single arched stone bridge, a sturdy massive structure that had probably been there for centuries, with a narrow lane across the span that ran beside a rock wall on either side of the cobbled roadway. Slightly more than halfway on the bridge's opposite downslope sat a small tollhouse, cantilevered out over the fast moving torrent.

The lieutenant called over the sergeant, who in turn gave orders to Clancy. When he returned to his reconstituted squad, Clancy said, "We're elected. We've got to get down there and check the bridge. It's probably mined so I'll need a volunteer to check it out."

No one offered.

"For christ's sake, do I always have to do it myself?"

Art fixed his eyes on this newer bridge, bringing back all the horrors of the span that killed Maeve and O'Malley and Caroline. Momentarily, he held his life cheap, and totally out of character, said he'd take the assignment. Whether it was the war or the way it demeaned life or some bugle-blooded defiance from his thickly stubborn Irish past or a sickness with life after so many defeats, there was no sense why, but the words volunteered themselves before he could retrieve them and he would have to abide by their consequences.

Clancy, surprised at Art's decision, said, "OK. It's the kid from the fruit carts showing us a little something. We'll all go down, along that sunny part of the slope, and hold up at the edge of the stream—down there by that line of trees—while Mahoney checks the bridge. We have two hours of light. It's going to be a lot easier than swimming in that cold water and it'll save us time from building another one of those damned pontoon bridges. Maybe we can get the whole battalion across that thing."

The eight men left in the squad slithered down the hill taking positions along the bank. So far, no fire from the other side, though they could hear shots in the distance. Clancy motioned Art ahead with an encouraging nod of the head and watched him as he bellied along towards the mouth of the bridge, knowing something was wrong with the picture.

"The son of a bitch forgot his rifle."

For Art, it had been a conscious decision; rifles are an awkward nuisance when crabbing along the ground, like dragging a broken claw. Instead he borrowed extra grenades from a nearby soldier before inching forward. Seeing no wires or detonators, he slid along the cobblestones and began crawling up the age-smoothed rocks towards the crest of the arch.

He kept alert to any loosened stones or disturbed crevices where mines might be hidden. Fifteen feet along the stone roadway he was interrupted when artillery bursts started falling around him in the water—PLOSH!—and behind him. A few minutes later, his own artillery answered but with much greater frequency, blasting away at the Germans a quarter of the way up Corned Willy, obviously friendly fire called up by his lieutenant, who was watching Art's progress from the top of the hill. A U.S. observer plane flew overhead and after fifteen minutes of shelling, the racket stopped, first the enemy fire from above, then their own guns from the rear. Soon the smoke began to clear along the stream and Art, who had scrunched into a drainage hole along the wall, peered around. During the exchange, he felt the bridge shudder at least twice from direct hits. He looked for damage but all he could see was additional rubble ahead.

He didn't try to move for a long time. He looked back at Clancy who was visible behind him, and he motioned Art along as if to say the bridge was still intact, something Clancy couldn't attest to, but the lieutenant on higher ground was able to confirm its integrity by hand signals. Moving slowly, Art finally passed the crest of the bridge, now out of Clancy's vision. He looked back up the hill and saw the lieutenant urging him on. He wondered if they thought he was dawdling, but he was so frightened, time skewed out of control.

The tollhouse was halfway down the far side and Art felt certain a mine was cloistered inside, waiting to perform its requiem service. They'll be prayers in St. Anne's and a marker in the park but they'll be no grave box because there won't be anything left to bury, Art thought. He bypassed the structure, which appeared to have boarded openings on all sides. He squirmed all the way to the end of the bridge, past some blasted fragments. As he looked back towards his commanding officer on top of the hill, the first bullet zipped by his ear, then another. His whole squad was now firing into the woods ahead of him and soon the whole platoon had opened up, attempting to protect him. He sensed there were snipers, but instead of running forward and taking cover under the bridge, he made a crouch run for the tollhouse, pulled open the door fully expecting that he would be blown to pieces and then, reprieved, hunkered down, still alive.

But he heard the sizzling noise and luckily saw the wire and the mine. Missing his bayonet, he took the wire in his teeth and chomped it in two, his mouth bleeding. Bullets were flying around him and splinters from the wooden pieces covering the windows stung his face and hands. He crouched down in the tiny space, noticing that the trigger mechanism on top of the mine was still intact, six inches away from him. He dare not move, but finally found the courage to disengage it.

The lieutenant had waited long enough. He called for a second barrage on the far bank, instinctively knowing trouble was waiting across the river in the trees and sent the entire platoon maneuvering down the hill under cover of the shelling, meanwhile ordering Clancy's squad to rush the bridge. That's when the machine guns began hammering at them. The Germans, avoiding detection until now, under pressure themselves from the American artillery, had waited until this larger force came on the scene and immediately knocked down three of the attackers, who floated out of life belly-up. One of the machine guns was lined up with the bridge and locked on the remaining squad members who were splayed against the stones. It was heavy going now; fear reigned and death walked both banks. The lieutenant gave word to his own machine gunners and they lit their candles of hell's fire. Meanwhile, Art waited, huddled up in the stone house, his head between his legs, his combat pack protecting his spine from flying debris.

Clancy yelled to Moriority, "Crawl up there. Try to get under the bridge on the other side. Take Mahoney with you."

At that, debris from German artillery kicked in the door of Art's tiny citadel. Aside from additional splinters in his face, he was unhurt. Looking out the broken panels he could see the cart track. Alongside the narrow roadway was a stone-lined drain. That depression was as far as fate allowed Moriority to progress. He had been hit in the stomach and he sank into the depression.

"Mahoney, for god's sake, get me in there."

Art knew there wasn't room for the two of them in the small enclosure, especially with the defused mine sitting in the corner. He was not about to change places with his mother's harasser. He had already volunteered for suicide once this day and with the amount of flying steel still in the air, the day might yet demand its toll, so he decided to leave Moriority where he was.

The automatic bursts continued from both sides of the river, but it was a standoff. The platoon realized it was going nowhere until the German machine guns were silenced and the defenders could see that they had held up the American advance. Elsewhere, north and south, there was constant shelling and above them on the hill as well. Knowing that their own forces were moving back, the Germans who were dug in on the opposite bank accepted their fate, aware that their job was to hold the bridge as long as they could. But first there would be a short respite. The guns would have a chance to cool down. Even though the Americans had momentarily chosen patience, they knew nighttime would bring a resumption of the fighting.

Clancy and what was left of his squad had retreated back to the bank. German bridge blowers now edged through the woods. The platoon poured fire on them. Using howitzers, they kept the dynamiters away from the stone arch.

Noticing a wooden cover on the floor opposite the mine, Art moved his feet sufficiently to wedge the cover from its groove, and found a hole in the floor that looked down on the raging stream below, the hole about the size necessary to relieve a distressed tollkeeper. Or in an upright position, catch a fish.

Moriority's moaning was making Art sick. In the air the sharp smell of cordite.

Hundreds of years ago, what was collected in this tollhouse? Carrots from farmers, wine from neighbors? Who would profit here from easy transit? Not he. Certainly not Moriority, dying in the drain. Art knew he was never destined to cross over life comfortably, barriers had impeded his growth. He was stuck again at this collector's place where defeat meditated upon existence, crouched, practically in the fetal position. So, why didn't his catastrophic imagination encourage him to burst out the door and run down the bridge, lob grenades at the reluctant killers defending the hill who themselves would rather be home in a Brunswick bed? Because he knew they would kill him, that he would be dead before he reached firm ground, and pay the supreme tribute for such a rough crossing. So he waited, wondering what his patron warrior queen, Mab, would have urged upon him. Wondering as well who the hell it was that set the price of passage he chose not to pay?

What was his blind nation doing here in this trap sprung by devious ancient confederations, bedding with old whores? How many legions had crossed this bridge to nowhere, urged on by false promises, loaded with loot and doubt?

When it was dark and Moriority's gut no longer bubbled, Art heard a voice.

"Mahoney, are you in there?"

It was Clancy. Owen glanced at Moriority and gnashed his teeth. "Couldn't you have helped him for christ's sake?"

There was no reply, so Clancy said, "You forgot this."

Clancy passed him his rifle.

"Follow me."

Down the sloping bridge they went, followed by the rest of the platoon, the company and the entire battalion. All they found on the other side was darkness. The Germans had decided to skip.

But Clancy couldn't save Art later and Art couldn't save himself as I Company fought their way to the top of Corned Willy. It was shrapnel that hit Art in the right shoulder. Clancy, seeing his neighbor lying in the mud, called back for stretcherbearers and then continued forward with the terrible business of the day. Art would not reach the top of that hill and look east towards the Moselle and Germany beyond, or celebrate the end of the war standing on his own two feet.

The day he was hit, Art swung in and out of consciousness. He was being carried off the field in a blanket stretched between two rifles. Then he was lying outside of a tent seemingly forever, while screams of pain reached him, sometimes those of his own making, and someone stuck him with morphine that worked its way through the streams of his veins. Then there were field angels sewing him up and a long jarring ride and the next day an old convent. Another day passed into night, until finally he was taken back along the railroad to the cleanliness of a place called Angers. And the first night there while he was still half-delirious, a redheaded nurse came to comfort him. And he cried for himself and the world and his own history until a gruff voice told him to stow it and shut up and let other people get their sleep or they'd haul him up the hill to the flu barracks from which, they guaranteed, he would never leave France.

The Armistice came soon after and everyone in the ward got drunk including Art. A few days after that, he was able to sit up and then again in another few days, his mail caught up with him. There were six letters from Gracie and oddly, one from his father but none from his mother, and he tidily arranged them in order, reading the most distantly posted letter first. It was the last letter that informed him that his mother had died in the world-circling flu pandemic.

He was defeated again from any purpose in life.

* * *

People of the world will never forgive or absorb the disaster of World War I unless mankind can figure out a way to recreate that blood-soaked generation, raise it from its misapplied aspirations, and regather its lost accomplishments on some ghostly altar to wipe out the abiding sadness it caused throughout the century that their loss was avoidable. The careful nurturing of that polite generation and the sturdy loyalty of their patriotism was for naught, and much of what followed was an attempt to disguise the loss in gulps of undrinkable gall. That war could have been easily sidetracked and the cruelty of that knowledge drove good men mad and disfigured the good intentions of others for life.

*Connecticut Charles Ives, the fiery bandmaster, for instance, was 44 and he had written reams of joyful music to celebrate the American genius: pieces honoring Emerson, Hawthorne, Whitman, Lincoln, the Alcotts, Washington, Thoreau and Foster. He had glorified the American holidays of Decoration Day, Fourth of July and Thanksgiving. He had done what Glinka had done for the Russians, tried to give his country a national music, and encourage what Dvorak taught Ives' own teacher, who then misunderstood the message though Ives didn't. Instead, Ives took the parlor songs and band numbers and minstrel show tunes and arranged them in an explosion of creativity that was so ingenious and difficult that he was never given the pleasure of hearing most of his own music in concert. If that disappointment wasn't enough, the horror of the war then so unraveled his soul that he broke down and wrote little original music ever again, dickering with the million notes of his war-stunted scores. The country band atmosphere of his old world was dead and would never return and its loss nearly killed him. He saw nothing but chaos ahead; his times had evaporated in world conflagration.*

The Armistice came so fast that it took people by surprise. No one thought the proposed American campaign set for the spring of 1919, aimed at driving the Huns into Germany, would ever be cancelled. The war's sudden end dislocated whole nations; German troops bolted out of their trenches towards the Fatherland the night of November 11 to avoid conscription in labor camps; the English were prayerfully grateful that the slaughter was over; the French delirious. In America the outpouring of wrath against the German nation changed the country forever and gave it a taste for international politics. At war's end, there was a swirling paroxysm of joy. Yet some from the warrior ranks were in shock; T.R., bitter over his aviator son Quentin's death and Wilson's refusal to give him back his old regiment, would die in two months. Hitler, agonizing over the German surrender terms, would use the defeat as a rationale for unfolding the foulest iniquities of all time.

Shattered as well, Art eventually headed home. It had not been a Europe of grand tours and nights in Montmartre. He had seen the mud of Europe and little else. But the debt to Europe had been repaid, so his country was now free to grow up.

An ugly, unnecessary war, its worst episode the battle of Paschendaele in Flanders. Beneath that stinking hill lies the Tyne Cot cemetery, where thousands of the fallen—the common wealth of English-speaking manhood—are forever platooned together. Planted there is the tablet for one of that mudhole's victims:

*A. Merryweather*

*Some day, some time, we'll understand*

That day and time has not yet come. Will never arrive.

## Chapter 14

Once home, Art's unhappiness was so intense that he didn't perceive at first how quiet and dull the apartment was without his mother's voice and laughter. When his senses sharpened and he began to listen again, not just to the broken instruments of his psyche, but the sounds and then the smells of his parent's home, he was jolted to discover that the four remaining members of the family occupied a cheerless, empty place. Already Martin was hinting at the prospect of farming Marie out to Kitty's parents. How could three workingmen possibly care for a young schoolgirl?

His homecoming was more bitter than sweet. His mother's death, without tangibility in France, slapped him with its reality when he stepped into her kitchen where her apron still hung on a hook behind the door, her recipe book open on the counter. When he crossed the threshold of her store, he was able to distinguish her cologne from the smorgasbord of sliced-up delicacies and aromas. He again felt her loss when he entered into the shared remembrances, seeped in sorrow, of his father and brother and sister and friends.

He had never been closer to his mother than the time when she had nursed him following the long-ago deaths of Maeve,

Caroline, and O'Malley. Their mother/son relationship had since changed on his part from the instinctual love of a child, natural and flowing, to one of more intertwined feelings, based on the reality of accumulated affection rather than faith alone. Art had remained devoted to her, hardly distinguishing between his feelings for Kitty and the Virgin he prayed to. Mother love had always been a secure place in his cut-open life.

That first night home was agony for Art; he could hear Martin crying through the walls, a sound he had never heard before. Francis, on the other hand, had accepted his mother's death but his sister's eyes showed the lost child inside.

In the middle of that long night, Art woke from a fitful sleep to hear the soft notes of a piano. Turning over, thinking he was dreaming, he became increasingly aware of a melody, which hauntingly entered his consciousness. Now awake, he listened closer and heard the strains of Maeve's *Wild Rose* song. He shifted his legs out of bed and followed the sounds down the dark hallway until he reached the dining room and in the corner behind a screen he saw the keys of Maeve's piano performing the melody of her favorite song on her own instrument. He hadn't noticed the pianola when he re-entered the house earlier in the day, his thoughts crowded out by the experience and loss of the last year. But now, it was as if his mother and Maeve were welcoming him home.

"It must have gotten unstuck somehow," his father said in the morning.

Gracie came by, conflicted by his grief and aloofness, frightened by his bandages. She hardly recognized him. Deeper lines were etched across his face; she heard a throttled voice without emotion. When had the boy in him dissolved, Gracie wondered—the shy, introspective adolescent who protruded through the denseness of church doctrine, through his body's crazy teenage hormonal chattering and the ethnic stew of the South Side? Where was the personal melody he had played in a kingdom choir of boys? Gone to a throaty baseness caused by the choking of his slaughtered mates.

Gracie vowed to be patient and watch to see what would return and what would go forward. Maybe Art would soon warm and the song in him would come back. She remained subdued as he gained the center of attention in the neighborhood, being sure to smile back whenever he glanced at her, but chilled by a distracting coldness in his eyes where hard, unspoken questions seemed to be lurking. She remained present and accounted for, but her emotions yearned for renewal and personal re-connection. She needed something from him to refire her blood.

Celebrating their first Sunday mass together, the Mahoneys proudly marched down the aisle but bereft, like a cut-out portrait, no longer a whole family, an empty space where Kitty had walked. Much of the parishioner's attention was directed towards Marie, the motherless child, whose life and buttons were now fastened by stubby-fisted men. After church, friends hurried up to Art only to suddenly stop in front of him, unable to contain themselves, crying so hard that all he could do was hold them with his good arm, neighbors and customers alike. The flu epidemic had wiped out a half million American lives, twenty million worldwide. And had washed away Kitty Mahoney with it.

Sunday noon, the remaining men in the family took time to sit together for the first time in years and actually talk to one another. Like many postponed discussions among males, this one was awkward.

Martin began, "We've been lucky. We were able to live with an angel—have a woman who feared nothing in the face of love. She lived for her parents who brought her into the world, for me after we pledged ourselves, and for you that she gave life to. Struggling over steamtables and crusty black pans. Now we have to find a way to repay her," Martin said. "We'll keep her memory inside us holy and try to live a life that will honor her. But I'd like to see some outward expression as well."

Art searched for words, "Pa, I'm sick that she's gone. But it's no angel I see but a haggard woman who never had a chance to be herself—always wrapped up in somebody else's ironing. For what? So some Chinese pig farmer can track halfway around the world and spread his disease around the latrines and body-garbage of French trenches? She died because that stink spread across the world and she became a victim of its filth."

"Hold a minute with your talk," Martin said, who wanted nothing but a sweetened requiem and holycard memory. "Don't go turning light into dark on me. She deserves to be remembered well. That's how we do it in this family. In the end we stick together in the summing up. Don't try to degrade any life. Families should bind together at the grave."

"What about before death?" Art asked. "Is that all life is supposed to do? Make you tired? Is all we're supposed to have is a limitless capacity for pain? I'm not trying to take away from her memory. . . .Don't you think I remember her—smiling through the steam? Do you think I never saw her care for me with her eyes, telling me to pull up my socks, getting down on her knees, her face close up, with nothing but love standing between her eyes and mine, her fingers lacing me up?"

"Son, you'll have to keep some things inside—the good and the ugly both. What I'm hoping for here is to find a way forward. Not. . . .How do we cope ourselves?. . . .Or . . . What kind of a schedule can we put together for Marie? We don't have time or money enough to grieve in public, only inside ourselves. But, right now, what I'm looking for is some word from the two of you—not about practical things that will overwhelm us soon enough—but some pledge between us as to how we can honor her."

"I want to say something here," Francis said. "You're right, Pa, about remembering her. Maybe we can make some kind of memorial for her"

"How so?" Martin asked.

"Like trying to fix up that old church Back of the Yards that's falling apart. Maybe we can help bring it back clean again for Ma."

"That's more what I had in mind. Why don't you call the Bishop's office and check it out. . . .Does that sound right to you, John-Arthur?"

"I'll do anything you say," accepting the common restrictions that surrounded him.

It would have been disruptive to rage at the injustice of his mother's early death or spill his anger any further through the family. Barely able to control the fury within himself, he nevertheless had little choice but to agree to family, social and church conventions around him, all of which formed institutional barriers against his individualism. A side chapel with a nice bronze plaque might be dedicated to Kitty but where was his mother's lost pleasure in watching her family's growth and what of her grandchildren? And how was the anger of a spiritually dismembered son to be quelled?

That day Francis checked Scotty's toolbox and sought out the pastor at St. Claire's.

In the afternoon, Art dutifully resumed his stand at the deli, relieving Francis, catching up on the latest ploys of the Prairie Avenue gang. The hoods from over east had moved into the Garfield-Ashland territory again and, now that the war was over, were demanding payoffs, which Martin as usual refused to pay. There had been a patriotic interlude when their extortion had been suspended, but as soon as the Armistice came, the gang began threatening retailers in an effort to rebuild their dwindling treasury so they could properly welcome their older brothers home from service. This time Martin's petition to church and state went unheeded, owing to the welter of postwar matters still pending—burial of the dead, visits to the amputation wards, homecoming parades, monuments to be erected in the parks, American Legion posts to be built, baseball parties to be held in Sox field for the benefit of widows and orphans. Who had time for a couple punks over by the lake?

The only name that Francis could recall was Moriority's brother, who led an attack on him one night after closing. Art was livid when he heard about the assault on his younger brother, and grew to fury when he learned that the gang had been hassling Kitty just before she got sick.

Returning home had a sweet sickness to it, like the taste of gas in his mouth at the front. Happy to see his family and Gracie, he had thought of little else except their welfare.

As he said to Francis, "All of us came back feeling you can never escape what's happened to you. You're just a guy from the neighborhood and you have a girl like Gracie who cares for you. And before you know what you've done, you're forced to walk through hell. And it took its toll....There are things," remembering when he was buried alive in a shellhole with mangled bodies covering him, "I can never tell you. I'll try to be normal again but it won't be easy. Maybe get a job driving a truck and Gracie and me can get together, if she can stand the wreck I've become. And tinker with cars and skate in winter and learn a few new songs for the piano. But I'm not the same or ever will be again. But we didn't go to France for nothing and people will have to respect that."

Muldoon's, the neighborhood's drinking outpost, became Art's first stop one night when he finally stirred himself from the house with Francis in tow, both glad for the diversion. The saloon was celebrating one of the city's greatest sports victories—a White Sox pennant win—but Prohibition was coming soon to slam Muldoon's doors shut forever. Gracie, not yet family, said she understood that he had to let off some steam and carouse with his friends.

Midwestern cities clung to their drinking parlors even though the end was near. Standing on every other corner in Chicago, Milwaukee and St. Louis, was a saloon, usually anchoring a rounded two-story faux tower. These bars had been the city man's social center for thirty or forty years, famous for their pails and schooners of beer and roast beef sandwiches. But the bluenose battleaxes were about to close them down from one end of the country to the other. Saloons were in their final days of glory and every night reunions were celebrated, and the returning doughboys added to the cheer. There were other quieter places to research certain aspects of citylife, but if it was a question of ward politics or Sox baseball or local sports heroes, there was no better place to study than Muldoon's, for somewhere along the zinc bar was some old codger who could separate fact from fiction for those seeking the essence of any important civic truth. The saloon even had its own icons, the minor ones included old team photographs and wide angle shots of the Hibernian Society's annual dinner, but the most sacred shrine behind the bar, in an elevated central location, encased in glass, was the actual derby worn in the St. Patrick's Day parade of eighteen and ninety three by Bathhouse John himself—a dusty reminder of past favors, glorious blather and a corruption that the poor tolerated.

There Art found a couple of his old buddies waiting for his release from national and familial duties, and when he came in, he received a big cheer from the entire community—though most of the regulars only dimly remembered his face and only a handful his name.

"Oh, Martin Mahoney's boy. . . .That's the wounded one, I suppose."

"Martin, whose missus died in the flu?"

"Rest her soul."

There was much clapping on the back, and Art remembered out of the past that's how his cousins greeted him each summer down on the farm. Then handshakes all around with the usual questions.

"Which outfit was you with, son?"

"Were you in the big drive in them Woods? Must have been hell."

"And did you see them saucy mamzells in Paris, France? I'll bet that was something."

"What'll you have, buckaroo? It's on me and my brother Dick here."

Art didn't like being the center of attention, though he had been dreaming of his homecoming for a long time. In his own way, he quickly deflated their enthusiasm, quietly accepted their good cheer, urging them to get on with their drinking, because he wasn't going to give them a big show and dance and regale the assembled stoolpots with episodes of glory or tales direct from sin central. It was steady, slow Art Mahoney who was home, no special thing, home to a place that was no longer a home. But how would they know, and why should they care?

When the saloon had settled back into its usual confusion, spiked by bursts of laughter and odd bits of song, Art, Francis, and a couple of his old schoolmates slid into a booth in the ladies' parlor out back with its separate entrance for the skirts, except at Muldoon's few women would ever venture in except on Saturday night or for an after-mass pick-me-up on Sunday, and never alone. The men began to swap gossip and stories in the back room under the still operating gaslight, and after an hour or so, Art said what was on his mind.

"The way I've come to see it is like this. In some ways, I feel so bad that I'd just like to chuck it all in and bum around the world. And if I don't watch out, I can see myself as one of those rumheads out there, spending the rest of my life on a sore assbone. I'll never say it again but it was like the end of the world over there and to add to it, my Ma's gone and my family's breaking up. Hell, I've enough grief to sit on one of those stools for the next twenty years."

But it wasn't long before he began spending all his free time with Gracie. They were awkward at first. She reveled when she knew for certain he had survived, but when he arrived home and she observed him close at hand, thin and wounded, her second reaction was to put her own desires aside and allow him time to adjust, not realizing how long that process was going to take. Art was conflicted by the changes in himself, at what he had become and experienced, though he wasn't able totally to express his disgust or self regret. He assumed Gracie would not understand the terror that had afflicted him, but he needed her help to return to normality. He was operating on emotional empty and prayed for deliverance from the coldness in his heart. This left Gracie at a point in their relationship when her loyalty was tested and eventually a kind of rigid personal devotion set in hard. He wasn't prescient enough to understand the emotions that engulfed her, nor she his, but Gracie was nothing if not tenacious and gave him time to mend, submerging her own needs. What he did possess was a sense of personal pride that had allowed him to triumph over fear in the Meuse-Argonne.

Finally they could be alone.

"Aren't you going to ask me how I did while you were away?" Gracie asked. She stood with one hand on her hip in a neo-flapper stance. She had trouble hiding her forthrightness.

"I was going to," Art said with a smile, "but I was afraid I'd get an answer I didn't like. . . .But knowing you, I'll bet I'm going to hear it anyway."

"I never did a thing you wouldn't have been proud of. What I kept saying to myself was: Would Art approve?. . . .You can see plain I revolve around you."

He said, "More likely the other way around. You're the one who's the magnet. I'm just like those little iron filings that gets swooped up in your hand."

"I'll bet. . . .Did you think of me often over there?"

"Only every other minute," She knew it was the truth when he said, "I would have never made it through without you."

Thrilled by the reconfirmation, she said, "Oh! Art. Just hold me. Hold me 'til I pop."

They danced to the phonograph, a recording of a Kern show featuring a song called *Sir Galahad* about the days of knights and ladies with tall conical hats. But instead of getting Art's feet moving, the lyrics about legends and myths brought back old memories. How a knight would wear his loving lady's glove.

He touched the Tara piece around his neck.

\* \* \*

He didn't tell anyone, not even Gracie, what he planned to do about the Prairie Avenue gang, but he had learned in the army to take action rather than collapse before fear and adversity. He went out and bought some surplus grenades and a .45 pistol, the only kind of handgun he knew how to shoot, and waited for a Saturday afternoon when he assumed the gang's clubhouse would be full. He walked in the front door of the one-level storefront, withdrew the pistol from his coat and held it down at his side, planning to inflict material damage only. Inside, the Clancy gang members were preparing for a dance that night, decorations bright with patriotic flavors, as if they were expecting another contingent of returning veterans. He raised the pistol.

"All of you. Into the middle of the room," Art waved them.

The look of amazement at this first ever invasion of their sacred precincts by a mad intruder stunned them into obedience. To look at him was to know he was both willing and able to do harm, and none dared to experiment with his first six shots, though they could see that he held two more clips in his signaling hand. In his belt crouched two grenades.

"What? Who's this crazy man?" one of them asked.

"My name's Art Mahoney and my. . . .We run a deli on Laflin and I never want to see any of you within sight of it again, or I'm going to kill you. And if any harm ever comes to any of my people, I will bury as many of you as I can."

From under his coat, Art pulled out the grenades. Terror gripped his audience as he laid them gently on a table.

Art shouted, "I'm going to show you what I mean."

The members were shifting about in fear. "What are you doing, you fool?"

"I'm blowing this place up," Art said.

"Get the women out of here."

At that, a big guy with a patch on his eye, entered from a back room, and said, "Private Mahoney, my friend, what the hell do you think you're doing?"

It was Owen Clancy and Art was smacked with cross currents of emotions, happy to see that he was alive, concerned that he might have lost an eye, unwilling to have his mission here interfered with.

"No disrespect, but me and my family don't intend to live with your threats, so if I blow this place apart, maybe you'll understand that I mean what I'm saying. I'll give you thirty seconds to get out of here." And with that, he reached down.

"Hold! Hold! Mahoney, for god's sakes, listen. I'll personally guarantee that you'll be left alone."

Art looked at him, gauged in five seconds everything he knew about the man, remembered that Clancy had once saved his life along that bloody river in remote France, but that he was also the leader of this gang, nevertheless agreed. But to be sure they remembered him, he put a bullet hole through the glass case that housed Alderman Tooley's sash and stick.

"Don't forget your grenades, Private Mahoney. You're always leaving things."

They wanted to go after him, but Clancy would have none of it then or later.

# Chapter 15

Before Art was fully able to uncover all the layers of complex family patterns that beset his own household, he began spending more time with Gracie's kin, the Clevelands. That house was ruled by Mary Agnes, nee Coyne of Connemara, twice a widow. Her first husband, Kevin O'Flaherty from Mayo, was born north of his bride's harbor village. The young Irish couple had both entered the world on the edge of the tide; their fathers before them fishermen off the dark west coast of Ireland, the entry way for bitter Atlantic storms and the airy hallway of a million Irish superstitions, myths and dreams. The ways of the Irish West flowed in both of them, but Kevin died soon after reaching the mountains of Colorado following their emigration to the New World. Later, Mary Agnes married again and began her family. But Gracie's sailor father died when she was twelve and she would spend much of her life suspended between his love at home and authority out on the ship, where he practiced his seamanship for the better part of thirty years in Great Lakes traffic. Mary Agnes, his future wife, had snared his attentions when she arrived in Chicago, where she entered service as the cook and white-aproned slavie of a rich family on the North Shore. The Cleveland marriage had produced five living children, of which Gracie was the eldest girl. Altogether they were three sisters and two brothers.

Gracie despised her older brother, Will, who was pampered and idolized by his doting mother. Mary Agnes had a bad case of older-son favoritism, a malady that applied to many tribes but nowhere stronger than among the Celts. The pair—oldest brother and eldest-born sister—feuded along the baseboards of their crowded apartment. Whose bedroom was larger and how many occupants and how much time was allotted for an individual visit to the single bathroom that served six people— these were the issues that comprised their daily vitriolics.

"Walks around like a peacock," Gracie would say of Will, "and smells like the inside of a vanilla bottle."

Will referred to Gracie behind her back as "The Skeleton."

When Will proved to be a delicate passenger on the rough waves of Lake Michigan, his father choose Gracie for ship's company. By ten she had captured his freshwater heart anyway. He was only beginning to see the outlines of her maturity—that blessed time when a father sees his daughter miraculously emerge—before he suddenly died. Her father didn't live long enough to see Gracie's spirits grow into young womanhood, and the result was that his passing partially inhibited the development of her self-confidence. But, unlike Art, she chose to join in the life around her, wondering, even at an early age, because of her father's death and other dark beginnings, if she would have to pay later in life for force-feeding her maturity which became the growth and groan of the life she willed for herself through her nearly irrepressible nature.

Gracie also harbored a jealousy of others, namely, her next youngest sister, Rose, who was both beautiful and delicate. The youngest sister, Marge, still in grade school, was exempted from Gracie's enmity and became the scamp of the family, the pervading spirit of their Irishness and least likely to provoke envy. Last in line was the youngest Cleveland, brother Jack, just entering the tutelage of the nuns, lost without his father.

Of her siblings, Gracie and Art found Jack to be the one who needed nurturing. No plan between the couple was made without at least considering the possibility of including Jack in the day's activities. It was Jack who was most interested in his sister's soldier boyfriend and who pestered them for tickets to the movies and the circus. And as hard as he tried to substitute for Jack's father, Art could always see the drawn lights of sorrow in the boy's eyes. So, away Art would take the boy to enjoy every kind of seasonal activity. There was ice skating in the winter, boat trips on the lake on a summer's day, rides at Riverview amusement park, a trip to see the crack express trains to California and New York, their engines breathing quietly in their iron blankets, resting between journeys, a bare trail of steam snoring out from their banked slumber.

At the big Cleveland dining room table, there were different games for different ages. Grace, Art and Rose were teaching themselves to play bridge while Mary Agnes, Marge and Jack preferred Hearts. Will, the eldest, played a nervous game of poker but slapped his cards elsewhere with his cronies. Sometimes, Art and Grace would bring Marge and Jack over to Laflin to play a round with Martin and Francis and sister Marie. Once, when they brought Mary Agnes to visit Martin's clan, there was a little gossip under the stairs of the wide back porches in the neighborhood.

Mary Agnes was always ready, like Gracie, with an opinion.

"We're having one of Pa's sisters over for Easter," Gracie said to Martin as they played a hand.

"I'm dreading the day," Mary Agnes responded. "She's going to come over and wear her blackest dress and tell pity stories about how's she's aged and how ill she's been. She's younger than I am, lord's sake, and blathering on how she's suffered all these years though she's never seen a day's work in her life. Coming around gloomy as a closet."

"Puts a drag on the holiday," Martin suggested.

"On any day," Mary Agnes said. "But you know what I'm going to do? I'm going to pull out the whitest, prettiest dress I've got and come out looking like it was my wedding day."

"Which wedding would that be, Ma?"

"Hush, or I'll send the little people around to pickle your tongue."

It was 1919—a year of celebration for most but a duration of sorrow for the Mahoneys—a time Art hoped to launch out on his own and pull down a salary. Once home, he tried to carve an independent path but he was stymied by his father's hopeless sense of business and the messy family finances, so he threw his energy into working long hours in the store taking the evening shift after spending all day on the alley route, aware that the family had suffered a double loss and had worked grueling hours owing to Kitty's death and his absence in France. He owed them a commitment until the family was more secure, so he put off his own plans. As they were all quite hopeless with the cashbooks, Kitty's sister and sometimes even old man Rapp, who still maintained a share in the store, came by and straightened out the records, until Art could take over the task, teaching Francis in tandem, in the hope that the older brother could leave confidently and find some new employment before the other returning soldiers gobbled up all the good jobs. He was ready to break free and begin the business of setting up his own household because he and Gracie were beginning to feel the need of having their own place. To her credit, Gracie pitched in and came over to operate a Saturday shift in the store after returning to the neighborhood from her job downtown. Art, after a long day in the alleys, always knew where to find his Saturday night date, downstairs in his mother's apron. The pair would also rise early for first mass and rush to the store to serve the Sunday morning stampede. Even though working together brought the couple and family closer, it was mostly labor ill-spent because none of them, except Gram, who worked elsewhere, could cook worth a damn.

The need for a solution to Marie's upbringing was a constant worry in the otherwise male household. It was Gracie who offered an idea; by then she felt free enough to do so.

"I don't know if this makes sense or not but say when we get married and have our own kids, I'd have to stop working anyway, right? Maybe then, we could take in Marie, and after a time, she might even help us with a baby. Or babies," she said, poking Art.

He smiled at her. She was generous in all aspects of their relationship, and here was another instance. He realized he was afraid to lose her.

* * *

One bright hot afternoon in the summer of 1919, the family decided to pack up and go to the beach, leaving Gracie's younger sister in charge of the store

"All we'll miss are some ice cream sales," Martin said. "Time for us to be together as a family."

They had fought all year to maintain their economic balance, but Martin knew that he had to heal the heart wounds of his family as well, create some family memories, and try to instill fresh hope. Like a divine seeking the healing waters of some harmonious park, a cleansing spa that would wash away past sorrows, he led them towards the lake. What they all needed was a benediction by nature or series of experiences that would help knit them together again and rehabilitate their nest. So the senior Mahoney, against their dollar needs and shyly affirming family harmony, left the store in charge of Marge in an attempt to re-enact the closeness of normal family life. But because it was a forced solution, they moved through thin, artificial air that didn't encourage the breath of rediscovery. Instead, he led them onto the sands of a choking desert.

It was their one half-day holiday that year; it was all they could afford—a nickel ride to the beach. Martin, always thoughtful, supervised most of the day's details. The father with his two skinny sons and small daughter, along with Gracie, who had helped prepare the picnic in the back kitchen of the store, paraded down Laflin towards Garfield and mounted one of the new buses cranking towards the breezes from the lake.

They spread out on the sand in the white people's section, Martin grumbling about the stupidity of maintaining separate beaches for the colored who could be seen cavorting a hundred yards away, as if the water cared—the water of the wider world, not this provincial inland sea, that had washed oceans of black people, the first of mankind, for a million years. Down went the blankets and soon Francis was helping Marie build a sandchurch with an old spoon and a pot on holiday from Kitty's pantry.

Art and Gracie, wishing to be alone, walked down the beach, while Martin, lonely and deprived of Kitty, tried to suppress his frustration. He was good at that, the priest in him trying to suffocate his emotions, but even Marie noticed the sadness in his face.

Martin was proud of all three of them. Art had turned into a fine young man, even a brave one. In many ways, his eldest was like himself, steady and giving. Francis, though quiet, made up in inner strength what he lacked in personality and communication skills, but Martin knew which virtues were the more important. He had fathered even-tempered boys—on the surface at least—and a little dream of a girl, a child he didn't know yet how to manage, though he trusted his own instincts. But how was he going to help her navigate through girlhood with his wooden masculine code?

Martin's emotional direction, more and more, lay towards Francis. Now that Art was settling down with Gracie, their father turned his attention to his second-born. If I can get Francis out of the store, Martin thought, the boy might be able to apprentice as a carpenter—if I could only convince the union guy who ran with the carts. Francis had improved rapidly on the skills that Scotty had taught him back on the farm, adding mechanical skill to his wood-based repertoire. Or maybe, like he says, he's serious about joining the religious brothers.

Martin reviewed what the boy had told him in his quiet halting way. "Dad," Francis had said. "I want to ask your advice. I've been thinking about going into the church."

For the failed priest, it came as a surprise.

Martin tried to think back how his father, old Frank, reacted when he announced his intentions to take holy orders. He remembered Frank had been understanding regarding the loss of farm labor that would result from his son's departure, telling him he had to follow his star and let him go with a blessing. Martin knew he would do the same.

As Art and Gracie walked along the matted sand, down towards the colored section of beach, they passed a blanket party sponsored by the ever-appreciative Alderman Tooley—a gathering that included the same gang of hoods that practiced their extortion in the neighborhood. Owen Clancy was among them and the army pair spotted one another and nodded. They probably could never be friends, but their mutual respect, born in war, was there, along with a surprising lack of hostility that probably stemmed from some ingrained psychological tool that induced camaraderie among warriors. Battlefields breed humility. As the strollers reached the invisible separation line between the races, Art noticed that a young black man had crossed over into the liquid equivalent of whitewater.

"That black kid on the raft has crossed the line," one of the Clancy club members shouted. "He's going to pay."

With that, a couple of the more aggressive instigators from the O'Toole party rose and beefing up their chest muscles and strutting cockily towards the shoreline, began yelling, waving their arms. Then a dozen other members followed the first belligerents, Owen Clancy excluded, and continued to raise a ruckus, shouting at the prejudicially errant swimmer.

Perhaps it was a sexually competitive thing, the jealousy of seeing colored men anywhere near unclothed white women, the automatic conclusion that such potential union would be stained with strange passion. White men could barely understand that their shallow feelings could be overmatched by a sensitive black man able to share a deeper love with one of the illusionary vestal virgins, waifs still trapped at Victoria's altar but beginning to bob their hair and show a new found curiosity about unconventional lifestyles and experimental sex. And how did patient black women react when some knees-up white hussy came and took one of their beaux out of circulation, with flippy whitegirl skirts edging up her calves? Black men who had walked down the Rue de la Paix after the war with a pert French lady on their arm began to know something about their own attractiveness—the white guys, furious if any colored flirted with one of their missy's, became insanely enraged at any sign of integration.

"Why can't coloreds swim here?" asked Marie, back at the blanket.

Her father said, "Because we haven't learned tolerance."

"What's tol-rence?"

"That I have as much respect for you as for myself," Martin repeated the worn words.

Francis said, "People downstate better learn some of that."

A few months before in East St. Louis, a race riot had broken out and two dozen died over white indignation concerning the decisions made by Negro migrants from the south that had traveled north for warwork. The newcomers announced that they planned to reside permanently in the community. Hostility turned to murder. Who did these blacks think they were. . . . hanging around a white community? Time for them to go back to Dixie. Trying to improve themselves. Right in East St. Louis.

Here colored men down the beach heard the white guys shouting, and saw one of their own in potential trouble. Some of the whites began entering the water. A hollering match from both sides—"Watch you don't touch him."

"Stay over there where you belong."—"Leave him alone."— "Get the son of a bitch."

Rocks started to fly.

"Stay away from him," Art shouted from the shore.

"Don't hurt that boy," Gracie echoed.

The rocks knocked the boy off the raft. The whites began swimming out, punching at the boy—thin and black in the green water. Some black men waded in further down the shore, yelling in anger. The boy, filled with fear at the approach of this armada of white muscles, began to panic as blows landed on his head and shoulders. But the black men could not swim fast enough to keep the boy from drowning. Like sharks on a kill, the whites kept pummeling the boy until he sank beneath the thrashing waves of anger.

Owen Clancy was now yelling from the shore to leave off but it was too late. Fresh water poured into the unconscious boy's lungs. The two groups of men began throwing punches at one another in the water and others began brawling along the beach, and clubs and knives appeared from picnic baskets.

Art had a choice to make: go to the boy' defense or protect Gracie. He barely hesitated.

He pulled Gracie back from the fight, while Martin gathered the other members and began a retreat from the shore. Looking back, they could see thirty or forty, then sixty men battling in the sand, some down, some with blood on them, one in the process of dying. Word spread later in the day that rioting had continued further north along the shore.

"It's as bad as the war," Martin said, packing his young in a cab, not waiting for a bus.

Marie was trembling and the others were in high anxiety as they looked back to see people running from the fray.

For the next three days, colored and white gangs fought their way through the South Side, a full-scale race riot. Gangs erupted on the streets. Ragen's Colts came out in force along with the Shields and Hamburgers from Bridgeport. Some pulled blacks from streetcars and beat them. A sizable number of homes were burned and dozens of people cut up. Hospital emergency rooms bloomed red from the bloodied participants and, before it was over, a total of thirty-five died on neighborhood streets, more blacks than whites. Hundreds were injured.

Some of the clashes occurred on the Mahoney block. Gangs of both color had been seen, mostly at night, roving through the neighborhood, with arson the principal aim of the one and murder the other, which terrified the Mahoneys because not only was the store an easy target but because they harbored a child upstairs. They took turns guarding the deli, which they opened on a limited basis. From the front window, they watched the passing state militia, called up on duty, marching through the streets.

The night of the big battle on Laflin, Martin was on watch and saw the gang of thirty or forty coloreds coming from the south at the same time that an O'Toole contingent came around the corner from Garfield. The blacks, making a quick assessment of the other's strength, decided to have it out and a brawl ensued. The opposing groups moved forward aggressively into the heat of the fight, their colliding bodies mangling in blood-letting fury. Chains and knives flashing in the light of the lamppost, cries and shouts, hammers flying—a conflict of revenge and hate. It lasted about seven minutes, then the injured began whimpering away, the battle a standoff. Once enough blood had been traded, the combatants mutually gave way.

People, watching from above, began tentatively coming out of their apartments. A few barrel-chested guys, with clubs in their hands, arrived either late or in a well-planned tardy way. Neighbors surged through the battlefield, helping white kids that had been injured and pinning down the injured blacks until the police arrived. Martin surveyed the debris—a lost shoe, a torn discarded jacket, a dropped crowbar. As he stood there, a black figure, bloody and bent over holding his shoulder, slid along the side of the store.

"Mister, can you help me. . . ."

Tall and skinny, there were red splotches on his black skin.

"Come with me," Martin said instinctively, pulling the kid into the store, then helping him into the back kitchen before he collapsed.

Art, who saw the end of the brawl from an upstairs window, came down looking for his father, checking to be sure Martin had not been caught up in the entanglement, entering the deli through the back door. He found his father kneeling over the wounded boy, trying to stem the blood. The boy had a big gash on his head and as Martin began probing the boy's body, he uncovered the shoulder wound.

"Are you crazy, Pa? What are you doing?"

Martin, irritated, "What does it look like I'm doing? Let's get him down in the storm cellar."

Martin examined the welts rising on the boy's arms and the puffiness ballooning up on his face.

"For god's sake, you'll have the whole neighborhood down on us," Art said.

"That's right. . . .It's for God's sake," Martin said to his son." We'll take care of him for God's sake."

"They'll tar us all," Art said. "Where's your sense?"

Martin looked his son in the face. "Don't have any. Or if I do, it's a peculiar brand. Now go for the doctor." He seldom used a paternal tone; it wasn't necessary. But now he told his grown son what to do and commanded him to action.

"OK. But take a clean bandage and press down hard on that head wound," Art said.

"I will," said his father. "Go!"

Art flew out, dimming the lights as he did so, bolting the front door as he departed.

He found the neighborhood doctor busy with a roomful of injured whites; the medic's living room had turned into an emergency ward. Bodies lay on the floor, spoiling his wife's favorite rug.

"I need help," Art said. "Where can I get it?"

"Next block," the doctor said. "Nurse at 5716."

Art moved quickly along the pavement, skipped up the stoop, and began ringing doorbells until a chubby Irish lady came to the downstairs door, still in uniform.

"Bad injury. Up at the store in the next block. The deli. Can you come?"

Nurse Holahan found her kit and followed Art.

"Where's the wound?"

He heard the brogue and was happy to hear it. He knew from the war that the Irish were famous for their well-trained nurses. Plus, she might be more tolerant than the local angels in aprons.

"Bad gash on the head," Art said.

"Stitches?"

"Yeah."

"You OK?"

"Yeah. I saw a lot of it in France."

"Good. You can help me. . . .Hell to pay at the hospital these last couple days."

Police were flooding the street now.

"Come around through the alley," Art said.

He never told her the boy was colored. In her white uniform, she fairly fluttered into the back kitchen. When she saw the shade of the boy's skin, her eyes squinted momentarily and her forehead wrinkled.

"What's this?" she asked.

"One of the fellows," Martin said. Authority had returned to him and the tone of his priest's voice registered with the nurse's heritage.

Biological tension evaporated and the three ministers concentrated on the boy, the nurse examining the wounds. They crabwalked him down the stairs to the sub-basement. From upstairs, Art hauled blankets, towels and the extra cot. Meanwhile, bandages came flying off the shelf and small bottles from Miss Holahan's kit. In one corner, a space was arranged for the patient and an upturned box served as a dressing table. Soon, a kettle was steaming, the bleeding contained.

"You gonna get the police?" the black wanted to know.

"No. Don't worry." Art said. He was nearer in age to the youth and took on the role of confidant.

"Can I get out of here?" the kid asked.

"Hold still," the nurse said. "I'm going to put in the stitches. Then we'll get to his leg," where she noticed another wound.

"You'll be OK here," Martin said, holding the boy down during the painful sewing. "When you're ready, you can go. Meanwhile, we'll take care of you."

As brave as the boy was, he let out a couple screams that motivated them to close all the upstairs windows, steaming up the already hot-soaked kitchen.

"How you feeling?" Art asked him when they were alone.

"What do you care, white boy? Just be sure you don't squeal on me or I'm going to fix you good."

Art said, "Hey. Don't threaten me, kid. I've got more battle mileage on me than most."

The black kid backed off. "Just because I'm laying here bandaged up doesn't mean I'm some patsy."

Art said, "If you were tall enough to come into this neighborhood, nobody's gonna call you scared. But coming in to burn us out was nuts. What'd you expect—A fire department welcome mat?"

"Got to burn some of it down, buddy. Can't let you just drown our kids."

"I was there," Art said. "Bunch of nuts did that. Crazy people lit up with beer and hate."

"They was your color. Not mine."

"Stupidity doesn't know about color," Art said. "Problem is how to quit the fighting. I know it's not easy on your side."

"Not easy is right," the kid said. "Like being the only peach in a rotten apple basket."

"You know what the dumb part is?" said Art. "I've hardly ever talked to a black man before."

"Same likewise white."

"You'd think there'd be a way to talk before we up and kill each other."

"I guess we're starting here," the black kid said, relaxing for the first time.

"Yeah! Give it a try," Art said, as if he were talking to himself. ". . . .It was all such a bad beginning for you coloreds. What a rotten history."

"We don't see ourselves as part of no history—this country's, or any other white man's history. To you, we're just pieces of baggage on a boat list. Like we were packaged up and sent away. Families cut out and shipped like meat from the Yard."

"Suppose keeping your families together is the hard part."

"When we don't, it's because we don't have time to heal the wounds. Bad news keeps coming. The *Defender* says that already this year, ten of us have been burned at the stake. Not shot or lynched, mind you. Burned to death. What do you make of that, soldier?"

"There's nothing to say," Art said. "There seems no end to craziness."

"Gawd, this thing hurts," the boy said touching his scalp.

"Better rest now."

The boy stayed that night, Art beside him on the floor.

As caring a person as she was, Nurse Holahan brought the wrath of the neighborhood down on the Mahoneys. Elements of the Clancy gang, already disturbed by the family's exclusion from the extortion racket, quickly organized a group of vigilantes when they discovered the next evening that one of the coloreds in the Laflin raid was being coddled by the store owners. It wasn't that Miss Holahan meant any harm; being newly over, she simply didn't understand the subtleties of race relations on the South Side.

A couple dozen nightriders came under a dark and rainy sky. They came pounding on the front door of the deli rousing the pair in the rear. Both Art and the boy understood exactly what was happening when they awoke to the commotion.

"Out! Get out the back," Art told the boy, who was trying to get into his clothes.

Art ran to the front of the store just as the large window of the storefront caved in. Grabbing a broomstick he tried to knock the heads of some of the leading avengers who were trying to kick in the remaining shards of plateglass and gain entrance through the opening. As he flipped on the lights to better estimate the number of invaders, he could tell from the horde of voices that he would be outmanned even if he had the assistance of Martin and Francis. Art could hear them mobilizing for the rescue upstairs with much yelling out the window. He wished that he had his Springfield rifle. The pressure on the front door burst it open and in poured the defenders of the white race. Beating as hard as he could on the rushing mob, Art could not stop the intruders with their pulsating red foreheads.

"Where is he?" a couple of them shouted as they pinned Art to the floor.

A half dozen sped to the back but the open back door gave them their answer.

"He got away."

"This guy's not getting away."

They started a fire on Kitty's old stove. Martin and Francis tried to force their way in, but were soon in the same grip as Art, engulfed by the intruders. Some rope appeared and they were tied up as smoke poured from the kitchen.

"Crazy coots," Martin yelled. "I've got a little girl upstairs."

"We're all going to burn some day," one of them taunted.

After the trio was subdued, some guy yelled, "Help yourself to some ham and turkey. Then let's get out of here."

In another couple minutes, they could see flames shooting out of the back as they wiggled towards the smashed-in front door. There in her nightgown stood Marie.

"Get away from the door, honey," Martin said, as he and the boys loosened the poorly strung rope.

Art yelled to Francis, "Just open the water in the sink and let it run. Then get away."

Art pushed his father out, waited a moment for Francis, and then the four of them stood outside as neighbors gathered to see Kitty's dream die. When the firemen arrived, with a few Clancy fire bucks hanging from the side of the wagon, they let the fire burn long enough to demolish the store.

The fugitive patient, escaping just in time, had disappeared in the rain through the back alleys, moving as quickly as he could towards his home near the lake—the lake where the body of a black boy tumbled slowly through the dark water near the bottom.

\* \* \*

It was all part of the general horror the Mahoneys had experienced that year—a terror that had quickly extinguished whatever minimum joy Art's homecoming had brought.

1919—the weird year the gyres changed. The new times had attacked the Mahoneys with desperate fury. In that pivotal year people both looked back on the dead remnants of western civilization and trembled with fear and queer excitement at the birth of the unknown modern age ahead. Fate had descended on this one family; its star-borne time had arrived in swirling chaos, bringing confusion to the Mahoney's firmament. With blurred vision backward and forward, the Mahoneys were forced to wrestle blindly with the year itself. The deli was the first to go, and then Marie was shipped off to her maternal grandparents, the three men unable to lace her up or sew her buttons or provide her mothering. Hauling Maeve's pianola behind them, the male trio then moved to smaller quarters along Laflin and all three took part-time employment in an effort to maintain the fruit truck business, but soon that scheme became untenable, for without the disposition of excess produce in Kitty's active kitchen, the unfresh food on display in the truck lingered and soon turned their customer base toward greener suppliers. Finally, Martin sold the truck itself and they all found full-time jobs. Art, always interested in engines, found a job driving a laundry truck. Martin went to work as a sales assistant in a downtown office, and Francis, in true South Side fashion, put on an apron and went to work for one of the meatpacking companies in the Yard. The final chapter of their attempt to independently maintain the family off the farm that was once the bright hope of Kitty and Martin was complete—it had all came down to weekly paychecks. Their American dream had been cashed in and drawn down.

That part of their lives—their rural migration to the city— was over. The Iowa cow herders buckled into their urban uniforms—Art in his milky white suit and matching cap, Martin in his stylish go-to-town outfit, and Francis in his bloodsoaked butcher's hat.

Behind them, the war. And the feathered bird that the English called the Edwardian age was dead in its gilded cage. In America, the Ragtime era ended; on tap came the mind-popping acceleration called the Jazz Age, named after the rambunctious music that Martin and Francis had first heard Jim Europe play at the now abandoned Fort Des Moines. Black man's music destined to cross the watercolor line, beach rights or not.

# Chapter 16

Back into their lives again came Al, the boy orator from Nebraska. That fall, a certain itchiness in the general population had begun to express itself, pointing towards wilder times. Self-sacrificing idealism was on the wane. An erosion of values struck as the country's cynicism about the true causes and manipulative aftermath of the Great War mounted. The impact was demoralizing to a nation that had just feasted on a banquet of patriotism, left now with a bitter aftertaste of dead and wounded. Gangsterism would soon invade the city where previously the villains had been big businessmen and corrupt city and state officials. The final blow in Chicago came when it became known that mere baseball players could spoil innocent dreams, denting the nation's fans like a beanball to the head, leaving them dazed and bewildered. It was a deceit as big as El Dorado and the bunkum of Barnum combined, and somehow Al was involved in it—the infamous Black Sox scandal.

"You know how reporters are," Al said, when he came knocking at the Mahoney's door, suitcase in hand. "They hear rumors about shady deals, stray facts. Hear them before other people. Then there's this subtle subversion. The powers that be, they use reporters as go-betweens and before you know it, you're in a swamp up to your neck. The long and short of it is, the hypocrites in the cityroom have fired me and I need a place to stay. All kinds of bad actors are looking for me, so I hauled out before the riff-raff appeared."

As crowded as the Mahoneys were, they welcomed the rent money and were happy to assist their young friend, so Al came and stayed, giving the boyhood pals a chance to catch up on each other's lives.

"Sorry to hear about the wound," Al said, sympathetically questioning his army friend once they were alone.

"Better off than a lot of others," was Art's typical response. He knew he had been lucky. "So where did you wind up?"

"This is what happened," Al told him. "Because I was wiring up half the trenches in the division, I had plenty opportunities to get to know the brass at headquarters, so after awhile they kept me around to trouble-shoot any communications problems that popped up between HQ and the battalions. Then because I had a little experience on newspapers, I started to distribute *Stars and Stripes* on the side and began contributing some pieces. Me with my big mouth, I'm soon telling the editors how to run the paper. Before you know it, I'm in Paris in the propaganda section. It's an easy transition, if you have the knack. You just paint a happy face on the war and try to make everything smell good—a little publicity, some bending of the rules, some hokum and you can lick any problem. . . .So, now that I'm back, I decided to quit the papers and I'm going into the advertising business. I learned from those guys in the propaganda department that there's a formula for leading people by the nose, and all those bunkos from Paris are coming home to start advertising agencies, so I intend to be a big cheese in one of them. It'll be one part circus, one part vaudeville and three parts hoopla. It beats the tents and it's five times cleaner."

Al said, "And I've changed my name. Meet Allen Osprey, no more Al Osmond. That should keep the bloodhounds down. . . . What happened was that the guys who were fixing the World Series couldn't keep quiet, so word leaked to the papers that something fishy was up. I caught wind of it, put a couple things together and started to raise the roof. That's when the bad guys wanted to lay their ham hands on me. And I decided to find my old pal Art."

On the weekend, the pair of army buddies sat at Maeve's pianola decorated with its powerful wingspread eagle caught mid-flight in colorful stained glass, the militant-looking bird's fluffy underside tinged with red. They sat for hours laughing and playing—double-handed—the old songs, the ones that

Maeve taught Art, the ones Al played in the circus and at labor rallies, the novelty and sad ones both. And Al repeated what Ives said—that there must be someplace in the soul all made of tunes of long ago. Performed by these now grown men stitched together in pain and joy, who had overseen each others' path in war and peace, trying to connect old America and new.

The music made it easier to rekindle their once warm feelings for each other; another reconnection clicked into place when a few months later they found the successors of the artists and writers they had visited before the war. Chicago's cultural caravan was now parked downtown at a different German restaurant, a sausage and sauerkraut hangout with dark paneling that framed paintings of jolly and rotund monks acting up in their wine cellar. Among the missing guests this time were the China hands that were all off helping Sun Yat-sen insinuate democracy onto imperial slaves, a task doomed to failure. But the newspaper scribes and book writers still gathered together.

When Art and Al entered Schlogl's restaurant in late1919, the Midwest Renaissance was winding down. Finished with his job as itinerant Socialist, Carl Sandberg had written his Chicago poem, Masters had published *Spoon River Anthology*, Sherwood Anderson was serializing *Winesburg Ohio,* Vaschel Lindsay had written *General Booth Enters into Heaven* and

Dreiser had completed most of his Chicago-based novels. T.S. Eliot, living in his new country, had already published *Prufrock* thanks to Harriet Monroe, who was still printing *Poetry* magazine. Piano-playing Margaret Anderson, the gorgeous one, currently home for a visit, had transplanted to the West Village and was serializing *Ulysses* in the *little review*. Almost on stage was the region's budding contribution to the 20's midwestern flowering—Hemingway, Fitzgerald, Lewis, MacLeish, Wilder, and Virgil Thomson. Within another year, the Chicago Crowd would be a national institution and there would be a round table at Schlogl's years before the Algonquin carved out its more publicized version.

Again Al and Art sat with the raucous news reporters, print yeomen under the daily scrutiny of the omniscient memories of their older editors. The last time the pair mingled with this group, they had collectively produced a publication called *American Centennial* whose profits kept its authors in beer and pretzels at King's restaurant for a month. That was back before the war when people cared more about their traditions and beliefs and stood or fell on their reputations. Since the war, there would be no looking back and less interest in family or society credentials. It was "right now" that counted.

"Al! Where you been? We heard you sold out to an ad agency. What's that name again—Barnum, Hokum and Steerwrong?"

"Anybody remember Barnum's fish story?" one of the older editors asked. "When *Moby Dick* was published. . . .Barnum goes to Newfoundland and hires a fishing rig and tells these clamdiggers to go out and find him a white whale for his museum. Can you hear the fishermen now?. . . .'Which way do we row?'. . . .And when these guys don't find one, he sends out two more expeditions and spends a lot of money. Finally he lands a whale and somehow—not so easy to do with a mammal that size—paints it white and sets it swimming in his aquarium on Broadway. . . .The sheer balls of the man."

The stories continued until one of the writers conjured up a new game. The lowly scribblers of the daily press were challenged by the acolytes of Apollo at the next table to upgrade their daily doggerel. In those days, there was a penchant among publishers to run considerable lines of verse in their papers. The aim was to entertain the public by fashioning slick, smart language, a practice the aesthetes found to be in doubtful taste.

"We're merely attempting to get you to raise the standards of your poetry," a regulation-size thin poetess called over to the penny-a-words.

An editor tossed back, "Madame, we have the unfortunate obligation to be certain we're understood by our readers, a feature your work sometimes overlooks."

"You can cater up or cater down, you know. Jokey verses don't have to be the only thing you serve up."

"They'll be going at it now," Al leaned over and said to Art.

The upshot was that the two tables decided they would write a collective piece on the origins of the midwest, and for the next few hours scraps of paper were floating through the air, criss-crossing the room like the knotted daisychains that festively stretch across a Munich beerhall, some of the more worked-over lines soaked in lager.

The poets were more aggressive this time, and the major part of the product was concocted among the more flamboyant opera-cape and walking-stick crowd.

"What shall we call it?" someone asked.

"How about something to do with the Northwest Passage?"

"How about just the *Midwest*?"

Soon language was emerging:

A frozen-eyed force walked the wavy iceland
And from its parted lips came a cloud of frosting air.

    Crystals floated down the shifting floe,
    And before the light fell away
    A drifting whitened form appeared.

    Snow for ten thousand years heaped high
    'Til overwrought the massive pile
    Began to slide a yard a year.
    In an eon's time, inclement mountains
    Hid within the bosom of the mass
    And cascades flowed before its tumbling crest.

    In the hulk, cold claws tugged up primal rocks
    And roughly yanked them south
    Past sleeping blocks of ice
    That gouged out pockets of frozen lakes.
    Subterranean avalanches laden
    With the black savings of scraped-away forests
    Roiled in the undertow.

Then around a corner of the universe
Came the sun dismantling the ice-blue heap,
Massive rivers running off its fingers
Dammed into great pooled lakes,
Or sprung free to flow down the continent.
Until crumbling, the glacier withered where it stood.

The force now spread its settling hand.
Hills dropped out of the ice.
Slush melted into fresh ponds.
Washed away black soil covered the central plain.
In misty evaporations, upland formed where
Kettled smooth, long hills left evidence of the
                                        vanished giant

Art, not interested in the poetic exercise, disappeared and
followed the sound of music into the adjoining banquet room.
In one corner, the most beautiful woman he had ever seen,
immaculately turned out, sat at the Mason & Hamlin playing
MacDowell's *To A Water Lily*. They were alone and she
glanced up and smiled as he approached. He saw in the woman
the spirit he had known in Maeve. People spoke of
extraordinary women in those years as "temples" of beauty, art,

and grace. By that standard, this woman a cathedral. He stood by the piano—a grown man of combat—and was unable to stem for whatever reason the tears that spontaneously began to saltslide down his cheeks. When she looked up at him and offered him an angel's countenance, he drowned in the bluest pair of eyes he had ever seen and saw that she was crying as well. Only the music passed between them, never a word. They exchanged faint smiles. When she finished, she rose, touched his arm, then his face, kissed his mouth and walked away.

Though emotionally drained, there were some feelings and expressions of beauty he could not resist. But could not retain.

\* \* \*

In succeeding weeks, friend Al and Gracie began to hit it off, both outgoing and talky. Once when they were alone, they had a chance to gossip about Art and discuss what their futures held.

"Art. He's the best kind of friend," Al said. "Never expects anything. Always there for you."

"He's been loyal to me and that's what a woman really needs to feel."

"The two of you are going to have a good life together."

Gracie said, "It'll work out. Might be hard along the way. Art doesn't have much more sense than his Dad when it comes to making money. But I love him, so I'm sticking by him."

"I don't mean to tell you your business," the Wiz said, "but Art's not going to take life by the horns. Just because he's playing it safe doesn't mean that you should just let life work you over. That'll make you smooth as a stone and just as inert."

"I sure would like to spread my wings a little."

"Gracie, you've got the spunk to do big things and spunk's all you need to get by. Let me introduce you to some guys downtown starting up an ad agency. They could use a scrappy girl like you."

"I'm still not sure about that advertising stuff. I hear some of it on the radio and it sounds a little puffy."

Al said, "It's all baloney. Everybody knows that. Except it works. But so long as you know it's bogus, you put on a straight face, deal with it and collect your coppers."

The idea, once introduced, appealed to Gracie, and before long, Al had placed her in a start-up agency that was showing promise of growth.

However, the year's bad streak continued to spread its stain when Art began his new delivery job. He was immediately swept up in the labor trouble rampant that year; the teamster's union was soliciting all truck drivers to unite, including the six drivers at Commonwealth Laundry. Desperately needing the pay and threatened with dismissal if he went on strike, Art was caught in the classic squeeze between those that hired and those pushing for worker's rights. But the organizing effort soon collapsed and Art, happily, was able to hold his place without violence, loss of pay or pride. Throughout the country, it was the same. Choices had to be made, but the power of ownership usually won out. People simply wanted an end to all forms of fighting. So, the union movement went into serious decline, while American socialism itself died and widespread reform was buried with it. People were sick of conflict and Republican normalcy took over. That's how the twenties came dancing in.

* * *

Art and Gracie remained sweethearts month in and year out without finalizing their vows. Instead, with unspoken sureness, they took it for granted that their relationship would culminate some day in a life together. Difficult as it was to deny their emotions, they knew they were bound to each other on a deeper level, in the marrow of trust. When they embraced and kissed, passion would ignite their flimsy resistance and it took willpower on both sides to restraighten their moral lines as well as their rumpled clothes and hair. What they would give to make love in their own place. Neither of them had ever slept with another, and they maintained separate fantasies as to what pleasure marriage would bring. Gracie would become excited when they slipped into the park to lie on the grass and hold one another. Afraid to let her passions run free, she angrily fought them off. He would ask her what the matter was, but she would evade his questions.

Most of the time, they spent their leisure hours in each other's apartments. Art maintained friendly ties with Gracie's two youngest siblings, Marge and Jack, all of them content to play jokes on one another, the younger ones comfortable enough with Art to awkwardly display their growing independence. Gracie would tell stories about the advertising agency where she was working and Art would tell funny tales about delivering laundry to the professors, gangsters and other characters to whom he carried his starched goods. Art would sometimes ask if Gracie ever saw Al, and she said she would see him sometimes walking along Michigan Avenue with his friends, smoking and laughing.

"Say hello to the old wizard," Art would say, "the next time you see him."

Often, they listened to Ma Cleveland's stories about her childhood in Ireland where her grandfather owned fishing boats and how she would sail out with him from Ballynakill Harbour toward Clare Island on a summer's placid day and tales about her Lake Michigan winter exploits with husband Bill Cleveland racing into port against the thickening ice of their inland sea. Ma would reach back and reminisce about her arrival in the eighties and tell about the time she worked as a serving girl in the big house of the publisher on the North Shore, and stories about the two daughters in the family, emancipated at an early age, who embraced Mary Agnes in their liberal views and billowy sleeves.

"They used to come in the kitchen and arm wrestle me for the cakes and pies," Ma Cleveland said. "Hellions they were. Smoking and sassy—long before the new century. Not like them puny eastern girls that the boys would bring home for Thanksgiving. My girls were healthy, would come to dinner in their riding britches if they chose, even when everyone else was dressed in diamonds. And careless! They would leave expensive jewels thrown in drawers. Spunky midwestern girls—all spit and no curls."

Ma Cleveland was easy to like and she had friends everywhere, including all the blacks for whom she cooked lunch in the steel plant. The men, black on black from the furnaces, would bring her presents, things they had carved, and show pictures of their children. And she would bring discarded clothes from her growing children and those of her neighbors and lay them out on a table in the mess hall with a little sign that invited the workers to help themselves. Chicago, of course, had been balkanized by rivers of immigration from Slovenia to Slovakia and Poland to the north and every place in between and she befriended them all. Many in the country still boasted about the old myth of helping neighbors, but for most that was a recitation of a memory of something gone by. Now a worker helped himself, then his family and then maybe his own kind. General sharing had once in fact been the mainspring of a much-lauded American generosity, though it was in truth a passing farm custom. But Ma Cleveland never forgot others in need, those who like herself had uprooted their lives and instead of finding life easier, discovered drudging work here.

Gracie had inherited most of her Ma's better qualities, maybe not the openness across racial lines, but they both acted boldly and glad handed everyone up and down the street, friends to all, squandering the richness of their liveliness on any citizen walking by. But Gracie lived behind a few closed doors. Art thought her moody moments were mainly a result of her problems with her older brother, but in reality there was another reason, sibling jealousy. Her more attractive sister Rose had a rich beau from a wealthy family who sported her around in a roadster, and Rose had managed to mature in a more agreeably social way than her older sister and was by far the best student in the family. For Rose, there were fraternity parties in Champaign-Urbana, and she was popular up and downstate with a ready smile for all, but a warm heart for only a few.

Will, the mother's favorite, was often absent. He worked for the railroad and was often called down the line to Elkhart or Toledo, where he trained with other clerks of the yard. When he was home, he expected extra privileges as the male head of household, rather like a crown prince, and unfortunately Queen Mary Agnes catered to him. Art shared his dislike of Will with Gracie, who battled within the family against any concessions to her older brother. Meanwhile Art tried to hide his true feelings, remaining as best he could aloof from their ongoing internal squabbles so as not to interfere, trusting he could better arbitrate when something important occurred.

As the twenties blossomed and the real twentieth century began, cultural and political unrest swept the world as it tried to digest the loss of its millions of dead from the flu and war, as well as the impact of new forms of thought and government like communism. But the Mahoneys and Clevelands swayed with the minimal tides of their backwater and experienced little of the world upheaval, except for transitory changes like the new women's fashions. There was definitely more talk about money and material things and less stress on religious and ethnic matters. Sexual barriers were burning down too, though there was considerably more smoke in this cauldron than fire, as old norms tend to die hard. Church attendance at mass remained high, but parts of the service became routine and oftentimes there was a hollowness of conviction, as if most parishioners slept-walked through Sunday service while only a few practiced its strict tenants on a daily basis. The world had speeded up and some things were left behind. Generally, people were more lax. Buttoned up Puritanism was unzipping, replaced by a loosening of older ties and rites. Art followed the changes in his haphazard way both on the street and in the papers, reading about the migration to the cities, the introduction of speedier trains, and random observations such as the fact that there were fewer eagles along the Mississippi. But moral losses were hidden in the whirlwind of activity that spelled out the new decade's impatience.

"I think people are less sincere nowadays," Martin concluded.

\* \* \*

By Christmas of 1922, Gracie and Art had been keeping company for five years and they decided to announce their engagement. They couldn't afford a party, but some of their friends and family chipped in for a New Year's Day buffet. He had a hundred sixty dollars in the bank and she had a hundred and seventy-five, so they opened a joint savings to better discipline themselves and each agreed to add two dollars a week to their account book where they were happy to see their names registered alongside each other. To scrimp, they ate with their respective families, attended free dances at the church, stayed home and played cards after meals, and only rarely splurged on a quarter movie. They were confidant that they could stretch out their loyalty a little longer and marry in a few more years. They were both appreciated at work, she typing away on ad copy and he exchanging dirty piles of linen for clean. The dream would materialize. They just had to hold on.

What shortened their wait revolved around the rivalry among the two older siblings and their competition surrounding time spent in the Cleveland bathroom. It came to a head one holiday night when Art came by to pick up Gracie. They had planned all week to ride downtown and see a movie in one of the new oriental palaces that had been ornately designed to display the celluloid dreams of Hollywood. When Art arrived at the Cleveland apartment, Gracie had not started to dress; she was angrily ranging through the rooms in her robe, yelling at her brother Will who was ensconced in the bathroom. Intermittently, she would pound on the door and Will's only response was to turn up the water volume. Appeals to her mother who never criticized her eldest child went unheeded.

Gracie spoke sharply at the closed door, "Art's already here, Will. Please get out of there so I can get ready."

She was so upset she began to cry and Art tried to soothe her, saying that they had time, or as the minutes passed, suggested that they postpone their show date to another time. By then, Gracie was screaming through the door.

"C'mon in the bedroom, Gracie," her youngest sister said. "I'll help you get dressed," steering her towards the room where the three sisters slept. "You'll look pretty. Don't bother with that gorilla."

Gracie's anger and frustration was so great that it took Art two hours to calm her down, alternately walking aimlessly along the neighborhood sidewalk, and then retracing their steps to the park where they could hold each other in the cold night while she cried some more. Enraged by her brother's insensitivity, and sputtering out the belief that his actions were deliberately meant to demean her, Gracie said that she was going to move out on her own. She couldn't take it any longer even if it meant she and Art had to postpone their wedding.

That's the night they decided to get married and that's what they did one sunny day in 1923. She wore a white flouncy gown, cut mid-calf to show off her white pumps, her belt low and wide in the twenties style, with flowers tucked in the loose enclosure of her bodice. She wore a short string of fake pearls and long earrings, and a brimmed hat with buds aloft. Art, tall and grinning in his new dark suit, topped off his outfit with a fedora propped on his head in such a way that it seemed to have a life of its own. The bottom of his trousers were still riding above his shoes, cut in the style of the Irish revolutionaries, whose careers he followed in these, their troubled times. At the last minute they invited Will though they mainly ignored him. When they had threatened to act out their anger and keep him away, Ma Cleveland started piping up a song of filial loyalty and forgiveness. Trying to maintain the peace, the family congregated amicably, her sisters as bridesmaids. Young Jack Cleveland and Art's brother Francis stood beside the groom.

Instead of the usual honeymoon, which they could not afford owing to the purchase of a suite of used furniture, they changed clothes after the ceremony and, following a dessert tea back at Ma's, they took an excited Jack downtown with them for an excursion out on the lake aboard the *S.S. Wilmette*. They arrived back in their one-bedroom place after enjoying a full day, including pot roast at King's restaurant, ready for the long-postponed journey through the wide tunnel of dreams where they could brush off the dust of reality and settle into each other's arms as they listened to the music from Maeve's player piano that followed them to the new apartment.

They were both so flustered when it came time for disrobing that they hardly spoke; her throat was choked and his stomach was jumping. They dressed in their new wedding sleepwear, she in a flimsy gown and he in his pajama bottoms, and when she entered the room, they were both so embarrassed they couldn't speak. They lay down and held one another and he began prodding around under the blankets and neither of them had any idea what they were doing. Art had this protuberance sticking out and he tried to poke around but she was so afraid of his advances that she trembled with fear and apprehension. She didn't know what he was trying to do; all she could feel was pain, and soon she detected blood. Her whole body revolted against his efforts, and because he had no experience either, Gracie became hysterical, crying and accusing him. Until finally, she got up and dressed and Art in pure mystification watched her go out the door and back she went to her family. It had been a mortifying experience for both.

Gracie came weeping to the bosom of her family that she had permanently left only hours before, falling on her mother's breast. Ma Cleveland pushed the younger children into their bedrooms while Will stood there and began grinning, and for the first and only time in her life, Gracie heard her mother raise her voice in anger at her eldest child, who was so shocked that his only reaction was to escape to the bathroom.

Her mother calmed her. Now that she was married, Gracie would need to learn of the intimacies of sexual partnering. The daughter was appalled by this amorous information, frightened by its animalism and shuddered at the prospect of performing such bloody bodily functions. It all sounded like a great deal of writhing around, not unlike what she and Art just managed.

"Is that what that funny uncle was trying to do to me when I was seven?" Gracie asked.

"Don't talk to me about that scum of a brother. I nearly killed him for trying to harm you."

The complications of sex jolted her.

After talking for an hour, Ma tried to make light of a woman's innocence about such things, said it wasn't so unusual what happened. Her mother tried to assuage Gracie by convincing her that a conforming lack of sexual knowledge governed their times and she was only one of its victims.

"Then why didn't you say something to me?"

"I thought you'd hear about it on the street. . . .Now, you'll have to go back to Art."

"I can't."

"You must go back. There's no place for you here. We've already changed your girl's room around and sold your bed."

Ma commanded Will to walk Gracie back to the apartment, a march they accomplished in silence. Art had been demolished by her departure and when the door handle turned and Gracie returned, they flew into each other's arms and she quickly undressed and returned to her spousal place. They held each other quietly for a long time.

"I'll try it again if you want," she said.

"Just sleep," he said and they cried together quietly before slipping off.

The sexual deprivation of the young, caused by the teachings of the church and maintained by refrigerated families and the real fear of pregnancy had smothered their natural instincts and had reached out to spoil Art's and Gracie's beginnings.

With all that, they had a beautiful remainder of the summer together. Romance in the midwest often blossoms seasonally, on July and August nights, and almost always near a lake, either along the shores of the five great ones that wound around their lives or some other damp enchantment—Lake of the Clouds, Land of Lakes, Chain O' Lakes—god's tears. Lovers with ukuleles strumming and singing *We were sailing along on*

*Moonlight Bay*. . . .Promises made, some kept, floating in a canoe on fresh water pools, Indian names mostly.

Vocalizing, "... *You have stolen my heart. Now don't go way.*"

Music drifted across the water from the dancing lights of the lake club. "*And we sang love's old sweet song on Moonlight Bay.*"

Art and Gracie knew about fashionable Lake Geneva—Rose's beau had a family place there—but the newlyweds never rode beyond Fox Lake, closer to Chicago, and easier to reach by train. By the end of that first summer, because Gracie was already pregnant and owing to their finances, they spent just one weekend away. They called it their delayed honeymoon and walked along the shore, losing their way in the dark. In bed, more adventurous now, Art with softness and Gracie with her hand on him, stimulating him with that dare-you look she had. The pair, close in embrace. *Love's old sweet song.*

## Chapter 17

There were times in '24 and '25 when Art and Gracie were content if not genuinely happy. There were soon two baby boys that needed care. With their births came a growing feeling of accomplishment that any decent family can bring its members. Other Mahoneys were moving on with their lives. Martin, dapper as ever, had taken up with a younger woman as he neared retirement, the young woman a sister of a prominent monsignor, a move that kept Martin within the hierarchical boundaries of his youthful calling if not his vows. Uncle Francis, unmarried, held a white-collar job at Armour Packing in St Louis, his position signaling a personal family victory—the rise above the slaughterhouses that had sustained the Mahoneys when they first arrived on the South Side nearly thirty years before. Curiously, Francis's mentor was an ex-boyfriend of Kitty, who had been disappointed but open-hearted about his loss to the young seminarian. His mother's old beau took Francis under his wing, a generous act of personal loyalty, perhaps upholding some ideal that Kitty had inspired, as if having once pledged himself to his lady fair, he was automatically indebted to her offspring as well. Thus this third-to-last encounter between the Irish Mahoneys and German-based Rapps was a peaceful employment arrangement. In addition, it gave Francis the opportunity to expand his church-building mission to Missouri. He was always on the lookout for fallen chapels, ready to reapply broken stones. People who knew him kept suggesting he was needed more in Ireland, littered as it was with liturgical ruins. Meanwhile, sister Marie, in school, resided with her grandparents, working part-time in the Rapp deli, keeping her expectations, for now, low.

Baby John-Arthur Junior came first, then Matt in '25. In the beginning, Gracie continued to work part-time, thanks to home help received from her side of the family. With the expense of a larger apartment further south on Laflin to contain his growing family, Art took any driving assignment he could find to augment his day job. He'd be up half the night making express deliveries or spend Sundays jacking furniture, keeping a step ahead of the bill collectors. He prided himself on his driving skills and had a knack for tuning car engines, eager to tear them down or find a replacement for an old chassis.

Midwestern guys thrive on annual trips to get away from the trials of domestic and wage-earning conflicts, places where they can swear, drink, smoke cigars, play cards and piss on trees. Most liked to go north to fish and hunt, camping out near cold lakes deep in the Great Woods along the Canadian border. But

Art's passion was to see fast cars run hot. He and his buddies with oil-soaked pants preferred to make their yearly jaunts in the opposite direction, toward Indianapolis where they could watch the fastest cars in the world spin around the big oval on Decoration Day. He and his friends would streak south—masses of people and shrieking racecars only hours away—days lit loud with the screaming sounds of the 500's engines. The Chicago guys would arrive at the speedway the day before in time to catch some of the preliminaries, eagerly computing the chances of their favorite cars and drivers to win the main event. Then sleep in their borrowed car to watch the final race. The spectacle sustained Art throughout the year until he could again drive through the night in order to suffer near-death by dust and oil fumes, and thrill to the fiery competition.

At home, John-Arthur Junior grew into a beautiful baby and his Aunt Marge gave up school to care for him when Gracie returned to work. Marge had turned out to be warm and bubbly teenager, sly and less edgy than Gracie, a more giving person with a good sense of humor. She adored the couple's first baby, hoping the experience would be a prelude to her own dreamshapes.

Marge, tiny and thin, featured bobbed hair that fell slantwise across her forehead. Fun to be around, she was a great kidder and adored men of all dimensions and types. She was only 14 when she first came to take care of the Mahoney offspring, leaving the classroom and the nuns behind. Though poor families like theirs sacrificed much, even in the relatively prosperous twenties, they struggled to maintain their pride. But they never gave in to sloppiness, appearing in public on Sunday in immaculate and even stylish outfits. Gram Cleveland's three girls, taking after the old girl herself, were a vivacious trio.

Weekdays, Marge would rise before dawn, walk across the neighborhood and be feeding young John-Arthur by 7 AM, allowing Gracie time to get downtown to her desk in BBDO's secretarial pool. Art, wearing his ice-cream suit, would have already been underway on his laundry route by then. By mid-afternoon, part-timer Gracie was back home, allowing Marge to get ready for her night course at secretarial school. If toil was the curse of the working class, the whole of the South Side seemed damned. But it was a feisty kind of damnation. As in....God, we know you're only testing us.

Substitute mother Marge, hardly out of dolls herself, had the responsibility of caring for what she considered to be the perfect image of God, a baby boy. She doted on little John-Arthur, tended his every need and helped Gracie out with laundry and dishes when the baby was down for a nap. The next year, along came Matt doubling her work. Marge worked for little or no money and with a good disposition. Bertold Brecht was not the only one to find a saint Back of the Yards. Even happy-go-lucky Jack Cleveland lent a hand, usually in the form of running errands. The Mahoney boys' raising became a family project. When Gracie was feeling better after the second birth, she remained at home, freeing her sibling to find work of her own. As the youngest girl, Marge had helped hold Gracie's family together, the best kind of a sister gift.

Luckily, neither of the babies was too demanding. Gracie, a deadweight infant on each hip, continued to slim down, matching the styles of the boy-cut fashions of the times.

"At least I don't have to cook and run a store like your Mom did," she would say in admiration of Kitty's stamina. "How did she ever do it?"

Gracie would sometimes dreamily view the society pages and see pictures of contemporary women dancing at the North Shore clubs. "They're all my age," she would say. From time to time, Rose would appear in the those pages and Gracie would feel a twinge of her old jealousy, belittling herself, asking why it was that pretty girls always won out? But she would rebound quickly, reject her disappointment, and get back to her tasks with an open heart, tending Art and the children. Maybe she was the lucky one after all.

There is a time in a young family's life, while the children are still toddling along the hallway, when the months slip by in quick order. Normally it was a time of grinding work on the part of the breadwinner, oftentimes fearful of being fired, living from paycheck to paycheck, forever tired. Parents watched children grow out of clothes and eyed the mounting bills. Homemakers worked from dawn to nearly midnight, cleaning, cooking, caring—wondering if they were still attractive, often too sleepy to perform their nightly beauty routines. Tending their family was how the mid-twenties passed for the Mahoneys. If they had known, or had been able to enjoy them, these were the good times.

In terms of life's passing, it was a time of harvest for them, as if some crops were meant for early reaping. The accumulation of a young family's shared love, needs and satisfaction, though trying, contented them; while the explosion of their passion brought them maturity. But a new sense of cultural awareness suggested possible alterations. For them, this was a busy, but in some ways a hollow time, especially in terms of personal development, as if they gladly sacrificed their more selfish ambitions for the greater good of the family. There was little time to spend on one's own improvement, too busy with economic and childrearing demands. This at a time when the literary, musical, and theatrical life of America was exploding as if the muses finally took their heads out of a European cloud and looked west. 1925 was a halcyon year for the developing arts of the land, and Gracie somehow sensed that.

Something began to change in the windings of their marriage. Art had reached a plateau in his growth and was happy to glide along a conventional surface. Gracie, however, was still striving toward a higher level, though she couldn't exactly express what that might be—yearning echoes for something better. With the pair at different elevations, adjustments began to occur. Art remained passive in many ways; consequently Gracie, unsatisfied about something in her life, began to take control of the family's course.

"Art," she said one Sunday when the children were down for a nap. "What do you think if we started studying things, read together, so we can learn more about what's going on the world."

"We keep up pretty well reading the *Daily News*."

"That's all good," she said. "But look around. We don't have more than a dozen books in the house, and most of them we borrowed from your Dad's place. Maybe we should start, for instance, to read to one another. People in magazines say it's a good thing to do. We're close in so many ways, maybe we can get to know one another even better."

"I'm no scholar like Pa," Art said. "But sure, we can try if you'd like."

They started by reading novels. In the beginning they read aloud to one another, but soon Art was slipping behind, struggling through parts that Gracie had absorbed days earlier. When they both finished a book, they tried to have a discussion but it was fairly brief and awkward. So Gracie suggested that they should read biographies of the inventors and mechanics of the time, thinking these would be more to Art's liking, so they borrowed books from the library on Edison and Ford and Westinghouse, though they couldn't find one on Tesla, who had lit up the Fair back in Martin's time. These narratives did gain Art's attention, and Gracie even splurged and bought him a book on racing cars for Christmas. But soon, Art was putting aside his reading to grapple with more immediate needs. Eventually, he withdrew from the process, leaving Gracie disappointed but resolved never to stop reading again for the rest of her life.

With books as a background, Gracie began to study how to compose better letters. She would look up new words and try them out in conversation and then correspond with family and friends in her open, handsome writing style, spending more than normal on writing equipment and stationery. A dictionary appeared in the apartment, then a thesaurus, and she went out to a second-hand store and bought a bookcase in which to deposit her purchases. In time, she hoped to have her own writing desk, but that was out of the question for now, but she did ask for and receive a gold-tipped fountain pen for her birthday, which she treasured.

Art didn't object to the time she spent reading or writing; he would smile at her when she looked up from her page to reassure her that he supported her efforts.

Soon, she made an attempt to widen their circle of friends, seeking out more interesting types. Because the twenties were such social times, it was easy to join a group in the easterly neighborhoods through contact with some of her new pen pals, mostly old school chums, women that matched not only her social ambition but allowed her the opportunity to come in personal touch with the more sophisticated kind of people that she met working downtown. Marge would sit for the children and off she and Art would go with their Friday night bunch, bringing with them some of Kitty's favorite hors d'oeuvres that his mother had collected in a handwritten cookbook.

It was all part of a trend towards self improvement and personality expansion encouraged by the times. Guests discussed psychology and economic theory without having much background in these or other offshoots of sociology, but that didn't stop them. Because there was a John Dewey influence in the crowd, owing to their proximity to the University of Chicago, education was much discussed, providing Art and Gracie take-home ideas about how to rear their children. Some people were even reading philosophy, not a normal thing in the alleys of the South Side. Once, they bumped into Al at one of these shindigs where the guests sat crowded on the floor, upended knee to knee. Al was an attraction as usual, mystifying partygoers with his tricks and illusions.

"Still the old Wizard," Art said.

"Yeah! You never know when the ad business is gonna fade away and I'll have to run with the tents again."

"Do you think much about those times?" Art asked.

"Not really. It actually wasn't so long ago, but so much has happened that it seems like ancient history. . . .I guess the war did that."

"Sounds right," Art said. "Even when I go back and think of Maeve and Caroline and all them in their long dresses, it seems as far back as King Arthur."

"It's all about progress now and being up-to-the-minute, right? Like nothing ever happened before 1919."

"Sad in a way," said Art wistfully.

Al put his arm around Art and said, "Memories are fine. But we got to get on."

"Yeah!" Art answered, not really believing in what he said.

"I'm getting more into radio now," Al said. "Thinking about joining the Columbia Broadcasting System. Seems to me I've always been spreading her gospel anyway."

There was a rumbling from the next room, like the start-up of the new kitchen fridge. At the same time, a man brushed against a wall filled with pictorial scenes from the woolly west. A framed picture fell to the carpet near where Art and Al were standing.

"Sorry," said the offending guest to the hostess. "Let me help."

It was one of those pictures of a lone Indian on the plains that decorated every other house in the midwest.

"Look. There's a piece of paper fell from the back."

"I never saw that before," said the hostess. "What does it say? The artist's name?"

"It says, *Never Forget.* Then down below, it says, *Last one to bed feeds the horses.*"

Al and Art looked at each other, wondering if the other remembered a similar accident.

One result of the Mahoney's expanding social life was that Gracie became much more clothes conscious. Following the fashions of their group, she began paying considerably more attention to her wardrobe. They couldn't afford new clothes, but Gracie canvassed downtown until she found a second-hand boutique where she managed to upgrade her costumes with little expenditure. What she wore, she wore stylishly, carefully tending fabric and accessories. With her now thinner body that she had whittled down to meet the requirements of the times and by also binding her breasts, she began to attract attention from both sexes and Art was proud of her and showed it by encouraging her to dress up.

Those Friday night parties didn't come quickly enough for her, but she had daily company. The rest of the week was drudgery but she looked forward each evening to the time when she could pick up her latest book.

\* \* \*

In 1927, on a hot and sunny morning, Gracie began her day with laundry, starting early to beat the heat. It would certainly be too hot for soup, so she wouldn't have to bother with simmering stock. Still she sweated, bent over her washboard at the kitchen sink, soaking and rinsing—the wringer to the side, bottles of disinfectant close at hand. She was looking forward to the 4$^{th}$ of July in another two days and hoped the weather would hold long enough for her young family to celebrate outdoors. She glanced at John-Arthur, Jr. crawling on the floor and heard baby Matt crying from the crib. Walking into the bedroom, she checked the infant's comfort level and found that it was low, so she changed him and returned the baby to the crib. Then she heard little John-Arthur's piercing cry from the kitchen.

The boy was screeching, sitting with an open and spilled bottle of lye. She could see from the residue around his mouth that he had been drinking the caustic liquid. Gracie screamed out and picked him up, wiping off the foul excess from his lips.

"Did you drink it?" she yelled at him.

He was crying so much, he couldn't reply but from some message in his eyes and the evidence around his mouth, she could tell that he had.

She frantically placed a call to her neighborhood doctor and he responded immediately, coming through the back door within ten minutes. Meanwhile, her screaming had attracted the neighbors who arrived to offer conflicting advice. All the while, the baby was trying to empty the poison from his system. The doctor induced further discharges and settled into the opinion that the boy would be all right and it wasn't necessary to go the expense of a hospital visit. In those days, such medical advice was sacrosanct.

After he left, John-Arthur wailed on. A few neighbors stayed on, and gradually the baby calmed down, became almost quiet and then faded away in his mother's arm.

Art raced home after his company caught up with him on his delivery rounds, running up the back porch steps, coming in to find Gracie sitting with a dead child.

It was Art who was the more grief-stricken of the two. He took his son's death worse than Gracie, as if their dispositions determined their reactions—he as a fateful sign that life was crushing, she with a sense of reluctant acceptance that much of life was accidentally arranged. But Gracie felt the guilt, and no matter how bright her dresses would ever be, she would wear the invisible dark shawl of bad mother for years.

The next day they faced the horror of buying a small casket.

The senior Rapps, Kitty's parents, came to the wake and brought Marie, who proved to be sensitive to everyone's pain, still carrying the grief of her mother's loss, though few were as affected as Marge, John-Arthur Junior's caregiver. Old man Rapp brought his own opinions with him and was soon in an argument with Gracie and Art about their burial plans.

"The boy should be buried vit his grandmother in the Rapp plot," the old delicatessener said.

"That's a good idea, Grandpa Rapp," Art said. "But we've decided to bury him in Saint Mary's where my dad has space."

"You would save the expense and not have to put down the boy with nobody else with him. He could be vit my Kitty."

Gracie interrupted, "In a sense, it doesn't matter where he's buried. What's important is that his life ended before it began."

"Yah, but he didn't have to die, did he?"

Gracie, burdened already, blurted out, "But he did, didn't he?"

Martin saw the hostility building and gently turned his parents-in-law aside.

In tragedy, anguish empties the mind of everything but anger and simultaneously attacks the body with all kinds of pain. In trying to comprehend what happened to them, Gracie and Art quickly muddled over the oft-asked question of how a benevolent universe could be suffocated by grief. No use in trying to understand things and then be blind-sided by fate.

They felt only emptiness, the fruitlessness and abuse of life. With no immunity from its randomness. Gracie wandered the apartment waiting to hear John-Arthur's cry; Art buried the dream of a boy child growing up in a loving home and was driven to distraction thinking about all the things the father and son would never do. He sat and cried for three days after his son's death. Gracie, bearing the responsibility, had to face the arrangements of the wake and burial herself. Caught on the details, the holiday spun around them unnoticed. Besides, there was Matt to care for.

After John-Arthur Jr.'s death, Gracie began calling Art by the name she had used when they first met at the church socials. He became John-Arthur again within the confines of his own home.

Art was unable to recover from the loss. He couldn't rise to a state of ambition; he saw no sense to it. No matter how long or hard he worked, there was little extra cash, and no sense of adequate compensation for his struggles. Luckily, economic times were good so his pay kept pace with rising costs. Though they had no savings, they were able to pay their bills except for the doctors' fees. Investments were out of the question except for their $1000 burial insurance policy. Saving for death, their only assurance.

Returning to work, Art sought to find solitude a few minutes each day either during his short lunchbreak or by visiting the parish church on his way home from his rounds. He needed healing time to sit by himself and contemplate his loss, often slumping in a pew wearing his white vestments, trying to recapture a lost state of forgiveness and understanding.

His laundry delivery route took him east on Tuesday and Thursday, traveling toward the lake where he was able to service his Hyde Park customers in the university area. There, in good weather, he would pull his truck into Jackson Park along the drive that circled the pond near the old Fair museum where he could spread out on a bench, unwrapping the lunch Gracie had prepared the night before, amused with a little note she had included or some treat to remind him he came from a caring kitchen. Munching away, his garrison cap tipped back on his head, he was able to view Lake Michigan and the park's vista that stretched south to a wooded island in an adjacent pond.

After awhile, he got to know the Hyde Park noon strollers by sight, a woman with a small dog yapping at the end of a yellow leash; also an athletic woman who raced heel and toe along the path. The one person he regularly spoke to was an elderly gent who in the beginning of their casual friendship had probably deduced some form of despair ringing Art's countenance. The older man and he enjoyed talking about their families, both devoted husbands and fathers. A mismatched couple, each placid with a warm personality and a quiet sense of humor. In time, Art looked forward to meeting his bench partner, who worked at the university, because their discussions, amicable and meaningful, appealed to each, even though the pair operated on different levels. One day a student, walking by, was surprised to see the older man with an ice cream man, greeting him as professor.

One conversation remained with Art. It was so illusive that he could not quite remember the details but the sense of it remained whole in Art's memory.

"My young friend," the older gentleman said. "I'm always interested to hear about the things you believe in."

"I pretty much go along with the rules I learned as a kid in school and church. I mostly believe in what I was taught, things I inherited from the family."

"You must have had a lot of trust in your parents and teachers," the older man said.

"I did," Art said. "Both my ma and pa laid down a good base for my brother and me. . . .My dad had studied things out pretty much for himself when he was young. Told us to think and care about people more than money and success."

The professor said, "Good advice. We should try to avoid collapsing in the face of a material world, goods and meaningless relationships. Life shouldn't numb us with things, make us docile. We have to keep fighting for real clarity."

Art replied, "All good, but a lot of experiences leave people confused, and I'm one of them. The war is one reason. It had a kind of disgust for life that's hard to shuck off."

"Yes, but shouldn't we try to fight through hard times and try to give a direction to our life. Try to control it."

"I don't know," Art said. "It's all sometimes beyond me."

"Have you known much sorrow?" the teacher asked.

"More than my share," Art answered quietly. "I had a young son who died recently."

"Oh, my god, not you too. I have lost two boys."

"Two? How do you cope? I'm sick all the time about my boy. Just can't seem to get over his death. . . .How do you deal with that twice?"

"It's unbelievable pain, I know," the older man sighed. "Many times I nearly gave up ... Have you known that kind of pain before?"

" I loved that boy in a special way. I often wondered if I could ever love like that after things happened to me the way they did when I was ten. . . . Back then I loved a girl and a woman the way a kid loves with no holding back. And I was crushed when they both died. I don't think I ever got over that until the boy was born."

"Such magic in that first birth. . . .What I had to do," the professor said, "was I had to find a new way of looking at things. Had to figure out how things worked together. What the sense of life was. It took me a long time, but I learned. I got to know science and art and philosophy, disciplines like those. Then I tried to put all that into a kind of relationship, seeing how things bore on each other, how they might organize themselves and grow into some kind of whole."

"Did it work out for you?" Art asked.

"I think so," the older man said. "But it wasn't easy. And I'll never be through with it."

"I wouldn't even know where to start with something like that."

"Just start by reading," came the advice.

"I tried that but it didn't seem to work for me. Maybe there's a simpler answer."

"I'm not sure," the old man said.

They parted with a cordial handshake, at least able to understand the grief in each other.

* * *

In the summer of '28, Gracie again conceived, the couple feeling ambivalent about a new child. When the pregnancy was confirmed that fall, they pondered its effect. How would they feel about a new baby after losing John-Arthur, Jr. the year before? Hammered by doubt, feeling caught in a cross current, they wondered how any new child could replace their darling boy. Nevertheless one early April morning the next spring, the wrinkled bundle they called James-Francis after Art's adventurous forefathers came bawling into being.

* * *

After the Crash in '29, the relatively easy economic life they had all enjoyed for ten years came to a halt. Ma Cleveland, with two grown children still at home, moved away to the West Side to save rent money and be closer to her factory job, where she was still dispensing soup du jour and victuals for her hardy black and Slavic workmen. Mary Rose and brother Will were married by now and only Marge and young Jack remained at home with the white-haired Irishwoman, who plainly saw that she would have to continue working until the economic situation got better. She knew she was in for a long wait, so she began administering tougher rules for those who remained under her roof.

The Depression spread its disease into the bones of the American dream, crippling it for a decade. Things taken for granted soon became privilege for the few. There were ever-smaller opportunities. At first, the financial panic caused confusion, then anger and finally raw fear as jobs disappeared, savings eroded, and living standards spiraled downward. The South Side and West Side began to hunker down for a long period of deprivation.

Then, as 1930 rolled into a new decade, Art began to experience symptoms of illness himself—a drop in weight, loss of strength and energy, disturbed sleep, a copper tone to his complexion and general irritability. It was the last that worried him most, because he had always been an honor member of the good spirits club. By March of '31, he feared his sickness wasn't improving, so he began regular visits to the doctor, who after some poking and tests, was unable to provide a diagnosis. Nor could the specialists he subsequently saw. Art confided the problem to Gracie in a forthright way and she said she had noticed his decline and odd coloring but attributed it to lingering flu symptoms.

By April his condition worsened and he was forced to ask for a leave of absence from his job. Exhausted, he stayed in bed for nearly a month until he received the verdict from still another specialist who diagnosed his problem as cancer-related, though he was vague about the origin and its progress. All that Art knew was that he began to feel that he might be dying.

Panic spread through the family. Gracie, with two boys, was fearful that she faced imminent disaster if the worst prospect came true. How could she dig down through that kind of pain to find the ability to survive?

By June, Art knew he was going to die, so he tried to straighten out what paltry affairs were left for him to organize and began to slip away. He managed one day to sit and play some of Maeve's old tunes and then the old pianola and the romance of his boyhood went silent. He would sit on his bed and look over family photographs, spending hours writing on the back of the pictures the names of those depicted and the times shown. Gracie, following a doctor's suggestion, arranged for a rest at the Indiana Dunes on the southern edge of Lake Michigan—a short interurban train ride away—where he might improve in the fresher air. Matt, now six, was elected to accompany his father so the pair, passing by the site of the old Fair, rode around the bottom of the lake and came to a poor man's resort on the southern lakeshore. When they arrived, they discovered that they would be staying in a reconverted Pullman car, heavy with Victorian decorations, and that amused Art.

"Probably one the Pullmans the strikers ruined during the battle of '94. Must be some kind of labor justice that a workingman can call this kind of luxury home."

Art and the boy tried walking along the Dunes but Matt noticed that Art tired easily, so they mainly played cards and listened to a radio lent to them by the landlady. Matt, frightened by his father's down periods, pleaded with him to get well.

Art knew by now that death was near, but unlike the visage of war, there would be no armistice with the dark force. He tried to accept his fate, but the sense of failure he felt in leaving Gracie and the boys bereft caused him more misery than the disease that was annihilating him. The poverty into which he was certain to leave them defeated any attempt to face resurrection with a sense of peace. He began to examine his life's bedrock, first the farm and then Chicago. And meditated on the institutions that had defeated him—school, government. Finally he began to doubt the worth of his own family's members. But he never did blame the church. A few images remained—Kitty bending down to him on a winter's morning, Maeve at her piano, Caroline running through Eagle Point Park, the boys asleep in his arms, the roar of the engines at the racing oval and most of all curling up with Gracie. Beyond these, only loss.

On their last day at the Dunes, Matt came into the sitting area and found his father collapsed on the floor. Frightened, he raced over to the landlady's house and a doctor was soon in attendance. While Art was coming around, the landlady called Gracie, who then spoke to the doctor. They decided that the best thing to do was to get Art home as quickly as possible.

By the end of June, the doctors told Gracie that the end was near. The Clevelands and Martin and Marie came to visit and Francis traveled up from St. Louis. Francis had been living an ascetic existence as a beef salesman, a life in some ways not unlike a cloistered cleric—a role that had originally been assigned to his father. Inwardly, he was a quiet reflection of Martin and Art. He never married. And never missed a birthday or holiday with the family. The good uncle who lived a subsidiary life.

Gracie called Al as well, and he came the day she telephoned.

"What is it he's got?" Al asked Gracie at the door.

"Nobody knows. But all the doctors say he's going fast. . . .God, Al, what am I to do?"

"You're going to brave it through. And we're all going to help you."

They walked into the bedroom

"Here's our John-Arthur," said Gracie and just as quickly departed.

"How's my old buddy?" Al asked, setting aside a magazine he had brought. To Art, his head still seemed a little overlarge for his body size.

"Don't feel much like an eagle these days," Art said with a weak smile.

"Hey! You'll be up and steering your car to Indianapolis before you know it."

"Didn't make it this year," Art responded.

"Surely next," Al said.

"I'm glad you came," Art said. "There's something I'd like you to do for me."

He reached around his neck to unfasten the silver chain that supported Mauve's Tara medal. Holding it in his hand, Art said, "I'd like you to hold onto this and give it to the boys when they grow up. I'd let Gracie do it, but maybe you can tell Maeve's story better because you were there."

"Sure, but you hold on to it a little longer" Al said. "Keep it aside until you're feeling a little better." Then reminiscing, he said, "Listen, old buddy, I just want to be sure that you don't blame Jack and me for letting Maeve and O'Malley go off onto the bridge that night,"

"Naw," said Art. "You can't hold martyrs back from their appointed rounds."

"I'm glad you feel that way. Because I always thought you blamed us"

"No," Art said again. "I always thought you were one of the best of buddies from first to last. I always tell people I've only knew one genius in my whole life and that was you."

The window was open and a sudden wind or force started making the pictures rattle on the wall. The scene of a thatched Irish farmhouse fell from the wall beside the bed.

"Here we go again," Al said.

The message inscribed on back was: *Courage isn't enough, only wisdom is. . . .and. . . . Never remove toast from the toaster with a metal instrument.*

The magazine Al left was an old 1914 copy of *the little review*, which Art never read. Then the Boy Wizard played some old Joplin tunes and the one song that bound them together.

Art died the next week. When Gracie realized that the day of his death was on the second of July, the anniversary of the poisoning of her firstborn, she collapsed in double despair. In her head, she kept rationalizing and telling fellow mourners, "I at least had the satisfaction of being loved by a good man."

Art's corpse made a round trip from the hospital to the apartment on Laflin and his body was laid out on the dining room table. Gracie sat in a chair next to the table and neighbors and friends began arriving with food and condolences. Matt and James-Francis had been staying with Martin under the care of Marge, and before the crowds arrived the boys were walked over to view the box in which their inert father lay, though only one of them would be old enough to remember.

Old Man Rapp came in with his daughter Millie and immediately began rattling Gracie with his opinion that Art should be buried with Kitty in the Rapp plot in the German cemetery. But Gracie said she had decided to bury him in St. Mary's in a plot that Martin had purchased.

"But he should be vit his wife—to give my girl some comfort," said old George.

"Grandpa Rapp," Gracie said with exhaustion, "what does it matter?"

This was sacrilege to the old German.

"Yah! But Martin should never have split up the family. And vhy is the casket closed?"

Martin broke in and tried to set the record straight, "George, little John-Arthur is already buried there and that's where Art wanted to go. He told me himself."

"Yah. You see. Children should be vit their parents, yes?"

Rapp calmed down but listened in on the rumors during the next hour while food was served from the kitchen table. But it didn't end there. When Old Man Rapp found out that Gracie had allowed Art's corpse to be dissected in an attempt to discover what killed him, he was further incensed. He had hired a limousine for Gracie, Martin, and members of the family and again exploded on the way to the burial. "It's against God's rule to dissect one of His holy wessels," he said. "Why did you do that? You make some money or something?"

Gracie snapped back, "Because we're trying to find what killed him so we can protect the boys."

"The boys are fine. You just let those medical people valk all over you and let them play terrible games vit my Kitty's boy."

"You narrow-minded little man," she said, letting fly years of frustration over the old man's stinginess and thick-headedness. "What I choose to do with the body of my husband is no concern of yours."

She hit all the sore points.

"Easy Gracie," Martin said. . . ."She's upset enough, George. Let her be."

There was near silence on the way to the cemetery. Then at the gravesite they were all able to cry together. Returning to the apartment for a few hours, some of the mourners contemplated the meaning of Art's time on earth. Others did so for a long time and his boys for the rest of their lives.

Art had allowed life to govern him. He had let events flow over him instead of diverting them to his will. By the standards of the day, his was a good life, though obviously troubled by sorrow. True, life had pushed him aimlessly along, and a few times he had fought back—when he drove with the wagons onto Emerald Avenue, when he failed to lose his courage in the Meuse-Argonne and when he entered the Prairie Street clubhouse alone. Oddly, he only found remedies in various forms of violence. He had maintained a modest existence, kept his religion, and faithfully departed. At the funeral mass, there was praise for quiet men. Dying with him was a strand of a gentle Mahoney strain that had maintained a level of civility for two generations. Sadly, his shortened life had only been allowed to clock through three cranks of the twentieth century.

An incomplete, certainly an imperfect, life. Like most, he had done a few brave things, but he had been unable to transcend the early pain life offered. Art lived with his losses, but couldn't overcome or manage them. But what if his congealing teenage optimism had not been liquefied in the swill of the World War, the anguish of a baby's death and the mindless hustle of Chicago? Perhaps he didn't love either God or Gracie well enough—though it would have been hard to believe that from his outward behavior. But who knew what constituted his internal life? He hadn't been an introspective person, and perhaps his father failed him there, because the priest in Martin might have guided him differently. Or maybe Art wasn't smart enough or original enough or educated. He was surely stunted by his early loss. Perhaps the boy who had once sat quietly in the Holy Cross church shadowed in the flickering light of Christ's presence wasn't able to speak up against the holy ghosts that persuade life. He maintained a pleasant surface, actually a manly one, but he was crushed by the accidents and mores of his times.

What was it that forced him to carry the burden of his youthful sin? Perhaps it was his intransigent Catholicism which engendered an earthly pessimism when judged against heavenly comparisons. It may have been a pure child's love that ran deeper in him than others. If he had only sought and divined a working well. If he had learned to manipulate the well's ropes to haul up from his unconsciousness the cooling spiritual waters he needed for healing instead of gagging on the dead sea of guilt. He might have peeled away the book of years—the mummies and colors of past self—and searched down the deckered cobbles of the well's walls in search of a silver pail. Inquiring down the stones that held the sedimented layers of his grief, banded in striations like a lost circle of friends, he might have found peace. Squinting through the dark, down where life and death are brothers, he could have dropped a pebble and listened for a soothing echo—Kitty's and Caroline's call, a Maeve song or Gracie's love sounds along with the sobs of remorse. Voices stirring there in the wet basement of his memory. Down by the foundation.

He was gone and Gracie was left with finishing his family's business for him. He had drunk the lie of a conventional life and had been cheated of any accomplishments.

# Chapter 18

Gracie put her three pennies back into her purse after expending two others for her streetcar ride downtown along Madison Street. Of the remaining three, she would pay one for the coffee that would wash down the sandwich in her coat pocket and the remaining two she saved for the ride home. The rest of her paycheck was handed over to Ma Cleveland each Friday evening except for the dollar that was returned to Gracie for her week's needs.

She and the two boys had moved into the Clevelands' West Side apartment near St. Mel's on Washington Boulevard. Here, much like the stone fronts and back wooden porches of the South Side, the uniform three-story buildings stretched along a wide tree-lined thoroughfare. Logistics dictated that Gracie share a bedroom with Marge while Ma kept her own room; Jack slept on the living room couch and the two boys tented under the dining-room table.

Because Gracie couldn't afford a morning paper, the hour-long ride on the Madison Street streetcar gave her time to fixate on her immediate sorrows. Hawk-faced now and painfully thin, she had lost the attractiveness she had built up during the twenties. Even her clothes had become slightly frayed, reflecting her general condition. Worst of all, her threadbare coat would have to suffice against the increasing cold of a nasty Chicago winter.

John-Arthur Sr.'s premature death the previous July had left her penniless following the funeral. When added to her moving bills to the West Side and the expense of going back to work, her insurance money evaporated. Even storing their furniture with a Rapp relative who owned a moving business proved costly. Luckily, because of her favorable notice at BBDO in earlier years, she was able to find part-time employment there in September even though many in the city were jobless. Then, because of her typing and steno speed and ability to compose a catchy business letter, she was rehired a month later as a permanent employee. Everyone in the office was generous and considerate toward her, owing to her low spirits that oftentimes bordered on a state of depression. A fellow worker, Trixie Young, had helped her resettle in the typing pool and brought Gracie up-to-date on the new clients and their advertising campaigns. Gracie repaid the company's generosity by producing high-quality, creative work. She often ate her lunch at her desk when there was a rush job and many nights she had to call Ma Cleveland to say she would be working late if one of the account executives needed to produce an overnight presentation. Though she tried hard to put up a good front, a certain hopelessness crept into Gracie's personality as she fought a triple-front battle to be a good mother, a dutiful daughter, and cooperative office worker. But a look of defeat and fear often followed after her.

The streetcar was cold. It had a wet-wool-and-goulashes smell after an early November snowstorm the night before. She had been lucky enough to get a window seat so she could observe the urban scene along the forty long blocks to the Loop, the ride delayed by stops at every intersection. What she saw from her window were long sections of city storefronts, punctuated from place to place by a new movie palace (Marbro), a park (Garfield), an armory, a stadium, and finally Skid Row. As the car passed through this last neighborhood of drunks, she could see them hanging out in front of liquor stores or the dozens of flophouses, pawn shops, hangover bars and pool halls. She looked away because sometimes the bums would yell at the girls on the streetcar if they caught them gawking at them. It was 1931 and the Depression was well under way, and the population of Skid Row was increasing daily, even after computing the deaths of those who were carted away each morning after dying from the cold, blasted livers, common brawling, or plain giving-up. Try as she might, Gracie couldn't help glancing out at the degradation that passed like a cyclorama of despair—once proud farm and working men—and she couldn't help feeling a part of the same general collapse.

She had enough of disease, even though she had made her own small contribution to medicine, feeling some small satisfaction in her own behavior regarding the tests and autopsy that had been done with her permission on John-Arthur's corpse. The medical investigation had resulted in gains in pinpointing Addison's disease, an affliction of the adrenal gland that failed to produce the corticosteroids for her dying husband.

Making matters worse, the Rapp relations who were storing her South Side goods demanded high monthly payments that Gracie could not afford. For the past months, the Rapps had been insisting that she pay up or threatened her with consequences. When she was unable to come up with the fee, there was trouble. The Rapps sold her furniture to cover the overdue amount and burned the remainder of her possessions, including the photographs that Art had so carefully marked. The memorabilia of her childhood and her life with John-Arthur went up in smoke. Only Maeve's piano survived. Francis, resettled in Chicago, had rescued it from the auction block.

The entire strain was too much for Gracie. After a month of streetcar rides through hell, she finally broke down. Simply, angrily, collapsed. Her mother found her distressed daughter in her room one Sunday applying layer after layer of cosmetics on her face until she had built up a grostesque whiteface mask of herself. Everyone feared for her, but it was Ma Cleveland who came up with a solution. She still had relatives living downstate on the farm, so Marge was re-recruited to take care of the children while Gracie recovered over the winter months. Once deposited in a family farmhouse south of Peoria, Gracie sat morosely in her room, sleeping when she wasn't weeping.

Her two most treasured possessions—her husband and oldest child—had died in her arms. The pain and grief were unbearable, stalling out her emotional electrical system. Burned down to her animal essence, she was incapable of responding to anything except basic wants.

First, she had to get all the demons out—the fears and the horrors of unforeseen circumstances. She moaned in bed, crying, waiting for the emptiness, that once it arrived, brought the most appalling time of all. She was a dry sponge that no longer soaked up life. Her horizons were as flat as the land around her when she first ventured onto the cold porch for some fresh air.

Crouched in front of a fireplace most of the time, she slowly learned how to dig down into herself and teach herself a style of meditation. Her life in Chicago was encircled by family obligations. When she finally surrendered to the depression caused by all these responsibilities, she was able to begin to shunt them aside and catalog her problems. Somehow she glimpsed that she had to cure herself first. The former tenets of her belief system—the church, her outward spirit of generosity, and her trust in Chicago-hustle—were in need of resuscitation. She sat, hour after hour, both hands gripping innumerable cups of tea, trying to reorder her existence and come out of the fog in which she had lost direction.

One of the more difficult questions she had to face was: What had John-Arthur brought to her? Certainly she could count the blessings of his love and caring and devotion to her and the children. Plus his steadiness that had calmed her. On the other hand, from her point of view, he had dismissed what she perceived as his obligation and opportunities to achieve personal advancement.

At Christmas, the boys sent her home-made cards, sweet simple drawings that prompted a weeping that felt more cleansing than painful. Slowly, she began to connect with her relatives, the old farmwomen who nursed her. A few weeks after New Years, she was helping with dinner and the dishes, and soon doing her own laundry.

By February, she was thinking about returning to Chicago, but everyone convinced her to wait, especially Trixie Young, who was trying to protect her job at the agency and who could discern from Gracie's letters that she was still in an early recovery period. Besides, the new ad campaigns had not begun to kick in; creatively, work was slow. She finally made it home for James-Francis's birthday in April, the child blissfully unaware that there had been instability on both sides of his family. And wondering, confusedly, which among all these women he was surrounded by was his true and authentic mother.

Once she was back on the West Side, the family offered Gracie time and space to readjust, but after a few days, Ma Cleveland told everyone to treat her normally and get on with life. The boys were ambivalent about seeing their mother and that made her sad. Matt who had worn a frightened look for over a year, ever since being dispatched to the Dunes to attend Art's collapse, held back from her. James-Francis remained confused as to who she was exactly. Both boys, however, quickly softened to Gracie's entreaties and gifts. The following week, she went downtown, doctor's certificates in hand, to renegotiate her return to work. Bargaining better than she planned, she returned to the secretarial pool again on a part-time basis. Trixie had protected her against a tide of other applicants.

With her first pay, which Ma refused to take, Gracie went out to her second-hand store and bought a black dress with a small fur piece and a hat to wear to church. The outfit was appropriate for her widow's role, though her sisters couldn't help but notice the neckline was latticed to allow some upper body flesh to show through the funereal color. As the weather began to warm, she shopped again for a second dress—still black but with a cross-sweeping white fabric that fell across her shoulders and breastworks. This time, the sisters had something to notice top and bottom. Strap shoes and a little beret.

\* \* \*

Sports interest in the midwest reaches a manic stage during the long and often delayed spring season. As the warm weather spread, Gracie noticed that there was an increasing rise of interest in golf among the men in the office. By summer she had gone around to a used goods store and purchased a knockered-looking set of clubs in a ratty brown-cloth bag that appeared to have been removed from service sometime before the Spanish War. She proceeded to go out and buy an outrageously priced pair of golf shoes and made her way to a public course, her new beret entering lighter service, to find an instructor—Trixie dutifully in hand.

She began to smile more, and step out with her girlfriends and soon reacquired her former steady-paying position. She and her Ma never spoke about the increase in Gracie's social commitments, but there was an unsaid agreement between them that recognized that it was Gracie's duty to go out into the world and find a new husband and father for the boys. Even though the Depression was deepening, Gracie was allowed to keep half her salary. That enabled her to go to a hairdresser and warm her hair with a fancy perm.

Men in the office began noticing her as Gracie regained her looks, and began to wear lighter colors. She was selective about whom she entertained and seldom went out more than once with men in her building or from her old Friday Night crowd. Men sensed that her experience offered warm pleasures, but she primly excused herself from close contact. With the first anniversary of John-Arthur's death past, Gracie became more daring. As a girl, she had learned how to ride horses, and now began dragging poor Trixie Young out to a farm on weekends where she refreshed her equestrian skills.

That fall, around the time of FDR's election, Gracie's life began to expand. Because of her versatility, she was promoted, chosen to be the personal secretary for one of the founders of BBDO. That in turn helped both the recovery of her self-esteem and income. When her boss discovered that she had unusually good writing skills, he encouraged her to try her hand at composing some of his presentation letters and these he thought showed talent. What happened after that was unexpected.

Because her boss was head of the Chicago office, Gracie maintained daily contact with the agency's clients and soon made herself useful in a dozen ways, handling office and travel schedules, expense accounts, gift-giving, and charitable work. This last gave her access to a wider range of Chicago's boosters and offered her an opportunity as the holidays neared to attend a few events where an extra woman was needed at the mostly male-attended charity fundraising events. The company allowed her to expense a new dinner gown, thus helping defray any shabbiness to be found in her older models. With her basic sense of style, she was able to appear at the Sherman House as an accomplished young businesswoman.

It wasn't long before an advertising executive from one of the shop's client list began noticing her. His name was Miles Goddard and he was a tall German-blondish guy with wide shoulders and a broad face that held an ironic appeal as if to indicate he was ready for whatever came along. They began by connecting on the phone, and were both pleasantly surprised to find that there had been an attractive person on the other end of the wire when Miles arrived early one morning for a client presentation. There was much hubbub when he entered the agency, but he took time to stop by Gracie's outer office and introduce himself, and a charge of electricity that sometimes goes through sympathetic souls jiggled between them.

At a YMCA benefit dinner around Thanksgiving, they sat at the same table and enjoyed more than one conversation. He was hearty and she was open and it turned out they both liked to laugh and so enjoyed each other's company. They shared one dance and there was a smoothness about the way the two of them moved across the dancefloor.

There was little she could do to activate the relationship, so she relaxed and waited for developments. They appeared soon after the New Year.

1933 was one of those banner years that occur deca-annually in every great city even though this occasion was during a ruinous time of economic despair. Ever optimistic, with its heart in its throat, its fingers crossed, amid the worst Depression in the history of the country, there was to be a new Chicago World's Fair.

Early in the year at a Hull House affair, the families of the old porkapolis along with new upstart businessmen like those from the advertising and broadcasting fields converged on the Drake Hotel one evening in late winter. The event was to honor Jane Addams after her reception of the Nobel Peace Prize the year before. BBDO's table included both the agency's social secretary, Gracie Mahoney, and client Miles Goddard, among others. The pair allowed their attraction for one another to expand that night in the lively ballroom by the lake. They danced together, ate side by side and had sufficiently detached themselves from the rest of the table that their coziness was noticed by her boss, who didn't seem to mind. Then as now, keeping a client happy as well as prosperous was the aim of any agency president.

Among other questions, Miles asked her if she rode and Gracie told him about the horsefarm where she exercised in the western suburbs. One day that spring, he invited her to his riding club in Lake Forest. They met and mounted up, and rode along the marked trails north of the city. Miles, aside from being a powerful and vigorous man, was a fine horseman, so well-seated that he had taken polo practice with other members of the club and had soon joined them as a member of the team.

Dressed in jodhpurs and boots, the pair searched for and discovered each other's dash and drive.

He was also a sailor and when the weather turned mild, they went out in his 30-foot gaff-rigged sloop, the foredeck covered each sunny weekend with young bucks and beauties, enjoying a day away from their Michigan Avenue offices. Gracie, familiar with these waterways and decked out in wide white ducks with a string-top jersey, radiated with a newfound sense of herself. Sun-bathing with their friends, they beamed along, trolling the city's waterfront, watching fairgoers steam off from Navy Pier, the weekend sailors laughing loud enough that their voices carried onshore at Touhy and the other passing beaches.

When Martin heard that Gracie was dating, he wasn't displeased. On one of his every-other-Sunday visits to the West Side to see her and the boys, they got talking about her future and he let her know that he thought it would be right and proper to find a protector for herself, Matt, and James-Francis.

"Of course, marrying a German has a lot of advantages," said Kitty's priest.

"I don't think we should get ahead of ourselves," Gracie said, smiling at the old gent.

"And tell us, Martin, when are you going to bring the Monsignor's sister around yourself? Marrying Irish isn't so bad, you know," Ma Cleveland added.

After dinner, Martin took the boys aside and promised them a trip to the new World's Fair when school was out.

"When I was a boy," Martin said, "did I tell you that Chicago had a fine-looking Fair down in Jackson Park. Maybe the new Fair will bring as good a promise to you as mine did for me."

The Mahoney-Clevelands sat after dinner and Martin waxed on, "This Depression thing is like when the family first came over. There was no money. Pray that people can work themselves out of the poorer classes and into the middle level so that we're all neither too poor nor rich. Hard times shouldn't sink us all."

Gathered in the living room, they turned on the Cleveland's newly acquired table radio. Gracie had been alerted by telephone to tune in. A theme from the studio organ was pouring out the strains of *Columbia, Gem of the Ocean* .... "Welcome to the Wizard's Lair. . . ." came a familiar voice.

"It's Al—John-Arthur's friend," Gracie said. "What a guy! He's gotten himself on the radio."

". . . .Welcome to a new program called *American Centennial* coming to you from our studios atop the Palmolive Building celebrating the music of our past, songs about the rails and nails that went into building up the country."

He planned to feature music that had a way of bringing on a rampage of American spirit.

Al continued, ". . . .If you'll indulge me. I'll play along on the studio piano to begin. Then if we get soulful, I might switch over to the organ and trick a tear or two out of you . . . .I'll start with a tune my old buddy Art liked—one I got to play for him before he died."

"He told me I should listen," Gracie said.

And out of the radio came the strains of *Wild Rose*. The reaction from the West Siders was electric.

When the song died away, Al said, "MacDowell's songs remind me of the taming of America. A civilized wash-over after the rough life of the pioneers. He offers a taste of a softer and more fulfilling kind of life as if beauty was not just for the rich, but someday'll be available to all of us. . . .I daydream sometimes about a tapestry showing us all arranged together— Huck Finn, Uncle Remus, Walden Pond, Gettysburg—All bound up in the same picture. Something like Gottschalk tried musically in *L'Union*."

Allen Osprey's voice cranked through the wobbly diaphragm of their new Zenith radio.

Continuing to listen, they heard Al play some Chadwick and Beach. The former boy wonder, ever the advocate of the laboring class, trailed off ". . . .Remember to stay tuned for the President's address. Let's hope he chats about the workingman this time and lets the unions have their say."

The program memorialized something for Gracie. Perhaps it was the music. Startled, it awoke a feeling in her spirit that allowed her to begin to take down John-Arthur's heavy drapery from across her mind. The winter was behind and the truth was that the threads of her life with John-Arthur were beginning to fade.

* * *

The hot July day that Gracie stepped off the el and entered the art-deco spectacle that was the 1933 World's Fair, she was dazzled at the sight of the flag-drenched "Century of Progress" celebrating Chicago's unprecedented one hundred-year growth from a swampy portage at a French trading post to a city with a population of three and a half million. With Gracie that day were her friends Trixie and Flossie dressed up and ready to promenade. This wasn't the boys' mother's first trip to the exhibition; she had led her two sons through the grounds on an educational mission only the week before, making sure their trail bisected the stuffed beasts in the Field Museum, and allowed time to paddle up the slope to the Shedd Aquarium.

An act of faith in the middle of the Depression, the Century of Progress Fair reflected the role of science as a contributor to the midwest's knack for turning chemical, biological, and electrical developments into cash profits. The exhibit halls strung along the waterfront near the Loop displayed a cold simplicity, clean boxes with no effort to obfuscate their modernity, having disrobed the embellishments that architecture had proudly worn since the Renaissance, stripped down to Bauhaus bare, with perhaps a feather or two here and there to remind the viewers of what they were missing. Exhibits were objectively scientific, in contrast to the Columbian Fair, which had promoted a more traditional culture enlivened by the beaux arts. The modern midwest clearly demonstrated that it had chosen an industrial future and in doing so had half-drowned the arts. Progress in this century was to be measured by the success of science linked with industry, and stow the frou-frou. The consumer had triumphed over the magician. The older fair was generally remembered with greater feeling—as a poetic vision of something exceeding their best dreams, the staff of a spiritual life. This new fair was exceedingly materialistic.

Stretching high above the fair spanned a Sky Ride that offered a tram's-eye view of the spectacle below. Its two steel towers, Herculean-like, strode over the basin, wearing their raw iron much like the Eiffel Tower and Ferris Wheel at previous fairs. Gracie looked up to see Rocket Cars traversing the space from tower to tower above a great splashing fountain.

The trio of post-flappers was there to celebrate. Exactly what was hard to say, perhaps their own sense of freedom, each unmarried and on the lookout for companionship. Seemingly invincible, they pranced through the grounds and wore their pride for all to admire. Dressed like most women in light colors, Gracie accented her frilly dress with white accessories—hat, gloves and like-trimmed shoes. Male fairgoers complimented them as they patrolled along, the males decked out in white shirts and ties, a few in white ducks. Caps and straw boaters were in evidence but they were giving away to fedoras, though Panama hats had reappeared now that the weather turned warm.

Trixie, taller than Gracie, was a model of sarcasm, an expert at mining irony, never missing an opportunity to open a vein, commenting in rapid fire on the mortality of man. "See, that one, over there" she pointed with her eyes, "the one with the scrambled–egg tie. . . .Got his hair caught in the ringer."

Flossie, on the other hand, was generous to a midwestern fault, "He just needs a little something to hold it down, a nice hand to smooth it out."

"And we know the name of the honey who'd like to do that, don't we?" Trixie shot back.

"C'mon you two. Men later. First, the sights. Let's head down the boardwalk."

Gracie was eager to see the House of Tomorrow, displaying its array of modern conveniences like air conditioning, an all-electric kitchen, indirect lighting, floor-to-ceiling venetian blinds, and a solarium. They sauntered slowly, arm in arm, taking in but not acknowledging the many male glances.

Flossie said," My folks in Lafayette tell me there's a big picture of Indiana over in their state building. . . ."

"We passed that ages ago," interrupted Trixie, never one for cornfields.

As evening approached, after innumerable stops for beverages, first tea, then beer and more lately gin fizzes, they entered the Radio & Communications Building, part of an immense complex called the Electrical Exhibition. The trio was eventually directed towards a broadcasting studio that was planning to demonstrate a live broadcast.

"Good," said Trixie, "we can rest our bunions."

They were ushered into a glass-plated booth along with another fifty or so fair tourists where they watched the mechanical preparations preceding an on-air radio show. Gracie looked up to see her friend Al seated beneath a wide-spoked microphone.

"I'll be. . . .Guess who?" Gracie said.

"You know him?" Flossie asked.

"You been holding out on us?"

"It's Al. He's a little eccentric," Gracie replied, "but he's been a good friend."

"Even if they're strange, it's hard to find good friends," Flossie said, thinking she was making a contribution.

Dripping sarcasm, Trixie said, "So I'm to understand."

Al, opening the show, began surfing through the American musical idiom, a medium that was currently expanding at clipper rates. He started by playing Gershwin.

Because Al had been concentrating on his script, he was unaware of the viewers behind the glass. But once that he had a moment to gauge reactions among the studio audience tucked behind the plate window, all dutifully lined up from his perspective like an open can of sardines, he spotted Gracie. As the music played, he had an opportunity to observe the small slice of Chicago's population before him—blacks, square-jawed

Germans, Slavs with high cheekbones, distinctive-looking Orientals, the freckled Irish, olive-skinned Jews and other Mediterraneans—viewed all the various shadings of the species except the land's most important specimens, the Native Americans..

What Al realized was that even though we were a vast country with an extraordinary past and make-up, the American people were startlingly beautiful taken altogether, as much in the mind as in the eye. It was a bogus nation in many ways, he thought—not fixed by a unifying racial past or single culture, but exotic in its own multicolored way.

When the music stopped, Al said, "I'm looking into the booth where fairgoers have come to rest their feet after standing around watching all those scientific experiments out there and what I see is every race and nationality under the sun. And a trio of beauties—killer-dillers from the South Side. I'm looking in this fishbowl and see right in the middle of the pond sits my best friend's best friend."

He felt compelled to push himself to another level.

"I'd like to play a MacDowell piece for my old buddy—the second movement of the composer's *First Piano Concerto,* a work he loved."

When the notes faded away, the boy Wizard said, "I never knew a piece of music that opened its arms so wide. Ask me why I believe in old Columbia, I say it's expressed here soft as flutes. I even read into the music a search for a sense of peace. Seven whole minutes when the noise of ignorance is softened by decent voices. I think the concerto is a call to good people to come together and keep common faith against arrogance, religious narrowness and uneducated boobism. If that's too much of a mouthful for one piano piece, remember the shy need a way to speak up for the things that are beautiful to them, which allows them to live in some honorable kind of way."

Al concluded, "You all can have any kind of society or America you want. The one I want I found in an old man's prayer— *Women should remain our beacons and teach us to balance ourselves. . . .*I'd add blacks to that. And the white light the Liberator once offered—*Our country is the world. Our countrymen all mankind . . . .*If we practice what that implies, charity to all, folks might even find a way to liberate themselves."

When the show ended, Al was busy wrapping up details, so he and Gracie didn't have a chance to speak. They waved a wistful goodbye through the partition of glass, no longer absolutely pledged to their mutual love of John-Arthur Mahoney.

The South Side beauties entered the evening through the gates of the lively "Streets of Paris" attraction, soon sexually dominating an outdoor café that opened to the wide inland sea. They stayed for hours, accumulating a dozen men who came to exhibit their confidence and run amok with their dazzling personalities. Gracie and her friends drank and danced the night away in the arms of one or another of them.

"How can you take two people named Trixie and Flossie seriously?" one of the suitors asked.

"Because they aren't only names. They're friends who help make me happy."

Gracie's thoughts turned fleetingly to John-Arthur, storing them in the locker of her past, and thought as well of their boys a few miles away, holding them in the basket of the here and now. Her piano player and his melody were slipping away.

Forgetting is easier for some—or more necessary.

* * *

The first third of the century, which had started so brilliantly, had been cut down in pain twice—first by the Great War, which was followed by a spike-up in the twenties, now spiraling downward again in economic ruin. Whether America would rise again, fall to revolution or simply come apart was an open question in 1933. The World War had caused huge disruptions; it not only destroyed idealism throughout the Western World and spoiled hope, but it also prompted a boom-and-bust cycle that the world economy could not bear. But thin threads were beginning to spin out a new tapestry, needles hesitating in midair, clicking in wonder, questioning if all the mixed-up together peoples of immigrant America—English-Africans-French-Central and South Americans-Dutch-Chinese-Scotch-Irish-Turks-Germans-Jews-Scandanavians-Italians-Slavs-Asians—if they retained the spunk to create a united state.

\* \* \*

*Over the Mississippi, a lone eagle rose high above the remains of the old glacier, the bird unaware of poverty, religion, man's sorrow or women's grace. Even with its sharp eye, it could not behold the sun god gleaming from the western mountains, watching the east encroach. Could it make out the rainbow above? Below, Indian mounds were visible as well as the opening to their old lead mine that gaped into the underworld. Aloft, the eagle soared, flicked its eye and was able to see ten-year olds running through its park, cart wheeling.*

A "very well written" novel of the Roaring Twenties
*Last Proud Gallop* by Gerald F. Sweeney

The Lost Generation is emerging. It's 1919 and the Jazz Age is about to erupt. Six vibrant youths seek fulfillment in the postwar period between the demise of Victorian values and the rise of the Flapper, set against the wealthy and power-driven background of Long Island's polo set.

". . . .very well written. The characters are so well developed that they don't often have to be identified in dialogue exchanges"—Easton *Star Democrat*

"Although long gone, the hazy era reawakens in Sweeney's narrative with dynamic and dimensional characters with strong, timeless voices."—*Dan's Papers*, Bridgehampton, NY

Available at Booklocker.com

CPSIA information can be obtained
at www.ICGtesting.com
Printed in the USA
BVHW070406271118
534057BV00001B/4

9 781601 451552